THE
CAGE

ALSO BY MEGAN SHEPHERD:

The Madman's Daughter
Her Dark Curiosity
A Cold Legacy

THE
CAGE

BY MEGAN SHEPHERD

BALZER + BRAY

An Imprint of HarperCollins*Publishers*

Balzer + Bray is an imprint of HarperCollins Publishers.

The Cage
Copyright © 2015 by Megan Shepherd
www.epicreads.com

Library of Congress Cataloging-in-Publication Data
Shepherd, Megan, author.
The cage / Megan Shepherd. — First edition.
    pages cm
Summary: Cora wakes up in a cage on an alien planet where she meets the Kindred,
her mysterious alien captors, and along with other teenager abductees must find a
way to escape back to Earth.
ISBN 978-0-06-224305-8 (hardcover)
1. Alien abduction—Juvenile fiction. 2. Extraterrestrial beings—Juvenile fiction.
3. Telepathy—Juvenile fiction. 4. Human-alien encounters—Juvenile fiction.
[1. Alien abduction—Fiction. 2. Telepathy—Fiction. 3. Human-alien encounters—
Fiction. 4. Science fiction.] I. Title.
PZ7.S54374Cag 2015   2014030624
[Fic]—dc23   CIP
                                                                   AC

Typography by Michelle Taormina
15 16 17 18 19 PC/RRDH 10 9 8 7 6 5 4 3 2 1
❖
First Edition

For Jesse.
I'd travel to distant planets with you, and beyond.

THE
CAGE

1

Cora

THERE ARE CERTAIN THINGS the mind cannot comprehend. People fall into the same routines of thinking day after day: toss an apple and it falls to the ground. Pick a flower and it withers. Fall asleep in your bed and wake there the next morning.

But *this*. This was like dropping an apple and having it fall toward the sun.

Cora Mason dug her hands against her temples to steady the churning sea between her ears. She'd woken in a foggy daze minutes ago—or maybe it was hours—in what seemed to be an endless desert. Her bedroom windows were now rust-red dunes rising in hundred-foot swells. Her ceiling was a cloudless sky. Her bedside lamp was a blazing sun searing her skin.

Wherever she was, it definitely wasn't Virginia.

And it wasn't like any desert she'd ever heard of. This wasn't cacti and thirsty clumps of dry grass. This was an impossibly vast smear of red as far as she could see.

Was she dreaming? In dreams, her mouth never felt this dry. When her father had first been elected senator, his security detail had trained Cora and her brother, Charlie, in what to do in the event of a kidnapping—stay in one place, don't fight back, wait for help. But that had been a decade ago. She'd just barely started kindergarten. Did the same logic apply to a sixteen-year-old? There were no footsteps in the sand, no tire tracks, no indication of how she'd even gotten there.

A starburst of pain streaked through her head. She hissed, pressing her temples harder. Only moments ago, she'd been in a car with Charlie, her down-lined parka pulled tight against the cold, cranking the heat as they drove to a ski resort to meet their parents. She'd had her feet on the dash, scrawling lyrics in a notebook.

"What do you think of this line?" she had asked. "'A stranger in my own life, a ghost behind my smile, not at home in paradise, not at home in hell'?"

Charlie had grinned as he took a left into the resort. "Not bad," he'd said, "but a senator's daughter can't sing songs about hell."

Now, surrounded by sand, Cora felt panic clawing up her throat. She was supposed to be in that Jeep. She'd waited nearly two years for this. The four of them together as a family. No more custody battles. No politics and reporters. Just winter in Virginia. Parkas and snow. Her parents waiting with hot chocolate, not a couple anymore, but not bitter enemies either. She and Charlie had been close enough to see the resort over the next rise. Were her parents there, waiting, wondering how she'd vanished? Were they safe?

The breeze stung her eyes, carrying a strange smell—granite and ozone. As she scraped her tongue with her teeth, she could taste the smell in the back of her throat. It triggered another memory. A dream. Hazy images of a man's handsome face—bronzed skin, heavy brows, closed eyes—that danced in the back of her mind like a will-o'-the-wisp. The dream beckoned her, but the more she reached for it, the farther away it floated, always frustratingly out of reach. Was he someone real? Or had she been unconscious for so long that she'd dreamed of an *angel*?

Or . . .

Am I dead?

She hugged her legs close. Dead people didn't sweat as much as she was. She was alive; she just had to figure out where. *Stay in one place,* the security guard had taught her. *Wait for help.* But if she stayed, she'd die of thirst or sunburn. She hugged her legs harder, fighting the urge to panic, and remembered the advice her mother had given her when things got too overwhelming.

Count backward. Ten. Nine. Eight . . .

She forced herself to her feet. She'd find shade, or water, or some kind of town, and wait there for help.

Seven. Six . . .

She started walking. One more step after the last. One more dune after the last.

Panic lingered in her joints, making her feel loose and unhinged, like her legs might walk away from the rest of her body. The blazing sun dried her tears into salty crusts that she tasted each time she licked her lips. She shaded her eyes and squinted upward, hoping for a helicopter, but there was only an eerie quiet.

Where were her kidnappers? What was the point of leaving her in the middle of nowhere?

Five . . .

Ahead, the valley floor sloped sharply into a towering dune that was higher than all the others. She blinked up at the wall of sand, her body wobbling as she started to climb. Up, up, crawling more than walking, sliding back one step for every two forward. She brushed sweat off her forehead with her sleeve, then froze.

The clothes she was dressed in weren't her own.

Her down parka and ski boots were gone. She was barefoot, with skinny black jeans and an oversized shirt advertising a band she'd never heard of, with thick black cuffs on each wrist. A punk look? She was more lace skirts and cotton dresses. The only concert she'd ever been to was her neighbor's garage band, and she'd left with her hands over her ears after ten minutes.

Now, she ran the tissue-soft fabric between her fingers. A white strap flashed beneath it. She peeked down her collar, and fear bubbled up her throat. Beneath her clothes were a white camisole and white panties. Not hers. Whoever had put her here had first dressed her like a paper doll and then left her for dead. Her stomach lurched at the thought of strangers' hands all over her. But whose hands? Who would do this?

Don't panic. Keep counting. Four . . .

She was unhurt, as far as she could tell, except for the sunburn. But would she stay that way? She needed her father's security guards. Or Charlie. All those years when they were kids, while her dad worked in Washington and her mother slept half the day away, Charlie had looked out for her. He was the one person she could always rely on, if you didn't count Sadie, which you couldn't because she was a dog. He'd told her old episodes of *Twilight Zone* as bedtime stories. He'd taught her where to hide her notebook of song lyrics from their snooping mother. And six months ago, he'd picked her up when she was released from Bay Pines juvenile detention facility. He'd even punched a reporter who shoved a microphone in her face and asked how an upstanding senator's daughter went from straight As to eighteen months for manslaughter.

Three. Two . . .

She pawed for her necklace like a lifeline. It held a charm for each member of her family: a theater mask for her mom; a golf club for her dad; a tiny airplane for Charlie, who wanted to be a pilot. All she'd wanted was for them to be together again, as close as the clinking charms on her necklace. She'd been so near to the resort where they would all sip hot chocolate like a family again—but her fingers grazed only air.

The necklace was gone.

Sweat chilled on the back of her neck. She threw a glance over her shoulder, suddenly overtaken with the feeling that she was being followed. The dunes were empty. Breathing harder, she climbed the final few feet to the top of the highest dune. *Please, let there be a road. A telephone. A donkey.* The only thing she desperately didn't want to see was another dune, and another, and another, stretching forever.

She crested the dune with burning lungs, brushed the sand from her hands, and squeezed her eyes shut. She took a deep breath and finished counting backward.

One.

She opened her eyes.

2

Cora

FROM THIS HIGH, CORA had a 360-degree view. The desert stretched in choppy waves behind her, but to her left was a field of rich black soil, and fruit trees reaching their branches toward the sun, and rows of rainbow-colored vegetables: purple eggplant, yellow squash, red tomatoes, golden corn.

A farm?

Cora crumpled to the ground as pain ripped through her skull. She cried out, squeezing her temples. Had she been drugged? Was that what the dream of her beautiful angel had been, a hallucination? She blinked furiously, but the farm didn't go away.

Count backward.

Ten . . .

She forced herself to look to the right and nearly choked. Opposite the farm, a stony outcropping covered with sea-green lichen sloped into a valley of windswept trees. Enormous oaks, and firs, and evergreens; all covered with a dusting of white. Not like the leafless winter forests of Virginia, but an arctic tundra. A cold breeze blew, carrying a snowflake that settled on Cora's sunburned palm. She shoved herself to her feet.

Screw counting.

She shook her hand wildly, pacing. Even more impossible than everything else was the slice of water directly in front of her. Gently lapping waves stretched to an ocean bay that made her stomach plummet like she was sinking. She spit out the phantom taste of salt water. An ocean didn't belong here. *She* didn't belong here.

Sweat poured down her temples, despite the tundra wind. On the far side of the bay, mountains loomed, and even what looked like a cityscape. A desert, a farm, an ocean, a forest—habitats that couldn't exist right next to one another. It had to be a secret government biosphere experiment. Or a rich maniac's whim. Or virtual reality.

The granite-and-ozone smell clogged in her nose, and she steadied herself until the sensation passed. She wasn't a little girl—she could handle this. She *had* to. As her breath slowed, a dark shape appeared at the bottom of the hill, where the ocean lapped against the farm's edge.

If she squinted, the shape looked like a person.

"Hey!" She tumbled down the path. Her feet tangled in the grass underfoot as the trail led between rows of peppers bursting with ripeness.

"Hey! I need help!"

The path gave way to a small beach. The person—a dark-haired girl in a white sundress—must have been panicked, because she was curled in the sand, frozen with fear.

"Hey!" Cora stopped short at the edge of the sea, as black-deep water and reality caught up to her all at once. The girl wasn't curled in panic. Facedown in the surf, hair matted, water billowing around motionless legs.

"Oh, no." Cora squeezed her eyes shut. "Get up. Please."

When she opened her eyes, the girl was still motionless. She forced herself to step into the surf, wincing as it swallowed her ankles, and dropped to her knees. In Bay Pines, one of the delinquents had suffocated herself with a plastic shopping bag. Cora had been writing song lyrics in the hallway as the police wheeled the body away: glassy eyes, blue lips.

Just like this girl.

Except this girl also had angry bruises on her shoulder, like someone had grabbed her. For a few moments, all Cora could hear was blood pulsing through her ears. A tattoo flashed on the girl's neck beneath the bruises, a collection of black dots that meant nothing to Cora and never would, because she could never ask the girl about them. Behind her, the forest was perfectly silent, with only the soft falling snow to tell her that the world hadn't stopped.

She stood. The water seemed colder. Deeper. Maybe those bruises meant the girl had been murdered. Or maybe the girl had drowned trying to escape from someone. Either way, Cora didn't want to be next.

She raced out of the water. *Stay in one place. Don't fight back.* That was the advice she'd gotten as a kindergartener. But how could she stay in one place with a dead body?

Footsteps broke the silence. She whirled, searching the spaces between the trees.

There.

White clothes flashed between the branches. Two legs. A person. Cora's muscles tightened to run—or fight.

A boy trudged out of the forest.

He was about her age. He wore jeans and a rumpled white shirt beneath a leather jacket, looking like he'd stumbled out of a pool hall after a night of loud music and beer. A pair of aviator sunglasses were shoved into his jeans pocket. As out of place as Cora—though he was barefoot, like she was. Cute, in a messy way. His dark hair fell around brown eyes that looked as surprised to see her as she was to see him. For a moment, they only stared.

He broke the tension first. "Aren't you . . ." His words died when he saw the body. "Is she *dead*?"

He took a step forward. Cora scrambled backward, ready to bolt, and he stopped. He popped a knuckle in his left hand. Strong hands, Cora noted. Hands that could have held a girl under water.

"Back up," Cora threatened. "If you touch me, I'll claw your eyes out."

Sure enough, that stopped him. He dragged a hand over his mouth, eyes a little glassy. "Wait. You think *I* killed her?"

"She has bruises on her arm. She struggled with someone."

"It wasn't me! I don't know what's going on, but I didn't kill anyone." He paced to the edge of the surf, where the water brushed his toes—not afraid of the water, like she'd been. "Look, my clothes are dry. If I'd done it, I'd be sopping wet." He rubbed his temples. "She must have fifty pounds on you, so I doubt you killed her, but *someone* did. We should get out of here before they come back. Find a phone or a radio. We can try that barn."

A phone. She longed to hear her father's voice on the other end, telling her that it was all a misunderstanding . . . but a girl was dead. Whoever the girl was, those bruises were more than just a misunderstanding to her.

"I watch TV," Cora said. "I know how this goes. You act all friendly and then strangle me behind the barn. I'm not going anywhere with you."

He rubbed a hand over his face, digging deep into his scalp, as though his head splintered with pain too. "In case you haven't noticed, this isn't TV. There's no one but me and a murderer, so I suggest we help each other."

Cora eyed him warily. Her first day in juvie, a gap-toothed girl had offered her a contraband Coca-Cola—a welcome present, the girl had said, to help her adjust. Two days later, the girl had punched her in the ribs and stolen her sudoku book.

You might have grown up in a rich-girl bubble, the gap-toothed girl had told her, *but in here you have to learn the rules of the real world. First off: never trust a stranger—especially one who comes offering help.*

3

Lucky

AFTER LUCKY WOKE IN a snowdrift with a splitting headache, wearing someone else's clothes and missing his granddad's
watch, he'd narrowed down the possibilities: either he was going
insane, or someone at the mechanic's shop had dropped a wrench
on his head and this was some freakish afterlife. Now, standing
opposite the girl with the wheat-blond hair, he knew.

He was definitely dead. And not just dead—he was in hell.

That was the only way to explain Cora Mason.

It had taken him a few moments to recognize her. Ever since
waking, it had been a challenge just to put one foot in front of the
other, fighting the knife of pain in his head. Then, suddenly, there
was a beautiful girl with hair so light it matched the sand. She
might have been a vision, except visions didn't dress like they were
headed to a rave.

Then she'd looked up, and her features had rearranged themselves, and *shit*—he knew her. The senator's daughter accused of

manslaughter. He'd followed her story for the last two years, surrounded by her painfully pretty face on television, read reports about how the accident tore apart one of the country's top political families.

It had torn him apart too. It didn't matter that he'd never met her. He had been the one responsible for ruining her life. Only two people knew it: he and her dad—a man who made Lucky's fist ache with a desire to punch something.

"Who are you?" she demanded.

He rubbed a hand over his chest, where the guilt was still tender as a sucker punch, even after two years. "Call me Lucky. From a little town in Montana called Whitefish. I woke up in the middle of a snowdrift in that forest a couple hours ago; before that, I was working on the busted throttle lock of my motorcycle. That's all I remember."

He stopped short, swallowing his words, the ache in his head pulsing like a second heartbeat. Memories of home played in the back of his head. His granddad's sun-wrinkled face. The smell of chicken feed. Motor oil slick in the lines of his hand, so hard to wash away. He'd been fixing his motorcycle so he could drive to the army recruiting office in Missoula. *With your grades, college isn't an option,* his school counselor had said, and slid a brochure across the desk: red, white, and blue font commanding him to do the right thing.

It didn't matter if enlisting was the right thing. It mattered that his dad, and his granddad, had sat in that same damn chair and gotten that same damn brochure. It mattered that Afghanistan was a long way from the accident that had left his hand busted, and from his mother's gravestone with the plastic flowers, and from Cora Mason's face in the newspaper.

A wave pulled the girl's body out to sea, and Lucky lurched for it. "Shit. Help me grab her before she floats away. The police will want to check the body."

Cora eyed the water like she'd rather step into quicksand.

"Okay . . . then we'll do Plan B. You stand there and look cute, and *I'll* haul out the dead body."

He approached slowly, giving Cora space as he waded into the surf. He'd never seen a dead body before. Would it be warm? Clammy? The dead girl looked foreign, maybe Middle Eastern, and she had to be close to six feet tall. An old scar marred her chin, in the shape of a lopsided heart.

He cracked the knuckles in his left hand. They were always stiffer when he first woke up.

"You ever done this before?" Cora asked.

"Pulled a dead body out of the ocean? Can't say I have." He grabbed the girl under the arms and hauled her to shore. As soon as he was out of the water, Cora helped. They laid her on the sand, and he did a quick check of the body.

"No wallet. No ID."

The dead girl's dress strap had fallen. Lucky fixed it, wishing his hands weren't shaking. He stood up, dusting sand off his palms like he could wipe away the grit of death, and met Cora's eyes directly for the first time. They were surrounded by dark circles in real life. The photographs in the newspapers hadn't captured that.

"I'm Cora," she said.

Now would be the time to tell her that he knew her name, and a lot more. He could tell her about September 3—the day he'd tried to kill her father. It was two weeks after the accident. He'd broken into his dad's gun safe. He'd driven to an airfield where

Senator Mason's son was learning to fly a Cessna 172. He'd parked the car and told himself he could do it. He had to. His mother was in the grave, and Senator Mason was patting his son on the back. Carefree. Guiltless. He'd tried to open the car door, only to find two men in black suits on either side. They'd dragged him out and taken his gun. Then they'd made him an offer.

"Nice to meet you, Cora." He looked away, wiping his mouth. "I'm going to check the barn for a phone. You should come. We're safer if we stick together."

She glanced behind her toward the cityscape. "Yeah, but . . . don't get too close."

He held up his hands in mock surrender and climbed the path. It wound them through the orchard, where a stream ran between the trees, spreading an eerie calmness through the air. He ducked a hanging apple, and his stomach lurched. How long had it been since he'd eaten?

"So what's your theory?" he asked.

"Theory?" She held her arms tightly across her chest.

"Where we are. How we got here." He paused. He really should tell her about that day in the airfield. But she cast a questioning look at him, all wide blue eyes, and he lost his resolve. "I mean . . . it's snowing fifty feet away, and here it's seventy degrees. There's a desert over that hill that goes on for miles. And I swear that sun hasn't moved since I woke up hours ago. The clothes you're wearing . . . are they yours?"

She brushed the strap of the camisole. "No."

"Same for me. Why would someone change our clothes? And put us in these weird locations?" He raked his nails across his scalp to help him think. "I've been through every possible explanation:

it's a joke. An experiment. But it's too weird, changing our clothes. That takes time and planning. Whoever is doing this is messing with us intentionally. I just can't figure out why."

"I don't care why," Cora said. "I just want to go home."

Her voice broke, slicing into Lucky's chest. He stopped. "Hey. It's okay. To be afraid, I mean." He gave her a smile, just a tug of one corner. "I am too."

The barn was just feet away. He started for it, but she grabbed his arm. He flinched, not expecting her touch. Her fingers were smaller than he'd imagined. So fragile. Who would do this to a girl who'd already been through so much?

"Those markings on your neck," she said. "The black dots. What do they mean?"

Lucky blinked. He had no idea what she was talking about, but her eyes dropped to the place just below his left ear. He reached up a hand that brushed hard bumps, like grains of sand embedded in his skin.

He dropped his hand.

For years he'd worn his granddad's watch, even back when the strap had been too big, but it had vanished when he'd woken. He felt lost without its weight.

"I don't know." His eyes went to her neck. "But you have them too."

4

Cora

CORA'S HAND FLEW TO her neck. Raised bumps, like a connect-the-dots game.

Pain throbbed through her head, and she doubled over in the sunflower patch next to the barn. She hadn't imagined that anything could be more frightening than her first day in Bay Pines. Charlie had driven her there with the family's lawyer, so that the press wouldn't get photographs of Senator Mason checking his daughter into detention. The officers had patted her down for contraband and given her khaki clothes that smelled like they'd been washed with rat poison. They introduced her to the cinder-block dorm room she shared with a cornrowed Venezuelan, then threw her to the wild in the cafeteria. She'd been one of the youngest inmates, and the richest. They might as well have squirted a target on her back with ketchup and mayonnaise.

Now, as she felt the raised dots, she had a new bar for what qualified as "terrifying."

"The dead girl had them too," she said quietly.

Lucky let out a mirthless laugh. "That's real comforting." He tugged on the barn door handle. "It's locked. I might be able to take it off its hinges, if I can find something to use for a makeshift screwdriver."

"I'll look for another way in." Cora circled the barn until she reached a large black window, six feet wide by three feet tall. The feeling of being watched felt like nails down her back. The window was in good repair, which was odd given the weathered state of the barn. She knocked on the glass. A hollow *thud* sounded. Something was wrong, like it lacked an echo.

She pressed her face against the glass, but a rip of pain tore through her head, and she winced and pulled back. It was too murky to see inside, anyway. More like a television screen than a window. Suddenly a shape moved, just a flicker, and she scrambled back. The tingling sensation down her back ran deeper, and she whirled toward the farm, half expecting to see a knife-wielding stranger rushing up behind her.

Nothing. Barely even a breeze.

Lucky came around, shaking his head, eyeing the window like it creeped him out too. "Get this—the door isn't real. The whole barn is fake, like a movie prop. We'll have to go to that city."

Cora glanced toward the sea, where the distant cityscape crouched on the far side of the bay. What if it was where their captors lived? Wouldn't they be walking right into danger?

She rubbed her eyes. Exhaustion was catching up with her. "No. We should stay put and wait for help. My dad's in politics. Once he realizes I'm gone, he'll have the entire country looking for me."

"I don't care if your dad is the president of the United States.

My dad's a sergeant in Afghanistan. You think he just kicks rocks around while insurgents are firing at him?"

On the black window, the shadow keeled slightly to the left. Cora took another step away from it.

Lucky's face softened. He cracked his knuckles, less of a threatening gesture this time, more like an old wound. "If we find a phone, your dad is the first person we'll call. I promise. Here's Plan C: we stay away from any more of these black windows. And if you see anyone—hear anyone—you run. Neither of us is going to end up like that girl in the water."

She nodded. "I can live with Plan C."

They set off down a path made of a material that looked like pavement but felt softer, almost spongy, through a meadow of tall grasses. It was all uncannily beautiful, but that only set off Cora's nerves. Beauty had a way of masking something darker.

The path crested a rise, showing the far-off city, only it looked much closer now. The structures blurred together in a dizzying way that didn't seem right, and she rubbed her eyes, wondering if exhaustion was making her head foggy. As they walked farther, she could start to see details. First the rooftops, then glimpses of windows, and pavement, and flashes of color from potted flowers.

She stopped.

It wasn't just exhaustion messing with her head. The buildings were real, but they were hardly the skyscrapers that they had seemed from a distance. They were between one and two stories high, and there couldn't be more than ten of them. It was as though the buildings had been placed in just the right locations so that, from a distance, the rooftops lined up to give the appearance of something substantially larger.

The shadows on Lucky's face deepened. "I swear this looked like a city from far away. You think it's in our heads, like virtual reality?"

"I don't think so. My dad invests in tech, and there's no virtual reality that comes close to this." Her mind whirled, playing back conversations with her father, coming up with no explanation. "This must be real. Designed to make us feel a certain way and go certain places, like elaborate optical illusions. The same with the distances. It should have taken us hours to get here, and it's been what, half an hour?" Sweat trickled down her forehead, though the temperature couldn't be higher than the mid-sixties.

Lucky motioned for her to follow him to the nearest building. As they circled it, a neon sign flashed above the front door.

CANDY SHOP.

Cora had mentally prepared herself for anything—tanks and guns and terrorists—but not for a place to buy *taffy*. Could Lucky be right, that this was an elaborate set for some movie?

A dozen shops circled an eerily idyllic town square, all built in different architectural styles, with signs above the doors. The drugstore had intricate Middle Eastern designs over the windows. The hair salon was set up like an old-fashioned French burlesque. The flashing lights of the arcade looked straight out of 1980s Tokyo. An enormous weeping cherry tree stood in the center, like a pin stuck in the center of a map. No cars. No people. The only sign of life was a tall Victorian house flanking one side of the square, with lights blazing in the upper windows.

"It's like Epcot Center," she muttered. "All different cultures and time periods crammed together."

Lucky cocked an eyebrow. "Dead girls don't float up on the beach in Disney World."

"Not as a rule, no."

He jerked his chin toward the house. "If the lights are on, maybe there's a phone. Maybe even a—"

His words were cut short by a shout coming from the shops. The yell came again, high-pitched and scared, followed by a deep bellow.

The saloon-style doors of a building marked TOY STOP crashed open, and two boys spilled out.

5

Cora

CORA REACHED FOR HER necklace, forgetting its absence, and felt her heart thudding beneath a too-thin layer of skin. Two boys. Both strangers. One—the biggest guy Cora had ever seen—was about to pummel the other one to death.

She spun toward Lucky. "What do we do?"

He jerked his head toward the cherry tree. "Stay here. If anything happens, run." He wrapped her fingers around a branch, rooting her, and took off. A gust of wind lifted one of the tree's weeping branches to brush her cheek, as though laying claim to her.

She jerked away. "Yeah. I don't think so."

She ran after Lucky. The larger of the two boys—a Polynesian built like a small country and dressed in a three-piece charcoal suit—had his hands around the neck of the other boy, a twitchy redhead with pale skin, who inexplicably wore what looked like a French revolutionary war jacket.

Lucky jumped onto the porch, and Cora flinched. A fight

between teenagers was like a fight between dogs: the worst thing you could do was get in the middle.

"Break it up!" he yelled, laying a hand on the hulk's shoulder.

He was braver than Cora, or else he hadn't been around as many fights as she had. Girls had fought all the time at Bay Pines, and after getting sucker punched that first day, Cora had learned that the best tactic was to hide in the bathroom and wait for the guards to break them up. Only there weren't any guards here—just a kid in a leather jacket.

The hulk whirled on Lucky, smacking away his hand. Tattooed black lines swirled around the right side of his forehead and eye, a look both ancient and menacing—completely mismatched with his tailored suit. For all his bulk, though, there was a softness around his eyes that said he couldn't be much older than she was.

"Mind your hands, eh?" He spit at Lucky in a rough accent. The redhead kid took advantage of the distraction to dart into the toy shop, probably looking for a back exit.

"Get back here!" The hulk shoved open the saloon-style doors, with Lucky right behind.

Cora climbed onto the porch. Inside, the shop was set up like an old-fashioned general store straight out of a Western movie. It even smelled old, like grain in burlap sacks and coffee and cotton, though there weren't any of those things on the shelves, only brightly colored toys of all shapes and sizes. The hulk had the other boy against a glass countertop, hands around his throat. In the corner, a dark-haired girl in a black dress rocked back and forth, emitting a high-pitched wail.

Cora pushed through the swinging doors and knelt by the girl. "Hey, you okay?"

A strangled sound came from the girl's throat. She was Asian; her full lips were pressed together; dark brown hair with a pink streak fell in her left eye. Beautiful—the kind that didn't happen in real life. Cora positioned herself to shelter the girl from the fight and glanced over her shoulder.

Lucky had managed to separate the boys. "What's this all about?" he demanded.

The hulk spit on the ground. "I'll ask the questions around here, brother. And I'd rather talk to that pretty blond friend of yours."

Cora jerked her head up. Her muscles reacted faster than her brain, pushing her to her feet as the hulk headed toward her.

A whir of movement flashed, followed by a *crack*. Cora flinched as a spray of blood fanned across the floor. She jumped back, staring at the blood, until it all made sense. Lucky had smashed his fist into the hulk's nose.

The tattooed boy stumbled backward until he collided with one of the creepy black windows. It didn't shatter. It didn't even creak. He dragged the back of his forearm across his bleeding nose as if that was all the tending it needed.

"How about *I* ask the questions?" Lucky flexed his hand. "Let's start with your names and finish with what the hell's going on."

The redheaded boy in the military jacket rubbed his neck. His eyes were blue-green, with heavy lashes that made him look like a kid playing dress-up. A small spattering of black dots, not unlike Lucky's, clustered below his ear. The hulk had them too. Cora glanced at the girl in the corner—her straight hair hid her neck.

"It's no good asking the two of them anything." The hulk jerked his chin toward the others. "I've been trying to get answers out of them for the better part of an hour. She hasn't stopped sobbing, and he's close-lipped." He shook his head, rubbing his chin.

"I'm Leon, by the way. From New Zealand." He spit a line of blood on the floor that landed an inch from the Asian girl's foot. She rocked harder, hands pressed tightly over her head, fingers gripping her hair so hard that Cora was afraid she'd pull it out.

"Easy." Cora rubbed the girl's skeletal shoulder, ignoring the tension and weariness in her own muscles.

"Her name is Nok," the red-haired boy said, still rubbing the splotchy red marks on his neck. His voice was deeper than she'd expected from someone so thin. "I'm Rolf. From Oslo, in Norway. She and I met a few hours ago when we woke up in different shops. She's Thai, but she speaks English well. Said she lives in London now. Except for a bad headache, she was okay before we ran into this Neanderthal and he started demanding to know what was going on."

"*Do* you know what's going on?" Cora asked.

Rolf shook his head. "Your guess is as good as mine. She doesn't know either. Before she had the panic attack, she told me she was a model; the high-fashion type with big magazine spreads. Someone famous, I think. There must be people looking for her." He crouched next to Nok and said softly, "He's not going to hurt you. He's just a stupid *bølle* who picks on anyone he can."

Nok peeked out from beneath the pink stripe of hair and scooted closer to Rolf.

Cora stood. "I'm Cora; this is Lucky." She glanced around the toys in the shop. "I think we should try to set off a flare, or make a sign that an airplane could read with some of this stuff."

"This isn't bloody Robinson Crusoe," Leon said. "There's an arcade and a movie theater, and you're talking about spelling some S.O.S. shit out of rocks."

"No . . . she's right." Lucky leaned against the countertop. "We need to find a way to make contact with someone, and we should keep searching the town. There could be dozens more of us."

"Not dozens," Rolf said. "Just one."

Cora turned, rubbing her pounding temples. With its high collar and epaulettes, Rolf's military jacket gave him an air of authority that didn't fit with his neurotic blinking. His fingers found some sort of metal combination lock built into the edge of the glass countertop; it had a row of gears that he spun now absent-mindedly, spreading a deep, nearly ominous rumble throughout the room. "Another girl, I think. Three girls and three boys. Six all together."

Rumble, rumble, rumble.

"Three and three makes six, eh?" Leon grunted. "You must be some kind of genius."

Rolf cleared his throat awkwardly. "Hardly. I just have a gift for observational reasoning. It's what I'm studying at Oxford. Well, that and robotics. And Greek philosophy."

Cora frowned. "Wow. How old are you?"

Rumble.

His cheeks flamed. "Fifteen." He shook his head quickly. "But that doesn't matter. Observational reasoning is really just deduction, at its core. Any of us can deduce. Nok and I explored each of the stores when we woke. There were six chairs in the diner. Six umbrellas on the boardwalk. Six dolls behind the counter." He nodded toward the glass case beneath the countertop, which held the dolls he had mentioned, and a child's painting kit, and a bright croquet set. "We explored the house, too. There's a few bedrooms upstairs, a living room downstairs. There were six dressers with six sets of clothing in the bedrooms. Judging by the clothing, there's still one girl missing. She'll be wearing a white sundress."

Cora's head shot around to Lucky. His mouth was set grim. "Yeah. About that." He rubbed the back of his neck. "We found her. She's dead. Drowned in the ocean, just over that rise."

Rolf looked up in surprise, pushing at the bridge of his nose, a gesture like a person with glasses might do. Even Nok stopped cringing. Her eyes were still damp, but Cora saw something else, just for a flash. Nok's mouth tightened. Her eyes narrowed a hair. And then, just as fast, she was wailing again, leaning into Rolf, crying harder.

Cora had seen plenty of girls at Bay Pines put on a show for the guards, to gain sympathy. She knew good acting when she saw it. But why would Nok put on an act?

"Dead?" Nok whispered in a trembling voice. "Like, from an accident, yeah?"

"She had bruises on her neck," Lucky said.

Leon gave a sudden shiver like a dog shaking off spray. He stalked to the door, rubbing the back of his neck. Trying to act like he wasn't scared, but he was sweating hard.

Cora took a deep breath. "We have to stay calm and wait for help. We'll be rescued."

They all turned at the sound of her voice. Rolf started spinning the gear again, filling the room with that ominous metallic rumble.

"Who will rescue us?" Nok said. "We don't even know where we are, or why they took the six of us." One bony hand snaked up to twist her hair.

Rumble. Rumble. Rumble.

Cora eyed each of them in turn. Nok was a famous model; Rolf had to be a prodigy, to be studying at Oxford at his age. Cora wasn't exactly famous, but her father was. Was this about ransoming them for money? She eyed Lucky. Beneath that leather jacket, was he someone famous? He was cute, sure, but not movie-star cute; not pearl-white teeth and well-rehearsed smiles. As if to prove her point, he kicked the row of glass jars, forgetting he was barefoot, then doubled over and cursed.

Leon snorted. "You're wasting time with theories. Me, I don't give a shit. I'm getting out of here, and any of you are welcome to come with."

Rolf spun the gear slower, so that it barely made a noise. "We can't leave."

"Like hell we can't. I'll pick a direction and walk. Those roads have to lead somewhere."

Rolf shook his head. "They end just behind those buildings. I already tried them." He looked down at his toes. "Well, they don't end, exactly. I followed one that led away from the town square. In about three blocks, the road led me back to the town. I didn't take a single turn, but it looped me back here anyway. I tried another road, and it was the same. It doesn't matter which direction you head. You'll just come back to where you started."

The toy store fell quiet. Only the sound of Rolf's spinning gear, and the humming black window, filled the silence. A shadow had appeared behind the window, moving slowly. It didn't seem so much like a person now; it was too tall and too stiff.

"That's impossible," Nok blurted out.

Rolf's fingers stopped. Without the sound of the rumbling gear, the room—the town—was even more eerily quiet. "According to the rules of physics, it isn't."

27

6

ROLF

ROLF FOCUSED ON THE marigolds beyond the toy-store doors. *Calendula officinalis.* It was easier to think about plants than about the kids staring at him. When he had started classes at Oxford, four years younger than every other university student and the only red-haired kid in his dorm, they'd teased him incessantly. Now he didn't even have his glasses to hide behind. Their abductors had taken them—and yet, as he blinked, his vision was inexplicably perfect.

"I must have hit you too hard, brother," Leon said. "That's insane."

A glance at Leon's tattooed face sent Rolf's fingers spinning the gears on the combination lock faster. His twitchiness was a bad habit, he knew, but not an easy one to break. "It's called an infinity paradox. It exists, but only theoretically. I'd wager that if you followed any of these paths, eventually you would end up back where you started. There's no way of telling how far the boundaries are, or if there even are boundaries. It's highly theoretical."

"So we're trapped?" Nok's eyes were full of fear. "Even though there are no walls or bars?"

Rolf froze. Staring was all he could manage with Nok. The pink strands of hair perfectly framed the left side of her face, a geometric wonder. He had first seen her standing on the boardwalk, hair tangled in the breeze. Her face had looked defiant—but he'd been wrong. The moment she'd turned and seen him, surprise had flashed over her features, and then tears. Big, rolling ones. She'd thrown her arms around him, never mind that he was a stranger.

He shoved at glasses that were no longer there. "Ah . . . yes. Trapped. I also believe the infinity paradox is responsible for the headaches we've all been complaining about. Our minds can't handle this much unpredictability."

He thought his logical explanation would put her at ease, but Nok went pale. *Stupid.* He'd never been confident around girls, especially beautiful ones. He came from Viking descendants; wasn't he supposed to be beating his enemies with sabers and ripping trees in half? All the Vikings ever gave him was an unmanly shade of strawberry hair.

Cora tugged on his military jacket, getting his attention. "What about the ocean? There's no path in the water that can loop a person back. Maybe someone just needs to swim out far enough to get past this infinity paradox."

Rolf paused to consider this. It most certainly wouldn't work, but at least she was displaying creative thinking, which was more than he could say for the others. "Perhaps, but judging by the fact that a girl already drowned, I'm not sure it's the best course of action."

His fingers found the comfort of the combination lock gears, spinning them again. He hated being put on the spot. Back in Oslo, all he'd wanted was to live in the flower garden at Tøyen, near to where his parents worked. He'd spend hours digging around the *Rosa berberifolia* and *Bellis perennis*. Dirt used to ring the beds of his fingernails, brown-black and permanent, like it had been tattooed on. *You can't play in the dirt, min skatt,* his mother had said, washing off the dirt. *You were made to use your brain, not your hands.*

He sighed, squinting at the small etched numbers on the spinning gears of the combination lock, blinking hard, still confused by his perfect new vision. He'd seen numbers like the ones on the gears before. It was a Fibonacci pattern even the most basic math student would learn: one, one, two, three, five, eight, thirteen, and a blank for the last number.

On impulse, he spun the final gear until the next number lined up with the others—twenty-one—with a satisfying *click*. A copper-colored token rolled out of a trough at the base of the counter. There were strange grooves on either side of the token . . . a foreign language, or symbols. He inserted the token into a slot above the trough to see what would happen.

A glass door swung free. Hundreds of peppermint candies rained to the ground.

He cursed, jumping back as the flood of candy hit his feet. The others jumped back too. The falling candy was the only sound in the room, along with a sweet smell that made him famished. It felt like forever since he'd eaten anything. At Oxford he'd had lunch every day at an Indian takeaway place just below his dorm . . . he'd kill for a curry now, or for his mother's egg-butter cod with flatbread, or even one of Snadderkiosken's overcooked burgers.

Cora crouched down to inspect the candy. "How'd you do that?"

"The numbers on the combination lock form a simple sequence."

"Simple? Maybe for you." She inspected the gears. "Look, the numbers have already reset themselves into a different order. I don't think it's a lock. I think it's a *puzzle*. Solve the numbers and get a token."

Rolf cleared his throat, leaning in to see. "It's possible. Scientists use this sort of puzzle to gauge the intelligence of lab mice and chimpanzees." He glanced at the humming black window. "These windows could be viewing panels. Our captors might be watching us now, timing how quickly we solve these number tests, and perhaps the greatest puzzle of all—why we are here."

As if to prove his point, one of the shadowy outlines shifted to the right.

Nok recoiled. "Is that *them*?" She collapsed against Rolf. "But those shadows are too big to be people, yeah?"

He tried to ignore how nice she smelled, like spring in Tøyen gardens. "We can't be sure of anything. I imagine that whoever put us here wanted a group of teenagers who all spoke English, even though we're from different countries. Nok is Thai, but she lives in London, I'm Norwegian, and I live there too. Leon is New Zealander. Lucky is . . ." He paused. He didn't trust cool-looking American guys in leather jackets as a rule, but he liked the way Lucky spoke, calm and certain, and he definitely liked the way Lucky had punched Leon in the face. "The two of you—Lucky and Cora—are both American. That can't be right. It doesn't fit the pattern."

"I was born in Colombia," Lucky said. "My mom moved to

the States when I was two and married my stepdad there."

Rolf almost smiled—his theory had been correct. "So perhaps they want us for our different ethnicities, not nationalities. And I suppose they want us all to speak English because *they* speak English, which means they're probably Americans or Brits or Australians."

"I don't care who they are," Leon said, glaring at the panel challengingly. "As long as they bleed."

"Do you think that's why this place is so strange?" Cora asked. "With all the weird angles, and time periods stuck together? Maybe they're trying to do some psychological test, like how much stress a mind can take?"

"If it is a psychological experiment," Rolf said, "then they won't tell us their purpose. It would skew whatever data they're trying to collect. But there's something else we need to think about. Every experiment has a control. A test subject who isn't being manipulated, so they can ensure accurate results. Someone on the inside. A mole. Which means the more pressing question is . . . how can we trust each other?"

Everyone went silent. Both Cora and Leon rubbed their heads like their headaches were only getting worse. Rolf realized his mistake too late. He hadn't meant to sow seeds of doubt—it had been a perfectly reasonable line of thought. But now he could practically hear the sound of their shifting eyes evaluating each other. He glanced at Nok—a girl who needed him. And Lucky—who had defended him. Had he already ruined his chances for friendship?

Stupid.

Next time he'd just study the *Calendula officinalis* and keep his mouth shut.

7

Cora

"A SNITCH?" CORA'S VOICE cut through the silence.

Nok was clutching her scalp, sobbing again. Even Leon, who acted so tough, paced over the peppermints, crushing them into a sticky mess. Cora could feel their panic—it beat in time with her own. But panic wouldn't help this situation.

She looked at her reflection the black window, forcing the tight muscles in her face to ease—her clenched jaw, her wrinkled forehead—until she looked calm on the outside. It was something she'd had plenty of practice with.

At a political rally for her father outside Virginia Beach, long before her parents' divorce, someone had called in a bomb threat. The security guards had whisked her away to a tent. Her father had come an hour later, unharmed, and wiped the tears from her eyes. *A Mason never lets the world see her cry,* he had said. *No matter how scared she is, she smiles.*

Cora couldn't quite bring herself to smile now, but she at

least kept her voice steady. "None of us are snitches," she said.

"Oh, yeah?" Leon asked. "How many run-ins has a pretty girl like you had with snitches?"

Cora turned away from her reflection, and fought the urge to tell him about Bay Pines. "I'm just saying that we shouldn't turn against each other five minutes after we've met. We don't know what's going on. We don't even know what's in the other shops."

Lucky pushed off from the counter. "You're right. And we should find out."

Cora met his eyes. *Stay in one place,* the voice of her father's guard whispered—but it didn't look like help was coming.

She gave a nod.

One by one, they went outside and filed into the arcade, which was nearly identical in layout to the toy store: a glass counter to one side, a black window, and arcade games lining the opposite wall. It was dark inside, with flashing lights that Cora had to squint into, and sounds that took her back to the arcade in Richmond that she'd loved as a girl. After school, her mother would drop her off at the mall with a few girl friends, and while they shopped for cheap earrings, she'd play the claw game with the bored mall cop.

She reached for her necklace, forgetting it wasn't there.

"Looks like you were right, Rolf," Lucky said, motioning to the glass counter, which had a copper slot for tokens and contained a circulating ring of brightly colored prizes: a guitar, a boomerang, a small red radio that made Cora wonder if they could rewire it to send a distress signal. "All the video games are puzzles. Must be testing our hand-eye coordination or something."

They went to the beauty salon next, which was styled in

gaudy French decor. Nok collapsed in one of the chairs, rubbing the velvet cushions. "Swanky."

Cora eyed her sidelong. For a supposedly famous model, she had awful taste.

Lucky scratched his neck. "So where's the puzzle?"

Rolf's fingers were twitching against his legs, his gaze going from the photographs on the wall to the floor. Cora leaned in. "You know, don't you?"

"Yes, but I was . . . going to give you all the opportunity to figure it out. Look at the photographs on the wall. They're pairs. It's a matching game." He flipped the photographs to matching pairs, and a token rolled down a metal trough built into the counter, identical to the one in all the other shops. He stuck the token into an identical slot in the countertop, and a jar of red nail polish tumbled onto the floor. Nok poked the bottle with her toe like it might bite. When it didn't, she slipped it into her pocket, despite the odd looks from the others.

"What? It's my favorite color."

On the wall, the photographs reset themselves mechanically into a different set of images. Now they were famous sites of the world: the Eiffel Tower, the Taj Mahal, along with outlines of various countries. Cora's head was still foggy, but she touched the closest painting, the Eiffel Tower, and spun the one below it until she got to France.

Tokens rained out of the slot.

Rolf hurried over. "Ten tokens?" He blinked too fast. "That doesn't make any sense. If anything, the game I solved was harder, but I only got one." His blue-green eyes blinked in confusion.

Cora rubbed her eyes. "I don't even want them—you guys take them."

"I've got all the nail polish I need, sweetheart," Leon said.

Rolf ran his fingers over the tokens, comparing them to the one he had won. "It just doesn't make any sense. It counters the philosophy behind conditioned responses. The most effective way to reinforce a lab rat's behavior is through random rewards. For example, if a rat runs a maze ten times, you only reward it six out of the ten times. The uncertainty makes the rat focus harder." Rolf frowned at Cora's pile of tokens versus his meager one. "But with a system of random rewards, you still have to be consistent from rat to rat. Even rats sense unfairness. It causes them to get extremely frustrated."

"Maybe the people who put us here aren't scientists," Lucky said. "They could just be twisted. This could be some sick kind of torture."

Everyone was quiet. Cora eyed Lucky carefully, looking from the way he habitually popped his knuckles like they ached to the small scar on his chin. What had happened to him to make his mind go to such a dark place?

"Don't think like that," she said. "At least not yet. Come on."

The group filed back outside.

Cora shaded her eyes, looking down the row of buildings.

Nok cocked her head, pink streak of hair falling into her face. "Do you hear that?"

At first Cora heard nothing, but then faint notes reached her ears. A song. It sounded like recorded music, old-fashioned, that made her think of crooners dressed in tuxedos. Then the lyrics began.

A stranger in my own life . . .

It was coming from one of the shops. The diner. Lucky started toward it, but Cora clamped her hand onto his.

"Wait," she whispered.

A ghost behind my smile . . .

A coldness started somewhere at the base of her skull and spread. The memory returned of riding in Charlie's car, wanting so badly to reach that resort where their parents waited for them, her crumpled notebook in her lap, making up lyrics. *Those* lyrics. The same ones playing now. She whirled toward the source of the music with a feeling like the world was spinning just a little too fast.

Not at home in paradise . . .
Not at home in hell . . .

A sign flashed above the diner: THE GREASY FORK. It flashed again and again, beckoning them.

"Hey, you okay?" Lucky asked.

"This song." Her voice came out hoarse. "These lyrics. They're . . . mine."

8

Cora

VERTIGO HIT CORA AS if the past and present were intertwining.

"You mean . . . you know this song?" Lucky asked.

She shook her head. "No. I *wrote* these lyrics. It was the last thing I was doing before I woke up here. Someone must have stolen my notebook, hired a singer, and recorded the song. That's so elaborate. Why would anyone do that?"

Everyone was silent.

She reached for her necklace and felt only emptiness.

Leon tugged off his tie and let it fall to the grass. "They're twisted shits, that's why." He climbed the diner stairs with a look like he'd kill whoever was in there. After a minute, he stuck his head back out.

"There's no one here." He sounded disappointed.

Cora started up the steps. Inside, old-fashioned lamps cast a smoky glow over the red-and-white checkered tablecloths. There was a long counter, and three tables with two chairs each. A black window hummed from the wall, murky shadows floating behind it like ghosts.

"There's the source of your music." Lucky pointed to a jukebox against the back wall. "It must be programmed to play automatically at certain times."

A stranger in my own life . . .
A ghost behind my smile . . .

Cora closed her eyes. This song was supposed to be private, meant to live only in the pages of a notebook. It was about the night of the accident, when her mother had first threatened to file for divorce. No one wanted a scandal, so Cora had attended her father's political fund-raiser at the last minute in her mother's place. *A Mason smiles, even if her heart is breaking.* She'd worn a green silk dress with lace down the back. On the car ride home, while her father drove, she'd rested her head against the cool glass and listened to the smooth voices on NPR, watched the stars overhead, and made a wish that a smile really could solve everything.

When she opened her eyes, Lucky was looking at her strangely, like he had when they'd first met on the beach. She touched her cheek self-consciously, wondering if her face looked as sunken and heavy as she felt.

"Hey." Leon slammed his fist on the jukebox. "Are they just going to play this song on repeat? What gives?" His head dipped as he searched for buttons. The controls slid around, but nothing happened, almost as if they weren't controls at all.

"Perhaps it is another puzzle," Rolf said quietly.

Cora leaned against the counter, still feeling dazed. The army. The helicopters. The police. They should have arrived by now.

Leon stabbed a finger in Rolf's direction. "If it's a puzzle, solve it, genius."

Rolf trudged over to the jukebox. His fingers flew over the blocks, but nothing he tried worked. Lucky took a try too, but he didn't make any more progress.

The song continued.

Outside, the sunlight faded to the golden color of late afternoon, not suddenly but all at once, like someone had flipped a switch. Cora whirled toward the doorway.

"Did you guys see the light change?" Nok pointed outside. "That's impossible, yeah?"

A clicking noise came from the countertop, and a trapdoor opened, revealing six trays of food. Curry over rice, looking so normal and innocent that it was terrifying.

No one made a move.

Rolf's eyes were wide. "I think it is safe to assume we're in a heavily controlled environment. It appears our food arrives not according to solving a puzzle but in correspondence to the light changing. Perhaps because food is a resource we require, whether we can solve puzzles or not. I would imagine this is supposed to be dinner."

Leon grabbed one of the trays. "Dinner. Breakfast. Whatever, as long as it goes down and stays down."

"Don't eat it." Lucky pointed to the sixth tray, which was empty. "One of us is already gone, remember? The girl Cora and I found. It could be poisoned."

Leon ignored him and dug into the curry. Cora and the

others watched in horrified fascination. He only paused midbite, cheeks full. "In case you were wondering, it's bloody delicious."

Halfway through Leon's meal, the light outside changed again, dropping from dusk to night abruptly. The trays sank back into the counter, as if the food had never existed.

Cora went to the doorway, where Lucky stood with his arms folded across his chest. Across the square, the lights of the Victorian house had come on, blazing in the darkness. The front door was wide open.

"The army isn't coming, is it?" she asked quietly.

Lucky popped the knuckles of his left hand. "I don't think so."

She shivered, though the night was mild. "Whoever put us here turned on the lights in the house. They want us to go there, I think. Pretend this place is real, like dolls in a play world. It feels wrong—like they're setting us up for something."

"Something like what happened to the girl on the beach?"

Cora hugged her arms. "Maybe."

"It's useless to resist." Rolf's shock of red hair popped up between them. "We're like the lab rats. The scientists control the experiment; the rats have no choice but to obey."

"And if they don't?"

"The scientists will throw them out and get new rats."

"Throw them out . . . like *kill* them?" Nok asked from inside the diner. At Rolf's nod, she turned even paler.

"What's the worst that can happen?" Leon grunted, pointing at the house. "There are flowers. And a porch swing. It's hardly a torture den."

He started for it, and the others, one by one, followed.

Inside, the house was just as Rolf had described it: a living room downstairs and a bathroom and three bedrooms upstairs, perfectly normal except for a few odd details, like carpeting inside the fireplace, that made Cora question the sanity of their captors.

Leon poked at a framed portrait of a toaster. "This from IKEA?" he asked Rolf.

"I wouldn't know. And anyway, IKEA furniture comes from Sweden, not Norway."

"Eh, it's all the same up there. Cold days. Long nights. Pretty girls."

Cora rolled her eyes and grabbed his shoulder, pushing him toward the stairs. "Keep going."

"It'll be safer if we all sleep in the same bedroom," Lucky said as they climbed. "Girls on the bed, guys on the floor. I'll take the first watch."

"Let me," Cora said, rubbing her dry eyes. "I'm an insomniac. I'll be up half the night anyway."

He shook his head. "You look like you're about to fall over from exhaustion. All the more reason you should try to sleep. We need all the rest we can get."

Leon gave him a wry salute and went to another room to get more pillows. He came back and threw one to Rolf. "Nighty-night, darling." He flipped off the light.

Rolf and Leon lay down on the floor while Lucky settled into the doorframe and Cora and Nok curled up beneath a blanket. Cora's weary muscles unwound slowly, but the familiar cloudiness of insomnia settled behind her eyes—it didn't matter how tired she was, she knew sleep wouldn't find her. But she must have slept at some point over the last few days, because she'd had the dream about that beautiful man with the bronze-colored skin. She wished he'd opened his eyes, in the dream. She wanted to look into the face of an angel.

At home, when she couldn't sleep, she'd sneak downstairs and borrow her mother's keys and cruise the Virginia back roads, listening to NPR. There had been a story once about the ways the human mind devised to cope with trauma: denial, bargaining, lethargy. The broadcaster talked about teenage girls in refugee camps who were starving and yet, when questioned, listed their biggest problem as trying to find a nice boy to take home to their parents. He said that the human mind is able to adapt to anything.

Cora wasn't too sure about that. When she'd gone to Bay Pines, she had been the outsider: a wealthy girl from a politician's family, charged with murder. When she'd left Bay Pines and returned home, she was an ex-con who knew how to make a shiv out of a toothbrush. That didn't fit well with lacrosse team and cotillion classes.

She rolled over and let lyrics form in the back of her head.

How much can we change . . .
When change is all there is . . .

The black window seemed to hum louder, or maybe it was just in her head. She didn't know which was scarier—seeing their captors, or knowing they were there but not seeing them at all.

9

Nok

NOK SHIVERED IN THE darkness. From where she lay, huddled under the thin blanket that smelled like chemicals, all that was visible through the window was the smear of night. In London, she'd never known true blackness. There'd always been headlights and fluorescent bulbs, streetlights and billboards. Here, it was so deathly quiet. No city noises to drown her memories. She pressed a hand to the base of her throat, expecting the familiar clot of asthma—but her breath came easily.

She rolled over. "Cora, are you still awake?"

"Yeah."

"I know this sounds crazy," she whispered, "but I think whoever put us here cured my asthma. And when we first met, Rolf said he used to wear glasses, but his vision is perfect now. They must be super-advanced scientists to do all that, yeah? What if they aren't . . . human?" Nok drew the blanket higher around her neck.

The other side of the bed was quiet. "You'll never fall asleep if you start worrying about that," Cora said at last. "Think about something better. Home. Tell me about London. The life of a model must be so glamorous."

Glamorous? Nok rolled over onto her pillow. *Not exactly.*

The story she'd told the others had been a detour from the truth. Her childhood had been banana leaves and *khee mao* noodles and dirt roads the color of rust. Her adolescence had been a rare trip to Bangkok with her three sisters, peppermint ice cream from blue glass bowls, a model scout who'd seen her from the street outside and scribbled an address on a napkin he slid to her mother.

Like winning the lottery, her family had said.

Then there'd been a plane ride, twenty other bony girls bound for Europe, giggling and striking silly model poses. The plane landed in London. She couldn't speak a word of English. They'd taken her to a neighborhood filled with sirens and trash, up seven flights of cramped stairs to a flat packed with five girls to a room, sleeping on floor mattresses, cheap clothes and cheaper makeup strewn everywhere. Home, the model scout had said.

She hadn't needed to speak English to understand that it was *not* like winning the lottery.

Nok blinked back to the present. "Home? Right—London. Oh, I've a gorgeous flat there. In Notting Hill, by the river. Penthouse suite with a balcony, a massive bathroom with a chandelier."

"I've been to London. . . ." Cora paused. "I didn't think Notting Hill was near the river."

Nok's heart thudded. She knew that—she'd just spoken in such a rush. "Chelsea, I mean. I moved last year. My flat in Notting Hill was a postage stamp. I couldn't stand it." She craned her head, trying to see on Cora's face if she'd sensed the lie, but there was only darkness.

"Right." Cora's voice was softer. "A chandelier. Wow."

Thank you, Nok mouthed to the heavens. If Cora did suspect anything, she was going to keep it to herself.

The bed bounced, as Cora must have flipped over. "We have a nice house too. My dad invested in tech companies at the right time. Now he's in politics. He doesn't know this, but I painted glow-in-the-dark stars on my bedroom ceiling when I was twelve. You can only see them when the lights are off." She paused. "It seems silly now."

Nok's own secret sweated from her pores as her mind raced for a safer topic. "What . . . do you think about the guys?"

"They're okay," Cora said. "Leon's kind of an ass."

Nok laughed before she could stop herself, and clamped a hand over her mouth. "I never go for those muscle types. Or the good-looking ones, like Lucky. Too full of themselves."

"You think Lucky's cute?"

"You *don't?*"

Cora didn't answer. Nok rolled over on her pillow, staring at the ceiling. That awful silence. One of the boys started snoring. It mingled with the hum from the black panel, and Nok's throat started to close up. Her hand shot to her neck. Blackness swamped her from both sides: the night outside, the black window. She could feel eyes behind that dark glass studying her. She didn't care about being watched—she'd spent her life watched by photographers from behind dark camera lenses.

When she closed her eyes, she could still see their flashing bulbs. Delphine, her steely-haired talent manager who seemed never to age, standing by the doorway eating black licorice, while a photographer who couldn't be more than seventeen hid behind a curtain snapping his bulb like squeezing a trigger. *Bam. Bam. Bam.*

Look beyond the camera, Delphine had said. *Look into the heart of the photographer—not this greasy-faced boy, but every man. Because it will be always be a man, even if a woman is taking the pictures, because it's a man's world. They always want something. Vulnerability. Weakness. Need. When you give it to them, you control them completely.* Sugary black saliva dribbled from the corner of Delphine's mouth as she bit into another licorice stick. *And controlling men is the only way women like you and me will survive.*

"What did you say?" Cora asked.

Nok didn't realize she'd mumbled aloud until Cora's hand squeezed hers in the darkness. "Hey. You should sleep. Lucky's keeping watch, and I don't sleep much either. You can close your eyes. It's safe."

Nok searched the dark ceiling for flashing bulbs but found none. No photographers. No Delphine with her dribbling black licorice.

She didn't let go of Cora's hand. She squeezed her eyes shut and thought of banana leaves and *khee mao* noodles. Her name meant *bird* in Thai; she missed the birds back home.

If she was being honest, the birds were the only thing she missed.

10

Cora

CORA STARED AT THE ceiling, feeling the absence of the glow-in-the-dark stars as strongly as the absence of her necklace. Her eyes were bleary with exhaustion, but her mind wouldn't quiet.

She sat up to see if Lucky was still awake.

The doorway where he was keeping watch was empty. Alarms rang in her head, and she jumped out of bed and checked the other bedrooms, then jogged down the stairs, and stopped.

He sat in the front doorway, head tilted back, eyes closed. He looked peaceful. She could almost believe she was home, a normal girl at a house party that had gone on too late, stumbling upon a cute guy passed out in the doorway.

His head rolled toward her, and his eyes opened. He scrambled to his feet. "Is something wrong?"

"No. I . . . I was just awake. I thought I'd keep you company."

His shoulders eased. He nodded toward the floor, a silent invitation to join him. Cora hesitantly sat in the doorway opposite him, hugging her tired muscles. He tossed his jacket to her as a pillow.

Outside, the jukebox was silent now. It could be midnight, or it could be five in the morning.

Lucky looked at the dark sky. "There aren't any stars here. In Montana, people watch the stars like people in other places watch movies. My granddad used to wake me up when there was a new moon and drag me out to the fields. Said he had Blackfoot blood in his veins, and wanted to teach me his people's legends written in the constellations." He'd been smiling at the memory, but it faded. "I miss him and his old lies. He wasn't any more Blackfoot than I am royalty." He rubbed the place on his wrist where a watch would normally be.

Cora paused. "Is your granddad the one who gave you the watch you're missing?"

His eyebrows rose. "How'd you know?"

"You reach for it when you talk about him." She touched her throat. "I had a necklace that disappeared when I woke up here. It had a charm for each member of my . . ." She stopped. It all sounded so silly. Her life couldn't be summed up by a string of charms. Besides, if she talked too much, Lucky might remember the news stories from two years ago, and he'd never trust her if he knew she'd been in juvie.

Her hand fell away. "Tell me more about your granddad."

Lucky snorted. "He's a grumpy bastard. He got messed up after fighting in Vietnam. I moved out to Montana to live with him a couple years ago—my mom's deceased and my dad's in Afghanistan. Third tour. He only gets leave every six months."

His head was pitched downward so his hair hid his face. She

wanted to tuck those strands back and read the words between his words: a mother who died too early. A father who wasn't there. A grandfather ruined by war. Where did he fit into all that?

"I'm sorry about your mother."

He shrugged a little stiffly. "It was a car accident. Isn't that how they always go—moms who die too young?" He paused and then cleared his throat. "I was little. Five years old. I don't remember much. I didn't see it happen." His words were a little forced; maybe he didn't want her to feel sorry for him, but how could she not? She knew all too well the devastation of squealing brakes, tearing metal, burning plastic. She ran a finger across her lips, not sure how to convey the rush of sympathy she felt. She wanted to squeeze his hand. Press her cheek against his and whisper she was sorry. But her mother was still alive—how could she ever sympathize?

"It must be hard not to have your dad around either," she said at last. "But it's a noble thing he's doing, serving in the army." She winced. She sounded like her dad on the campaign trail, not a friend.

Lucky was quiet for a while, massaging his hand like it felt stiff, but then he brushed his hair back and grinned. "Have a soft spot for soldiers, huh?"

She smiled. "Of course."

"I was on my way to enlist when I woke up here. Just . . . saying."

His words slowly sank in, as her cheeks warmed. Oh, he was definitely a charmer.

He went back to rubbing his hand. "My granddad didn't want me to enlist, but there aren't a lot of options for a kid like me. I'm not exactly academically gifted. Besides, if you get in at eighteen, you can retire by thirty-eight with a full pension. Thought I'd head to Hawaii after my service. Cash government checks and grow old on a beach somewhere with a girl and a guitar."

Cora perked up. "You play guitar?"

He examined his left hand, flexing it slightly. "Not so much anymore." He watched his tendons working, frowning like he was reliving some bad memory. "I busted my hand a few years ago. Got mad and punched a wall. But I still like strumming around, alone so no one can hear how bad it sounds. Music helps me make sense of things."

Cora's heart squeezed. "Yeah, I . . . I know exactly what you mean."

Their eyes met, and she told herself not to look away. Her bleary eyes and tired muscles seemed to fade when she was around him. At last, she cleared her throat. "Maybe whoever put us here will fix your hand. Nok said her asthma was cured, and Rolf's bad vision."

He raised an eyebrow. "I didn't realize we'd been taken by such thoughtful kidnappers."

She leaned into the pillow of his jacket, soaking up the smell of him lingering in the seams. "I think Nok's tougher than she seems. She acts meek, but . . ." She paused. She'd caught Nok in a lie about her living situation in London, but Nok hadn't struck Cora as dangerous or malicious. Just scared. And Cora wasn't one to judge—she was keeping secrets of her own. "Anyway, I like her. It's been a long time since I've had a girl friend." She ran her finger over her chapped lips, regretting saying anything. "Please don't ask why."

"I don't care why."

She smiled. "You're good at this, you know. Keeping everyone calm. You'll be a good leader, in the army."

"Leader?" He snorted. "All the army teaches you is how to follow." He leaned in conspiratorially. "You want to know how I really get the others to listen?"

"Besides punching Leon in the face?"

He smiled, ignoring the comment. "Chickens."

"Chickens?"

He nodded solemnly. "My granddad bought a chicken farm after the war. Preferred their company to humans. They're not so different from people. You'd be surprised."

"You're serious?"

He smiled in a self-conscious way that formed the hint of a dimple in his left cheek. "When laying hens get flustered by a dog or a hawk, you have to reassure them or they won't produce. You put gentle pressure on their wings. Makes them feel safe. Not many people know this, but chickens are smart. They respond to a hierarchy. That's where the whole idea of pecking order comes from." His smile faded. "Whenever my granddad introduces new chickens to the flock, he plays them music. The same song over and over. It lulls them into complacency."

Cora shook out his leather jacket and wrapped it tightly around her shoulders. "You think whoever put us here is doing the same thing, with that jukebox?"

He paused. "Maybe. Nothing really makes sense. I mean, why the five of us? Six, if you count that dead girl. Were we just in the wrong place at the wrong time? I don't know why they'd want me. I'm just a part-time mechanic who's failed more classes than he's passed."

He leaned his head back, so his hair fell away and showed that dimple. Her first night in Bay Pines, she'd been so scared and alone. She'd cried into her pillow so her roommate wouldn't hear. Now, the same sting pushed behind her eyes. She wiped away the start of tears.

He was quiet for a moment, then reached out an arm. "Come here."

"What are you doing?" she asked.

"I'm going to chicken you."

Cora's surprise melted as he pulled her into a hug, like he would a frightened bird. She started laughing and crying, either or both or somewhere in between, but she felt less alone. Friendships were important; that was something she'd learned at Bay Pines. The dimple didn't hurt, either.

CORA WAS GROGGY WITH half sleep when hazy morning light spilled through the open doorway. If she'd slept at all, it had only been fits and starts. No dreams of angels. Only nightmares.

She rubbed her eyes and found Lucky snoring against the doorframe.

They were very smart, their captors. Very clever. They hadn't gotten all the details right, but at first glance through the doorway, she could almost be fooled. The light was soft and pink, like a sunrise. The gentle sound of ocean waves echoed from the beach. The town would be convincing, if they hadn't thrown such disparate types of architecture together in an attempt to condense the world's thousands of cultures into a single town square.

The sound of jukebox music drifted toward her, and Lucky

jerked awake, muscles tense until he saw they were safe.

Leon came sauntering down the stairs, disheveled, and stared through the front door. "Bloody hell," he muttered. "I'd hoped it was a bad dream."

Nok came down behind him. She'd transformed her drab black dress into an outfit worthy of the runway. She'd ripped the hem to shorten it, cinched the waist with one of Leon's ties—he certainly wasn't using them—and thrown on a band T-shirt identical to the one Cora wore. Rolf came tripping down the stairs last, looking like a sleepy porcupine with his hair sticking up at random angles.

Nok rested a hand on her hip, striking a pose without even meaning to. "You don't mind me wearing one of your shirts, do you, Cora? There are duplicates of everything in the dressers upstairs. As if anyone would need *ten* of this awful dress. And if we're going to be rescued today, I might as well look good."

Cora forced a smile. *Smile, even when you aren't sure a rescue is going to come.*

Lucky stood, stretching his back. "I had some ideas last night about how we can figure out where we are and who put us here."

Leon patted him heavily on the shoulder. "Sure thing, Bright Eyes. Just not before breakfast." He sauntered toward the diner.

Lucky cursed and started after Leon.

Rolf rubbed the back of his neck like it ached, watching the two boys argue outside, and then finger combed his hair back into place. "Leon took my pillow in the middle of the night. Said he was twice my size so he should get twice the pillows."

He chewed on his lip and blinked. Though Cora was usually good at reading people, Rolf was an enigma. His red hair swept down to nearly hide his eyes, two blue-green mysteries in an otherwise expressionless face.

"You can't let him bully you," she said.

His face remained impassive, except for a slight twitch in one eye. "Guys like him have been beating up on me my entire life. We call them *bøller*—bullies. I tried standing up for myself once. I went to a private school in Oslo where a team of boys twice my size waited for me each day after school by the bus stop. Karl Crenshaw was their leader. He was a big Scottish kid, ugly, always made fun of my twitches. One day he beat me with a cricket bat. I was in a coma for two weeks."

Nok made a sympathetic pout, which shifted suddenly into a frown. "Do you feel that?"

Cora did. Her skin was tingling. The hair on her arms and the back of her neck rose like static electricity. She exchanged a worried glance with Nok. "We've got to get the others."

They ran toward the square as a crackling sound started, but Cora couldn't trace it. It seemed to come from *everywhere*. It built like pressure, a constrictive feeling like taking off in an airplane, and got stronger and stronger until Cora thought her body might burst.

As she rounded the corner, she saw Lucky ahead. He turned and met her eyes. She'd never thought she'd see someone so brave look so afraid.

A scream came from behind her, and she whirled to find Nok with a hand over her mouth, letting out frightened little gasps. A creeping feeling crawled up her neck—the same feeling she got around the black windows, only a thousand times stronger. Lucky crashed into her, holding her tight, preventing her from turning around.

"What is it?"

"Don't, Cora. Don't look."

Whatever was standing right behind her was terrifying even to someone as brave as him. But he couldn't stop her from looking. She had to.

She looked over her shoulder.

They weren't alone.

11

Cora

A NEW FIGURE—A MAN—STOOD next to the cherry tree. He had to be close to seven feet tall. Something about his black uniform suggested a soldier, though Cora had never seen clothes like his before. They fit closely to the muscles of his arms and chest and moved with him so seamlessly that they were almost liquid cloth—except for the row of knots down one side. He wore a utility band slung across his chest, which glistened with equipment that looked far more advanced than the prototypes her father invested in. He carried himself as stiffly as a soldier in an army recruiting ad, with buzzed hair and the straight back of a warrior—except for a few key differences. His impressive height. His skin, which was somewhere in between the color of copper and bronze and reflected the sunlight like metal. And his eyes.

They had no irises. No whites. They were entirely black.

Breath slipped from her. His was the face from her dreams.

The most beautiful creature she had ever seen, yet he no longer looked angelic. He was terrifying.

And he isn't human.

They weren't in a dream or virtual reality. They'd been taken by gods or aliens—or monsters.

The soldier flexed his glove.

Rolf fell to his knees. Nok crumpled next to him. The soldier's presence screamed danger, but there was something captivating about him too, like staring into a flame. It was impossible to look away.

Coldness pooled between her shoulder blades. She leaned closer to Lucky, her heart pounding. Had this man been the shadowy figure behind those black windows? Studying them, like Rolf said? Was he the one who had dressed her in a stranger's clothes?

Movement flickered to her left.

The black-eyed man's presence didn't seem to have the same captivating effect on Leon, who let out a war cry and lunged forward. Cora's breath caught. *Don't fight back,* that was the rule in situations like this, but Leon hadn't gotten the memo—or hadn't cared.

The soldier watched patiently, arms at his sides.

Leon collided with him.

Cora flinched. She expected cracking bones and spurting blood, but the moment Leon touched his shoulder, the stranger threw him. It was an effortless movement, no more than swatting a fly, but it sent Leon—who had to weigh 250 pounds—fifteen feet away.

All the strength from Cora's body drained into the grass.

Leon pushed himself up, shaking the sweat out of his hair, looking stricken. "That bastard—he zapped me with something!"

But the stranger held no weapons.

"Remain calm," the soldier said. There was no trace of an accent, but his pitch was monotone and deep, just as unnatural as his eyes. "You are not in danger."

"Who are you?" Lucky asked.

The soldier cocked his head. A second passed, and then another. Cora burrowed deeper against Lucky's chest. The man's eyes burned right through her, down to her innermost thought, hypnotizing her with a single look. She traced her eyes over his bare arms, his hands, his chest. The angel from her dreams—or rather, a demon. He looked so very close to being human, but he was beyond that, clearly from another place or time. Not just his metallic skin and otherworldly beauty, but the magnetic feeling he gave off. He radiated *otherness*.

"I am your Caretaker," he said.

"Take us home," Lucky demanded.

The Caretaker tilted his head as though perplexed by the idea. "That is impossible. You are on our aggregate space station, far from your solar system. These habitats are meant to replicate the lives you would have experienced on Earth. We hope they please you."

Cora drew in a sharp breath.

Not on Earth?

Her fingers fell away from Lucky and curled around the edges of a nearby tree, her stomach weightless even though nothing had changed. The tree beneath her hand wasn't real. The grass wasn't real. It wasn't attached to soil—only whatever made up their space station, metal and pipes and tubing and materials she'd probably never heard of.

A cherry-blossom petal fluttered to the ground.

It landed in the grass, and she jerked her head up. Nok sobbed loudly—real tears, nothing fake now—and Rolf took her hand, as though hand-holding could protect them. Leon was still on the ground, looking stunned.

Stay calm. Wait for help. Meaningless words now.

"Why did you bring us here?" Cora asked.

"We took you for your own benefit. My people are called the Kindred. We are the most advanced among the intelligent species and, as such, take responsibility for overseeing lesser races. We are stewards of endangered species such as yours."

"Endangered?" The word tasted wrong in Cora's mouth. Siberian tigers were endangered. Polar bears were endangered. Not humans.

The Caretaker flexed his black gloves. "Earth is a dangerous and unpredictable world. The practices of your species are unsustainable. So we have brought you here, to this enclosure, where we can ensure the survival of your race regardless of your planet's well-being. Here you have ample sustenance and a microcosm of the various habitats and cultures in your world. We have given you a variety of stimuli to exercise your minds and bodies. You will find these enrichment activities to be rewarding."

He produced a small token from his pocket identical to the ones they had found in the shops. It glinted in the sunlight, burning dark spots into Cora's eyes. "There are eight enrichment puzzles in the biomes, and eight in the settlement areas. Complete each enrichment activity and you will receive a token redeemable in any of these commercial establishments. The candy and toys are authentic artifacts from Earth that will help you maintain an emotional connection to your previous home."

She stared at him. Games. Toys. Candy. These creatures—the Kindred—thought they were children.

No, not children.

Animals.

Cora clenched her jaw, centering herself. Her headache throbbed, pushing her toward anger.

"Why us?" Lucky asked.

The Caretaker's black eyes shifted among them. "You each display valuable attributes. Strength. Morality. Beauty. You are, in your own ways, paragons of your species."

Nok started whimpering low, like a dog.

"We have three rules we require you to follow," the Caretaker continued, oblivious of her fear, "which are for your own benefit and that of your species. The first is to solve the enrichment puzzles. This will strengthen your physical and mental conditioning. The second rule is to maintain your health by eating the food we provide for you, getting ample sleep, and cooperating in routine health assessments. The third rule is to ensure the continuation of your species by engaging in procreative activities."

He spoke with such little inflection that Cora almost didn't get it at first. *Procreative activities?* She took a step back as though the Caretaker had just burst into flames. "You put us here to reproduce?" she choked.

The Caretaker turned to her. "We require immediate compliance with Rule One and Rule Two, but we understand that your species does not adapt quickly to new situations, so we have granted you an adjustment phase. By the end of twenty-one days, we expect you to fully engage in Rule Three. If not, you will face removal."

Removal. The word had a sinister ring. "Is that what happened to the dead girl we found on the beach? She didn't cooperate, so you killed her?"

The stranger's eyes shifted to Cora, and she got that involuntary shiver down her spine again. There was something so unnerving about him. So familiar. He'd been in her head—in her dreams.

"Girl Three's death was the result of an accident," he replied.

Girl Three? Was that how their captors thought of them, as nameless specimens? What did that make her, Girl One or Girl Two?

He continued, "She attempted to swim too far through the ocean habitat before we had properly adjusted the saline levels. On Earth she was a gifted swimmer; we had not anticipated how far she could go. The problem has been corrected. There will be no more accidents. Your safety is of utmost importance to us."

Cora turned toward Lucky and dropped her voice. "Are you buying all this altruistic stuff about saving us?"

His face looked grim. "Not even a little bit."

Despite the Caretaker's dazzling appearance, he was a liar. A kidnapper. A criminal. Well, after eighteen months locked up with teenage murderers and pushers, she had plenty of experience dealing with criminals.

Don't fight back. Don't try to escape.

That had been her father's security officer's advice for kidnapping situations, and she'd followed the same logic in juvie. She had kept her head down, barely spoken to anyone, scrawled her fear and frustration in her song journal instead of letting herself feel anything. She had waited for help to come, as she was supposed to do. She had obeyed the rules.

But help wasn't coming this time.

She was close enough to see the set of his jaw, the rope-like muscles in his neck. The metallic sheen of his skin hid most imperfections, but not the bump in his nose or the scar on the side of his throat. His chest rose and fell with each breath. Flaws. Breathing. So he wasn't a machine—which meant he could be hurt.

One of the apparatuses strapped to his chest gleamed like the hilt of a knife. *That* could even the playing field. But how could she take it from someone with such incredible strength?

"I need help," she blurted out. "My wrist. I hurt it when I woke in the desert."

Lucky shot her a warning look, but Cora didn't tear her eyes away from the Caretaker. She took a step toward him. He regarded her coldly, as though he could see straight through her lie. A crackling sensation began in the air, and the hair on her arms tingled. He was going to vanish as suddenly as he had appeared.

"Wait!" Cora took another step forward. "Don't go yet. I need help."

"Do not come forward." His voice was cold as the pressure built faster. He started flickering in front of her, and she knew he'd be gone in seconds, along with any answers. Right now—this moment—was her only chance.

She lunged for the knife hilt, but his hand was on her wrist in a second, and she let out a cry. Electricity pulsed through her bare skin into her nerves, tingling and jittery and just short of painful. Now she knew what Leon meant about being zapped.

Only it wasn't a zap, it was plunging into an icy pool of water. Falling toward nothing. Dying, all at once. She jerked her arm but couldn't get free.

Lucky called her name. Footsteps ran through the grass. But she was swallowed by the pressure. She *was* the pressure. It coated her skin, wormed into her head, until she thought she would shatter into a million pieces.

Then, just as suddenly, the pressure was gone. Lucky's voice calling her name was gone.

But the stranger was not.

His hand still held hers, his skin against her skin, flooding her with that wild sensation she couldn't name. They were no longer in the town square but in a plain room. The only light came from seams in the metallic walls and radiated out like starlight.

The Caretaker released her hand. She fell backward, blinded by the starlight, elbow slamming into the hard floor. She scrambled into the corner. Her elbow screamed in pain, but so did every other part of her.

The Caretaker stood over her, speaking rushed words she didn't understand into a device on his wrist. The static-like voice that spoke back to him in guttural bursts sounded furious.

She dared to peek between her fingers, like she had as a little girl watching a scary movie. A window was set in the wall in front of her, three feet tall and six feet long, but this one wasn't liquid black and opaque. It was almost like a one-way mirror, cloudy but transparent, and beyond it Lucky and Leon and Nok and Rolf argued soundlessly in the grass. She pushed herself to her feet with shaky steps, cradling her elbow.

"This is how you watch us," she whispered. "You can see us, but we can't see you."

The Caretaker paused in speaking into his wrist and looked at her. A muscle twitched in his ropelike jaw. He had called it an enclosure, a habitat, but she knew better.

It was a cage.

12

Lucky

LUCKY SHOVED ASIDE THE cherry tree's weeping branches for the millionth time, but there was no sign of Cora. "She can't have just vanished!"

Rolf's face was beet red, his fingers twitching frantically. "He took her—don't you understand?"

"I don't, actually. I have no idea what's going on!"

Nok collapsed, burying her face in the grass. She sobbed in big racking shudders, clutching her head like it ached, smearing snot all over the grass. Jesus. Not that he could blame her—he'd nearly pissed his pants when that metal-skinned creature had appeared—but *someone* had to hold their shit together. Not that he was any type of leader, but in a group with a fashion model, a twitchy recluse, a bully, and a girl whose life he had ruined, he guessed he was the closest thing.

Leon cast Nok a disgusted look. "This isn't the time for breakdowns, sweetheart. Get up!"

He kicked her.

"Hey!" Lucky shoved Leon, hard. "Don't be a jerk." Was everyone insane? They were acting like terrified preschoolers, picking fights, throwing tantrums. "She's scared, you bastard."

Leon kicked her again, harder this time.

"Oh, hell no." Lucky started toward Leon, but Nok pushed herself up from the grass, cheeks slick with tears. Hot anger twisted her mouth. Her knee connected with Leon's groin in a satisfying *smack* that sent him doubled over to the ground.

"Christ, woman! You trying to kill me?"

In response, she started kicking him harder with her long, bony feet. "How does that feel? You like that?"

Lucky exchanged a look with Rolf. He knew he should pull Nok away, but he had to admit that it was satisfying to watch. Nok gave one more kick before Lucky grabbed her.

"That's enough. Not that he didn't deserve it."

Leon rolled over, staring at the sky with glassy eyes. A husky grunt came out of his mouth.

Lucky released Nok. "Stop fighting for one second and let's think this through. We need to find out where that creature took Cora. She couldn't have just disappeared."

Rolf shoved his spindly fingers through his hair. "Yes, she could. We're not on Earth anymore. They can bend space and time. We don't even know what they want."

"They want us to sleep together!" Nok sank to the grass next to the supine Leon, their earlier fight forgotten. "They want us to have babies so they can do god knows what, probably torture them or raise little human slaves." Her face went white. "What if they eat them?"

Rolf crouched next to her and patted her back stiffly. "I'm sure that's not the case. Otherwise they'd just eat *us*."

Nok's face went paler. Lucky let out a silent curse—Rolf was only making it worse. He rubbed his face, hoping to jar some sense into himself. He'd been looking right at Cora when she'd vanished. She'd tossed her head back to look at him one last time. The last time someone had looked at him with such fear in her eyes had been his mother, right before she'd died. He'd told Cora he'd been five years old when she died, not fifteen. He'd told her he hadn't seen it, when he'd been in the very car. His mother had yelled out his real name—*Luciano*. Then squealing brakes and twisting metal. Rain and broken glass. Waking up disoriented in a hospital, attached to an IV. His dad there, still wearing his fatigues, eyes sunken from the flight from Afghanistan, saying the worst words in the world.

"She didn't make it."

He'd ripped the IV out of his arm. Shouted. His dad tried to hold him down. His granddad's face, with its gray beard, peering through the glass window in the door. Then he was out of bed, and he *burned*. He slammed his fist into the cement wall. Blood spurted from his left hand. He'd had the random and misplaced thought that no one would ever call him Luciano again.

Only his mom used his real name.

He'd seen the other driver. A fancy politician type who would get off on a technicality. It made his blood burn enough that, as soon as he was out of the hospital, he drove to the airfield with his dad's pistol tucked in his waistband. He wasn't planning to kill the senator, exactly. He just wanted to point the gun and see the look in his eyes.

Revenge can't bring your mother back, the senator's men had said when they'd stopped him. *Neither can money, but it can give you opportunities you'd never have. Your grandfather's farm is going into foreclosure. . . .*

He'd hated himself for it, but he'd taken their money.

It had been an *awful* lot of zeroes.

"Nok." He forced himself to sound calm. "It's going to be okay. Seriously. Stop crying."

She looked up from her hands. A collection of black dots flashed on the milky white skin of her neck, standing out as bright as stars against the night sky. It triggered a memory. His granddad showing him the stars.

Constellations.

That's what the black dots formed on Nok's neck, he realized. A constellation. Cassiopeia, to be exact. He grabbed Rolf, who protested weakly, and pushed back his hair to see identical black dots.

Dazed, he turned to Leon, who held up his hands.

"Keep your hands to yourself, brother."

"I think the marks on our necks are constellations. Yours"— he craned his neck to see Leon's neck—"looks like the Big Dipper." He felt his own neck. "Mine is Orion. And that's what Cora has too, if I'm remembering right."

Nok abruptly stopped crying, feeling her neck.

"That makes no sense," Rolf said. "Constellations aren't fixed in the sky into certain shapes. If you looked at the same stars from any other planet, they would appear different. And we aren't on Earth."

"Well, I have no idea why they marked us with stars, and I have no idea why they put Leon in a suit and Rolf in a military jacket, and I have no idea where Cora is right now. I have no damn idea why any of this is happening."

Rolf cleared his throat. "I might."

Lucky spun on him. Rolf's cheeks burned as he continued. "It isn't so crazy, you know—that they could be telling the truth. Humans *are* destroying the planet. Maybe it will take another few thousand years, or maybe it will happen tomorrow. But maybe they did take us to preserve our species."

"You *believe* them?" Lucky said.

Rolf pushed at his nose like he was used to wearing glasses. "I'm saying that we should consider all options. As far as the marks on our necks, I don't know why they used constellations, but I can guess *why* we're marked. Rule Three. Procreation. The symbols match us in pairs. Nok and me. Lucky and Cora. Leon and . . ." He blinked. "Well, the girl who died, I suppose."

For a moment, no one spoke. Lucky's stomach twisted. The Kindred had matched him with the girl he'd sent to juvie. It couldn't be a coincidence. Was it some kind of retribution for what he'd done? A sick experiment?

He ran a shaky hand over his face. He'd been so close to a fresh start. Two months until graduation, until he was shipped off for some boot-camp crap and then on a plane to some faraway country where people would likely shoot at him, but he didn't care. He'd been prepared for insurgents. He hadn't been prepared for this.

Maybe he should just stay away from Cora. He'd already hurt her enough. But the thought of that black-eyed monster laying a hand on her made him livid. Maybe it was time to tell her the truth.

If she ever came back.

13

Cora

CORA RESTED HER FINGERS on the viewing panel. Beyond the glass, Lucky and Leon were hurling accusations at each other while Rolf clutched Nok, who was sobbing.

I'm here, Cora wanted to say. *I'm right here.*

"You are not supposed to be here," the Caretaker said. "I must return you."

He seized her shoulders. Electricity tore through her. She tried to twist away, but he lifted her so high her feet dangled above the ground.

"Put me down!"

Incredibly, he did. Her feet connected with the floor. She winced as her hurt elbow popped. He took notice and turned her arm palm up, then gently inspected the bruised bone of her elbow. His fingers tightened over the bones, and with a snap they realigned.

She stumbled back to the safety of the wall. "How did you do that? And how did we transport here?"

He touched the knife hilt. "You thought you could harm me with this, but it is not a weapon." He pulled it out, a thin strip of metal that ended in a needle as long as her forearm. It dripped with something that looked like blood, but darker than a human's. "It allows me, and anything I am touching, to dematerialize. Now take my hand."

She shook her head.

"I thought it was a dream," she muttered. Memories of his beautiful face stumbled into her head. "But it wasn't. It was real. I remember your face because you were the one who took me, didn't you?"

"I must return you to your habitat."

He reached for her. She jerked back, staying close to the edges of the room. Her eyes searched for any possible exits but found nothing. The light was bolder on the far wall, beneath what looked like a pulsing blue cube; starry light poured through wall seams that were shaped like a rectangle and tall enough for a person to pass.

Was it a door?

Don't fight back. Don't try to escape.

But this wasn't a man she was going to be able to reason with. This wasn't a guard at Bay Pines who could be bribed or flirted with. Wherever they were, the police weren't going to find them. The only thing left *was* escape.

"You cannot escape," he answered.

She whirled. Had he read her thoughts—or just seen the intention on her face? Either way, she forced her chin high.

"I can try."

She shoved off from the wall and dived toward the doorway, just as he lurched toward her. She braced to feel his superhuman grip on her arm, but a burst of static came from the communication device on his wrist. It distracted him long enough for her to dig her fingers into the glowing door seams and pull until her muscles screamed, but nothing happened.

Then, abruptly, the door slid open on its own.

She fell through and slammed onto a hard metallic floor on the other side. Four sets of perfectly polished black boots stood in front of her, attached to bodies that, when she dared to look up, showed four sets of black eyes. Kindred. Just like the Caretaker. They were all between six and seven feet tall. All with skin that shimmered like metal, ranging from dark bronze to ruddy copper, and dressed in cerulean blue uniforms with knots along the left side—three had six knots, one had seven. Two had a slimmer build, with glossy black hair tugged back in stiff knots and uniforms tailored to their curves. Females.

None of them had the Caretaker's knifelike apparatus strapped to them, but they all wore some form of equipment slung around their hips. It spanned their thighs and looked like the protective wear an athlete might wear, but it was covered in flat buttons. When the black-tipped fingers of one of the females pressed against the buttons, Cora realized they were keypads.

The four Kindred stood in front of a metal table that bore a body, lying flat as though sleeping, long dark hair still stained with salt. On the girl's chin, a scar shaped like a lopsided heart.

The dead girl. Cora screamed.

Powerful hands grabbed her from behind and lifted her to her feet. The Caretaker let her go, and she braced herself against the wall, head spinning. "What are you doing to her?"

The Caretaker's wrist communicator buzzed incessantly, but he ignored it. "They are examining Girl Three's body, as per protocol. They are researchers who are here to monitor your safety and record data about your interactions."

"She's *dead*! What do you need to monitor?"

The Caretaker's black eyes slid to the others. "Every time a ward dies, we take the opportunity to examine the body, to record any changes in your species' physical evolution."

"Evolution happens over aeons. You can't track it with one person."

"Your limited mind cannot understand our advanced technology, nor the finer points of evolutionary theory."

There was an ominous ring to his words. The girl with the heart-shaped scar was naked now, no more white sundress; and from what Cora could see, she didn't have webbed fingers or extra toes or anything evolutionarily advanced. She was just a girl, like Cora. It hadn't been that long ago that Cora and Lucky had dragged her out of the water.

"You are frightened." For once, the Caretaker's voice sounded softer, and she jerked her head toward him in surprise. Had he seen how her hands were trembling? "There is no reason to be. We do not mean to harm you. That would go against the responsibilities we have assumed."

Before she could respond, another section of the wall slid open and starry light filled the room, blinding her. She shaded her eyes. Footsteps approached quickly. The air shot from her lungs as something slammed into her. She collided against the opposite wall with a sickening crack. She tried to breathe, but an enormous fist clamped around the back of her neck, thumb pressing into her windpipe.

When the door shut and sealed off the blinding light, she found herself inches from another Kindred. A man. This one was dressed in the same cerulean uniform of the researchers, but his build was more like the Caretaker's. Tall. Warrior-like. Though unlike the Caretaker, no scars or broken bones marred his face. He was just as strikingly beautiful as all of them, and yet his eyes were a little too sunken, a little too sharp, like a permanent knot had formed between them. He scowled, and a vertical wrinkle sliced between his eyebrows.

He spoke words she didn't understand.

Cora couldn't breathe. The man's touch sparked electricity, but it wasn't thrilling like it had been with the Caretaker. This was pulsing and painful. She clawed against his fist.

The Caretaker lowered his head as if this was his commander and spoke in rapid, insistent words. Was he trying to *help* her?

A chill ran up her spine as she realized that these creatures, as mechanical as they seemed, might actually think for themselves. Disagree with each other. Argue. She almost preferred to think of them as machines.

"Do not struggle, Girl Two," the Caretaker said. "This is the Warden of this facility. His name is Fian. He merely wishes to examine you."

Cora jerked her head toward the dead girl they'd been examining. She started to speak, but the Warden's hand tightened more around her windpipe. She fought the urge to claw his face off.

The Warden slowly took each of her hands—the electricity of his touch sickening her—and inspected her fingers front and back, turned her around to feel the muscles along either side of her spine, then pulled her jaw open to look at her teeth. Last, he touched her hair. It was the first time he had been at all gentle. He ran his fingers down the length of it to her chest, and then slowly wrapped one curl around his finger.

He wasn't inspecting her like a dead body. He was inspecting her like livestock.

He released her abruptly. He said a few words in guttural tones and then, without a single glance, left through the starry doorway. Inspection over. She slumped against the wall, heart pounding.

Had she passed?

The Caretaker spoke to the researchers, who filed out of the room. One of them, a female with a thin nose and high cheekbones, threw Cora one last look, though her face was a perfect mask of nonemotion. Did the woman pity her? Was she curious? Or was it merely protocol?

The door slid closed, and Cora sank to the floor. "What was that?"

"The Warden believes your actions indicate you are not suitable for this enclosure. He intended to remove you." His gaze veered to the dead girl, so fast she almost missed it. "I convinced him to reconsider, given your assets. I said that your presence in this chamber was accidental—that you had not intended to leave your enclosure." He leaned over her, his face a mask of indifference. "I saved your life."

He spoke so calmly. Cora could only stare, afraid he'd take that favor back.

"Now I must return you, and there can be no further *accidents*. The Warden does not offer second chances."

He pulled her to her feet, and the spark of his electricity

made her light-headed. Warm, invigorating, not like the Warden's touch. It eased the heaviness of her limbs. He reached for the apparatus strapped to his chest.

She pulled away.

"Wait—I can't go through that again. It feels like being ripped apart. Can't you take me back another way?"

He paused. For a second, she wondered if he really did pity her. She wondered if they were telling the truth about their altruistic mission, that they had saved her from a doomed planet. But then her eyes fell to the girl with the heart-shaped scar, and anger wove between her ribs. Her throat still ached from the Warden's grip.

Strangling her hadn't seemed very altruistic.

"Materialization is the primary means of transportation into your enclosure," the Caretaker said. "There is a fail-safe exit in case of a technological breakdown, but this current situation does not warrant its use."

"An exit? Like, a physical door?"

His only answer was to extend his hand. "Come. Soon you will be back where you belong, Girl Two."

He was waiting for her to take his hand, giving her this small measure of control. She took it hesitantly. The pressure shifted again, that terrible squeezing that suffocated every pore, and she clutched the Caretaker around the neck, afraid that if she let go of him, or if he let go of her, she would disappear into a thousand particles. His skin was hard as metal, but supple. And warm. So much warmer than she thought it would be. Not at all like the Warden's harsh grip.

In the next instant, pressure consumed her.

14

Cora

JUST WHEN CORA COULDN'T bear another moment of bone-splitting pressure, grass materialized beneath her feet. Distant waves crashed. The sun shone directly overhead.

They were back in the cage.

The breeze tangled in her hair, along with the metallic smell of the Caretaker's skin. She let him go as if he was a spark and she a dry piece of wood.

"Get away from her!" Lucky's voice cut like a knife. She turned in a daze as he and the others sprinted across the grass.

The Caretaker ignored them, eyes only on Cora. "Remember: three rules. That is all we require." His outline flickered like an old-fashioned television set and then vanished, just as the others rushed up.

Cora wiped her mouth, swallowing hard despite the memory of the Warden's hand clamped around her neck. "I'm okay. He took me to a room I wasn't supposed to see. It's where they observe us." She pointed toward the candy shop, head foggy. "It was behind one of these black windows."

Rolf frowned. "The candy shop wall that supports the black window can't be more than six inches thick—not nearly enough room for a viewing chamber." His lips moved silently as he seemed to be performing calculations. "The black windows must work on forced perspective technology that's more advanced than anything I've heard of. The walls appear straight, but they must bend to accommodate viewing chambers."

Cora dug her knuckles into her aching forehead. "I don't know, but there are more of the Kindred, behind the windows. Researchers. And the one who's in charge—they called him the Warden. His real name is Fian. He was huge like the Caretaker, with a knot of angry wrinkles between his eyebrows. He tried to strangle me, but the Caretaker stopped him. And I saw . . ." She paused. How would they react when she told them about the dead girl?

"So this is *it*?" Nok cried. "We're here for the rest of our lives? No more walks through Hyde Park, or old *Star Trek* reruns, or any of that?"

She was pacing wildly, near the breaking point, and Cora swallowed back the words she'd been poised to say. One horror at a time.

Lucky pulled Nok into a hug. Nok collapsed against his shoulder, though she was a good three inches taller than him, and let out a burst of runny-nose tears.

"We'll get out of here," he said softly, meeting Cora's eyes over Nok's shoulder. "I promise. We'll go home."

Home. What had Charlie done, when she'd disappeared

from the passenger side of his Jeep? She pictured her father holed up in a hotel room with his security staff, the head of the FBI on the phone. Maybe her disappearance had finally brought them all together; a family again, only without her. Or, for all she knew, the Kindred had wiped every memory they had of her.

She let out a choked breath.

She leaned in to them, her face pressed between Nok's cheek and Lucky's shoulder. To Cora's surprise, Leon crashed into her, wrapping his big arms around all of them. Rolf was the only one left alone, his fingers twitching against the stiff pockets of his military jacket. Cora grabbed his wrist and pulled him into the group embrace. It was the five of them, no longer strangers, any differences they once might have had now meaningless. Nok slipped her bony hand into Cora's and squeezed.

Girl Two, the Caretaker had called her. No longer a person. Now a specimen. Given a second chance only because the Caretaker had intervened.

"I know we're all strung out," Lucky said. "We can get through this, as long as we stick together." The group broke apart shakily. The morning light turned to noon in a single click, and Cora's song started on the jukebox.

"Great," Leon muttered. "Lunchtime. I feel better already."

"Food's not a bad idea, actually." Lucky cracked the knuckles in his left hand. "None of us have eaten anything in days, except for Leon, and he's alive, so it must be safe. Rolf, you and I will bring the trays out here so we all have some fresh air to help us think. Nok . . ." He paused, avoiding Cora's eyes. "Tell Cora what we figured out . . . about the marks on our necks."

He disappeared with Rolf into the diner. Nok stumbled

through an explanation about the matching constellations, and by the time Lucky came back with the trays of noodles, Cora understood why Lucky hadn't told her himself. They were *matched*? She could barely look at him without feeling mortified—although a small voice in her head whispered that he was the kind of guy she'd always liked. Not arrogant, like the boys she'd gone to school with. Not flamboyantly dramatic, like most of the guys in Charlie's theater classes.

The kind of guy with grease on his hands.

She looked down at her noodles. They smelled wrong—sticky sweet. The song ended and flipped over, starting again. Was it supposed to make them complacent—or torture them?

"So," Lucky said. "We should figure out what the hell is going on."

"We've been abducted by little green men," Leon said. "Or in this case, big bronze men. What more do you need?"

"I need to know why." Lucky turned to Rolf. "No offense, Rolf, but I don't believe they're telling the truth about why they brought us here. So what do we know? They took the five of us specifically. They want us to reproduce, which is . . . messed up. They're watching us from behind those panels. They want to study us in our natural habitat"—he motioned to the row of fake shops—"or whatever this is supposed to be. Why? For entertainment?"

"Maybe they want to see how we interact?" Nok offered. "Like, not just our daily lives, but under pressure. When situations change. Maybe that's why they've dressed us in clothes that aren't ours and thrown us together in random pairs and given us food that tastes wrong. I mean, this looks like *khee mao* noodles, but it tastes like a cinnamon bun."

"To what end?" Lucky asked.

Nok tapped her chin, thinking, and then a look of horror crept over her face. "What if they're going to attack Earth? Maybe this is all a war scenario. They might want to see how people will react under pressure so they can make it an easy fight."

Everyone was quiet. Cora's song played steadily from the jukebox, taunting them.

"Maybe." Lucky rubbed his forehead like his head ached. "It's one possible theory, and it explains some things, but not others. If that were the case, why would they care if we reproduce? I was thinking, maybe we really are like lab rats. The Kindred seem pretty similar to us, physically. They can speak our language, so our vocal cords must be similar, and they breathe the same air we do, so we must just be a few chromosomes away or something. Wouldn't that make us perfect test subjects?"

Rolf frowned. "Theoretically."

"They could be developing some new kind of drug but don't want to test it out on themselves first. We're the lab chimps now. And the drugs . . ." Lucky looked at the noodles.

Nok and Rolf both shoved their trays away.

"There's something else." Cora knew she couldn't withhold what she'd seen forever. "While I was in their control rooms, I saw the dead girl's body. They were examining it. Maybe experimenting—I don't know. They said it was protocol to monitor dead bodies for signs that humans were evolving, but she looked perfectly normal to me. It felt like they were covering for something."

Even Leon dropped his fistful of noodles. He always looked

so tough, but for once he seemed almost stricken. Cora recalled that the girl with the heart-shaped scar was supposed to have been his match.

"This is seriously shitty. All of it." He pushed off from the grass and sauntered toward the row of shops.

Lucky shook his head. "That guy is going to be trouble."

Cora watched Leon disappear in the town. "I'll talk to him."

15

Cora

CORA FOUND LEON SITTING on the movie theater steps, head cradled in his hands. "Leon, you can't just run off. We need to decide what we're going to do."

"We're going to die, that's what."

She paused. She'd seen him angry, and impatient, but never depressed. "We're not going to die. The Kindred brought us here, which means they can take us back. It's nonsense, what they said about humans destroying the Earth. Humans have been polluting for centuries. It'll take aeons before we actually destroy it—if we ever do."

He tossed a stone from the potted marigolds into the grass. "You remind me of my sister, you know that? She has hair just like yours. She never gives it a rest either—always telling me I run from my problems."

She sat next to him. "Your sister has blond hair?"

He snorted. "She dyes it. And she's got about fifty pounds

on you, but yeah. Long blond hair. Same annoying way of giving me a hard time." He tossed a pebble at her foot, not hard enough to hurt. The others' voices were barely audible from the town square. "I can't stop thinking about that girl. The dead one. How she and I were supposed to be together . . . or whatever."

Sweat trickled down his face. He tossed another pebble.

"Do you have a girlfriend at home?" Cora asked softly.

He snorted. "I'm not exactly boyfriend material, sweetheart. Dad's in prison. My two older brothers too. My little sister, Ellie, made me swear I wouldn't end up like them. She was the only one who believed I had a chance to do something other than get locked up." He glanced at the closest black window. "I guess that's what happened anyway, eh? How ironic."

Cora toyed with a pebble. "I'm glad she believed in you."

"Well, it didn't do any good. I never listened to her. I dropped out of school and took a job working for my brother. He smuggles electronics from Bangladesh—among other merchandise. Black market stuff. Just a matter of time before we were both caught."

The pebble slipped from her fingers. "Oh."

"I worry about her." His voice was quieter. "Ellie. If she's okay."

Cora's heart clenched. She liked this side of him, the one that cared about his little sister. She almost told him she'd been locked up too but stopped. Her father's voice was too fresh in her mind. *We'll never speak of what happened,* he had said. *Not to the media, not even to each other. You're not an ex-con, you're our daughter.*

But she *was* an ex-con. That's what they never understood.

She stood and tugged on Leon's massive arm. "Come on."

When they returned to the others, Nok was twisting the pink streak of her hair nervously. "You really think we can go back?" she asked.

"Of course we can't!" Rolf sputtered, pushing at the place where his glasses should reside. "That could be the reason they killed the other girl—for all we know, she was trying to escape. They gave us three rules. That's all. We should at least *try* to obey. There might not even be any walls or exits, anyway."

"There is an exit," Cora said. "The Caretaker called it a fail-safe."

Rolf shook his head. "It doesn't matter. They'd just see us through those panels and stop us."

"Why do you want to stay here so badly?" Cora snapped.

He blinked like she had slapped him. "It isn't about staying here," he said. "It's about staying *alive*."

Staying alive. Cora had experience with staying alive. At Bay Pines, girls made makeshift knives out of toothbrushes. Pummeled each other with pillowcases full of loose change. She'd tried to banish such memories, like her father had said, but some things were harder to forget.

"I might have an idea," she said hesitantly. "The Kindred are stronger than us, but not invincible. The Caretaker breathes oxygen, which means he could choke. He had a bump on his nose like it had been broken. He's not flawless."

"What are we going to hurt them with?" Rolf asked. "Meat loaf? Every inch of this place has been designed like a padded cell."

"There *are* weapons." She leaned in and dropped her voice. "Remember those toys we saw in the shops? The Caretaker said they were authentic artifacts from Earth. That means they're real, not soft like everything else. Those croquet mallets could inflict serious damage. We could use the guitar strings as garrotes."

"What's a garrote?" Leon asked.

"A weapon you can use to strangle a person silently," she explained calmly.

"Bloody hell," he muttered. "How's a girl like you know a thing like that?"

Cora bit the inside of her cheek. "I . . . watch a lot of TV."

Thankfully, Lucky saved her from having to explain further. "It's a good plan—and the only one we've got. We have twenty-one days before they remove us. Until then, we'll solve their puzzles—it will look like we're cooperating. But really, we'll map the different habitats to find the fail-safe exit and win prizes we can secretly turn into weapons we can defend ourselves with."

Rolf shook his head. "We can't even solve the jukebox puzzle, and you expect to escape from superintelligent extraterrestrials? Impossible."

Cora glanced at the black window. Was the Caretaker watching? Her skin still tingled at the memory of the spark of electricity. Did all humans feel it, or was it only her?

Lucky shot Leon a sharp look. "And don't even think about acting on Rule Three."

Leon held up his hands. "Why are you telling me? My girl's dead."

Nok let out a quiet sound of disgust.

Cora rubbed the constellation marks on her neck. It wasn't just her eyes that felt tired. It was her whole body; her face, her limbs, her mind. They had more to worry about than the Kindred.

Captivity did strange things to people. In Bay Pines, pretty girls had lusted after balding old male guards because that was all there was, and human nature was too strong—even stronger when family and routine were taken away.

"Tomorrow," Lucky said, "we'll divide into teams and start our escape."

16

Nok

NOK HAD BEEN ANKLE-DEEP in slime for the last two hours.

The day before, when Lucky had suggested they search the habitats, this wasn't what she'd had in mind. Lucky and Cora had gone to the forest. Leon had set out on his own for the mountains. Why she and Rolf had been given the swamp environment to explore, she'd never know. Next time she'd request someplace dry and warm, like the farm.

She looked at the sky between the breaks in the trees. Perfect and blue, but no birds. Around them, set into mossy banks, black panels watched. She shivered, thinking of the beast with the gleaming skin who had called himself the Caretaker. He looked like a man, but his shimmering bronze face reminded her of the iridescence of lizard scales. When she'd been a little girl, the monk in her village had read stories from a leather-bound copy of the *Ramakien*. There was an illustration of the god Phra Phai, with blue skin and a celestial beauty that masked his treacherous nature. That painting had always both terrified and enchanted Nok. That's how she thought of the Caretaker, as Phra Phai. God of wind, giver of life—and of death.

Ahead, Rolf was nearly invisible among the trees.

"Hey, wait!" she called.

Rolf came tromping back through the slime. "Sorry." He held out a twitchy hand to help her across a knot of roots, and her mood softened. How easy it was to manipulate boys like him. Shed a few tears, and they'd do anything.

Nok rubbed her arm, looking at the slime swallowing her feet. She'd gone along with Delphine's lessons because she'd had no choice: Delphine had controlled every aspect of their lives. The flophouse was supposed to keep them "safe" and the pathetically sparse food was supposed to keep them "thin." Instead it kept them starved and enslaved as they were driven around to shoots in an ancient black van with sticky seats.

And Nok had been *good*. She could look into the camera and give the man on the other side exactly what he wanted. A smile full of promise, an alluring tilt of her chin. But each time, resentment had grown in her, bit by bit, like a cancer.

She blinked. *Delphine isn't here.* For once, she didn't need coy smiles. She could just be herself.

"No . . . I'm sorry," she said sincerely. "I shouldn't have snapped at you. It's this headache."

"We'll turn back soon." Rolf helped her tread though the sticky mud. "Wouldn't want to stay out here after dark."

"Seriously," Nok muttered. "We'd probably wake up in the morning to find the Kindred had dressed us in Halloween costumes."

Rolf snickered, and Nok gave him a surprised look. She hadn't been joking.

They continued through the swamp, as Rolf pointed out each clump of green muck and gave her its name—alder twig, cattail, loosestrife. She'd never met a boy more in love with slime; it almost made her smile as much as it made her roll her eyes.

"Look!" He slushed toward a cluster of fungus. "*Pleurotus ostreatus*. I didn't know they grew in wetlands."

"Swamp mushrooms." Nok feigned rubbing a hungry stomach. "Mmm."

He grinned.

They kept walking. She'd warmed up to him, she realized as she watched him take careful steps ahead of her to avoid crushing any plants. Neuroses and fungus and all. She didn't mind that he was four inches shorter than her and looked like he hadn't seen daylight in weeks. Handsome boys were insufferable, always checking themselves out in mirrors. Judging by the cowlick in his red hair, Rolf hadn't glanced in a single mirror since they'd arrived.

"What will you get with the token?" he asked over his shoulder.

She patted her dress pocket, where a heavy bronze token rested. Rolf had solved the swamp puzzle after only ten minutes. It involved listening for a bullfrog croak (it had a metallic ring to it—definitely not real), then searching for water bubbles and reaching into the silty bottom to get a token before the bubbles stopped. "It isn't really my choice, yeah? We have to save up to buy something Cora can make into a weapon."

He glanced at her. "Well, if you could choose anything, what would it be?"

She took another slushy step through the slime. "More nail polish?"

No, stupid, she cursed herself. She didn't care a quid for nail polish—but Delphine was still hiding in some deep pocket of her brain, telling her to say what he wanted to hear.

"Ah, scrap that. I'd take the radio," Nok answered, more confidently. "The red one in the arcade. I liked the way the knobs formed a little face."

Her first few months in the London flophouse, she'd both loathed her parents and missed them painfully. The only comfort she had found was a little shortwave radio she'd discovered crammed on a bookshelf, which she could tune to a Thai station. Now she had a feeling she would never see home again.

Her foot sank deeper in the slime, which splashed the hem of her dress. She cringed. Rolf rubbed the back of his neck, blinking a little fast.

"I could try to carry you," he offered.

She snorted. She'd squish the poor boy. "It's fine, really."

As they kept walking, Nok wondered what kind of a baby they would have, if they did go through with the Kindred's insane plan. Maybe with her looks and his brains, it would be some super child. Or else with his twitches and her height, it would be the most awkward thing ever. She pressed a hand to her stomach, feeling sick. Were they really going to have to go through with it? Sixteen years old and trapped in an alien zoo didn't exactly make her feel ready to be a mother.

"Some of my friends back home got pregnant," she said. "Only one kept the baby, though." The girl had married a photographer—a real classy guy—and had brought the baby back to the apartment to show the other girls. Nok had held it uneasily. It wasn't entirely awful; it had smelled nice, at least.

Rolf stopped, blinking steadily, and faced her. "I don't know what's going to happen, Nok. But I can promise you one thing. Whether we end up having a child or not, whether they take it away from us or not, I'll always be there. For you, I mean."

She swallowed back a surge of tenderness. No one had ever been as sweet to her before. She cleared her throat, suddenly nervous. "Hey, look. More *Pluris ostrus* or whatever."

He smiled. "*Pleurotus ostreatus.*"

"Well, we can't all be geniuses."

The grin fell off his face as his cheeks reddened. He pushed at the bridge of his nose. "I'm not a genius."

"You think Leon can identify swamp mushrooms? Why do you downplay it so much?"

His fingers twitched by his side, performing some calculations, as though that might help him think better. "Girls don't like smart guys," he said at last.

She looked at him in surprise. Suddenly she regretted all her crocodile tears, all her acts of helplessness. She knew when a boy liked her, and Rolf had it bad—but he didn't even know who she really was.

"Let me be the judge of what I like," she said softly.

They reached the end of the swamp at last. As they climbed out, the moss lining the bank soaked up the slime on her feet, so that she looked utterly clean. She glanced at her reflection in the nearest black window and adjusted her hem.

The light overhead changed. Late afternoon.

"Nok, look." Rolf pointed ahead. "What's that?"

Through the swamp trees, distant lights came on. Nok's heart beat a little faster as she recognized them. Her headache returned tenfold, and she doubled over in pain.

"Impossible," she gasped.

17

Cora

THE FOREST WAS EERILY quiet as Cora and Lucky passed among the trees. It had been almost three days since they'd found each other on the beach, but in a place without clocks or lengthening shadows, did time even exist the same way?

Cora hadn't slept more than a few groggy hours, and it made her headache worse. At home, there'd been one sleepless night, driving the Virginia back roads, when she'd heard a radio program on a psychological experiment in which they put test subjects in a room without natural light. Strange things started to happen: people would sleep for days on end, then wake for a week at a time. Was she changing, like the people in the experiment? Her temper had gotten snappier—everyone's had.

She hugged her arms around her white dress. She'd found a dozen of them the night before, in the dead girl's armoire. Rolf had said it was wrong to wear the dead girl's dresses because the Kindred might punish her, but it was worth the risk to shed the punk look and feel like herself.

They followed the trail past a chalet with murky black windows. "They find a way to watch us everywhere, don't they?" she said.

Lucky glanced at the window. "I'll give them something to watch." He raised his middle finger.

Cora grinned, but then she glanced behind them at the trail that had somehow telescoped in distance, and pain shot through her skull. "Ah—my head. Feels like someone's stabbing screwdrivers behind my eyes." She leaned her head against a tree, fighting the pain. "It has to be like Rolf said. Our minds can't handle the unnatural angles and distances."

"It can't help that you've barely slept," he said. She looked up at the worry in his eyes as he crouched next to her. "Didn't you think I'd notice? You look like you're practically sleepwalking. I . . ." His voice faded as he caught sight of something behind her. "Are those . . . platforms?"

Cora shaded her eyes as she looked in the direction he pointed. Dark shadows in the trees formed into rough shapes that looked a bit like platforms and tree houses and ladders. "You think it's one of the puzzles?"

"It isn't an Ewok village." He stood. "We should check it out. I'll give you a boost, if you feel up to it."

Cora hesitated. In seventh grade she'd climbed a high ropes course at day camp. She'd been fearless, the first one to the top, and that night her mother had invited her friends over for cake to celebrate. But that was before that horrible weightless fall when her car had plunged three stories off a bridge.

You were fearless once, she reminded herself.

"Yeah. I can do it." He formed a stirrup with his hands. She stepped up and clambered up a branch, blinking through bleary eyes. Lucky hoisted himself up beside her, as effortlessly as if he'd spent his life climbing trees, and she gaped. "Maybe that's why the Kindred took you," she said. "Supernatural climbing ability."

He grinned and then pointed down. "It helps to know we don't need to worry about falling. The ground cover's spongy pine needles. I bet we'd only bounce."

"Yeah, they wouldn't want to bruise any of their precious specimens."

Slowly she climbed higher, until they reached a platform circled by a thick rope. She gripped the safety of the rope, trying to catch her breath. Ten feet away, a metal object gleamed on another platform.

"Do you see that?"

Lucky shaded his eyes. "Looks like a token chute, like in the shops." He crouched at the platform's edge, judging the distance, and then looked back at the rope. "The only way over is to swing across."

"*Swing across?* Go ahead, Tarzan. I'll wait here."

"I'll go first. Just watch how I do it."

He swung out. Alone in the tree, Cora grabbed the trunk harder, eyes squeezed shut. She waited for the terrible crash as he fell, but none came. When she opened her eyes, he was standing on the next platform, dusting pine needles off his shirt.

"See?" he called. "Easy."

"Easy for you," she muttered. He threw the rope back. She searched her brain for words of advice from her father, but none came. She couldn't smile her way through this one. She gripped the rope, blood pulsing in her ears. *Don't look down*. She jumped off, shrieking as she hurtled through the air. The world was a blur. Branches and leaves and Lucky, and then his gentle laughter was in her ear, and his body was pressed against hers.

"That wasn't so bad, was it?"

She pulled away to hide the burn in her cheeks. "Okay. I've met my vine-swinging quota for the day. I'm ready to head to solid ground." She punched the chute's red button. A flood of tokens slid out. Lucky pushed it too—just one.

"I guess I'm better at this than you," she teased.

He wrapped his fingers around his single token. The smile fell off his face. "That's the second time you've gotten more for solving the exact same puzzle. Listen, maybe we should keep this just between you and me. You know what Rolf said about how lab rats get angry when they sense unfairness. Not that we're rats, but . . . When you got more tokens before, Rolf seemed frustrated."

She shoved the tokens into her pocket nonchalantly, but Lucky's words stuck in her mind like a thorn. What could the Kindred hope to achieve by spreading unfairness?

"Well. At least we're done."

"Uh . . . not yet." He pointed toward the clearing. "We have to climb down."

Any sense of accomplishment she'd had collapsed.

Lucky went first, moving fast, and was on the ground in no time. Cora took a deep breath. Not letting go of the trunk, she crawled to the closest branch, her muscles shaking. Left hand, then the right. Not so bad as long as she didn't look down.

"You're almost there," Lucky called. "Two more branches."

His voice gave her enough courage to glance down. That was

a mistake. The ground was dizzyingly far, telescoping toward her, and her mind was already so sleep deprived.

Her hands slipped.

She grabbed for the branch again, but her hand glided off it, and she tumbled toward the clearing.

Lucky caught her. It was awkward and painful and she must have landed half against his head, because when she found her feet, his ear was red and his hair was ruffled.

"Whoa. That was close." His breathing was only slightly taxed, his eyes glinting with the thrill of having finished the puzzle.

She tried to comb her hair into some semblance of neat. "If I didn't know better, I'd think you were enjoying yourself."

"Rescuing a pretty girl? I don't mind too much." He still held her tight. He was warm—she had missed that. The only other boy who had ever hugged her so close was Charlie. Her brother had always smelled of cologne, but Lucky was pine sap and cut grass. *Home.* The burn spread to her cheeks.

He let go of her almost reluctantly, and she almost wished he hadn't.

Overhead, the light grew brighter.

"Noon." Lucky slipped his token into his pocket. "We should keep going before it's time to turn back."

"I hope Rolf and Nok are getting along," Cora said as they ducked through a perfectly engineered tunnel of rhododendron. "They're sort of a mismatched pair."

"Maybe the Kindred's research found that opposites attract. Look at us—I mean, back home, guys like me don't end up with girls like you."

"Girls like me?"

"Rich girls. Important girls." He paused. "Beautiful girls."

Beautiful? Not with her eyes sunken from lack of sleep. Not with her hair tangled and wild. At least she was walking in front, where he couldn't see her burning cheeks. The last thing she needed was to start blushing whenever he threw his dimple around. The Kindred would love that. The researchers were probably checking off boxes left and right. Attraction? *Check.* Witty banter? *Check.* Rescuing a girl in distress? *Check.*

"Maybe it doesn't have anything to do with opposites," she said. "Maybe there's some connection between the couples we don't know about. We both lived in Virginia for a while."

"Right. That's true." Lucky kept walking in silence. Cora tossed a glance over her shoulder. What wasn't he telling her?

They crested a ridge and stopped. Ahead, colored lights twinkled between the trees. One flashed blue, another orange. Neon signs.

"Is that . . . another town?" She squinted at the lights. "Maybe there are more kids like us. Or maybe it's where the Kindred live."

Music slowly trickled through the trees, finding its way to her ears.

> *Don't belong in paradise,*
> *Don't belong in hell . . .*

She shot Lucky a worried look. "That's my song."

They pushed through the last of the forest, toward an enormous cherry tree that rose in the center of a town square exactly like theirs. Pooled in the grass was one of Leon's ties. The same tie he had ripped off their first day.

"Oh, no," she whispered.

"It's our town," Lucky said quietly. "We've come back."

Across the town square, Nok and Rolf emerged from the jungle, looking stricken.

Cora ran toward them. "Did the paths loop you back too?"

Nok had gone pale. "Yeah . . . we didn't turn once, I swear."

A curse came from the boardwalk, where Leon came stalking up the beach. "Bloody hell. I must have tramped up that mountain for six hours, and in five minutes I was back. After a couple hundred feet, it started snowing. Looked like goddamn Siberia. Then I find sleds, a whole stack of them just sitting there, and a racecourse marked with colored flags. Rode a sled down the mountain and ended up right here on the beach."

"I told you all trails lead back," Rolf said. "It doesn't matter what direction we took, or what time of day we left, or how quickly we walked."

As though someone had flipped a switch, all the lights of the shops turned off, plunging the town into a darkness lit only by twilight.

"Um, was that supposed to happen?" Nok asked.

A single light flickered back on—the drugstore's. It was on the end of the row of buildings, next to the boardwalk. The front door had always been sealed.

Now, it was wide open.

"Finally," Leon muttered. "Valium. Percocet. They've taken pity on us."

Lucky shot him a look. "I doubt our captors want you to get high."

Hesitantly, Cora approached the open doorway. There was

no countertop. No toys or candy. No black windows. If there was a puzzle, it was well hidden.

"I'll go in first," Lucky said. "If anything happens, let me do the talking."

The five of them crammed into the drugstore, which looked the same size as the other shops from the outside but was considerably smaller inside. The odd angles made her head twist with pain. She spun, looking for numbers or buttons that might indicate a puzzle.

The front door slid closed.

They were packed together like cattle, pressed against the walls, and Cora's lungs started to seize up. She'd been claustrophobic ever since the accident, when her father's car had crashed into the river. The doors' automatic locks had shorted out, locking them in. Water had first swallowed her ankles, then her knees, then her waist, until her father had broken the door window with a flashlight.

"Hey!" Leon pounded on the door. Cora's heart was racing. Breathing was getting hard. Nok clenched her arms tightly over her chest. Rolf's nervous fingers were tap-tap-tapping away. Every once in a while he would rub the top of his nose, adjusting glasses that weren't there.

The bare walls made sense now. It *wasn't* a puzzle.

It was a trap.

18

Cora

"CORA. STAY WITH ME." Lucky gripped her arm. She must look pale. Her shoulder found the wall, which was sturdy. *I won't fall. I won't . . .*

Just as her legs went slack, Lucky caught her. The pressure in the room began to change. Leon bellowed. The hair on Cora's arms rose, and she clutched onto Lucky as the pressure ripped her apart, piece by piece by piece. For a terrifying moment everything was a blur, like the dizzying sensation of passing out, and she thought she might have found the release of sleep of last. But then it let up, and her vision returned.

They weren't in the drugstore anymore.

They were in a large chamber with an arched ceiling made of molded metal blocks that fit together in interlocking seams. It wasn't the same room she had rematerialized in before, though the same starry light came from the seams, filling the chamber with a muted glow. A jumble of equipment was hooked to the walls like a gun armory, only there were giant needles and sensors instead of knives and triggers. A blue cube the size of her fist pulsed above the doorway, and more were built into wall cabinets. A cold examination table sat in the middle.

Cora's nails dug into Lucky's leather jacket. "Look."

In the corner was a small cage. A human girl sat locked inside, with dusky dark skin and stringy black hair hanging in her eyes. She wore a dark scrap of clothing that left her legs and arms bare, and she was crouched like a feral animal, glaring at them through her braids.

"What the . . . ," Leon started. "Who the hell are you?"

The girl didn't answer. Either she didn't speak English or she didn't care. Her hands slowly curled around the bars.

"You deaf, girl? I asked—"

The door beneath the blue cube opened, silencing him, and a Kindred woman entered. It was one of the researchers, the one with high cheekbones and a thin nose, who had spared a glance back at Cora. She ignored the poor cramped girl in the cage.

Her black hair was pulled back in a tight knot, not a hair out of place. She now wore a stiff white uniform with cerulean trim and a row of intricate knots down the side. Seven knots, Cora counted. The other researchers all had had six. Did that mean she was a higher rank? Cora had been too distracted to count the Warden's knots—seeing as he'd been choking her to death—but she was sure it had been far more.

"I am Serassi." The woman spoke flatly. "I am your medical inspector. It is time for your physical assessments. You may disregard the human subject behind those bars. She is here for observation purposes only."

Another door opened, and the Caretaker entered.

Cora's breath caught. She would never get used to seeing him. His imposing size, his dreamlike beauty. Her body hummed with the memory of his touch, how foreign and frightening it had been, and how he had spared her from the Warden. Then she remembered the girl in the cage, and her fury returned.

They're monsters. Even him.

While the Kindred exchanged words, Cora balled her fists. If she'd had the guitar string garrote right then, she could easily have wrapped it around either of their necks and *pulled*. But she had nothing. She felt helpless.

Their conversation paused. The Caretaker's head jerked toward her an inch, as though he heard her thoughts. The back of her neck went cold, and that creeping worry returned, that maybe the Kindred could read their minds. But that didn't make any sense. If the Kindred could read minds, wouldn't they know about her plan to find the fail-safe exit and escape?

"We will call you in numerical order to approach the table," the Caretaker said. "The medical inspector will record your body mass and perform a series of tests to evaluate your health. This process will not be painful or unpleasant unless you chose to make it so. Boy One, you are first." He looked at Rolf. "Remove your clothing."

Cora's eyes went wide. Rolf's went wider.

They wanted them *naked*?

The first day in the cage, Cora hadn't showered or changed clothes because of the black windows in the bathroom. Eventually she'd had to. But there was a big difference between stripping in front of a black window and here, with the Kindred, not to mention the other captives and the girl in the cage.

Leon cursed. "Is he serious?"

Cora kept her eyes fixed on the Caretaker. Did he understand why they were so reluctant? Did nudity mean the same thing to his people? In the cage, the human girl watched impassively, rocking slowly back and forth. Cora started to wonder if she *was* even human.

"In adherence with Rule Two," the Caretaker continued, "we require you to cooperate. These tests are for your own benefit, whether your limited minds can comprehend that or not. Now approach the table, Boy One."

Rolf went white as porcelain.

"This isn't right," Nok whispered. "What'll they do to him?"

Cora watched her throwing him nervous glances. Nok might have been acting before, manipulating Rolf into protecting her with wails and tears, but her concern for him was real now, as was her fear.

Cora grabbed Rolf's shirt and pulled them all into a huddle. "We'll all face the wall, okay? We won't look. We'll give each other privacy."

"What about *them*?" Nok asked. "And that girl in the cage?"

Cora turned to face the Kindred, digging her nails into her palm to take her mind off her fear. "You have to turn around too, or else we won't do it."

It was a hollow threat. They could make them do anything, of course.

"Your request is impossible, Girl Two." Serassi cocked her perfectly coiffed head. "I must see you in order to perform my tests." Cora searched for some emotion in the medical officer's face.

A human might have smirked at her quaint modesty, or threatened her, but this was none of those things. This was perfect skin and unflinching gaze, as blank as a machine.

"Well, that's okay. You're sort of a doctor." Her eyes slid to the Caretaker. "But you have to turn around."

"Very well." He sounded amused. Serassi's head jerked in surprise, and she said a few words in his language, but he ignored her.

"Boy One," he ordered.

As soon as Rolf stepped forward, the Caretaker faced the wall. Cora was shocked that he actually did as she asked, as though she had a modicum of power over him. Cora and the others turned, but the caged girl kept rocking. Cora heard Rolf's clothes pool on the floor, then a *clink* of equipment, and a quick intake of breath.

"Doctor," Leon mumbled beside her. "More like a veterinarian."

Behind them, Serassi told Rolf—Boy One—to put his clothes back on. He returned to the wall and cleared his throat. "It's a type of sensor they run over your skin. It doesn't hurt, but it's quite cold."

"And the girl in the cage?"

Rolf's cheeks flamed. "She didn't turn around. She didn't seem to care at all. She looked . . . bored. I'm not positive she speaks English."

"Girl One," the Caretaker ordered. When Nok stepped forward, visibly shaking, he faced the wall again. The process was repeated on her, and she rejoined them.

"Boy Two," the Caretaker said. Lucky squeezed Cora's hand, and then his presence was gone. Cora took a deep breath. She was next. Even at Bay Pines, they'd had a small amount of privacy.

They'd had shower curtains. They only had to share a room with one other girl. When they went to the facility's doctor, they got a paper robe.

When Lucky returned, brushing the back of her hand reassuringly with his fingers, her hands shook harder. Her throat was dry. She was waiting to hear that she was next.

"Cora," the Caretaker said.

Her tired eyes sank closed at the sound of her name. Lucky tensed beside her. The girl in the cage stopped rocking, and Cora's eyes shot open again. Something was different.

She looked over her shoulder and met the Caretaker's black eyes, and saw half a blink. It made him seem suddenly very human, and that terrified her more than anything. She didn't like the idea of these creatures having lives, and hopes, and fears, and names.

That's when she knew what was different.

He hadn't called her Girl Two.

He had called her by her name.

Behind them, Serassi spoke a few rapid, mechanical words. Cora got the sense that he was not supposed to have called her by anything other than the labels the Kindred had given them.

He had made a mistake.

"Girl Two." The Caretaker quickly corrected himself. There was a harshness in his voice, like he was trying to make up for his slip. He faced the wall. His hands were tensing and flexing by his side.

"It's best if you just obey," Rolf whispered.

Cora walked to the table in the center of the room, anger braided through her nerves, her hands fluttering at the straps of her sundress. Serassi held a long and flat instrument. She didn't blink. She didn't offer encouragement but didn't threaten either. Cora tugged the dress over her head so she was in her white underwear and camisole. Her hands hesitated on the camisole's strap as her eyes shifted to the Caretaker.

Why had he slipped on her name, and not the others'? Why had he obeyed her request for privacy, when he ignored theirs? Why did she get so many tokens, when the others only got one? A strange sensation throbbed in her head, like eyes watching her thoughts. She shivered.

Serassi cleared her throat, and Cora pulled the camisole over her head. She tried to cross her arms over her bare chest, but it was pointless, and Serassi didn't appear to care. Cora hooked her fingers in the waistband of her panties and took a deep breath, then slipped them off quickly and balled them and her camisole on the table.

She was naked.

The room wasn't freezing, but without clothes, she shivered harder. She kept glancing at the Caretaker to make sure he didn't turn around, and the other captives too. The girl in the cage seemed to have fallen asleep. Serassi motioned to the table, and Cora stretched out on it. That was both better and worse, because it felt more like a real doctor's visit, and yet now she was nothing but a specimen. Goose bumps rose on her skin as Serassi ran the instrument over her limbs.

Cora replayed the sound of her name on the Caretaker's lips. He had made a mistake.

She was his mistake.

She couldn't imagine such mechanical creatures ever making mistakes. Was there more to them than their stiffness? Was there a beating heart beneath all that knotted cerulean blue? A mind capable of error, and emotion, and even mercy? Finally Serassi removed the instrument and told Cora to stand. She scrambled up and tugged the dress back over her head. A second later, the Caretaker turned around.

"Boy Three," he said.

Leon was already halfway naked as he passed Cora. Fearless—or at least pretending to be.

At last Serassi announced that the medical exams were over and they would be rematerialized back to the drugstore. Everyone seemed to sigh, relieved they wouldn't be in the same room with these monsters anymore—except for Rolf. Cora caught sight of his eyes darting around the room, visually cataloging the equipment on the wall, muttering silent words to himself, fingers twitching like he was working calculations. His gaze rested on one of the blue cubes set into the wall above the doorway. Both his murmuring lips and his twitching fingers stopped abruptly.

"What is it?" she whispered.

He blinked too fast. "N . . . nothing."

The pressure in the room started to build. Cora closed her eyes. She'd ask him about it later, when they were safely away from the Kindred. She never thought she'd be relieved to return to their prison.

One by one they started to flicker and fade: Rolf, then Nok, then Leon, then Lucky. Lucky clenched her hand as he flickered away, until she was holding nothing. She braced herself for the rematerialization sensation, but it never came.

The pressure faded away.

Her eyes snapped open. The starry light was brighter,

stinging her eyes. She whipped her head around in surprise.

"Take me back," she choked.

"Not you, Girl Two," the Caretaker said. "We require you to remain here."

She took a step backward at the same time that the Caretaker came forward.

19

Cora

AN ICE CUBE OF fear slid down Cora's back.

The Caretaker's head turned toward the female medical officer. "You as well, Serassi. Leave us."

Had he just given an order? Cora had thought he was just the hired muscle, but Serassi's mouth went thin, and she turned sharply and left through the opposite door obediently.

Cora pressed her back against the wall. The caged girl had fallen asleep; she mumbled in her sleep, useless. Apart from materialization, the door was the only exit—and the Caretaker would stop her before she could pry it open.

The Caretaker took another step forward. The dead girl flashed in her head. Then waking in the desert. And the Warden's hand around her neck. Something deep within her pulsed with anger, and she sprang like an animal. Her fingernails clawed the Caretaker's skin, splintering with sparks of pain as she dragged them across his chin and neck and uniform, ripping jagged lines that vanished almost instantly. If he felt any pain, it didn't register.

His hand clamped over her shoulder as he shoved her against the wall, knocking the air out of her. Blood seeped from her jagged nails. Her fingers throbbed. The wall seams dug into her back, their light warm and pulsing.

"Let me go!"

The Caretaker's hands tightened around her wrists. He wore gloves now that prevented any transfer of electricity, but she could still taste metal deep in her throat. She was glad he wore gloves, but in the next second, crazily, she *wanted* to feel that electrical sensation again. It was like a drug, the only thing that cut through her sleep-deprived fog, which only made her angrier.

"Do not try to fight," he ordered.

"I'm tired of not fighting!"

Surprise flickered across his face. His chest rose and fell quickly. It made him seem so very nearly human, and she drew in a sharp breath.

He's feeling something.

She stopped struggling. He seemed cold, acted stoic, but underneath that exterior there was a beating heart, a warm body, hot blood. Did he feel things like sympathy? What about pain? Desire?

His jaw shifted. Even without whites of his eyes, she knew he was looking straight into her eyes. He took one last deep breath, and the pace of his breathing slowed, and the heartbeat pulsing in his hands returned to a regular rate.

He released her wrists but didn't move away.

"Yes. In answer to your question, we feel all those things. Sympathy. Pain. Desire. They are unintelligent emotions—signs of weakness. Complete eradication of emotion is impossible, so we attempt to suppress our feelings in public. Some of us are better at it than others."

Cora dug the heel of her palm against her temple. "But . . . I didn't say anything." She dragged her fingers through her hair, then dropped them abruptly. "You read my mind, didn't you?"

He didn't bother to answer. She wished for the ability to steady her own pounding heart as easily as he had.

"That's how you know my song too, isn't it? You probed in my head and found my memories. That's why you keep playing it on the jukebox."

"The Warden thought it would calm you."

"The last thing it does is calm me!" Her voice echoed in the chamber. The sleepy girl in the cage stirred awake and looked at them. For a second, Cora realized how they must look. Only inches apart. Her back pressed to the wall. Flushed face and rumpled clothes.

Panic filled her. Would the girl think it was a tryst? Did that even happen between humans and Kindred? But the girl just gave a long yawn and started picking at her toes. Cora's chest sank in relief, but it didn't last for long. The Caretaker still watched her with those eyes that could reach too far into her head. How were they supposed to escape from creatures who could read their minds?

He hadn't blinked once, she realized.

He paced to the center of the room mechanically, returning to his stoic state, seemingly unconcerned with how much he terrified her. She reminded herself that it was the Warden who had tried to kill her, not him. It didn't make him any less of a monster, but maybe it meant he didn't intend to hurt her—at least not yet.

Her breath slowed a fraction. "Why keep me behind?"

"It has been three days, and you have not slept adequately. By not sleeping you are disobeying Rule Two: maintain your health." He tilted his head. "We are not as heartless as you imagine. We recognize that you, in particular, have certain fears—enclosed spaces, deep bodies of water—that prevent you from a restful slumber. I would like to help you. Tell me what you require to sleep."

"What I require?" Her throat felt dry. "To go home. For all of us to go home, and that girl in the cage too, while you're at it."

"That is not possible."

"Why? Has something happened to Earth? Is that what you meant, about how humans always destroy their surroundings?" Her voice rose in pitch, but he didn't answer. "We deserve to know where we are and if our families are okay!"

His eyes stayed trained on her, just as hers stayed trained on him. It was a staring contest she was determined not to lose, even against someone who never blinked.

"I want you to be happy here, Girl Two. I can bring you a different pillow. A nighttime snack, if you prefer."

She almost laughed, though it would sound hysterical. A pillow? Dessert? She hadn't slept well after she was released from Bay Pines, either. She'd taken those long drives at night, listening to the radio. Only one thing had helped: Sadie, her old basset hound, who curled up protectively at the foot of the bed. Sadie had creaky joints and smelled like autumn leaves and couldn't have protected her from an angry cat, but she had loved Cora unconditionally, in the way only a dog could.

She pushed aside thoughts of Sadie. Sadie was *her* memory, not theirs.

"Did you really expect me to sleep well, in a deranged zoo?"

"Your species has a history of thriving in captivity. You even place your own people in captivity, a very primitive practice."

Cora steadied an untrusting gaze at him. Was he referring to her own time in juvie? If he thought she had thrived in captivity, he was wrong. That unwanted sensation itched in her mind, and she rubbed her eyes.

The hard set to his jaw softened. "You misunderstand, Girl Two."

"My name is Cora."

"Just because humankind is a lesser species does not mean it has no intrinsic value. In fact, as stewards of the lesser species, we value you all the more because of your natural innocence. Your kind has not yet been corrupted by superior intellect. Your life here will be effortless. We will provide everything. All you must do is enjoy it."

"In exchange for what?" She shook her head wearily. "Nobody goes to all the trouble of abducting us from Earth and building an entire habitat out of the good of their hearts. Is that why you took kids, instead of adults—you thought we'd be too innocent to question your motives? I have news for you. I'm not that naive."

"We wish only for your safety and survival."

"The Warden nearly killed me. Was that for my *survival*?"

Her words snapped in the air. The Caretaker was quiet, as though she had struck too deep—or too true. Even the girl in the cage stopped picking at her toes and paid attention.

"You are mistaken," he said at last. "We have sworn a strict oath never to kill a human. This moral code cannot be broken—it would contradict our core mission. I am sorry if he unintentionally caused you pain, but he was not attempting to kill you."

Cora took a shaky step forward.

"You might actually believe that. You might actually want what's best for us, too—you're a Caretaker, after all. But I refuse to believe those researchers care about my safety. When I fell at their feet, they only watched like I was some experiment. And the Warden? He would have killed me without so much as a blink." She stopped walking when she was close enough to feel the heat from his body, and she dropped her voice to a whisper. "Tell me why you *really* took us, and why those researchers keep manipulating us. Is it for your own amusement? Or are we test subjects for new drugs?" She swallowed, almost losing her resolve. "Or are you studying us because you want to see how humans will react when you attack Earth?"

"Attack Earth?" For someone who suppressed his emotions in public, he sounded sincerely surprised—or else he was a good liar. "That is another endearing trait of your species. Your vivid imagination."

"Don't mock me," she said.

His face grew serious once more. "We have no interest in your planet. We are not a terrestrial species but an astral one. We have made our home among the stars for the last million rotations—thirty thousand human years. An ancient race known as the Gatherers took us from our planet of origin and elevated us to the realm of the stars, where we evolved into one of the intelligent species. Now it is our turn to elevate your species to the stars, just as the Gatherers once did for us. Perhaps in time you will also display signs of evolving toward intelligence."

"We *are* intelligent."

"Not in the way we mean. For us, the difference between the intelligent species and the lesser ones is perceptive abilities: Telepathy. Telekinesis." He paused, as though gauging her reaction. She thought back to Lucky and the others . . . had they shown any signs of telepathy? Telekinesis? No. They'd all seemed as helpless as she was.

When she didn't react, he looked away, as if disappointed. "Your theories are not only incorrect, but they display signs of paranoia. No one intends to invade your planet. No one intends to use you as a test subject. No one is manipulating you."

"Yes they are! If you've been studying Earth for so long, then you know how we really dress. You know what we really eat. You know it's unfair that I get more tokens whenever I solve a puzzle. You know the optical illusions mess with our heads. You've even matched us in random pairs using constellations—why *constellations*?" Her angry ramble ended abruptly, as she raked her nails over the marks on her neck.

"Every species with a home planet has created symbols out of the placement of stars. We use these symbols because they are soothing to you. And as to the pairings, they are not random. Our society is run by a program called the stock algorithm. It creates our law and determines our positions within the hierarchy. It selected your cohort because you all carry a high level of genetic diversity in your genes, and you also exhibit traits we find of particular value. You are all exemplary."

"*Leon* is the best humanity has to offer?"

"Boy Three—Leon—is a paragon of physical stamina, in addition to being from an ethnic group with rare genetic traits."

Cora closed her eyes. The foggy cloud of insomnia settled

back over her, so frustratingly heavy. They had been selected and paired together by some alien supercomputer. She and Lucky, out of all the kids in the world, had the best genetic compatibility. It wasn't a particularly romantic notion. Did she only like that dimple in his left cheek because of a computer? Had he made her blush because the Kindred had designed it that way?

"I don't believe you. And I don't understand why you're covering for them. You're supposed to take care of us. Why are you defending *kidnappers*?"

The room was too quiet. As it was, Cora's own breath was deafening.

"I will try to bring you a dog," the Caretaker said at last. "To help you sleep."

Sadie. He had read her thoughts about Sadie. He might as well have stripped her naked and stared into her soul.

As if he sensed her anger, he folded his hands. "We are not the monsters you believe us to be, Cora."

She pointed a shaking finger at the girl in the cage. "Then prove it. Let that girl out of that cage. It's cruel to keep her cooped up like that. If you won't take her back to Earth, then let her stay in the environment with us."

The Caretaker's mouth quirked in something like amusement. He exchanged a glance with the stringy-haired girl. "Have you seen enough?" he asked. "Are you ready to join them?"

Cora's head jerked around. Had the girl understood English this whole time? The girl gripped the cage bars with an impossibly thin hand, glaring at Cora with brown eyes shockingly lighter in shade than her skin.

"I am ready," the girl said.

To Cora's shock, she pushed the cage gate open. It hadn't been locked.

"She was not imprisoned," the Caretaker said, reading Cora's thoughts. "She requested the enclosure as protection from your group's unpredictable emotional outbursts. She wanted to be certain she was safe among you."

Cora gaped as the girl climbed out of the cage, all long legs and long hair and eyes that seemed to slice through skin. Serassi had said she was there for observation, but it wasn't *her* the Kindred were observing. The girl had been observing *them*. The dark scrap of fabric she wore was actually a leotard with thin straps and silk panels, beautiful and delicate, like a ballerina might wear. She picked at it like she was used to wearing something looser, or nothing at all.

This had been the Kindred's plan all along. Whoever the girl was, with her feral looks and her ballerina costume and her strange alliance with the Kindred, she had always been intended to join them.

This was the girl with the heart-shaped scar's replacement.

This was the new Girl Three.

The Caretaker dragged Cora over to the girl and grabbed ahold of her as well. The pressure began to build. The ballerina girl yawned, like she'd dematerialized a thousand times. Cora gritted her teeth as the pressure grew, and then they were back in the cage, standing on the boardwalk. Waves crashed gently behind them. The scent of roasting meats laced the air. The Caretaker let go. The new Girl Three slunk off toward the diner, sniffing the air. Had Cora made a mistake by assuming the girl was a victim like the rest of them? Rolf had said the Kindred would need a mole. Someone on the inside . . .

Alone with the Caretaker, she crossed her arms over her chest.

"Just stay away from us, Caretaker." She took a shaky step toward the diner, but he grabbed her arm.

"I have a name too," he said. "It isn't Caretaker."

She paused, squinting in the bright sunlight. Such a figure didn't belong on a sunny boardwalk among toy shops and candy stores. He belonged in dreams. He belonged in nightmares.

Why is he telling me this? she wondered. *And more important, why do I care?*

But she did. Either from curiosity or some sick fascination, she cared.

"What is your name?" she asked.

"I am called Cassian. And I am not your enemy." He stepped back. "Now return to your cohort and try to sleep."

He flickered and was gone.

Cora took a few shaky steps toward the diner, hand clutched over the patch of arm where he had touched her. Ahead, the new Girl Three waited by the cherry tree.

Cora's muscles ached, but sleep was the last thing that would come to her now.

20

Leon

LUNCH, ACCORDING TO THEIR captors, was tuna fish smothered in chocolate sauce. Each day the food got weirder—damned if he knew why—and the mismatch of flavors made his head ache, but all that poking and prodding had made him irritable, and when he got irritable, he got hungry.

Cora appeared in the doorway.

"Hey." He kicked Lucky under the table. "Your girl's alive."

Lucky shoved his chair back in such a rush that chocolate sauce sloshed on the table. Leon cursed.

"I'm okay," Cora said. "They kept me behind because I wasn't sleeping well." She jerked her chin toward the jukebox, which was playing that song that grated on Leon's ears. "I found out they can read our minds. That's how they know about my song. And that's probably part of why we all have headaches. It's going to make getting out of here more challenging—"

Leon froze as another figure filled the doorway. It was the

caged girl with stringy hair and long limbs.

"She's . . . joining us," Cora said.

Leon grunted in surprise. The girl didn't bother to introduce herself—maybe she didn't speak English, or speak anything at all. She sauntered over to a table, pulled Rolf's military jacket off the back of his chair, sniffed it a few times, then slid into it. It swallowed her small frame, and with the ballerina getup, she looked as mismatched as the cage itself. She plunked into Rolf's chair and started shoveling his food into her mouth.

Rolf started to object but stopped. "Well. I wasn't going to eat it anyway." He fiddled with the leaves of a potted flower on the counter.

"Hey. Girl." Leon barked in annoyance. "You talk or what?"

Cora shot him a look. "Ease up. She's probably been through a lot."

But to Leon's surprise, the girl lifted her head. Chocolate sauce covered her mouth. A ratty braid hung in her face, making her look wild. She regarded Leon coldly as she pinched her arms with hands that were deeply scarred.

Then she went back to her chocolate-covered tuna.

"Maybe she's deaf?" Nok suggested.

"Maybe she's a spy," Rolf countered, blinking quickly, his hands buried in the flower. "I told you that every group of experiments has a control."

"They don't need a spy." Lucky hopped off one of the tables and jerked a thumb at the black window, where two shadowy figures lurked. "They already know everything we do, especially if they can read our minds. Besides, she's one of us. Human."

Leon grunted. "You sure about that?"

But the truth was, he knew with one look into her eyes that

she was just as human as the rest of them; and just as screwed. He couldn't stop stealing glances at the scars on her hands. He wondered who had hurt her—Kindred or human.

"Seriously, kid, if you got a name, tell us," he said. "Girl Three doesn't have much of a ring."

Cora gave him a surprised look. "Leon, that was almost a nice thing to say."

"Don't get used to it."

Ignoring them, the girl stood and drifted around the room, fingers dancing over the murky black window, leaving ghostly traces of moisture that evaporated as soon as they appeared. Her fingers kept tracing the same shape over and over. *Letters,* Leon realized. Rough, childlike, clunky.

M-A-L-I.

"Mali?" Cora sounded out the word. "That's your name?"

The girl gave a stiff nod, but her eyes hesitated, as though there was more to say but she didn't know how.

"Maybe she means Molly, like with a Y," Nok suggested.

Leon grunted. "Are you all blind or what? She means just what she wrote. Mali. The country. Look at her hair and skin. She's telling you where she's from, dorks."

Cora's head swiveled back to the girl. "Is that true?"

The girl's fingers still danced on the window. "The Kindred know where I am from but not my name, so that is what they call me. I am young when they take me." She spoke in a strange way that Leon had to struggle to piece together. Each word was so pronounced and distinctive and in the present tense, even if she was talking about the past. It was almost like a speech impediment a little cousin of his had, like her lips didn't learn to form words right.

"How young?" Cora asked gently.

The girl held up four fingers. Leon's head ached harder. The Kindred took tiny little kids? Those black-eyed bastards were seriously messed up.

Cora kept her voice soft. "Are there more like you, who were taken as children? Are they in enclosures like this one?"

Leon had to give it to Cora, she had a way with crazy feral humans. Left to him, he'd have shaken the answers out of the girl.

The girl looked at her toes. She wiggled them as though bored. "No." Nok sighed with relief, until the girl added, "The others are not nearly as fortunate."

Leon slammed a fist against the table a little too hard. "There's more than one of this screwy playground?"

"There are nine other environments, each containing between two and twenty individuals, but they are much smaller. Several hundred humans live in the menageries, and a few thousand on the nature preserves. A few hundred more are kept by private owners . . . those are the worst of all."

For a moment, none of the captives spoke. Even Rolf's hands, fiddling with the plant, had gone still. Lucky moved a little closer to Cora, like he feared their captors would come drag her away at any moment.

Leon broke the silence.

"Well, shit."

"What's a menagerie?" Cora asked. So help him, she actually seemed curious.

Mali steadied an unblinking stare on Cora. "You will see soon enough if you continue to resist the Kindred. There are thousands of humans who are not prime stock who will kill to be where you are. Humans who do not obey. Humans who have flaws. Humans who are taken by species other than the Kindred."

"Hang on," Lucky said. "There are other species?"

"Yes. Four are intelligent. The Kindred. The Mosca. The Axion. The Gatherers."

"What about humans?" Leon barked. "Don't we count as intelligent?"

"Not unless we're psychic," Cora interrupted. "Only the psychic races have any rights."

Mali picked at her fingernails, bored. "This is why the Mosca take us—we have very few rights. Some are black market dealers. The Gatherers and the Axion believe parts of the human body contain chemicals and will cut or kill a human to get those parts."

"But how can the Kindred let that happen?" Cora asked. "The Caretaker told me they had a moral code that prevented them from killing humans."

"They do. The other intelligent species do not swear the same oath. They do whatever they want. They trade human hair and knuckle bones and gall bladders and teeth. The right ventricle of the heart is their favorite. They powder it into a tea to stop pain in various parts of their bodies." Spoken in her strangely flat tone, her words were even more ominous.

Leon set down his tuna. They made *tea* out of kids' body parts? What kind of superevolved beings believed in black magic? Leon worked in the black market himself—he knew all about the things she was describing, only on Earth it was called the illegal wildlife trade. Rhino horns. Alligator skin. Bear gall bladders. They could fetch a fortune, especially in certain Asian and African countries, among discriminating clientele. And yet the difference was, humans weren't *goddamn animals.*

Leon stood abruptly, chair scraping backward, and paced to the jukebox. His head felt like it was splitting in two. That same song, over and over. He pounded a fist against the jukebox.

"You must cooperate," Mali added. "The Kindred keep you safe as long as you obey the rules." From nowhere, her face cracked in a flat line that somewhat resembled a smile.

They stared at her, mouths agape.

Nok broke the silence with a ragged cry. "The *rules*? That's really what this is all about? We eat their food and play their games and have sex and they won't cut us up for some alien's tea? Screw it, sign me up. Come on, Rolf. The bedroom. Five minutes." Her voice was growing hysterical as she paced by the countertop. Rolf's eyes went wide. The only way to tell he was alive was that he was rapidly turning the same bright shade of red as his flowers.

Lucky came around the counter and grabbed her, forcing her to stop pacing. "No one's doing Rule Three. They can't make us do that."

"Yes," Mali answered. "They can." She started picking at her toenails.

"She should know, shouldn't she?" Rolf stuttered, finally coughing some air back into his lungs. "She's lived with them. Look at the scars on her hands. She was in a *cage* when we first saw her! What's worse, ending up like her, or obeying a few rules? I mean . . . it's hardly torture. We've all had sex before, right?"

"It would be more convincing if you weren't blushing like a girl when you said that," Leon muttered.

Mali slid her unblinking gaze to him, and he shuddered as if a ghost had passed through him. Those scarred hands. The hollow

127

eyes. That girl had been through god knows what. An instinct in him flared up, fighting against his sympathy. This girl was weak, he tried to tell himself. A victim. And he didn't associate with the weak. No one in his family did. He used his size to intimidate people. He'd gotten tattoos to show his family's powerful story. He'd taken a job with his brother smuggling electronics from Bangladesh—he wasn't a hero. He sure as hell wasn't interested in being *this* girl's hero.

"Don't feel sorry for her," he snapped. "She's probably lying."

The girl didn't flinch. Even with her thin arms and thin legs, she didn't seem intimidated by him in the slightest. In fact, he sensed something else far scarier.

A connection.

She didn't have a constellation mark on the side of her neck that matched his, but she didn't have to. The moment she looked into his eyes, something shifted. Some wall fell down, and an instinct to protect her rose. This girl who'd been through so much. This girl who didn't know how to be gentle, just like him. He didn't need the stars to tell him she was meant for him, and he for her.

His head throbbed harder, and he stomped out of the diner. Away from the girl with the light brown eyes. Away from what the Kindred wanted him to do. He'd always run away from his problems before, so why not now?

"Leon, wait!" Cora ran out behind him, her blond hair flowing like the trail of a comet. "Where are you going?"

"I can't sleep in the house with that girl there. I'm going to the jungle—there are huts there. I'll be back in the morning for breakfast and another spin through the rat maze. You all divide up the bedrooms however you like."

He didn't look back.

21

Cora

WHEN CORA RETURNED TO the diner, the ideas Mali had alluded to—private owners and abducted children—churned in her stomach. She'd thought, after Bay Pines, that she could face anything. That was when the only monsters in her life were bad-tempered guards and other juvie girls who stole her stuff while she was in the shower.

The others formed a huddle by the countertop, whispering, while Mali sat alone at a table and poked at Lucky's folded aviator sunglasses.

"Cora." Lucky beckoned to her and, when she neared, dropped his voice so Mali wouldn't overhear. "Rolf thinks we should listen to Mali—that it's too dangerous to try to escape."

Cora shook her head. "No. We stick to the plan."

Over Lucky's shoulder, Cora watched as Mali slowly opened the aviator glasses, one temple at a time, examined them, and then placed them on her face.

"You wish to find the fail-safe exit," Mali said cryptically.

"You cannot. The Kindred hide it with perceptive technology. It could be in this room and you could not see." She stood, squinting through the dark sunglasses, and wandered to the jukebox.

Rolf leaned in, moving aside the potted geraniums. "You see? Escape is impossible. These are creatures who trade human body parts. We don't want to go up against them. I'll solve their puzzles, but you know what I'm going to do with the tokens I win? Buy the painting kit. Take up art. Enjoy myself. Maybe I'll even buy the radio and listen to some music that isn't this same aggravating song on repeat."

"So that's it? You're giving up?" When she was little, she'd always been the good girl, top of her class, the smiling face standing to the left of her father. Even in Bay Pines, when the gap-toothed girl punched her in the stomach, she hadn't objected. But now . . .

She was done doing what everyone wanted.

"And you." Cora spun on Mali. "They kidnapped you. You should hate them. Has the Caretaker brainwashed you or something?" Cora could barely keep the anger out of her voice, thinking of how a powerful creature like Cassian could do anything to a tiny girl like Mali. Four years old, and stolen away from her family.

At this, Mali lifted the sunglasses. Her startlingly clear eyes cut to Cora's sunken ones.

"Cassian is my friend."

"Your *friend*?"

Mali's mouth twitched. "He saves my life three years ago."

Cora looked down at her torn fingernails, piecing through Mali's strange way of speaking, wondering how the man who imprisoned them could be the same person who would save a girl's life. In the medical room, just for a flash, she'd thought that he was different from the other Kindred. Was he?

Mali approached slowly, lifting and lowering the sunglasses. She looked like a deranged ballerina in Rolf's oversized military jacket. "Cassian is the Caretaker only recently. Three years ago, he is *malakai*—soldier paid to find and save humans kept by private owners. He finds me. He saves me."

"You were in an enclosure like this one?"

"No—three years ago I am kept by a private owner. A bad owner. He sells me many times." Mali brushed a finger slowly down the seam of Rolf's military jacket, paying more attention to the woven threads than her story. "After Cassian saves me, he takes me to a good menagerie. I am there one year and then I am in an enclosure like this but smaller for one year and then I am in another menagerie." She paused. "This enclosure is not like the others. The Kindred set the days to different lengths here. They change the distances. The clothes here are strange."

Cora leaned forward. "You mean they don't mess with the other kids' heads like they do ours? Why us?"

Mali was silent. Her face was a mask behind the dark lenses of the sunglasses, just like the Kindred, and then she pinched herself slowly on the shoulder. "There are rumors that humans can evolve to have perceptive abilities. That this is even happening now. The Kindred fear the day when humans are as capable as them."

Cora straightened, glancing nervously at the others. "Evolving? Is there any truth to it?"

Mali paused. "I see nothing with my eyes, but friends I trust tell me yes this happens. Perhaps the Kindred treat you different because they fear you are different. *Here.* In the mind." She tapped her head. Her words lingered in the air like whispers of prophets.

Then she sneezed and drifted back over to the jukebox.

Cora ran a finger along her lips, sorting through Mali's words. A hand sank onto her shoulder, and she jumped out of her fog. Lucky jerked his head toward the doorway, and she followed him to where they could talk in private.

"Go easy on Nok and Rolf," he said as soon as they were out of earshot. "They're terrified, and everyone's tempers are short. Leon too—why do you think he stormed out like that? He's scared. At least here we're safe. Beyond the walls . . . who knows."

"Lucky, they're talking about giving up on escape. That's insane. We can't spend our lives here."

"We won't. I have plans, remember? Retire at thirty-eight. Military pension. A beach somewhere with a beer and a girl who doesn't mind me picking at a guitar with my bad hand." He flexed his scarred knuckles. "Just give them a few days to calm down."

"The Kindred only gave us twenty-one days and we've already wasted some of that time. We can't let headaches stop us."

He took her hand in his reassuringly. "We won't."

Her face felt heavy, but she smiled. At least there was one other sane person around. Even though she hadn't known Lucky for long, she felt drawn to him in a way that had nothing to do with the constellation marks on their necks, and everything to do with his determination not to spend their lives as a sideshow.

"Um, guys?" Nok said.

The smile fell from Cora's face. Nok and Rolf had backed away from the jukebox, which Mali was circling, bobbing her head up and down, a predator ready to strike.

"She must not know what it is," Lucky said. "Maybe she's afraid of it."

Mali approached the jukebox hesitantly. Cora was about to tell her it was a puzzle they couldn't solve when her long fingers started to fly over the controls. Rearranging shapes. Stacking them. She worked out the first combination of shapes in seconds and moved on to the next.

Cora was speechless.

They'd been wrong about Mali. The jukebox wasn't foreign to her, or at least its puzzle wasn't. From the corner of her eye, Cora glimpsed Rolf's hand twitching—making the same shapes as Mali's, she realized. He had had the same intensely focused look in the medical room, studying the blue cube above the doorway.

"Hey," she whispered to him. "In the medical room, you were looking at their equipment like you'd figured something out."

His fingers went still. There was an edge to his blue-green eyes that hadn't been there before. He shook his head. "Looking around, that's all."

They were interrupted when Mali clicked the last shapes together, and a token slid from a trough on the side of the jukebox. Mali caught it with sticky fingers and inserted it into a slot, then pressed a red button.

The song ended.

Another one began. It was terrible, something poppy and vaguely Japanese, but it was wonderfully, marvelously new. Mali leaned against the jukebox and licked the rest of the sauce off her fingers. "That is a very basic puzzle. The Kindred give it to children." The Japanese song rose in volume, filling the space with high-pitched voices. "Some puzzles are more difficult," she continued. "Have you found the one in the bookstore yet? That one is very challenging." She drifted closer to Nok, who took a jerky step back.

"If she can solve that puzzle," Lucky whispered in Cora's ear, "maybe she can help us solve the others."

Mali suddenly spun, drifting over with that strange bobbing motion, and reached out to touch the curling ends of Cora's hair. "It is useless to speak in low voices. They know what you say." She tapped Cora's head. "They hear you *here*."

Lucky tensed. "They can even read our minds through the panels? Then any kind of planning we do is useless. We might as well scream it out loud."

"There are ways to block the Kindred." Mali twirled a strand of Cora's hair slowly around her finger. "It is not thoughts they read, but intentions like *escape* and *restlessness*. To read one single word requires much concentration and a strong mind."

"The Caretaker can read specific words," Cora said.

"He has a very strong mind," Mali answered, almost proudly. "And he watches you for so long that he can read even your softest thoughts. Not mine. I spend years learning to block him."

"So tell us how," Lucky said.

"I will." A slow smile stretched across Mali's face. "For a price."

22

Cora

MALI TWIRLED CORA'S HAIR tighter around her finger. "Your hair is quite pretty, do you know that? The Kindred have very dark hair and most humans do too. It is rare to find one with hair so light." She paused. "If you give me some, perhaps I will tell you."

Cora jerked backward. "You want my *hair*?"

"Only a small piece."

Lucky cleared his throat. "Yeah, that's not happening—"

"Wait." Cora took a deep breath. "I'll give you some—one lock. But you have to tell us first how to block our thoughts."

Lucky shot her a look like she'd lost her mind, but Cora ignored him. She shook a curl tantalizingly. "Do we have a deal?"

Mali wobbled her head—her version of a nod. "There are three ways to shield your thoughts," she explained. "The first takes many years to learn. It is similar to a form of meditation.

You must divide your mind into two streams of thought." She pointed outside, where the ocean was crashing against the beach. "Observe the ocean. The water is warm above and cold below. The mind is the same. Let the Kindred read what is above but not in the deep. Think hard about something—the song on the jukebox—but let your true thoughts sink below. The Kindred can tell that you are hiding something, but they cannot break through."

"That's it?" Lucky said.

Mali wobbled her head again. "It takes me seven years to learn this."

Cora and Lucky exchanged a look. She shrugged and practiced concentrating on the records flipping in the jukebox. Then she tried to split her thoughts to also focus on Lucky's leather jacket. But within seconds, she'd lost all thoughts of the record, and her headache only worsened. She tried again, but her thoughts jumped from one to the other, never both simultaneously, and the effort made her restless mind throb.

She rubbed her eyes. "What are the other ways?"

"The Kindred cloak their emotions in public. This gives them greater control of their perceptive abilities. But they cannot perceive your mind unless they also have a calm mind. If they are uncloaked, they cannot read anything. But it is very difficult to make them uncloak. They practice cloaking since they are very young."

"Then what's the third way?"

Mali pinched Cora's arm. She yelped and jerked her arm back.

"Pain," Mali said. "It is so strong that it hides other thoughts."

Cora clutched the angry red spot forming on her arm. "You've been pinching yourself this whole time. I thought you were just crazy."

Mali's head wobbled in her equivalent of a shrug. She held out her hand flat. "Now. Our agreement."

Cora forced herself not to flinch away from Mali's scarred fingers. It went against her every instinct to hand over a piece of herself, with her DNA, to a girl who was so cozy with their captors. "What are you going to do with it?"

Mali's face was very serious, and then her lips dipped into a smile—just for a second—and she looked young and friendly for once.

"I see why you are his favorite," Mali said, ignoring her question. "I think at first it is just the unusual color of your hair but it is more. You are determined. You have a sharp mind. That cannot help but intrigue him."

"Intrigue . . . who?" Lucky asked.

A shiver ran down Cora's back. She knew exactly who Mali was talking about. In her dream, he'd been an angel. The most beautiful face she'd ever seen, a body more powerful even than Leon's. So powerful it was terrifying.

Cora's hand unconsciously drifted to the tangled blond strands around her shoulders. The jukebox song kept playing, over and over. Lucky looked between Cora and the black window like he was missing something.

"Wait," he said. "You mean the Caretaker? Is that why you get more tokens than the rest of us—you're his *favorite*?"

"It doesn't matter." Cora yanked on her hair, ripping a dozen hairs. She hissed at the sting of pain but passed the hair to Mali, who examined it, then carefully deposited it in the upper pocket of Rolf's military jacket.

"You can just . . . go ahead and keep that jacket," Rolf said from across the room.

Mali sauntered to the doorway like nothing had happened. Cora repeated Mali's words to herself: three ways to block their thoughts. Through meditation, through pain, and when the Kindred were uncloaked. In the black window, a single shadow moved slowly to the left. Cora pressed a hand against her throbbing scalp. It hurt so badly that whoever was watching now wouldn't hear a thing inside her head.

She stood on tiptoes to whisper in Lucky's ear.

"I don't care how much Mali knows about them. I don't trust her. And I want out of here before we figure out why they've really taken us. So we need to find the exit. Starting in the grasslands, right now."

WHEN CORA HAD BEEN fourteen, her parents had taken her and Charlie to the Serengeti on a safari to see rhinos lazing in the sun and giraffes bending to drink from a watering hole. Now, as she and Lucky gazed out over the grasslands rippling with waist-high grass, goose bumps rose on her arms. It was beautiful, and desolate, and monotonous, just as the Serengeti had been. A near-perfect reproduction in miniature. The only difference was, now she and Lucky were the animals being watched.

"Sometimes I forget it's all fake," Lucky said.

There was a slight catch to his voice. Cora felt it too—that there was something so wrong, but also beautiful, about each habitat. As much as she might have hated the Kindred, she couldn't deny that they were masters at what they did.

"Over there." She pointed toward a hill. A few scattered trees dotted the landscape, along with a long, low building that looked like a rural Kenyan school.

They started through the tall grass. The wind was strong, coming in waves like the seas. As it bent the grass, it made a hollow sound, like whistling. It made Cora think of a song she'd once written, about how the fences at Fox Run, their gated community, hadn't been that different from the ones at Bay Pines. Even the names weren't that different: both were named after the wildlife that had been destroyed for the buildings to be built.

The school door didn't open when Lucky tugged on it. While he circled the building, Cora examined a few uneven cinder blocks, the first imperfections she'd seen.

"Nothing." Lucky came around the corner and leaned against the building, frustrated.

A low chime came from the school's bell tower.

He jerked up, head craned toward the tower. "Did you hear that bell? All I did was lean against a block. If that's all there is to the puzzle, they must think we're idiots." He pressed the same block.

The low chime rang again. Cora's body felt weary and her head foggy, but she forced herself to concentrate. She pressed two different blocks, and two higher-pitched chimes rang. Behind her, the wind whistled harder through the grass.

Lucky started pushing every block in sight, but no tokens came. Finally he kicked the schoolhouse in frustration.

"Wait." Cora grabbed his arm. "Listen."

She closed her eyes, letting the wind wash over her. The

notes began to take form, hollow and windy. It was three notes, repeated again and again. She pressed different blocks until she was able to match the exact pitch of the notes.

Tokens rained out of a slot in the school's door, too many to catch at once.

Lucky frowned. "There must be, I don't know, thirty tokens here. They just keep giving you more." There was hesitation in his voice. "I guess you really are the Caretaker's favorite."

Before, in the ropes course, he had joked about being jealous of her extra attention. He wasn't joking now.

"I don't know what Mali meant by that. She's crazy."

But Lucky kept studying the tokens.

"You've been alone with him twice now." There was a strange hitch to his voice. "On the first day when you beamed away with him, and then when he kept you behind after the medical test. Is there anything you haven't told me? Something he said or . . . did?"

For a flash, she was back in the med room with the Caretaker's body pressed against her, starlight radiating from the walls. She swallowed. "I told you everything. I don't know why I get more tokens, Lucky. I swear."

The wind picked up again, ruffling his hair. He was so handsome that it made her heart unsteady—but the look in his eyes was dangerous. Rolf had said that lab rats could sense when things were unfair. Rolf had already snapped at her a few times. Even Nok had kept her distance. Why would the Kindred want them to turn on each other? Or rather, turn on *her*?

"Lucky . . ."

"No. Forget it."

His knuckles popped, and just like that, the tension broke. He slid the tokens into his pocket like he couldn't get rid of them fast enough, and cleared his throat. "How about that three-note melody? Pretty awful. The Kindred must not be musically gifted."

She clung to the lighter tone in his voice and tried to work it into her own. "Don't say that too loud. We should at least *act* like it's good."

He snorted. "Something tells me you're a better actress than me. Probably inherited it from your mom."

She gave a tired smile. At least the tension was— *Wait a minute.* Her head whipped around. "How do you know my mom was an actress?"

The grin fell off his face. The wind grew colder, pushing between them. She'd trusted Lucky because he wanted to get home as badly as she did, and because he was missing a watch just like she was missing a necklace, and because if a super-intelligent race matched them together, maybe they knew what they were doing.

But Rolf had said there might be a mole.

Lucky gave a half shrug. "You know. That first night, when we were talking. I told you about my granddad, you told me about your family." He swallowed like his throat had gone dry.

Cora's suspicion started to slip away. She *had* told him that her dad was a politician—but she didn't remember saying anything about her mom. Her mind started to concoct all kinds of conspiracy theories, but she shook her head. No. Paranoia was too rampant here, and it was a short leap to full-on madness.

"Right." She rubbed her temples. "It's because I haven't slept much, and with these headaches on top of everything . . . it makes me forgetful."

Lucky hesitated, then reached into his pocket and tossed her a token. "No worries. Here. Buy yourself something nice, like a Slinky you can strangle that Caretaker with. He'd never expect that from his *favorite*."

She caught the token, and the uneasiness was gone. Any boy who could joke about murdering their alien overlords was someone she could trust.

She gave him a sly smile. "Just wait until you see what I can do with a toothbrush."

23

Nok

AFTER THAT CRAZY GIRL with the stringy black hair so casually told them about kids kept as pets and black market traders who sold knuckle bones, Nok had nightmares for three days straight.

She refused to take a step outside of the town.

If she ignored the lack of traffic and unmoving sun and weird mash-up of cultures, she could almost delude herself into believing she lived in a quaint town, somewhere beachy and flashy, like Florida. She told herself the headaches were just allergies.

Cora and Lucky were braver than her—or more foolish. They went out every day to the far reaches of the enclosure, still trying to find the walls, while Leon did god knows what in the jungle, and Mali wandered through the habitats like she'd never seen trees or pumpkins or beach umbrellas before—which maybe she hadn't.

Nok stayed behind, with Rolf, and earned tokens from the puzzles in town. The candy store was her favorite. She could have done without the pastel paint and the bins of every type of candy imaginable—licorice, mints, butterscotches—but the puzzle might as well have been designed just for her.

She approached the big metal cash register on the counter, an enormous silver thing that looked a hundred years old, with round buttons and a lever to open the cash drawer. The buttons had letters on them instead of numbers, and where the price should have been displayed was a card behind glass with nonsense words printed on it:

LIP LO POL.

Nok smirked. This one was the easiest yet.

She tapped a few keys, and the new word she'd spelled out appeared in the window box: LOLLIPOP.

A token rolled out of the register. She snatched it and started for the door, but paused at the glistening bin of butterscotches. Who was she trying to stay thin for now, anyway? She wiped her mouth.

Rolf appeared in the doorway. "You solved another anagram? Nice." He'd been in the arcade again, she could tell. He only rumpled his hair like that when he was playing video games.

He peeked at the card. "Lollipop? You never said they were so easy. Let me try one." He punched a button on the cash register, and another anagram card popped up. AT ECO LOCH. He frowned, trying to figure it out, until Nok took pity on him. She punched in a few keys.

CHOCOLATE appeared on the card, along with another token.

"Aren't you supposed to be some kind of genius?" she teased.

"With math and physics, maybe," he answered. She couldn't help but notice his hands were resting calmly at his sides. He rarely twitched his fingers anymore when it was just the two of them. "You're the one with a gift for languages. No wonder the Kindred wanted you. Smart *and* the most beautiful creature on Earth."

She blushed, letting the pink streak of hair fall over her eyes. It was true that she'd picked up English within weeks of arriving in London and had gone on to learn seven more languages from the other models. Delphine had only sneered when she'd asked if she could start taking translator classes. *Speaking foreign languages doesn't make you smart,* Delphine had said, chewing on a black licorice rope, *if you have nothing of merit to say. And you, girl, look prettiest when you keep your mouth shut.*

Rolf took her hand in his. "I have a present for you."

Nok's eyebrows shot up as he pulled her next door into the arcade. The video games blinked and beeped on their own like ghosts were working the controls.

Rolf covered her eyes with his hands. "I don't want you to see yet."

She laughed as he led her blind between the beeping games. After sharing a room with four other girls for so many years, she'd missed the warmth of another person.

"Okay. Look." He removed his hands. Sitting on top of the arcade's counter was the shiny red radio.

She drew in a breath. No one had ever given her a present before, except some of Delphine's photographers, who'd been hoping to take a little more of her than just a photograph. "You got this for me?"

Rolf ruffled his hair nervously. "You said you liked listening to the radio back in London. I don't know if this plays any Thai music." He was leaning very close to her, twisting a dial, and his cheek brushed hers. He jerked up, blinking fast. "Sorry . . . I'm sure it's plainer than what you're used to. You probably had a huge entertainment system at home."

She wrinkled her face, confused—she'd never even owned a TV—but then remembered that he thought she was a famous model.

"No, I love it!" She threw her arms around him. "Oh, but you must have used your tokens to get this, yeah?" She pulled back, looking at the radio reluctantly. "We were supposed to save those for Cora."

Rolf was quiet. He rubbed his temples, eyes squeezed shut, like pain was throbbing in his skull.

"What's wrong?" Nok asked. "This isn't about her getting more tokens again, is it?" It was a topic that had come up more than a few times, as each evening when the others returned, Cora's pockets were loaded with tokens. Last night, when they'd compared their haul, Cora had sixty. Rolf, who'd spent ten straight hours in the arcade, had earned six. "Just forget about it. You look like your head's killing you. You should lie down."

"That's just it, Nok. I thought the strange angles and optical illusions were giving me a headache, but it's actually making everything clear. I can think better now . . ." He shook his head, blinking fast. "I understand those rats now, the ones that revolt when they receive unfair rewards. It isn't that the rats are just stupid, jealous animals. Any solid society is built on the foundation of fairness. That's why monarchies topple. That's why governments experimented with communism. When you lose fairness, you lose what makes us human."

"Or what makes us rats," Nok offered, hoping for lightness.

But Rolf didn't seem to hear her. "You were right when you said I shouldn't be ashamed to be smart. That's why I like you. You see me for who I am, and you *like* me. So I have been. Letting myself think, I mean. And my mind is telling me something doesn't add up with Cora. All the times she's disappeared off with the Kindred. The favoritism. I'm not saying she's the mole, but . . ." He rubbed the bridge of his nose. "All I'm saying is she isn't the only one who can come up with a plan."

He picked up the radio.

"This is *my* plan: to make us happy. If a few tokens go missing here or there, Cora doesn't have to know. Besides, I already examined it. There's no transmitter, so there's no way we could radio anyone for help. It's just a toy. For you."

For a moment, the sounds of the arcade surrounded them, the flashing lights spilling out on Rolf's face, turning it blue, then orange, then red. Nok's heart twisted a little bit with each one. She hated that the others didn't see how valuable his genius was. She hated that Leon bullied him. Maybe he was right—they deserved a little happiness.

Rolf put his hands over hers, holding the radio tightly.

"I know this place was scary at first." The lights of the games reflected in his eyes. "But it really is engineered to keep us safe and happy."

She swallowed. "But Cora says—"

He was always looking away, at his toes or at the floor, but this time, he looked her square in the eyes. "I don't care what Cora says. I know I'm supposed to hate it here and want to go home, but the truth is, life was bad for me there."

She rubbed his hand, petting him like a wounded bird.

His eyebrows knit together. "I was testing eight years ahead of my age level. My parents had my entire life planned out: graduate from Oxford at seventeen, PhD in mechanical engineering at MIT in America, a MacArthur fellowship by the time I was twenty. It was suffocating. I felt like I'd be trapped for the rest of my life. I don't care about engineering, or Greek literature either. I want to work with plants. Have my hands in the soil. But that wasn't academic enough. And then here . . . and you . . ." His fingers were starting to shake. "I know I'm not supposed to, but I like it here. And I really, really like you."

The arcade games kept beeping and flashing, throwing colored pools of light over both their faces. Nok clutched the radio. Rolf's hands clutched hers. In that moment, she felt like the arcade was the only place in the universe.

"I lied before," she admitted. "Life was bad for me at home too. I'm not some top model. My parents sold me to a seedy modeling agency that's only a step above an escort service. I'd have been stuck with them forever, or until I was too old and they threw me onto the street."

She hung her head, worried he wouldn't like her anymore.

But his hands didn't let go of hers.

"I'd have done anything to save you from that life," he said. "I still would."

She looked up in surprise. She wasn't sure what impulse made her do it, but she kissed him.

Rolf went rigid; despite what he claimed about having had sex before, he went as stiff as though it was his first kiss. But then he kissed her back, a little too soft and a little unsure of himself, but to Nok it was perfect. She had kissed boys before, but always to get something. Delphine had taught her well. And yet when she kissed Rolf, all she wanted was to be kissed back.

The next day, when Cora and Lucky went to the alpine biome to explore, Nok and Rolf kissed again while sitting in the movie theater's red plush seats, and then the next day in the French salon, and it only got better and better.

In another week, they were obeying all the rules—even the third one.

24

Cora

SAND CLUMPED BETWEEN CORA'S toes as she searched the beach for a seashell. Since she rarely slept, she'd started rising before first light to collect seashells, which she left in a stack on her windowsill, one for each day. Today's would be the fifteenth. And yet the pink streak in Nok's hair hadn't grown out, and neither had anyone's fingernails or the boys' facial hair.

What was happening to time?

The dull ache of exhaustion throbbed in her head. She lost her focus and her toe snagged on something hard. She crouched down to find a snow-white shell. Like all the rest, it had no sharp edges, as though it had been worn smooth by years of sand and sea. Or, rather, engineered to appear that way.

The hair on her arms rose. Her headache increased, like pressure was building. She shoved the shell into her dress pocket and spun toward the town. Was the Caretaker coming? Or had that tingle on her arms only been the sea breeze?

She climbed the stairs to the nearest shop, the bookstore. Inside was a different world. England at the turn of the twentieth century. Two leather club chairs and a brocade-covered settee in the middle of the room, with a tea set on the coffee table. The shelves were made of elegant wood packed with beautiful cloth-bound volumes that smelled like must and rain. They weren't real books—she had already checked. They made up the puzzle, which involved categorizing the volumes by title and color. The real books were enclosed behind the glass countertop. *The Hobbit*. *Charlotte's Web*. The complete boxed set of Dating the Duke romance novels. All available for a few tokens each.

But it wasn't the books she was interested in. The hair on her arms was still tingling, and she faced the black window behind the counter, keeping her distance. She ran her thumb over the seashell's hard edge, reminding herself that nothing here was real. Not the shell. Not the bookstore. Not even time itself.

But the Caretaker—he was real.

Cora leaned against the counter. "Are you there?"

She had meant to sound accusatory, and yet the words came out as a whisper. She'd sounded almost curious. Guilt cut into her, and she whipped her gaze out the bookstore door. What if Lucky caught her trying to talk to Cassian?

She turned back to the window. Yes, she was curious about him. And yes, she knew that was sick, but she couldn't help it. It didn't mean she wasn't also desperate to wrap the metal guitar strings around his neck and *pull*.

She rested the pads of her fingers on the humming window. The vibrations entered her. The ache grew in her head. She pushed through the pain to peer into the murky blackness, longing to see a shadowy figure—*his* shadowy figure—and to know she wasn't alone.

"Cassian? Are you there?"

She wanted answers. Why he had saved her from the Warden. Why she got more tokens than everyone else. If all humans felt a spark of electricity when he touched them, or if it was just her. Her shaking fingertips coiled into her palm, making a tight fist against the panel. In her dreams, she thought he was an angel. A beautiful face to chase away the nightmares. He *was* beautiful. But instead of taking her away from nightmares, he had brought her into one.

The throb in the back of her head grew. Or rather, it changed. It spread at the base of her head like soft needles, not entirely unpleasant but strange. The colors of the bookstore seemed to grow brighter, and her balance tipped like she was drunk, and a sharp tug came from the other side of the window.

She shoved away from it. Her vision returned to normal, her skin calmed, but her heart still raced. Had he reached into her head? The sensation was different from the normal headaches that came whenever she looked at an angle that wasn't right. This one felt almost . . . pleasurable.

"There you are."

With a start, she turned. Lucky stood in the bookstore's doorway, hair still sleep tangled, but his eyes were bright. They darkened at her expression.

"What's wrong?"

"Nothing." The word came out too fast. She stepped away from the black window and set the seashell on the glass countertop. "I was just getting this. For our calendar." She smiled, hoping he couldn't tell how fast her pulse was racing. She tapped on the glass countertop and cleared her throat. "I noticed that the copy of *Robinson Crusoe* is gone. The radio's gone from the toy store too, and the teddy bear."

"You think the Kindred took them?"

"They must have, but it doesn't make sense." The black window hummed, and Cora pinched her arm, hard, so they wouldn't be able to read her mind. She pulled Lucky away from the window and lowered her voice. "If they knew we were planning to use the prizes as weapons, they would have taken the guitar strings and the boomerangs. Those are a lot more dangerous than a teddy bear."

Lucky gave a shrug, looking tired. "There's no understanding them."

The black window hummed louder. She tried very, very hard to ignore it.

They started down the long path toward the desert. They'd spent nearly every day in the biomes together, winning tokens and mapping the area. They hadn't found the fail-safe exit, or anything to indicate how large the enclosure was, but Cora hadn't lost hope.

Her legs burned as they climbed the tallest dune. Besides the vast empty valley she'd woken in, the desert was filled with Egyptian-like ruins. There weren't any pyramids or temples, only dusty sandstone walls that stretched into infinity, winding around each other in impossible twists and turns that made her wonder if it was more Kindred technology messing with her perception. At the very top of the dune, a copse of palm trees surrounded a pool of crystal-clear water. A black window, set into a crumbling sandstone wall, overlooked it. Even though the wall was only two feet wide, she knew there was somehow a viewing chamber behind it.

She shivered and looked away.

"I think it's a maze," Lucky said.

"It can't be a maze." Cora knelt by the pool to splash water over her limbs. Her skin still throbbed from whatever had happened in the bookstore, when her vision and balance had faltered, but she ignored it. "A maze has openings and dead ends, and this has none."

They started down the dune, sliding more than walking, heading for the closest of the sandstone walls. It ran forever in either direction; if they were going to go deeper into the ruins, they'd have to climb it. They followed it until they reached a place where the wall had crumbled enough that they could scramble to the top.

They balanced on the wall and dusted off their hands. Cora counted at least a dozen places where the circular stone walls were so collapsed they might be able to scale them. Others were deteriorating from the bottom, forming tunnels they might be able to crawl through.

A tingle spread through her nerves. "Wait—it *is* a maze. But not a regular one. See those places where the stone is crumbling at the top or at the bottom, making a tunnel? We have to climb up or under. It's a vertical maze, not a horizontal one. The tokens must be in the center."

Lucky raised an eyebrow. "Race you?"

Her limbs were heavy with exhaustion from lack of sleep, but his grin energized her. She took a deep breath. "You're on."

She took off, fighting the burn in her muscles, looking for a place to climb under the next wall, while Lucky tried his luck scaling the top. The sand warmed her bare feet; she found a tunnel and crawled through into a tighter ring, and followed it until she could scramble over. An oasis waited on the other side. She paused for a drink of water. When she looked up, her own face looked back at her from a black window. Her reflection showed deep circles and sunken eyes, but a grin.

The smile dropped from her face.

Smiling? She shouldn't be enjoying herself. This was a prison. It might not have Bay Pines's chain-link fences, but they were captive, just the same. The Kindred could be there now, studying them for some nefarious purpose. What if the Warden changed his mind and cut her up for the black market—blond hair going to the highest bidder, gall bladder up next?

Footsteps reverberated in the sand as Lucky rounded the corner, stopping when he saw her. He pulled off his leather jacket. He was breathing hard, but the dimple winked in his left cheek.

"Break time already?" He knelt by the oasis pool and soaked his face, tossing his hair back.

Cora ignored the lines of water running down his neck. "Your dad learned hand-to-hand combat in the army, didn't he? Did he ever teach you?"

Lucky's grin faded. He wiped the water out of his eyes. "Yeah, the basics, and I took a few years of martial arts. Why?"

"Will you teach me?"

His face creased in confusion, until he followed her line of sight to the black window. "Look, I get why you'd want to know how to defend yourself, but the Kindred are too strong. The Caretaker threw Leon like he weighed nothing."

"I need to know how," she said. "I can't stand feeling like this. Powerless."

He squinted at the sun reluctantly but then splashed another handful of water over his face. He stood and paced beside the oasis, drawing a wide circle with his toe.

"Come on, then."

She jumped up, wiping the sand from her hands.

"First of all, it's called combatives, not hand-to-hand. It can be any style of martial art or close-quarter combat system, but the one the army teaches is drill based. You practice certain techniques until they're second nature. The most important thing is to recognize the situation you're in and know what technique to use."

"And if I just want to inflict serious pain on someone?"

He smiled. "No offense, but you're not big enough to do damage to a flock of chickens. You need to focus on dodging blows and holds. Then we can talk about body-weight techniques where you might actually be able to hurt someone."

Cora nodded. "Show me."

They spent the next hour practicing stances and kicks, and how to throw her weight to knock her opponent off-balance, and which parts of the body were most vulnerable to attack—they could only assume the Kindred's bodies were similar to theirs. Cora's muscles blazed with exhaustion.

"This is called escaping the mount." Lucky drew an X in the sand. "If you're pinned in a choke hold or a joint lock."

She came forward ready to fight, but he hooked a foot behind her ankle and off-balanced her onto the sand. Surprise shoved the breath from her lungs. She started to push herself up, but Lucky straddled her chest.

"Not so fast. I'm going to show you a standard pin."

He gripped her left wrist, and her pulse pounded with exhilaration from using her muscles this way for the first time—and from something else: she'd never been this close to a boy before. Certainly not like *this*, with his groin resting on her stomach. She'd gone to an all-girls school before Bay Pines, and afterward the only boys who approached her were more interested in being on the news for dating a convicted murderer, like she was some kind of rite of passage for jerks.

Her heart thudded so painfully, she was sure he could feel it through the layers of their clothes.

"Ready?" His voice caressed her ear.

The sand felt warm against her back. She had never noticed before all the different colors in his eyes, flecks of copper and green and ocean blue.

"Your goal is to escape the mount," he explained. "For someone your size, it's less about strength and more about positioning. You want to do what's called a bridge, thrust your hips up and to the side to throw me off balance, and then slip out. If you're dying to punch someone, now would be the time, while he's down. You'll get the most force if you use an elbow to the temple."

The idea of thrusting her hips against him made her face burn even harder. Her lips parted. She didn't move.

"Any time now, Cora."

His throat constricted as he swallowed. Maybe he felt it too, this attraction. This place did strange things to all of them, and she was so starved for human contact, her skin longing to brush against the fabric of his shirt.

Lucky leaned closer, his face an inch from hers.

"Cora?"

"Yeah."

"Any time now."

Her head nodded on its own. She only vaguely remembered she was supposed to be doing an escape of some sort. Right now there was only one thing on her mind, and judging from the way Lucky shifted on top of her, she didn't think she was the only one.

"Hang on. There's . . ." His breath was ragged. "There's something I should tell you."

"Mm-hm," she muttered, letting her jaw lightly brush his shoulder. He let out a tight breath and lowered his head, so the side of his face grazed hers.

"Really," he breathed. "I have to tell you. Before . . . this happens."

"Just stop talking," she whispered. She tilted her head enough for her lips to graze his jaw, which tasted like the dryness of the sand, but saltier. She was aware of every grain of sand, every pulse of sunlight, every inch that separated them.

Lucky tilted his head too, until their lips were a breath away from touching. This was going to be it. Her first kiss. With a Montana farm boy who smelled like motor grease and fresh-cut grass, and was going to help her get out of this twisted playground.

She parted her lips.

"You call that fighting?" a deep voice called.

25

Cora

CORA SAT UP TOO fast and bumped heads with Lucky. His hands clamped over hers protectively.

Leon stood on the closest wall, smirking. "Don't let me interrupt."

Lucky pushed himself to his feet. His face was flushed. She knew she must look the same and glanced at her reflection in the black window. *The window* . . . she'd forgotten about it. Had they been about to make out in front of the Kindred? Just like the Kindred *wanted*?

Lucky picked up his leather jacket, shaking out the sand a little too hard. "You're supposed to be mapping the alpine areas, Leon."

Leon jumped down from the wall and sauntered toward them. "I was, and it's bloody freezing. I thought, *What better place to warm up than a desert?* And being the thoughtful guy I am, I came to help you two with the desert puzzle." He smirked. "But it seems escape isn't the first thing on your mind."

Cora looked away. "He was teaching me to spar."

"That what they're calling it these days? Hell, sweetheart, I can show you a thing or two about sparring, if you want."

"Back off," Lucky said.

Leon gave a deep laugh. "Ease up, brother. She's not my type. She reminds me of my sister." He ran a hand over his face. "Anyway, I've been watching the last ten minutes, and you fight like you've a stick up your ass."

"It's standard military combatives."

"Whatever it's called, you wouldn't last five minutes in a street fight."

Lucky jerked his chin. "Is that right?"

"Hey." Cora shoved herself between them. "Leon's right. We were distracted from solving the maze, and right now we don't need distractions." She fingered the shell in her dress pocket. "There aren't many days left before the deadline."

"*If* we make it to the deadline without starving." Leon turned to face her, giving her a pointed look. "Thought it was funny, eh? Where'd you put all the food, sweetheart?"

Cora frowned. "What are you talking about?"

"This morning. All the trays in the diner were empty. Except for the one you always take, last one on the left—yours had extra. A prank's a prank, sweetheart, but you don't mess with a guy's food."

An uneasy feeling spread up her back. "I didn't do anything."

"You were the only one awake early. And the Kindred sure as hell didn't do it—they're trying to fatten us up."

Something wasn't right. She gave Lucky an uneasy glance.

He popped the knuckles on his left hand. "If she says she didn't do it, then she didn't."

Lucky started for town, but Leon stopped him with a massive

hand to his chest. "Hang on, brother. You calling me a liar?"

Lucky rubbed his temples. "You want to fight over one meal?"

"A Maori defends his honor," Leon growled. "And his right to breakfast." He straightened, flexing his neck. "Or are you scared?"

Lucky gave a brittle laugh. "I'm not scared of you."

"You should be, given what I've seen."

They had forgotten she was even standing there. What would she do if a fight really did break out? This wasn't Bay Pines, where she could stand back and wait for a guard to come.

"Come on." She tugged on Lucky's arm. "Just leave it."

He didn't even seem to hear her as he shook her off, shoving his finger in Leon's face. "One sparring match. No punches to the face. No knees to the groin. Nothing dirty."

"You're on."

Pain splintered through her head. "You're seriously going to fight each other?"

"Hell yes," Leon said. "Last one standing gets the other's lunch *and* dinner."

Lucky jerked his head in a nod.

Cora stomped off to the shade. *Idiots.* In the circle, Lucky assumed a rigid boxing stance. Leon smirked and lunged forward, throwing a punch toward his shoulder. Lucky dodged it easily and they danced around each other, more posturing than punches.

Cora rubbed her eyes. "This is stupid. We should keep working on the maze."

"Worried I'll ruin your boyfriend's face? If I readjust his nose, give him a few black eyes, he might even look as pretty as that Caretaker. I bet you don't mind looking at him, eh? You're his favorite, after all."

Lucky lunged forward. He clipped Leon in the jaw, hard. Blood splattered the sand.

Leon jerked back, wiping his nose. "You said none to the face, bro."

"Rules have changed."

Leon growled. Cora shrieked as Leon threw a punch that cracked something. There was a flash of blood at Lucky's nose, but he twisted away and threw another punch. They were better matched than Cora had thought. Leon was big, but he was slow. He yanked his button-down shirt over his head and kicked it away. The tattoos on his face continued down his chest, hugging his right shoulder and rib cage.

The sand grated under Cora's feet. The Kindred wouldn't let the boys hurt each other—would they? She glanced at the nearest black window, but it only reflected the fear in her face. Why was the Caretaker letting this happen?

Did they *want* this to happen, so they could study it?

Leon threw a punch that nearly knocked Lucky onto the sand. The bet was forgotten. They paced around each other like animals, and then Lucky lurched. He managed to get an arm around Leon's neck, pinning him so that his face turned red, but Leon slammed him to the ground. He grabbed a fistful of Lucky's hair.

"Maybe those traders are on to something, eh? Maybe I'll rip that ear off your head, make my own bloody tea—"

He grabbed the flap of Lucky's ear. One jerk would be all it would take. Cora felt a wild desire flare out of nowhere for Lucky to fight back; to put Leon in his place, to tear flesh and spurt blood—but just as fast it was gone, and she was horrified by her thoughts. She was going as crazy as them. She lurched forward, but time seemed to have slowed. It was all happening too fast, sliding and slipping out of control.

Lucky spit in his face. "You do, and I'll skin that tattoo off your face—"

"Stop it!" Cora slammed into Leon. The force of her weight jerked him back long enough for Lucky to scramble to his feet. He breathed hard. Blood dripped from his nose. Leon was on his feet in a second.

Danger crackled in the air.

"This isn't a game!" Cora yelled. "Trying to rip ears off? Skinning each other? Have you both gone insane?" Her heart beat unsteadily, as out of control as the fight.

This is so, so wrong.

She turned away sharply and rested one hand on the ruined wall.

"Cora—" Lucky started, but she spun around.

"No. Don't bother explaining. They've put us here like we're animals, and you're only proving them right. Who do you think messed with the food? *Them.* The Kindred. I don't know why— probably to poke and prod us into fighting so they can study how we interact. You're giving them one hell of a research thesis." She left them alone in the desert.

"Wait!" Lucky called.

She didn't look back. Her head throbbed.

Rip that ear off your head . . .

Skin that tattoo off your face . . .

There'd been tension between them from the start. They were all so on edge, so strung out by headaches and from distances that didn't match up. This place was twisting them, and it was twisting *her*. For a second, she'd almost been rooting for Lucky to hurt Leon. . . .

She ran back to the house, jogging up the stairs. For weeks the five of them had collected tokens in a pillowcase. They had one hundred seventy-six, last time she counted. Not enough for the croquet set, but there was a kite for one hundred fifty that she could disassemble into a stake. She'd be ready, if the Warden came, or if another fight broke out between the captives. It was time for some law. If the others couldn't stay civil, she'd be the law herself.

She jogged up the stairs. The door was closed to the first bedroom, so she twisted the knob and charged inside, looking for the pillowcase.

The room wasn't empty.

Cora froze. "Not you too."

26

Mali

OUT OF ALL THE habitats, Mali liked the beach one best.

She sat in the shade of a red-and-white umbrella, toying with a deck of cards. Lucky's shiny aviator sunglasses were perched on her face. She scrunched her nose, trying to get used to the feeling of the sunglasses. She'd only ever heard about them from other captives she'd been with before, with her series of private owners or the two menageries she'd been in or the other enclosure. Now, as she wrinkled her face and flipped another card, she found them itchy.

A tingle began on her arm. She slid up the sunglasses to watch the hair rise. In another second, footsteps sounded on the boardwalk. Cassian sank into the deck chair opposite her, which groaned under his weight. He wore his dark uniform with knots down the side to show his rank. Five, now. When he'd rescued her three years ago, it had been twice that number. He had never told her what happened that led to such a demotion, but she could guess: he'd always let his fondness for humans get in the way of his duties.

She slid the sunglasses back over her eyes. "I am like you now." She tapped the dark lenses. "Black eyes."

He leaned forward, picking up a few cards that had fallen off her lounge chair. He handed her the cards, and she swirled the pile on the table. She folded her lips in a smile.

"Go fish," she said.

Though, like those of all cloaked Kindred, his face betrayed almost no emotion, Mali had learned to read subtle shifts in his features; that flinch meant he was almost smiling. Out of all of them, Cassian had the hardest time suppressing his emotions, but she liked him all the more for it. Go fish was a human game, but the Kindred had a soft spot for anything human, and she had convinced Cassian to play before. Their world—the public one—was so harsh. Sharp angles, sterile rooms, everything a monotonous shade of cerulean. It was only in their private lives that they revealed their true personalities. It was there, in the pleasure gardens and menageries, that the Kindred uncloaked their emotions. Their society had evolved to be so sterile that they had lost the ability to create music and entertainment for themselves, so they borrowed culture from humans instead. The quirks of humanity were all the rage in the menageries; the Kindred dressed like humans, listened to their music, played card games like this one.

Cassian patiently took the hand of cards she offered him. "I will play if you tell me how you are adjusting to the dynamic of this cohort."

Mali scowled beneath her sunglasses. Sometimes she wanted cards to just be cards. Sometimes she wanted Cassian to just be Cassian, and not her Caretaker, and not ask so many questions.

"There is no dynamic. There is no cohesion. Leon does not even sleep in the house. Nok and Rolf do not leave town. They fear the habitats."

"It is a difficult adjustment. It is never easy for any of the human wards. In time, they will learn that we are not to be feared." Cassian studied his cards methodically. "Nine."

Mali shook her head. "Go fish." She studied her own cards. "I want to know why this enclosure is different. Why you dress them in human clothes and give them strange food to eat."

"It is the Warden, trying something new." He took a card from the pile. "We will not harm them, of course."

A darkness wormed its way into the pit of Mali's stomach. Like most of the Kindred, Cassian often talked about his kind in the plural form. She did trust him; he had saved her life, even at risk to his own. But she didn't trust *them*. Not the Kindred. Not as a whole. Certainly not any of her previous owners, and not the Warden, either. Mali had heard rumors about the Warden, but had never known his name—Fian—or met him until Cassian had taken her from the menagerie where she lived and told her she had the chance of a lifetime, to join the grand new enclosure. Fian had insisted on inspecting her first; examining her teeth and ears and hands, then asking Cassian if he was confident that any human males would find such a damaged ward appealing.

There was one thing she had learned, living caught between the human and the Kindred world. It didn't matter what race you came from: there were good and bad among every species.

"Seven," she said.

He handed her a card and drew another. "The stock algorithm has predicted that Boy Two will grow into the group's leader.

He will welcome you into the group, but these things take time."

She set down the pair of sevens. "Lucky is more interested in escape than in being a leader. He is more interested in *Cora*."

It was Cassian's turn to ask for a card, but the cards stayed in his hand, untouched. "There is a history between them."

There was a strange tone in his voice Mali had heard only a few times before. She slid the sunglasses on top of her head and reached into the pocket of Rolf's military jacket. She held out the lock of Cora's hair.

"I acquire this for you. A present. For bringing me here."

Cassian stared at the lock but made no move to take it. "You know I do not share the same primitive beliefs as the Gatherers and the Mosca. A lock of hair means nothing to me."

Mali gave him a hard look. "It does if it is hers."

Mali had been transferred to enough private owners and menageries to know that as disciplined as the Kindred considered themselves, they weren't perfect. Among themselves, relationships between males and females were noncommittal; sex was for physical release, not for procreation or love. But sometimes deeper emotions did surface. *Fondness,* the Kindred called it. Sometimes for another Kindred, but sometimes—though very rarely and always forbidden—for a human.

Mali offered him the hair again. She did not care what Cassian's predilections were; she just wanted to repay the kindness he had shown her. In fact, she liked the glimpse of weakness. It made him seem almost human.

He folded her fingers around the hair, pushing it away from him a little hard. He picked up the cards and shuffled them roughly. The waves crashed on the beach as the light changed one degree lower. Mali wished, not for the first time, that Cassian could show her his true eyes as easily as she could slide up the sunglasses.

"The others notice that you treat her differently." Mali slowly replaced the lock of hair in her pocket. "They do not like it. There is an altercation this morning over breakfast. Everyone's food is missing except for hers. It is dangerous. Food is a basic need. I do not understand why the Warden manipulates them—"

"The Warden did not interfere with their food. If so, I would know. It must have been one of the wards."

Mali gave him a hard look. He had rarely lied to her before—why was he lying now? "Is the Warden changing things because of the rumors. Because he thinks that humans are showing signs of percept—"

"No." He cut her off hard. "And you should not speak thusly. You know what the Council did to Anya when she started saying such things."

Mali could feel sweat running down the sides of her face. She could still remember Anya's big round eyes, her blond hair the same color as Cora's, only it had been stick straight. They had shared a private owner, a high-ranking Kindred official, who had cut off two of Anya's fingers to give to a Mosca he'd lost a bet to. He had tried to cut off Mali's too, only she'd fought back. Cassian had found them ten rotations later. She'd never forget seeing him for the first time; the door sliding open, fear making her stomach knot, expecting the official's squash-nosed, broad face. But it wasn't the official. It was a young enforcer, a strikingly handsome one, who had taken one look at their tiny cages and smashed the locks open with the hilt of his communicator.

Do not fear me, he'd said. *I am not here to hurt you.*

He looked like the dazzling hero in the stories Anya used to tell her, but Mali knew better than to believe anything the Kindred said. She'd clawed his face when he'd reached into the cage, and hissed at him. It hadn't been until his guards had tranquilized her, and she'd woken up in a medical unit with fresh clothes, that she'd known she really had been saved. When the medical officer had come to repair her wounds, she'd asked for the scars on her hands to stay, as a reminder. Cassian had come to check on her, and she'd climbed off the table and wrapped her arms around him. It was only later that she learned of Anya's death. Despite the rescue, Anya had never recovered from the abuse. In another ten rotations, she was dead.

Anya, like Cora, had been very perceptive.

Cassian looked back at his cards.

Mali squinted at the ocean, trying to imagine herself back on Earth. There was so little she remembered. Camels. Hot tea. A carpet laid out over sand. If she concentrated very hard, she could picture her mother's light brown eyes.

"Cora should not be here," Mali said. "The Warden is right. She does not have the correct temperament. She is determined to return to her previous life."

"Did you tell her?" Cassian asked quietly.

"Tell her what."

His boot scuffed on the boards. At his side, his fist was clenching and unclenching. "That there is no other life for her. For any of them."

"No." Mali set down her hand of cards. She was tired of games.

"Do not tell them, at least for now. It is too large a concept for their limited minds to comprehend. It will take time before they are ready to hear the truth about their home."

Mali slid the sunglasses back over her eyes. She dismissed that wrinkle of annoyance she felt whenever he gave her orders. As long as they let her stay in this paradise where she could eat as much as she wanted and play games all day, she would do whatever the Caretaker asked her to do. She had found, long ago, around the time a Kindred had tried to cut off her fingers, that it was best not to question them. Ever.

27

Cora

CORA STOOD IN THE bedroom doorway, one hand still on the knob. Nok and Rolf were tangled in the bedsheets, more naked than not. They'd been giggling when she first entered, but that had ended abruptly.

"What are you doing?" Cora yelled.

"What does it look like we're doing?" Rolf sputtered. "Give us some privacy! Wasn't it enough to steal our breakfast?"

"I didn't touch your food! Just— Hold on. I've got to get something." Cora wavered a second, then darted into the room, holding her breath like she was under water, snatched up the clinking pillowcase—it felt heavier—and dashed out. She slammed the door behind her, and only then gasped for breath.

If that wasn't sex, it was pretty close.

She sank onto the bottom stair, the pillowcase of tokens sagging on the floor, and took the seashell out of her dress pocket. How long had it been? Two weeks? And everything was already going to hell. Nok and Rolf had clung to each other right from the start, so maybe she shouldn't be so surprised, but seeing them tangled in the early-morning sunlight with a black window looming next to them stirred something ugly within her.

It wasn't the sex—they were old enough to make their own decisions. It wasn't even that they were obeying the Kindred's rules, because she knew they were terrified of disobeying. It was because they had looked truly, blissfully, blindly happy.

They like it here.

The pillowcase slipped from her hands. Tokens avalanched to the floor, far more than she had collected. She must have grabbed the wrong pillowcase. Had Nok and Rolf been earning tokens on their own, or worse, siphoning off the ones she'd earned?

Now that she looked around the living room, at the candy wrappers on the side table, and a fort they must have made from sofa cushions, and even a radio—the red one she thought the Kindred had stolen—she realized she'd been blind.

Rolf and Nok never had any intention of escaping.

Footsteps sounded on the porch, and Lucky stuck his head in, still sweat soaked from the desert. "I've been looking for you everywhere." He leaned in the doorway, catching his breath. "I know that fight was stupid. Guys can be like that sometimes—I didn't mean what I said. It's this place. It makes my head ache so bad I can't even think." He squeezed a fist against his forehead and released it with an angry sigh. "It's my fault. I let everyone drift apart."

Cora knelt to pick up the scattered tokens. "Well, they all hate me now, thinking I stole their food. And good luck talking to Rolf and Nok. I doubt you can get them to stop making out long enough to listen." She stuffed the tokens into the pillowcase and then started past him onto the porch.

"Wait. I can fix this—" he began to say.

"I'm fixing it myself. I'm tired of these black windows. Nothing they give us here will break them, but I know something that will."

He followed her at a fast clip, trying to talk her out of it. She strode up the toy shop steps, shoving open the saloon doors. The croquet set sat between two dolls. She started shoving tokens through the copper slot.

"Maybe you should take a deep breath, Cora. Meditate . . . or something. I know that fight turned quickly. We've all been bottling up emotions. Not thinking straight. This morning I woke up and forgot my mom died. I kept waiting to hear her making breakfast downstairs."

Cora paused before continuing to feed tokens into the slot. She'd forgotten that Lucky's mother had died when he was little. He'd told her so quickly, like it pained him deeply to even think about.

The Kindred were taking those memories from him.

From all of them.

"It isn't about the fight." Cora fed the slot more tokens. "Not entirely. It's about the two of you arguing with each other, when it should be *them* we're fighting. It's about Rolf and Nok hooking up even though the Kindred are watching. We're forgetting what matters, Lucky."

She slammed the last token through the slot and pounded on a copper button beneath the croquet set. The glass door opened. She grabbed the blue mallet.

It felt powerful in her hand. Real.

She headed for the doorway.

The light had shifted to dusk. Music came from the diner, something with a hint of jazz, but it just made her head pound harder. Mali stood by the open door with her hands across her chest, watching Cora like she could see straight into her soul. A cry came from inside the diner and Nok rushed out, followed by Rolf, who clutched a guitar in one hand.

"You!" Rolf jabbed a finger at Cora. "What, breakfast and lunch wasn't enough? You had to steal dinner too?"

"I didn't steal anything!" Cora yelled.

"Stop shouting!" Nok wailed. "My head hurts!"

Rolf stomped toward Cora, his eye twitching. "Is this revenge for seeing us together? If you're jealous that you and Lucky don't have a relationship like we do, maybe that's your own fault!" He let the guitar fall to the porch with a clatter of errant notes.

Cora jumped back. What had gotten into him? She tightened her grip on the mallet. First the radio. Now the guitar. If anyone had a right to be angry, it was her.

"You've been secretly buying things from the shops, haven't you? We could have used those things, Rolf! If I'd had a garrote or a makeshift knife when the Warden had tried to strangle me, maybe I could have killed him!"

He rolled his eyes. "Wow. How brilliant of you to figure out my plan. Yes, I bought them and didn't tell you. Just like you took our food and didn't tell us."

"I didn't!"

Splinters of pain shot off from her head. It felt like her brain was splitting in two, and anger boiled from the fissure. She gripped the mallet tighter.

Rolf narrowed his eyes.

"Stop it." Nok tugged on Rolf's arm. "It doesn't matter why she did it—there's still enough food, if we divide up what's on her plate and forage in the orchard. Cora, just don't do it again. Please. Headaches are bad enough—we don't need hunger pangs too."

"I didn't take your food. Don't you see? The Kindred are doing this. They want us to turn against each other."

The others stared at her like she'd gone mad.

Mali yawned.

Cora spun and strode through the grass, bumping into Rolf so hard that he knocked into the guitar with another burst of errant chords, and then she stopped in front of the movie theater's black window.

Her father had taken her to a zoo when she was a little girl. They had gone to see the tiger. She remembered squeezing her father's hand as it paced back and forth, back and forth, watching them with unblinking eyes through the glass.

She felt like that tiger. She *was* that tiger.

She laid her palm flat on the humming window. Only a thick piece of glass had stopped that tiger from killing her. She hoped the Kindred could read her mind, and know she was biding her time until no surfaces separated her from them, and she could do to them what that tiger wanted to do to her.

"All right, Caretaker," she muttered, stepping back. "Take care of *this*."

She swung the mallet with all her strength against the glass. Nok shrieked. Cora cringed, expecting a satisfying *crack* and shatter of glass. The mallet was real wood, not whatever fake substance everything else was made of, and yet the moment it connected with the window, nothing happened. Not a crack. Not even a thud.

"Dammit!" She hurled the mallet to the ground.

Her vision started to fracture into little dots, as if the lights of town were a spinning kaleidoscope. Pain ripped through her head as lack of sleep caught up with her all at once. She sank to the ground.

Lucky crouched next to her. The sweat had dried on his shirt in the cool evening air. He nodded toward the croquet mallet. "Did you really think that was going to work?"

She pushed her mess of hair out of her face and sat up. "I don't know. I had to try." She watched the others tearing into her plate of food on the diner porch. "Look at them. They're like wolves. Don't they understand what's happening? These are creatures who took us from our beds. Who are forcing us to breed for their own twisted purposes. Who keep kids in cages and cut off their fingers."

Lucky crackled the knuckles in his left hand. "The Mosca cut off fingers, not the Kindred."

"They're all part of the same system! The Kindred protect us only as long as we obey them."

She moved closer, brushing his leather jacket, catching a trace of his fresh soap smell that reminded her of home. *Home.* Maybe at this moment Charlie was pulling his Jeep into the driveway, and Sadie was running out to meet him.

"I can't take it, Lucky. I'm going crazy." At Bay Pines she'd checked off the days on a calendar, but she had no boxes to check now. No end date. Just the seashells, but there was an endless ocean of them. Would she keep collecting them until they filled the house, spilling out the windows into the marigolds? For months? *Years?* She curled up tight, wishing she could disappear into herself. She needed help. She needed a way home.

She needed a sign that there was hope.

A soft, familiar *plink* sounded on the black window behind them. Cora lifted her head. When dusk had rolled in, clouds had come too.

A drop of rain fell on her bare toes.

She stared at the patch of water, dumbfounded. Every day in the cage had been identical. Sunny skies without a trace of clouds. It rained in the jungle, and it snowed in the forest, but always on a predictable schedule, and never in the town. Now the rain started softly, a few errant drops at a time. The clouds grew heavier, making the day darker. It had been so long since Cora had felt a drenching rain that she'd forgotten the way it smelled. So earthy.

Nok shrieked with delight, jumping up and down and clapping, her mood flipping on a dime, as though the fight had never happened. She took Mali's hands, swinging her around, trying to make her dance, but Mali just pitched her head toward the sky in distrust. The rain grew. Big fat drops formed rivulets and streams and rivers on the black windows. Rolf was trying to trace them with his finger, but there were too many.

"Why?" Cora turned to Lucky, rubbing her throbbing temples that were soaked with rain. "Why are they doing this? What do they hope to gain by changing things?"

"You're tired, Cora. You haven't slept."

"You know I didn't take everyone's food, right?"

A slight pause. "Sure."

Water flowed down his handsome face like tears, finding the valleys of his eyes, dripping off his jaw. Even if she hadn't known him at home, and even though the Kindred had dressed him in a stranger's clothes, she recognized sincerity in his face.

"They want to see what we'll do." She twisted her head toward all the watching windows. "They're standing there now, watching us. You see them, right? The shadows?"

"Sure. I see them." But his eyes stayed locked to hers. He tucked a wet strand of her hair gently behind her ear. "Do you trust me?" There was a strange hitch to his voice.

Her headache reverberated in her skull, louder and louder, but she nodded.

"Then come with me. There's something I want to show you."

28

Cora

LUCKY LED HER ACROSS the grass toward the weeping cherry tree that burst with thousands of blooms. "I found this place the first day, when you vanished."

Cora could barely hear him over the falling rain. He parted the weeping branches and she ducked inside, flinching as a skeletal branch grazed her arm. But the tree gave them shelter, and the smell was soft and perfumed, and it slowly untangled the tension from her muscles, knot by knot, until she could breathe. The ground was carpeted in velvety pink petals. With the dome of flowers around them, it looked otherworldly.

She hugged her arms tighter over her wet sundress. "It's beautiful, Lucky. But it doesn't help us."

"It isn't about that." He wiped the rain from the planes of his face. "It's the black windows. They can't see us here."

She blinked as it slowly sank in. The branches formed a perfect dome that hid them from prying Kindred eyes. For the first time in fifteen days, she wasn't being watched. Her throbbing headache lessened. She turned in a circle as mist caught in her hair like fairy-tale dust. She felt a million miles away from the half-mad dancing in the rain, and the croquet mallet, and the fact that their lives had been stolen. There was only the beating of her heart beneath her dress, and Lucky's warm hand taking hold of hers, and a thousand feelings of relief.

For once, it felt like home.

A petal landed on his shoulder. She brushed it off. He was so solid beneath her fingers. Real. On impulse, she threw her arms around his neck and breathed in the smell of rain in his tangled dark hair.

"You have no idea how badly I needed this." She could feel his pounding heart between two layers of ribs and skin and cotton. Her heart responded. She coiled her fingers in his jacket, wanting him even closer. She didn't want to think about the Kindred. Or the missing food. Or the others.

She tilted her chin toward his. In the desert, they'd almost kissed. It would have been a mistake there, with the Kindred watching. They would have been doing exactly what the Warden wanted.

But there was no one watching now.

She pressed her lips to his. A hundred sensations overtook her. Her heart fluttered and spun like the petals falling around them. He pulled back in surprise. For a few breaths his eyes searched hers, water dripping from his dark hair, and she almost thought she'd made a mistake.

He let out a ragged breath.

Then he kissed her back, harder, his hands threading

through her wet hair, pulling in a way that drove her mad. She matched his fervor. No thinking. Letting her heart overpower her head. Shedding all those days her father had told her to smile through pain. There were no black windows watching them. No Cassian was watching them. No other captives were shooting her sharp words and dangerous looks. An urgency swelled in her chest.

He turned his head away. "Wait. There's something I have to tell you."

She shook her head. "Whatever it is, I don't care." She pulled his shirt tighter, drawing him closer. All she could think about were his eyes in the rose-colored light and his arms around her. She'd had so little practice with this sort of thing, and her hand drifted to rub against her bottom lip. His face darkened like he wanted nothing more than to kiss her again.

"I've wanted to kiss you ever since you fell out of that tree," he said. "But there's something you don't know."

She rested her head on his shoulder, breathing in his scent, tugging at his leather jacket like she was afraid he would dissolve in the rain.

"Cora. It's about your father."

She let him go abruptly. It was strange to hear someone else speak about her life at home. It made it all suddenly real again. Her father. Charlie. Her mother watching *Planet of the Apes* on the sofa. Sadie barking at squirrels. "My father?" She shook her head in confusion. "What does he have to do with anything?"

Rain still dripped from Lucky's hair.

"He has to do with everything between you and me." Alarm started to beat in time with Cora's heart, and she steadied herself against the tree trunk as he continued. "I told you I lived in

Virginia for a while. I didn't tell you when. I moved away two years ago. April third."

"April third?" She pressed a hand to her aching head, trying to think past the fog. That date was stamped on her parole papers. The day she was admitted to Bay Pines.

He kept his eyes on the ground. "I should have told you that first day, but I just . . . didn't. I had seen you in the newspapers, and on TV. I knew that your father was a senator and your mother used to be an actress."

He *knew*?

She pressed her hand harder against her head, trying to ease the throbbing that cut like a knife. "No—don't apologize," she stammered. "I worried that someone would remember the news, but the others all live overseas, so it seemed unlikely. I should have told you about the conviction, but I thought you'd think of me differently. I promise you, I didn't do it."

He didn't even blink at her words. "I know you didn't kill that woman, Cora. I know who your father is because I met with his men three times after the accident. I collected checks from them. They were paying me to keep quiet about what I saw that night."

The aching in her head vanished. The sound of the rain faded, and the smell of the cherry blossoms. Slowly, her hand dropped. "What do you mean?"

"The night of the accident. Your father's political fundraiser. He'd had too much to drink. The car was swerving all over the bridge. All I could make out was your dress—green silk—as you were yelling for him to stop. The headlights were so bright. And then the car went over."

Dimly she realized that the rain had stopped outside, but it didn't matter. "How could you have seen that?"

A second passed, a second she knew would change everything. "I was in the other car," he said. "The one your father crashed into before he swerved off the bridge. I was in the passenger seat." His voice broke. "The woman who died was my mother."

Dread filled Cora the same way water had filled her father's car that night: rushing in too fast to stop. She had been accused of a woman's murder. Involuntary manslaughter. The woman's name had been Maria Flores, and her teenage son had been with her, though Cora had been so occupied trying to help her father get control of the car, she hadn't seen either of their faces through the windshield.

Luciano—that had been the son's name. Luciano Flores.

"Call me Lucky," he had said.

She doubled over, struggling to breathe. "Your *mother*? My dad killed your *mom*? You said she died when you were a little boy!"

"I . . . lied. I didn't want you to know."

Her body started to rack uncontrollably. Not just a nameless face anymore. Not just a grave with plastic flowers she had visited once, secretly, at night. She'd tried so hard not to think about that woman or the son she'd left behind. *Smile,* her father had said, *even when you're hurting.*

What a fool she had been. She should never have listened to her father when he told her to push aside her true feelings. Why had she taken advice from a man who'd had too much to drink and *killed* someone?

"God, Lucky. I'm so sorry."

Lucky was by her side in a second, his arms around her. "No. If anything, I'm the guilty one." He flexed his hand, the one that was always giving him trouble. "I . . . I tried to kill him at first. My dad kept a gun in case of intruders. But his men stopped me, and they offered me money instead if I corroborated some story he'd come up with saying you were behind the wheel. He said you wouldn't go to prison. He said you'd get off on parole. I didn't care—I had no idea who you were. I figured his daughter was just as bad as him. So when the police questioned me, I told them it was you driving. They asked how I was sure, and I told them with your long hair and blue eyes, that you were a hard girl not to look at." He shook his head. "I took his money and got on a plane to Montana. I knew if I stayed in Virginia, I'd change my mind. I'd drink too much one day. I'd kill him." He paced beneath the tree. He kept wiping at his face, even though the rain had long since dried. "I *let* him get away with it."

She closed her eyes. The memory of water choked her. Her father had jerked the wheel so hard, it sent them careening into the river. The impact had stunned her. It hadn't been until water poured in, and her father had shaken her awake, that they'd both managed to flee the drowning car, swim to shore, and wait shivering for an ambulance.

"He said a drunk-driving conviction would have ended his career and put him in jail for decades," Lucky continued. "But you hadn't had a sip to drink. He said you could claim it was an accident; that you'd just gotten your license and there was a glare on the windshield on a rainy night. Involuntary manslaughter. He said you wouldn't get more than community service."

Sitting on the riverbank, shivering in each other's arms, still reeling from the crash, they hadn't known the judge would make an example out of her.

Lucky said, "At the time, I was angry. I wasn't thinking

straight. It wasn't until after the trial that it started eating away at me. Had I sent an innocent girl to prison? You were always in the newspapers, looking so angelic, and I started to realize that it wasn't your fault you were related to him. He'd played you just like he'd played me." He shook his head. "I don't know what he offered you. I hope it was more than I got."

She leaned against the tree trunk, feeling her head pulsing. She hadn't told anyone the truth of what had happened that night. Not her mother. Not even Charlie. And now this boy who she'd only known a few weeks, who she'd just had her lips all over, knew her secrets.

"The Kindred must have known," she said. "It can't be a coincidence that they would put us together."

"Maybe they put us together *because* of this. So that I could make up for what happened. I didn't know what to think when I saw you standing on that beach. I thought it was some kind of punishment for my sins. Then I got to know you. You weren't anything like your dad. You were his victim. And *my* victim. And dammit—you were pretty. Even more pretty in person than on TV. You do this thing sometimes where you run your fingernails over your lips when you're thinking, and you have no idea how much that killed me. How much I wanted to kiss you." He paused. "I wanted to make it up to you. I've been trying. I had your back when they accused you of stealing food. I've run mazes and swung from trees because you asked me to. I nearly ripped Leon's face off because he insulted you."

She stared at him in a mixture of fascination and horror. The mazes? The fight with Leon? He took a step toward her, but she pulled back, wishing the shade didn't hide his eyes. In a certain light they were the color of coffee, but now they looked black.

"We came up with the escape plan together, Lucky. You didn't just do it for me."

A petal fluttered down to his shoulder. He didn't bother to brush it off. Cora just stared at that petal, wishing he would speak, wishing he would say he believed in their plan.

"I'm sorry." His voice was so quiet, it almost sounded like a stranger's. "You wanted to go home so badly that you thought some sharpened sticks were going to get us out of here. But Rolf was right. We'd never have escaped from them. I went along with your plan because I wanted to make you happy. I still do—"

He reached for her, but she jerked away. The petals underfoot felt slick now. Sticky. The branches tangled in her hair like they were trying to trap her. She shoved them away. "You were *pretending* you wanted to go home?"

A shaft of light broke through the flowers to land on his face. His eyes were still coffee brown, not black. "Of course I wanted to go home—especially the first few days. I just never believed we actually could. I couldn't bear to tell you how I felt. It would have broken your heart."

"And now you suddenly decide to confess everything? Why, because the rain made you feel nostalgic?"

"Because we're running out of time. Twenty-one days is coming fast. We're going to have to . . . sleep together. And before that, I wanted you to know the truth."

"Oh, thanks!" Her voice was laced with venom. "So I not only am supposed to sleep with a guy I barely know, but he also happens to be the one who sent me to juvenile detention."

"*Dammit.*" He was fighting not to raise his voice. "You think

I want it to be like this? I want to be back home with an old man and his chickens. I want to visit my mom's grave one more time. I want to meet you there, back home, and I want to show you the sky in Montana, teach you the constellations. But this is our home now. The others already know it. It's time we grow up and admit it too." He stopped abruptly. His words echoed in the quiet space beneath the tree. His eyes had gone dark again. Night must have fallen outside, or else the world only felt darker. "At least we care about each other. And I do care, Cora. I don't think I've ever cared about a person more in my entire life."

He reached for her, but she jerked back.

"Tell me one thing. Do you believe that I didn't steal the food?"

He was quiet, his eyes shadowed in black. "If you did, I don't care. I'm on your side."

Cora pulled back, ripping the fabric that bound them. Her plan seemed so childish now, using sharpened toys as weapons and fighting their way out—to what? How did she ever think she could make her way home, when she didn't even know where she was? And yet a force within her came screaming back up.

She wasn't ready to give in.

She stumbled away from him, tearing through the branches that pulled at her like a thousand clutching fingers. Lucky called for her, but she kept running, faster than she ever had, tearing past Nok and Mali, who were dancing in the rain, past Rolf, who was plucking unsuccessfully at the guitar.

Not even Lucky was on her side anymore.

29

Leon

NIGHT FELL ALL AT once. The rain stopped abruptly, lingering in puddles on the boardwalk. Leon crouched behind a bush and spied on the cherry tree. He'd seen Lucky and Cora disappear beneath its branches, and he could guess what was going on in there. Another couple forming according to those damn dots on their necks. First Nok and Rolf. Now Cora and Lucky. Didn't any of them have an ounce of self-restraint?

"Animals," he grunted. He stood up and sauntered back toward town. The lights were off in the shops and the house—the others must have gone to bed. The rain had soaked his clothes, but he'd long ago stopped caring. His dress shirt was worn and stained, rolled to his elbows and undone at the neck. The suit pants were caked in mud from crawling through the jungle. He climbed the stairs to the diner and tugged at the door—his stomach howled for food—but it was locked.

"Here." He turned just in time to catch an apple flying his

way. Mali stood in the shadows, her face unreadable beneath the long braids. "There is no food today. Only empty trays except for Cora's. I find this on the farm."

His stomach howled louder. What shifty game was Cora playing at, stealing all the food?

He took a hefty bite of the apple. "Cheers. Now if you don't mind, bugger off." He started down the steps past her. She so unnerved him, with those shockingly light brown eyes, that permanent scowl. Her hand shot out as he passed, clamping onto his bare forearm.

"Are you returning to the jungle." She spoke all her questions like a statement, something else that unnerved him.

"Not any of your business, is it, kid?"

Her hand fell away, but that cold stare kept him prisoner. She was like a walking ghost, haunting him.

Ghosts. He flinched as a shadow seemed to pass through him. He whirled toward the ocean, breathing hard. The feeling of eyes on his back. A presence that wasn't quite human. It had started the first day; he'd thought it was the Kindred watching behind the panels, but now he sensed it was something else.

Someone else.

Mali's eyes flickered to the cherry tree. "Cora and Lucky kiss behind those branches. They will soon obey the third rule."

Leon snapped out of his daze.

"You really are a little spy, aren't you?" He ignored the fact that he'd been spying as well. "Well, don't worry about those two. Cora looks sweet, but trust me, that girl's got a dark streak. She's not obeying a thing. And Lucky won't either, as long as she tells him not to."

"They have no choice. The twenty-one day mark approaches."

She took a step to her left, head shifting like a snake. "They must obey. We all must." Her hand snaked out to grab him, and he slapped it away.

"Hands off. Don't get any ideas about you and me."

"You have no choice."

"What's the Warden going to do, get his Caretaker to lock me up? Joke's on them. It was only a matter of time before I was behind bars back on Earth anyway. Here's a piece of advice: stay away from me. I'm not a good person."

A vision flashed in his head of a girl with green eyes and a heart-shaped scar on her chin. A headache tore through his scalp. She'd been the first thing he'd seen when he woke. He'd been on the boardwalk, head throbbing and vision blurry, and a beautiful Middle Eastern girl leaning over him with the most shocking green eyes.

"I'm Yasmine," she'd said. "I don't know where I am. . . ."

Mali tapped his forehead, jerking him back to the present. "The Kindred do not take bad persons."

Sweat poured down his forehead. He wiped it away, trying not to think of the girl with the heart-shaped scar. "You don't know a thing about me."

"Yes I do. Cassian lets me watch you before putting me here."

Leon froze. His heart started thumping extra hard. He turned on her slowly. "What exactly did you see?"

Yasmine's green eyes flashed in his head again. She had woken him on the boardwalk, and he'd jerked upright. His head had been pounding and he hadn't been thinking straight. All he knew was he was somewhere he didn't belong, and there was an ocean and shops and a beautiful girl. He'd grabbed her hard enough to bruise her. He hadn't meant to threaten her. But she must have been so scared already, and his size frightened people. . . .

"What did you see?" he growled.

"I see you taking care of Nok. You know she is scared so you sneak to the farm when no one is looking and get her a peach. You leave it for her on the bed."

He sighed in relief. Mali hadn't seen, then. That look of fear crossing Yasmine's face, and her tearing away, and him chasing after her, certain she had answers, still so dazed he didn't know what he was doing. She'd run straight into the ocean and dived into the water. Leon had yelled at her to come back. By the time he'd gone in after her, she'd stopped moving.

Drowned.

While trying to escape from *him*.

He stopped pacing and glared at Mali. God, he hated how she never seemed intimidated by him, no matter how he tried to push her away. He hated most of all how much he liked the shape of her face, and that stringy hair, and that cold look.

He jabbed a thick finger in her face. "Listen, kid. You may think you understand humanity, but you've been living with those bastards for too long. I'm done with this whole social experiment. They can mess with time, spy on me, I don't care. I'm done with this—you most of all."

He stomped past her toward the house, where he ripped off a few sheets from a spare bed and stuffed them into a pillowcase, then stormed out the back. The jungle called to him. He'd never belonged in this pretend town anyway. He should have taken Yasmine's death as a hint that he belonged alone. A cold shiver ran through him, and he whirled toward the ocean.

Was it Yasmine's ghost? Was she the one giving him headaches?

He turned back around and kept walking.

He liked the solitude of the jungle. No talking. No arguing. No stringy-haired girls with scarred fingers. There were the black windows, sure, but what did he care if he was on display? Let them watch. All they'd see was a guy not giving a shit.

"Be careful."

He nearly jumped. Mali stood behind him on the path. How she'd moved so fast to get there, he wasn't sure. In fact, in the moonlight and shadows, he wasn't sure she was real at all, and not a hallucination.

"There is a reason the Kindred create the town. Humans are not meant to live on their own. Away from the group you start to lose yourself."

The branches around her rustled, and when he caught up to her, ready to unleash a string of curses, she was gone.

Had she even been there?

Shaken, head throbbing, he pushed farther into the jungle. He'd slept in the huts before. With the sheets, he could make himself comfortable. He could scavenge food from the farm. He didn't need the others at all. If the Kindred wanted to punish him for it, let them try.

He paused and tilted his throbbing head toward the sky.

Sometimes he thought he could hear the moon moving.

30

Cora

NO MATTER HOW FAST Cora ran, Lucky's words clung to her heels. All this time, he'd been lying to her. About the accident. About believing they could go home. About believing she wasn't stealing food. She plunged into the shadows of the forest. There was no moon or stars, but her eyes adjusted. She followed the steep path toward the mountain biome, the farthest one from town.

Sweat slicked on her face. The path curved, trying to steer her back to town, but that was the last place she wanted to go. She leaped off the path onto the wild forest floor, where roots and twigs twisted at her feet. Snow began, softly at first. She ignored the blinding flakes and kept running until Lucky was far behind her and the town was a distant memory, until her foot caught and she slammed to her knees.

The shock of impact left her numb. Her frozen lungs fought to pull in air. She squeezed her throbbing toes and searched for what had made her trip.

There—a sled.

It was old-fashioned, with wooden slats and metal runners, though the edges were harmlessly spongy. Next to it were five more sleds. Leon had told them about this puzzle—some kind of racecourse.

Her body started shaking so hard that it threatened to shatter. She had been running off-trail for hours, and she'd ended up exactly where the Kindred wanted her to be. Running in circles. Her brother, Charlie, had owned a pet rat before he'd left for college. Sometimes he would take it out and let it ride around on his shoulder, but most of the time it ran on a wheel in a corner of its cage. Running, running, running. She felt like that rat. Running endlessly, going nowhere.

She shoved the sled down the mountain. "I'm not playing your games!"

The hair on her arms started to tingle. The pressure in the air crackled. She balled herself tight, pressing her back against a tree, not daring to look up. She knew, if she did, Cassian would be there. She clenched her jaw in anger. Well, if he really could read her mind, *good*. She focused on how much she hated him.

But when she did look up, and saw his two boots, and then him standing so stoic in the snowfall, the anger vanished. This was the person who had rescued Mali. Who had saved Cora's own life from the Warden. Could she truly hate someone who would do that? Did he deserve her fear—or her admiration?

Cassian's boots crunched softly as he approached. He crouched so they were eye to eye. He wasn't wearing a coat, but he didn't shiver. His head tilted to study the goose bumps on her bare arms.

"You should return to the house, where there is warmth, and try to sleep."

A snowflake landed on his cheek and melted quickly. The metallic sheen to his skin had a way of absorbing the low light so that he almost glowed in the darkness—a man made of starlight. She leaned her head against the tree and squeezed her eyes shut. She had never noticed before, but snow made a sound when it fell, like rustling leaves.

"I have brought you something," he said.

Cora opened one eye, begrudgingly curious.

He removed a small object from his uniform pocket and held it an inch from her palm. It took Cora a moment to recognize the delicate gold chain tarnished around the clasp, the golf club charm and the theater mask and the airplane. Her necklace. She had thought it destroyed forever, like Lucky's watch and their clothes and every trace of their previous lives.

There was a new charm attached to the chain.

A dog.

"Dogs are rare here." His expression was perfectly flat, and yet his voice fluctuated with the barest hint of emotion. "I searched hard for one, but they are considered low value, so they are not kept in this sector. I submitted a travel request to get you one, but the Warden denied it."

The charm was old, with a dent on one of the dog's legs. She couldn't imagine where he had found such a thing. It did a strange thing to her to see all she had truly cared about in sixteen years of life—her family and her dog—reduced to such trinkets.

It wasn't much to hold on to.

A cold breeze blew, and she shivered. He noticed and moved to the left, blocking the wind, but it didn't help. It was hard to imagine this otherworldly creature having a life. Did he live in a city? Did he go shopping and cook supper and spend his evenings listening to songs on the radio? And what happened in private with all that pent-up emotion he kept so tightly stored away?

He reached the necklace around her neck, but he wore no gloves. His bare fingers brushed the delicate skin of her neck, along with the sizzle of electricity. She jerked away.

"Don't touch me."

He regarded her like a puzzle he couldn't solve. "I wish only to give you this present."

When she didn't recoil again, he reached gently to brush the hair off her neck so he could fasten the necklace. She closed her eyes, anticipating his touch. His finger barely brushed her skin. *There.* That spark. It was such a foreign feeling, just short of painful. She wanted to feel it again and again. She felt the weight of the charms around her neck, so familiar and missed. When he let her go, she almost grabbed his hands back to feel that spark again. It was an addiction she didn't want to have.

She pressed her hand against the charm. "What does it feel like, when you touch me?" she whispered, as though by whispering she could pretend she hadn't asked.

"Very soft," he said. "You are very soft. Cora."

Her fingers started throbbing over the charm, along with her heart. Unfreezing, piece by piece, but she fought against it. She curled a fist around the charms. "This won't help me sleep. I don't want a piece of home. I want all of it."

"Be careful, Cora. Defiance is not a desirable human value. The Warden believes that your attempt to kill me, naive though you were, betrayed a defiant spirit. He was not pleased."

"You think?" Cora rubbed her throat. "He nearly strangled me."

"Our moral code would prevent him from attempting to murder you. Though there are other ways to get rid of an unpredictable human subject. I was able to convince him your actions came from fear, not defiance, and that your other traits—resilience to captivity, extensive knowledge of Earth, even the rare coloring of your hair—made up for the difference. I told him it would not happen again." Cassian leaned closer. "It *cannot* happen again."

She squeezed the necklace harder. "Why are you telling me all this?"

"I want you to trust me, Cora."

The way he looked at her, with a flicker of concern behind those black eyes, made her think he might really be on her side. That there were forces even bigger than him, and he was bending the rules for her. But how could she ever trust the man who had taken her?

His head tilted slightly.

"In time, your hatred of me will diminish. You will come to understand that I brought you here for your own good. If a necklace is not enough, I can give you more." Cassian closed his eyes.

The snow stopped falling. The last flakes settled a little too slowly, like in a dream, and then, between the breaks in the clouds, faint lights appeared. Just a few at first. Tiny dots. She could almost have mistaken them for fireflies, if this had been any other place. They multiplied until the sky was a shimmering dome.

Stars. He'd given her the stars.

Her hand pressed against her mouth, holding in a silent exclamation. She didn't know how he'd made stars appear with his mind alone, but she didn't care. Nor did she mind the ache that spread through her head, the same familiar ache that came whenever they manipulated the environment. She had missed the stars too much to care. It was like seeing old friends after too long apart. She had painted stars on her bedroom walls when she was twelve. She used to climb onto the roof and watch stars appear on the horizon. Making wishes. Picking out the constellations.

Her fingers drifted from the necklace to the black marks on her neck. Orion. She thought about Lucky, and that brought a stab of pain. She tried to think instead about how she never wished upon a star for *this*. Maybe back home she would have spent her life as an outsider, torn between two worlds. But nothing, especially not fake stars in a fake sky, was going to change the fact that he was her captor and she his prisoner.

She was done being caged.

This couldn't be her life. Four walls made of endless trees and mountains and a ceiling made of limitless sky, and a man with black eyes who thought giving her the stars could make this world real.

"Mali might have taught you some tricks," he said, "but you cannot hide your thoughts from us forever. The Warden knows you are attempting to find the fail-safe exit. He knows you refused Boy Two's sexual advances. His researchers are collecting observations, Cora. If you continue down this path, he will soon have enough data to build a case to remove you, whether the twenty-one day mark comes or not."

She ran a nail over her lips, taking in his words, and then dropped her hand when she remembered Lucky saying that habit had made him want to kiss her. "Is that why I get more tokens for solving the same puzzles? Why he only plays my song on the jukebox, and why the others don't get food anymore, but my plate is full?" She swallowed. "Why is he trying to drive a wedge between me and the others?"

He stood abruptly. "You do not know what you are talking about."

She stood too, moving to face him. "You're trying to break us, aren't you? That's why you're messing with us. That's what the headaches are about. It's the rumors that Mali told us about. Humans evolving. You're trying to push our minds to the limit. You want to see if we can be perceptive, like you can."

"The researchers do not need to test that. We *know* you cannot be perceptive."

"I know that too!" She grabbed his arm. "But you're just the Caretaker. The hired help. You don't know what the Warden might be planning—but you could find out. You owe us that. If you believe in your mission to take care of us, and I think you do, then you have to defend us even from your own kind."

He pushed her hand off his shoulder. It was rough, a gesture of anger. He was going to leave her on her own, just like Lucky had.

With an angry cry, she lurched for the materialization apparatus. If he wouldn't find out what the Warden was planning, she would. But just as her fingers closed over the smooth metal, his hand gripped her shoulder, hard enough to sear her with pain, and then she was flying. The air exploded from her lungs when she connected with the ground. She pushed back to her feet, head swimming, and lunged for him again.

"*Stop.*" His command was sharp, not at all regimented. Cora ignored him and scrambled against his chest to grab the apparatus, while he tried to stop her without inflicting damage. His knee pressed against her chest, pinning her to the snow that seeped through her white dress, just hard enough that she couldn't breathe.

Her throat burned. Was this it? Was he going to turn her over to the Warden for this final act of defiance?

Suddenly, his knee was gone. Air rushed back into her lungs just as he grabbed her wrists, pulling her close.

"Let me go," she managed to choke.

"No." His grip tightened. He reached for the apparatus on his chest, the very thing she had wanted. "You still do not comprehend the magnitude of the danger you would face outside of the life we have given you. You are only safe here, under my care. It is not a kind world, Cora, beyond the walls."

From somewhere even deeper than her fear, deeper than her gasping lungs, curiosity whispered. What was out there, beyond the walls? She didn't want to be curious, but how could she not be? This was the stuff of legends, and gas-station tabloids, and dreams. This was the truth about the universe.

He clenched his jaw in a gesture that looked startlingly human, as if this was actually hard for him. Sweat broke out on Cora's skin.

"Are you turning me in to the Warden?"

"No." He pulled her closer, so they were only inches apart. "I am going to give you what you want. Answers. And when you see what is beyond the walls, you will not be so anxious to disobey us anymore. You will find that life here—life with me—is far superior to anything out there."

Her heartbeat throbbed in her veins. "Life with you?" she echoed.

The muscles in his throat constricted. "Life in the environment, watched over by me." His hand tightened over hers.

Pressure consumed her.

31

Cora

WHEN THE STATIC-LIKE PRESSURE ebbed away, Cora opened her eyes.

A row of cabinets. A metal table. They were back in the medical room.

Before she could speak, Cassian dragged her toward one of the wall cabinets. He took out a metal bar the length and thickness of a pencil. When he snapped his wrist, it opened to reveal a set of shackles.

"My colleagues would question my motivations if I were to transport an unrestrained human subject. Hold out your hands."

Cora pulled back. Her head felt deep in a fog; was it really only hours ago she'd twirled beneath a fairy-tale tree with Lucky while the others danced in the rain? The sting of his betrayal felt as fresh as the snow melting down her legs. "Tell me where we're going first."

He gripped the restraints impatiently. "If you insist on asking questions, I can summon the Warden. He would be happy to give you answers—perhaps while he was handing you over to the Axion for dismemberment."

Cora grudgingly held out her wrists. The shackles clamped over her. The metal was flexible, just like the Kindred's clothing, and molded itself to every contour of her wrists. Cassian guided her toward the door, which slid open automatically.

Light glinted from the hallway, and she shielded her eyes. It was a strange kind of light, bright enough to sting her retinas but richer somehow, multidimensional, like a kaleidoscope. As her eyes adjusted, she saw it spill over Cassian's face and the empty metal floor, not constant but moving like it was fractured on water, giving the hallway an underwater sense even though it was perfectly dry. Cassian didn't slow his pace to allow her to marvel. He pulled her along at a brisk clip.

She was in the Kindred's world, now.

It was an overwhelming and terrifying idea, until she realized that each detail might tell her valuable information about their society—she might even find a way to escape. But her hope faded as they continued down a hallway that had no remarkable features. No air ducts. No elevator shafts. As far as she could see in either direction, the hallway was the same. Her headache returned, throbbing gently. Was it more of their space-bending technology?

After what must have been ten minutes, a faint rumble sounded in the distance. She glanced at Cassian, who was taciturn as always. The sound grew. The hum of machinery. Footsteps. Even voices, though too garbled to tell if they were speaking English. An end to the interminable hallway came suddenly, with brighter light and the rush of wind.

Cora's footsteps slowed. "Where are we?"

"Do not speak here. Do not stop walking. Do not stare—some of the other species consider it rude."

"*Other* species?" she hissed.

The hallway ended before he could respond. The sound of voices swelled as they rounded a corner into an enormous chamber that rose thirty feet high, packed tightly with people. Painfully bright lights radiated from interlocking wall seams onto a mass of bodies dressed in all shades of blue. Kindred. Hundreds of them, weaving to and fro like at a busy airport, some striding with determined steps, others grouped to one side, speaking in low voices. Stalls were set up haphazardly in the center of the room and clustered around the edges like hunched cockroaches. They displayed objects Cora didn't recognize, except for a few. A rice cooker with Chinese lettering on it. A potted lemon tree. A stack of license plates from different countries.

Maybe it was a museum of stolen artifacts from Earth and other planets, but from the way the Kindred argued in that flat way of theirs, she got the sense that transactions were happening. It was certainly like no store or supermarket Cora had been to. No one carried baskets or bags, so where did they put their purchases? Did they use money?

"For once in your life," Cassian said, "obey what I tell you. Or else someone will question why you are here."

He led her deeper into the chaos, veering abruptly left and right, as though he saw some sort of organized system that she didn't. A few Kindred slid their black eyes to her, but their faces registered no curiosity. They were like automatons, masked and unfeeling. Three in the crowd wore Cassian's same black uniform, but most wore a simpler variation of the uniform the Warden had worn, with a row of knots down one side, though some of the Kindred—both male and female—clothed themselves in white robes with a single knot at the shoulder. They kept their eyes low to the ground and did not speak.

No other colors flashed among the crowd, except a shocking blur of red: two figures who might have been normal height if standing upright, but whose backs were so hunched that they couldn't be more than five feet tall. They wore dirty rust-red jumpsuits and masks that fractured their eyes like insects', and they had an odd way of walking, a little fast and jerky. No patch of skin or face or hair was showing; there could be anything under those jumpsuits, but the way their backs twisted so unnaturally screamed that they weren't human.

She nearly collided with someone while trying to study the insect-masked creatures. She started to apologize but froze. A man's leather belt was directly in front of her, at eye level. Her head pitched up, and up, until she was looking into the face of a creature—a man, as far as she could tell—with startlingly green eyes and skin a watery shade of gray. He had to be eight feet tall. He ruffled fingers at her that were long and willowy as water reeds, and she gasped.

Cassian dragged her away by her wrist cuffs.

"That was an alien!"

She supposed her words sounded ridiculous—*Cassian* was an alien too, but she had never really thought of him that way. Her eyes ran over his features; they had looked so foreign to her at first, but compared to the other creatures, he seemed strikingly close to being human. As his dark eyes cut to hers, she felt a kinship she knew she'd never feel with the other species. At least he *had* eyes . . . who knew what was underneath those masks.

"That was a Gatherer." His tone was flat. "And they, in particular, do not like to be observed. They especially do not like to be bumped into by lesser species. If you must stare, the Mosca could not care less." He jerked his chin toward the two hunchbacked figures in insect-like masks. "All they care for is unloading their wares, consuming alcohol, and falling asleep in some hallway."

Cora gave the two Mosca a wide berth as they passed. The sea of cerulean-clad Kindred moved so stiffly around them, their heads held high, as though to show that they were superior. Most of the booths were run by Kindred, but a few were staffed by more of the Mosca in masks and rust-red jumpsuits. They tended to huddle on the floor, their voices droning in fits and starts behind their masks.

Cassian led her past a stall stacked high with comic books: some in French, some Japanese, a few English. A short Kindred man—only six feet tall—stood stiffly behind the table, dressed in a uniform with only two knots on the side, with a jean jacket slung over his shoulders and sunglasses perched on his nose, looking so strikingly out of place that she had to stare.

She ducked to read the title of his comic book as they passed. *Aquaman.* A date was stamped on the bottom left corner. She did the math quickly—the comic book wouldn't come out for another two years.

Her head started to throb. How was that possible? Had they been gone from Earth for *two years*? Or did the Kindred have the ability to manipulate time even more than she thought?

Cassian kept walking so fast that she barely had time to think. She tried to turn to see the comic book again, to confirm she hadn't imagined it, but they were too far past the stall. "That comic book. The date—"

But Cassian shot her a cold look, to be quiet.

Cassian stopped abruptly as two Kindred soldiers in identical black uniforms approached. They exchanged words with Cassian that sounded harmless, though Cassian's fingers dug into Cora's arm like a warning. She looked over her shoulder amid the crowd, half expecting to see Fian's creased face bearing down on her.

"Hey, give that back."

She whipped her head in the other direction, following voices in English. In the booth across from them, three human children dressed in costume—a boy as a cowboy, as second boy in a princess crown, and a girl in a baseball uniform—were chained to a post, arguing over a dirty stuffed dog. They couldn't have been more than eight years old.

The boy in the princess crown grabbed the dog. He was missing his two front teeth and half of one of his fingers. The cowboy let out a racking cough, and the creature running the booth, one of the masked Mosca, tore the dog away.

"Worthless. All you childrens." His voice, behind the mask, came in fits and starts like a static-filled radio program. "When I go back to Earth next, I will get little childrens who know how to behave. I will to bring them back here, and then will throw the lot of you childrens out."

Cora instinctively moved closer to Cassian. He glanced at her dilated pupils and sweating brow, said a few final words to the guards, then led her through the rest of the market quickly.

They plunged into another hallway, this one blessedly

empty. It was all she could do to put one heavy foot in front of the other through the murky light that made her feel as though she were moving underwater.

"Why were those kids chained up back there, and missing teeth and fingers?" she whispered insistently, rubbing her knuckles against her tired eyes. "Were they for sale?"

"They were, yes, but do not fear. That was one of the more reputable trading halls. Those children were protected by basic laws. If they were selling the children for individual body parts, they would not have done so out in the open."

Cora stopped in the center of the empty hallway. "So it was a *pet* store?" She looked at him hard. "It's nice to know that's how you think of us."

"I told you that you would not like what you saw. You should feel fortunate. The Kindred only take humans of the highest-quality stock. The Mosca take whatever they can get; those humans often suffer a poor fate." He paused. "It is a deplorable practice. In my previous position, it was my responsibility to save and protect humans mistreated by private owners."

"How heroic of you."

"Keep walking." His fingers curled around the bar imprisoning her wrists as he pulled her farther along down the hall. "We did not come here to see a trading hall. We are going to see the menageries. Be warned that until now, you have only ever seen one aspect of our world: the public one, where we cloak our emotions to demonstrate the highest standards of intelligence, obedience, and above all, emotional control. But as much as we would like to, we cannot suppress emotions forever. They have a way of coming out, and that is why we live very different private lives." He reached a door but stopped. The light from the seam in the door danced over his features, casting his eyes in shadows.

"What are you waiting for?" she asked.

"I am wondering if I am doing the right thing." His voice was distant, as though he was speaking more to himself. "Perhaps I am making a mistake."

Cora stepped closer, letting the light play over her face, which she knew must look sunken and worn. "Sometimes mistakes are worth making."

The muscles in his neck constricted. His hand tightened and flexed at his side as he turned away from the light, and shadows ate at his features. "The ways in which humans and Kindred think are so very different. Mistakes in our world are to be avoided at all costs, because they betray a lack of intelligence, just like lesser emotions. It is sometimes difficult to understand you when you say such things—that sometimes mistakes are worth making."

He stepped back into the dancing glow.

There was more than confusion written on his face. There was curiosity too. This black-eyed creature studied her like he truly did want to see inside her head, more than just thoughts and images, but to see *her*, understand who she was and why she thought what she thought.

He wanted to understand humanity.

Good luck, Cora thought. *I'd like to understand it myself.*

3 2

Lucky

LUCKY STORMED THROUGH THE town square, past the flashing lights of the arcade and the thumping beats of jukebox music. Each one punctuated what an idiot he was. He'd stayed up all night, but Cora hadn't come back. He should have known she'd run away the minute he told her the truth. Why did he ever think she'd forgive him for putting her in prison? Because she smiled at his jokes? Asked him about his granddad's farm? God, what an idiot he was.

He raked a hand through his hair, fighting against the pain in his skull. His mother's eyes burned behind his eyelids. He was back in their car on the rainy bridge. Arguing over the radio station, country or top 100. Then the glare of headlights. The car spinning out of control. His mother calling his name. *Luciano.*

And he'd let her murderer go free for a pile of cash.

He followed the sound of guitar music to the farm. The

others were playing the orchard puzzle. It involved picking apples, each one stamped with a different constellation, and tossing them in bins with the same mark. Nok plucked at the guitar with unskilled hands, while Rolf and Mali tossed apples back and forth, laughing, trying to hit each other more than the bins. A pile of half-eaten apples rotted in the sun.

He stared at them like they'd gone insane. "What are you doing?"

Rolf caught an apple from Mali. "There wasn't any breakfast this morning. That makes the third day. There's not much here, but it will keep us from starving. We aren't going to play Cora's games. She's egging us on for a fight. All I can conclude is that she's jealous because we're happy." He took a bite of the apple, then tossed it in Lucky's direction. "Catch!"

The apple hit Lucky's shoulder and bounced on the grass. Rolf looked at him expectantly, then pointed enthusiastically toward the apple. "Throw it back. I want to see what kind of arm you've got. Aren't all you Americans good at baseball?" A grin cracked his face, like he was making a joke between two friends.

Lucky kicked the apple into the stream.

"Listen. Cora's gone. Last night I followed her into the mountains, but she just vanished. I thought she was hiding out, but when I went back this morning, her footsteps ended in the snow. There was a second set of prints too, bigger than a human's. The Caretaker must have taken her."

Nok and Rolf only blinked calmly, and it made Lucky's stomach flip. Didn't they care?

He turned to Mali. "Where did he take her?"

When she didn't answer, he grabbed her thin shoulders and

shook her. Mali just allowed herself to get thrown around like a rag doll. "I do not know."

"You have to! You've seen beyond the walls—you grew up in their world."

"They tell me what they wish me to know. I assume they remove her."

He let her go abruptly. "But it hasn't been twenty-one days yet."

Mali gave that odd head wobble that was meant to be a shrug. Lucky kicked over one of the bins in disgust; apples rolled everywhere. "They can't just change the rules! They said we have twenty-one days to obey Rule Three. If they took her before that, then they should take me too. I haven't obeyed yet either."

"Perhaps he comes for you next."

Lucky froze. His head pounded so hard he could barely think. "Comes for me? Well, good. Then he'll take me wherever he took her, only this time I'll be ready. Nok, give me that guitar."

Nok looked up innocently through her long eyelashes. "You want to play?"

"No, I want to break it apart and wrap a string around the Caretaker's neck when he comes back. Cora was right. It isn't safe—they can take us at any moment. I should never have listened to you all."

"Listening to us saved your life." Rolf kicked an apple with short, sharp jabs, one eye twitching like his head stabbed with pain. His voice was suddenly bitter. "If the Kindred hadn't—"

"Rolf, shh," Nok hissed.

"No! I'm tired of everyone acting like idiots instead of using their brains. I thought Cora was smart, but she let her emotions get the best of her. She's gone crazy with these stupid ideas of escape that are just going to get us all in trouble. You don't want to end up like her, Lucky."

Lucky dug his fingers against his temples.

"Don't you get it?" Rolf sputtered. His face was splotched with red, but his fingers weren't twitching. "Tell him what you told us, Mali. About Earth."

A creeping feeling spread through Lucky's veins. He eyed Mali warily. "What is he talking about?"

"I am not supposed to tell." Mali shot Rolf a hard look. "The Kindred believe your minds are not yet ready to understand. I only tell *you* because your mind seems stronger than the others."

Lucky braced himself. He didn't care about whatever stupid thing Mali and Rolf had argued about. He sensed that he was about to learn something that he could never unlearn. For a moment he clung to his ignorance. If he didn't know, he could pretend everything was okay. He could close his eyes and think of home and his granddad and that horse that kept kicking over the fence so the chickens got out.

"Earth is gone," Mali said.

The ground fell out from under him. He collided with the grass, leaning against an apple tree, the smell of blossoms so thick around him he might choke. His head throbbed. He raked his fingers over his face and scalp, trying to ease the pain. Earth was gone, along with his dad in Afghanistan and his granddad and his mother's grave with the faded plastic flowers and all the horses and the chicken houses he'd repaired last summer and everyone he had ever known, ever loved, ever said hello to as he crossed the street.

Nok crouched beside him. Her fingers were so soft against

his head that he wanted to lean his head into her. His mother had had soft hands too.

He remembered her eyes meeting his as the car careened out of control.

Luciano.

And now even her grave was gone. But so was her murderer. Lucky might not have pulled the trigger that day on the airfield, but Senator Mason was dead.

Lucky lived. And Cora lived.

"Poor Lucky," Nok said, brushing aside his hair. "I know it's hard. I was upset too, but there's nothing we can do but be thankful we weren't there when it happened."

Rolf crouched over them, casting a cold shadow. "She's right, you know. You have to think about this logically, Lucky. Put aside your emotions. The Kindred knew what was going to happen to Earth and picked us, out of everyone, to survive. There's only the six of us and a few thousand humans scattered throughout the Kindred world. The Kindred were telling the truth all along. The rules aren't there to be cruel. They're there to save humanity." He rested a hand on Lucky's back. "We have a duty to keep ourselves healthy and keep our species going."

Lucky felt as though his head was splitting in two. The house in Roanoke he grew up in, with the patch of forest behind it. The strip mall where he used to skateboard. The school where he'd only had two months left to graduation. The army recruiting center. Everyone, and everything—gone.

"*We* were our own enemy," Rolf pressed. "Humans. We were so cruel to each other, and to our planet. We didn't deserve what we had. Look at Cora—she's sabotaging us, and herself as well. That's human nature."

Lucky looked between Nok and Rolf. Neither had spoken much about their pasts, but he could see in their eyes that they had always been outsiders on Earth, just like him. Rolf's twitching and Nok's hiding behind her pink streak of hair. The same for Leon, who faced the entire world like it was out to get him. The same for Cora, who'd been wronged by her own father—and by him.

Maybe the Kindred were right to take me.

Maybe he belonged in a cage more than he ever did on Earth. Maybe they all did.

His face was wet, though from tears or sweat or spray from the creek, he wasn't sure. He sat up. His knuckles popped from the old accident scars. He rubbed the aching joints.

Rolf's fingers were twitching again. "The Kindred saved our lives. They fixed Nok's asthma, and my poor vision. I bet they even healed that hand you keep saying gives you trouble. Try it. Nok, give him the guitar."

"I told you, I can't play anymore."

"Just try. Let this be your proof. Earth ruined your hand and took away your music, and the Kindred gave them back to you."

Lucky dragged a hand over his face. Now that he really thought about it, his joints didn't actually feel that stiff. Had cracking his knuckles just been an old habit?

"Give me the guitar."

"You aren't still planning on attacking the Caretaker with the guitar strings, yeah?" Nok asked.

"Just give me the goddamn guitar."

Nok handed it over. For a moment, Lucky cradled the wood in his hands. He'd missed the feel of wood. Everything in the cage, even if it looked real, had a synthetic quality. Nothing was quite the right weight or texture, but this was. The wood slipped into his hands like an old friend. The strings were taut.

For a brief second, everything hit him again: they were the only ones left.

He closed his eyes and gritted his teeth. He struck one note, then two. He hadn't played at all since the accident. Punching the hospital wall had damaged his fingers too badly for fine dexterity. Now, though, the joints didn't pop or grind. His tendons moved fluidly. Sound came out that tore his heart in two all over again. He played for the hand that the Kindred had miraculously fixed, and he played for a lost world, and he played for a girl who, wherever she was, didn't even know that they would never go home again.

33

Cora

AFTER LEAVING THE KINDRED marketplace, Cassian led Cora down hallways that were not glinting with starlight like the ones they had left behind. These were narrow, with low ceilings and murky light coming from the hairline cracks in the floor. The narrow halls wound like an animal den, twisting and dank and unpredictable. She grazed the walls with a hand that felt too heavy and came away with a chalky dust.

"We are in the deepest section of the aggregate station," Cassian explained. "These tunnels are dug out of rock. Kindred stations are never permanent; they last one or two hundred human years at the most. We are a transient species. We locate a sizable asteroid and build our stations around it, ship by ship, interlocking until we have an entire functioning system with residential, governmental, commercial, and recreational sectors. When it is time to move on, we merely reverse the interlocking and go our separate ways."

They passed the shadows of more Kindred. Unlike the ones in the market, these weren't stiff but slinking, loose, skittering like animals. Uncloaked.

She inched closer to Cassian.

They rounded a corner. At the end of the next hallway, under an island of light, a Kindred woman with loose black hair down to her waist stood before a node of four doorways. She was dressed in a light green gown that was elegant and flowing, almost humanlike. So different from the Kindred in the market, who all wore cerulean uniforms or white robes. The woman leaned on a podium and gave an unexpected yawn. The movement was so jarringly fluid—so uncloaked—that Cora jumped.

"Uncloaking is necessary for our well-being," Cassian explained as they approached. "We abhor the lesser emotions—jealousy, lust, fear—and yet to be alive is to experience such states. There is no escaping them, only delaying them until an appropriate time and place. That is why we have these menageries, where Kindred can go for emotional leave."

"What happens in a menagerie?" She wasn't sure she wanted the answer.

"Anything to express or enhance emotion. Games of chance. Intoxicants. Brothels—though not here. Some menageries allow Kindred to do virtually whatever they want with the lesser species, and humans are a particular favorite because, as you have noted, we are quite similar physically."

His black eyes settled on her, and she looked away. "When you rescued Mali, was she in a brothel?"

"No. She was part of a fight ring with three other human girls and a chimpanzee." He raised an eyebrow at her surprise.

"Have you not seen her fight yet? Do not underestimate her."

They reached the Kindred woman dressed in her flowing gown. An almost maniacal smile stretched across her face. She wore glasses with painted blue eyes that made her look more like a doll than a living creature.

Was this what *uncloaked* looked like up close?

Something about the way she tipped her head down coyly at Cassian was a little familiar, not to mention seductive. Cora threw him another look. What exactly did he get up to, in *his* uncloaked time?

The Kindred woman made a high-pitched hissing sound that might have been a laugh, almost as though she could read Cora's thoughts. Cassian responded to her curtly and led Cora past the woman.

"I informed her I was here in an official capacity. It is rare to be cloaked here, particularly when escorting a lesser species. I do not want to draw more attention to ourselves than we must. We will use a service passageway."

He pushed open a doorway with his hand. It was the first time a door hadn't opened automatically, and she wondered how exactly their telepathy worked. Her thoughts plunged into darkness as soon as they entered the hallway. Only faint light came from the small drill holes in the walls, but Cassian guided her forward as though he didn't need light, or else knew the passageway by heart. It opened into a viewing room. Unlike the cage's, there was nothing scientific feeling about this. It was simply a rock-hewn cave with a wide window overlooking a chamber below.

Cassian motioned to the window. "We can see out, but they cannot see us."

Cora approached the window hesitantly. After passing through such dank corridors, she had expected something repugnant, but the chamber beyond was a complete contrast: well lit, with a gleaming stone floor and stately columns at either end like a Greek temple. Cells were built into the temple facade opposite them. Each cell looked about ten feet tall by ten feet wide in front, but then seemed to open up, impossibly, into much larger spaces. It had to be a visual illusion—more advanced Kindred technology.

Each cell was decorated in soft silks and columns; one was a bedroom, with a young human girl asleep in a gilded bed overlooked by statues of Athena and Zeus. Another cell contained a wooden table stacked with scrolls, and a human boy with very dark brown skin, dressed in a toga. His pupils were dilated. Drugged.

Cora drew in a tight breath. Their worn faces didn't look so different from her own sleep-deprived one. "Why do you do this to them—just to entertain yourselves?"

The bright lights of the temple reflected on Cassian's stoic metallic face. "There is some educational value, but yes. These children are primarily here to entertain the uncloaked. We enjoy viewing vignettes of what life on Earth must be like."

"What about that oath you swore to protect lesser races?"

"No one is harming them." Cassian's voice was carefully devoid of emotion. "They are perfectly safe in their enclosures. They have ample food and a facsimile of their natural habitat."

If her hands hadn't been bound, she might have slapped him. Did he truly believe *this* was fulfilling their oath?

"Each menagerie adheres to a different theme," he continued. "This one is called the Temple. It is modeled after humans' early philosophical foundations. There is one on the third level of the aggregate station that is modeled after prehistoric Earth, called the Cave. There are seven menageries on this station alone."

Mali had once mentioned the Kindred's penchant for dressing like humans. Now Cora understood that the Kindred woman at the doorway was dressed so strangely because she was in costume.

"Why human places, human times?"

"When we uncloak, we crave experiences, and there is no society, nor habitat, better suited for the cultivation of experiences than the human world. Of all the species, intelligent and lesser, humans are the most vibrant."

"What about *your* world?"

"The concept of a homeland fascinates us because we have not had one since the Gatherers elevated us to live among the stars. The environments on Earth, the weather, the shape of the land and the way you build your structures into it—the idea is quite foreign and quite . . . charming. Your kind is just as interesting. Like your planet, you are all so varied, so prone to warfare and destruction, but also beauty." He paused. "Can you blame us for wanting to watch such fascinating creatures? To act like them, even?"

She could only stare at him. The Kindred had no homeland, so they wanted to experience humans', and they'd kidnap kids and lock them up to get it.

She tested her shackles again. They held too tight.

"This menagerie, or one like it, is where I would have to take you if the Warden orders your removal—assuming he lets you live. These are all children who had to be removed from their enclosures or private owners for one reason or another."

"Why are they all *children*?" Her voice was barely audible.

"We do not only take children. We prefer to take them, however, because of their malleable natures and heightened ability to adapt."

"But what happens when they grow up?"

His face darkened. No longer a man of starlight, but of shadows. "Many grow unruly as they age. They are sent to unmanaged preserves; there they are free to be as savage as their true natures dictate." He pointed through the window toward the last cage. "This girl is the one I wanted to show you."

The last cell was a tableau of a Greek throne room, with a little girl of about ten years, who had wheat-blond hair shorn close to her scalp. She sat on a leather stool, hands clasped in her lap, staring into a hearth that crackled with what must be simulated flames.

"That girl was relocated from Iceland four years ago," Cassian said. "She was put in an enclosure like yours, though less advanced, with only two biomes. She refused to eat, which disobeys Rule Two. After several rotations she had to be removed, and was sold to a private owner, from whom she escaped. She escaped from her next two owners as well, but was caught each time. She will be here for the remainder of her life. We administer drugs to her to keep her docile. We must do that with the rebellious ones. For their own safety."

Cora could only stare. The girl would be there—staring at the stone hearth, isolated, drugged—for *the rest of her life*?

"That could be you, Cora," Cassian said.

It wasn't hard to imagine—with her wheat-blond hair, the girl almost looked like a younger version of Cora. In the cell, the girl raised a sluggish hand to scratch her shorn scalp. She was missing two fingers, from the middle knuckle up. Cora's own fingers started throbbing.

Cassian leaned in close. "Do you still intend to disobey our rules?"

34

Cora

CORA'S HEAD SPUN. THIS little girl. The boy in the scroll room. The other girl, asleep under the watch of statues. They were just a few of many who had been taken. A living display, a breathing museum, to satisfy the Kindred's fascination.

Her stomach twisted.

"I am trying to keep you from this, Cora," Cassian said quietly. "Do not make me bring you to a place like this. It would only—"

He stopped when the door below opened. They both leaned toward the window as two Kindred women entered the chamber below, wearing Grecian costume dresses, their hair loose, their faces plastered with the exaggerated emotion that meant they were uncloaked. They strode directly to the Icelandic girl's cell.

Cassian's cold gaze slowly slid to Cora, and she got the sense that whatever they were about to witness was going to be even worse than it already was.

Below, the taller Kindred woman reached through the bars

and beckoned to the girl, who stood and approached slowly, walking like she was dizzy. The Kindred woman said a few words that Cora couldn't hear through the viewing panel.

"She wants the girl to clap," Cassian explained. "To perform a trick for her entertainment."

The girl slowly brought her disfigured hands together like a wind-up toy, which made the Kindred women gasp in delight.

The Kindred woman's lips moved again.

"Now she wishes for the girl to bow," Cassian translated.

The girl bent at the waist, sweeping her arm with a slightly dizzy flourish, and the Kindred handed her a token. The token fell from where the girl's missing fingers should have been, but she picked it up with her other hand and slipped it into her pocket.

"The humans in these exhibits collect the tokens and redeem them for prizes," Cassian explained. "The more tricks they perform, the more rewards they earn."

Disgust crept up Cora's skin. This was what the Kindred thought of humans? That other than a handful of elite ones suitable for breeding, they were no good for anything but performing cheap tricks?

The shorter Kindred handed the girl another token, then leaned forward with her lips pursed. Cassian explained, "She has asked for a kiss, this time."

All the tension that had been knotted in Cora's body unraveled, plunging to her feet.

A *kiss*?

The shackles felt too tight. Her lungs constricted. Sweat broke out on her forehead and her vision started to blur as the horror of everything descended on her all at once.

The Kindred could do anything to them, she realized.

Kiss them.

Kill them.

Drug them.

Destroy them.

The insanity of this place hit her like a blow to the chest. The world didn't seem to move in real time. It jerked and jolted between slow motion and fast forward. Her balance keeled, just like it had that day in the bookstore. Her vision sharpened and blurred too, as the colors of the room pulsed too brightly.

Cora pressed a hand against the glass. Cassian said a few words that she couldn't process. She couldn't stop staring at the little girl below. The girl bent forward and met the woman's lips through the bars of the cage, giving her a peck, chaste and sexless, like a deranged kissing booth. A small sound came from Cora's throat. She realized she was swaying.

Strong hands shook her. The bright colors faded to normal. The sound of her own pulsing heart dialed down in volume. Cassian shook her again, hard.

"Cora. What is happening to you?"

She tried to speak, but her lips were too dry. Cassian checked her pulse, lifted each eyelid, even looked down her throat. Examining her, just as the Warden had done, like she was merely a problem to be solved.

Lucky was right. They'll never let us go.

"Describe what is happening." His voice came urgently in her ear. "Are you experiencing strange sensations? Visual disturbances?"

She shoved Cassian and his questions away and braced

herself against her knees, but her hands were too sweaty and slipped off. She stumbled toward the floor. Cassian caught her. Her hands were still bound, but she grabbed the strap across his chest, holding tight. She pressed her face against his chest, eyes squeezed closed, as though to block out everything that was happening.

"Take me away from here. Please."

Through his clothes, his heartbeat was nearly as fast as her own, and she wondered why he cared enough about her panic attack to ask such odd questions. He hesitated only briefly before removing her from the viewing room, sweeping her up in his arms and carrying her when her limbs were too sluggish to move on her own. He spoke in a rush to the blue-eyed Kindred and took Cora through another doorway to a Parthenon-style room that was blessedly silent, empty save for a circular fountain in the center, surrounded by a ring of artificial stone benches.

A bathroom. No matter how intelligent they were, the Kindred still had to pee somewhere.

Cassian set her down on the soft cushions around the fountain. He removed his gloves and dipped his hands in the water, then touched them to her face, trying to cool her down, but his touch never cooled her. The water just made it spark more.

Her eyes were closed. She panted for air. Once her head cleared, she grabbed the strap across his chest and pulled him close. She slapped him, hard, across the face.

Her palm stung.

He didn't flinch, of course—she could never hurt skin as hard as metal. But his throat constricted. He was very close to her, water dripping off his hands onto her dress.

"Why did you strike me?" he asked.

"Because you're one of them. You're a monster just like those women down there."

"I am trying to protect you from that. It is the way the world is, and I want you to understand how dangerous it would be without my assistance."

"Our enclosure is no different from this one! Run your mazes. Play your games. You're sick, all of you."

Cassian's black eyes shifted between Cora and the door back to the menagerie. "I brought you here to show you how *desirable* your environment is."

"Because there we're only forced to kiss each other, you mean? Here we have to kiss *you*?"

His eyes darkened to a deeper shade of black. "A kiss is a very common trick. I do not understand why it bothers you to this degree."

She let her head fall back on the cushions. "Because it's more than a kiss. It's Rule Three. Procreation. Taking love and making it a trick, or an obligation. You'll never understand that."

The fountain gurgled calmly into the silence.

"Help me understand," he said, and he sounded sincere. Cora opened one eye, surprised by this. "We have nothing like it in our culture. I'm . . . sorry. I did not understand what it meant to you."

His black eyes moved back and forth, back and forth, searching her own. He had said that he wanted to understand humanity, but it wasn't so simple.

"It's not a trick." Her temper was cooling beside the bubbling fountain. "It's not like clapping your hands or giving a bow."

He paused. "What is it like?"

She wondered, fleetingly, what the Kindred did to show affection if they didn't kiss. He sounded genuinely curious. *Help me understand.* His face was so close to hers that she would only have to tilt her chin to show him exactly what a kiss was like. That would teach him more about humans than months of studying them.

What would that electric spark feel like, between their lips?

A drip of water from the fountain landed on Cora's cheek, and she jerked out of her thoughts, shocked by where her mind had gone. "It's personal," she snapped, and wiped the drip off her cheek. "It's something special between two people who care about each other. It's very emotional. Something you'd know nothing about."

His hand had stopped flexing, but his eyes stayed on her lips.

"You do not know what I am like in private," he answered. "When my emotions are uncloaked."

"No. I don't. I don't want to, not if you're anything like the rest of your kind." When he didn't respond, her blood burned hotter. "If you're so fascinated, why don't you give one of those kids on exhibit a token for a kiss? I'm sure they'd be delighted to show you." Her words were poison. She wanted him to say yes. She wanted to know he was as bad as the rest of his kind.

"I'm not interested in learning about kisses from them," he said simply.

His black eyes didn't move away from her lips for a second.

35

Rolf

ROLF STOOD AT THE top of the mountain, ankle-deep in snow, gazing at the line of little red flags. At the bottom of the racecourse, Mali waited in her oversized military jacket, sled slung over her shoulder. Lucky stood behind her, looking like he hadn't slept in days; he'd only come when Nok had dragged him along.

Rolf pitied Lucky—up to a point. Earth was gone; it was a fact. Fighting the truth was like fighting gravity. The news had hit Rolf hard at first, too. He'd thought about the little curry shop two blocks from his dormitory, and about the secret patch of tulips tucked away behind the manor in Tøyen gardens, and how he used to count the beautiful red bricks on the walk to school (11,321) as a boy—but there was no logic in mourning what was already gone. Besides, it meant no more bullying from his classmates. No more parents' rigid expectations. No more being stuck with an entire race of people who were too stupid to see they were destroying their own planet.

But Rolf wasn't stupid.

He arranged his sled to match up with the red flags. He wasn't good at the physical puzzles, but this one wasn't about strength or speed but reflexes. It involved throwing one's weight at the precise angle and time to turn the sled through the flag course. He'd never sledded with the other children in Tøyen gardens, afraid of being mocked. But he was *good* at it. Who knew?

"Just go already!" Nok jumped up and down by his side, a smile stretched between her red cheeks. Her lips were stained bright blue from candy. He still couldn't believe how beautiful she was, and that she was *his*. On impulse, he pulled her close for a kiss. She laughed and kissed him back.

He'd never understood unspoken rules on Earth: social norms that flew over his head, polite conversation, a hierarchy of coolness where he'd always been on the bottom rung. But here, he understood the rules. There were only three! Clean, logical, efficient. The only thing that didn't make sense was that the food was still missing. At first he'd thought the Kindred just favored Cora, but it made no sense, because the Kindred had sworn to keep them healthy. So it had to be Cora stealing on her own, but if she was gone, who was stealing it now? The only conclusion Rolf could reach was that Lucky had been mistaken when he said the Caretaker had taken her—she must still be here, hiding out like Leon. Maybe they were even working together.

Nok tugged on a red curl hanging in his face. "Go, silly. It's my turn next."

Her candy-blue lips pulled him from his thoughts. The same shade of blue as the cubes in the Kindred's medical room.

There had been one above the doorway. Several more built into the cabinets. Both the door and cabinets had opened automatically according to the Kindred's thoughts—and then it had hit him.

The physical equipment was different, but the theory was similar to the research his colleagues at Oxford's robotics lab had done on brain waves controlling prosthetic limbs. The blue cubes had to be thought amplifiers. Which meant the Kindred weren't as powerfully psychic and telekinetic as the others believed. It also meant that, if the cubes could be modified, it would hamper the Kindred's abilities. A fact Cora would die to know. A fact he would never tell her.

"If I'm going," he said to Nok, pulling her into his lap on impulse, "then you're coming too!" She shrieked in surprise as he pushed them down the mountain together. It was a challenge with her added weight and his restricted view. The wind flew by them, making Nok squeal with delighted fear and clutch him harder. They passed trees in a blur: *Abies recurvata* and *Ducampopinus*. Her hair brushed his cheek. The snow kissed their faces. He adjusted their angle, and they moved faster, faster, until Lucky and Mali had to jump out of the way as they shot straight into a snowbank.

They flew off the sled, tangled around each other, and landed in the soft snow. Rolf was half buried in it, numb except for the fire raging in his heart.

Earth? Good riddance.

Lucky picked up the token that had slid out of a trough at the bottom of the sledding course. "Here. You earned it." Heavy worry lines framed his face. He had to be as aware as the rest of them that it was the twenty-first day, and Cora showed no signs of returning. But he tried for a tired half grin. "I've never seen anyone navigate the course that fast."

Lucky tossed the coin to Rolf, who caught it triumphantly. He'd always wanted a friend as cool as Lucky. Soon, once Lucky got over his grief, he'd have a girlfriend *and* a best friend.

They tromped home through the snow, and he and Nok paused to make a snowman that looked like the Caretaker. Then they returned to town and goaded Lucky into pulling out the guitar. The town square was summery warm. Nok stripped off her snow-soaked dress and jumped into the stream in her underwear, while Lucky played an old country song he said his granddad had taught him. Rolf mentally laid out a new plan for the farm. *Asparagus officinalis* by the barn and *Phaseolus vulgaris* beans along the fence. Under his leadership, they wouldn't even need the diner.

Nok didn't bother to get dressed after her swim and lay out on the grass to dry in her underwear. Christ, but she was beautiful. Her long limbs gleamed in the sunlight. She tapped her toes in time with Lucky's music.

"I love a guy who can play guitar," she said dreamily, rolling over in the grass.

Lucky grinned back, and Rolf sucked in a sharp breath. His fingers started tapping, and he forgot about the *Asparagus officinalis* and *Phaseolus vulgaris*. Why was she looking at Lucky so adoringly? Rolf had been the one who won the guitar. *He* was the one keeping them alive. Nok let out another peal of laughter at some joke Lucky had made, and red flared into Rolf's cheeks. His eye started twitching.

He stood abruptly and headed for the house.

"Where are you going?" Nok called.

He got the pillowcase of tokens from their bedroom, then pushed through the saloon-style toy-store doors, slamming tokens into the counter. He got the painting kit so Nok could draw the birds she missed. The Curious George book set so he could read to her every night. He stuffed all the toys, along with handfuls of candy, into the pillowcase. He carried everything back to the town square and emptied it on the grass.

"What's all this?" Nok dug through the toys with wide eyes. "It looks like Christmas!"

"Yes, Norwegian style. The gnomes have decided you've been very good boys and girls," Rolf said, emptying the rest of the pillowcase. "It's time for a celebration."

Nok tore through the presents, showing Mali the best ones and explaining what they were for. Rolf smiled until Lucky silenced the guitar with a hand on the strings.

"A celebration of *what*?" Lucky's voice had an edge.

Rolf glanced at Nok, letting his gaze slide to her bare back, her bare legs. "A celebration of making it to the twenty-one-day mark and still being here."

A shadow passed over Lucky's face. "We aren't all still here."

Rolf paused. He should have picked his words more carefully. Lucky still thought the Caretaker had taken Cora, but Rolf knew that logically, she had to still be there.

"We've all lost people we love." Rolf tried to keep his voice diplomatic.

Nok found the painting set and started setting out the pots of rainbow colors in the grass. She selected a fat brush and dipped it into the green.

"The way you two are acting," Lucky said testily, watching

her, "playing around while Earth is gone, makes it seem like you don't even care." When they didn't answer, he went back to plucking on the guitar, sunk into a dark mood.

Oblivious of their argument, Nok drew a flower on the back of her hand, a purple lollipop sticking out of her mouth.

Why should she grieve? Rolf wondered. All she'd lost on Earth were parents who'd sold her into indentured servitude, and an apartment full of sickly thin girls, and a talent manager who might as well have been a whorehouse madam. He didn't have much to grieve, either: his parents had never been affectionate; always pushing him to work harder, isolating him from kids his age. The only people in his life he'd interacted with had been a steady stream of bullies: Karl Crenshaw and the cricket bat. The schoolmates who made fun of his glasses. A professor who had forced him into public speaking.

They're all gone now, Rolf consoled himself. He picked up a lollipop from the pile and spun it lazily in his mouth.

"Hey, Mali," Nok said. "Take off your jacket. I want to paint on you, yeah?"

A branch snapped near the side of the movie theater, and Rolf spun on his heels. Was it Cora and Leon, spying on them? He'd never trusted that lumbering Neanderthal. Nothing had delighted Rolf more than when he'd banished himself to the jungle.

Rolf took a step closer to Nok, protectively. Mali had shrugged out of the military jacket, and Nok was using her body as a canvas, drawing bright blue swirls all over her arms. Empty chocolate wrappers surrounded them. Nok's lips were stained bright purple from lollipops.

"You too, Rolf," Nok said. "Take off your shirt. I'll paint you next."

He cast one look back toward the jungle behind the movie theater, searching for the moving shape of a tattooed Maori or a small blond girl, but the leaves were quiet now.

He sat in the grass, pulled his shirt over his head, and closed his eyes. Rolf would be a canvas if she wanted him to be. He'd be anything for her. He'd be *everything* for her.

Nok dotted his nose with paint, and he fell just a little bit more in love.

36

Cora

CORA COULDN'T STOP SHAKING as Cassian led her down the dank burrows back to the austere upper levels. The shock of seeing the menageries had lulled her into silence. Caged kids. Missing fingers. Drugged eyes. Cora's chest knotted with longing for this whole nightmare to be over. She wanted to play in the backyard with Sadie. She wanted to pick up where she'd left off, be back in Charlie's Jeep, scrawling lyrics.

> *Home is the place you never know . . .*
> *Until there's nowhere else to go . . .*

Cassian's head cocked toward hers; it was usually difficult to gauge where exactly he was looking, but this time she felt the heat of his gaze. "I thought showing you this alternative would make you content in your environment. Yet in your head, you are only more determined to return to Earth."

Cora nodded.

"Cora, your home . . ." He stopped. "Never mind."

They walked in more silence, Cassian's hand balling into a fist and releasing. There was something he wasn't telling her, but no matter how she searched his dark eyes, she couldn't see into his head.

A door slid open, revealing the star-lit medical room. Cassian held out a hand to stop her. "*This* is your home now. You must accept that." He removed her shackles mechanically. While he readied the materialization apparatus, she leaned against the examination table, running a fingernail over her lips. The pull of home was too strong to give up on. She glanced at the doorway that had closed behind them.

Planning escapes had practically been an extracurricular activity at Bay Pines; Cora and her roommate used to lie awake at night swapping far-fetched ideas, most of them stolen from bad action movies. She'd never taken their planning seriously, but four months after she'd been there, a girl two rooms down had succeeded. She'd bribed a guard to unlock her room at night, then sneaked to the kitchen, which was run by outside contractors she'd paid off to smuggle her out in a vat of food scraps so the guard dogs wouldn't smell her.

Cora bit on a jagged fingernail. The space station was hardly a juvenile detention facility, but maybe she could use some of the same tactics. Trading information. Bribery. Cassian had said that the Mosca only cared about payment. . . .

Cassian's head jerked to hers, and Cora pinched her thigh, hoping Mali was right that pain could block the Kindred's ability to read minds.

His black eyes scanned her face. "You are trying to hide something from me."

She pinched herself harder. "No."

"You should not inflict pain upon yourself." His chest was rising and falling a little quickly. It made her remember his face so close in the fountain room, his lips just an inch from hers. . . .

He shoved the apparatus into his chest and darted out a hand to pull her close. He whispered in her ear.

"Obey the rules. Please."

It was no longer an order. It was a request, and one of the few times Cora had heard his voice sound anything other than mechanical. "I'm not the only one watching you," he said. "I cannot protect you forever."

HE RETURNED HER TO the empty drugstore. Beyond the doorway, sunshine spilled over the green grass. Cora stumbled toward the light.

She blinked a few times, clearing her foggy head, reminding herself that the crickets chirping weren't real. The sunlight was fake. It was as much a fabricated prison as the menagerie. At the heart of it, they weren't any different from those drugged kids.

Nok and Rolf were stretched out on the grass, dressed only in their underwear, playing with the painting kit. Not far away, Mali was toying with the radio, twisting the volume to make the voices rise and fall, rise and fall. Blue paint coated her arms. Rolf had blue streaks over one arm too, and was in the midst of painting a yellow swirl on Nok's stomach. He dotted her cheek with paint and she laughed, trying to take the brush from him, getting gooey blobs of paint all over them. Their candy-stained lips met, and the brush fell from his hand. They started making out, right in front of Mali and the dozens of black windows.

And the Kindred thought humankind was evolving? If anything, it was *de*volving.

A hand clamped over her shoulder, and she jumped.

Lucky stood behind her, guitar half forgotten in one hand. His dark eyes raked over her. The last time they'd been together, everything had changed. She had thought she'd found a friend in him. More than that. Someone who made her feel less alone, a boy with a broken hand and a dimple in one cheek, and yet it had all been a lie. *We need to grow up,* his voice echoed in her head. He had betrayed her the night of the accident, and he had betrayed her here too, when he'd said he didn't believe in escape. Cora's heart didn't know how fast to beat.

Should she shove him away? Or forgive him?

He answered the questions in her head when he let the guitar fall into the grass, forgotten. He pulled her into his arms.

She clenched her eyes shut. She couldn't bring herself to hug him back. She couldn't quite pull away either.

"What happened?" His voice sounded older.

She shook her head against his shoulder. "Where's Leon? I want everyone to hear this."

"No one's seen him in days."

"Days?" Cora pulled away, confused. She glanced toward Nok and Rolf, who hadn't yet noticed that she was back. "I've only been gone a couple of hours."

Lucky was very quiet, searching her eyes with his own. "You've been gone three days."

Her heart pounded harder. The Kindred controlled the

sunlight, so they could set a day to be however long they wanted. So did this mean instead of four more days until she faced removal, she only had one? It was already the *twenty-first day*?

Mind racing, she hurried over to where the others were sprawled. Nok glanced at her briefly, then went back to mixing paint. "Hey. You're back."

She spoke casually, like Cora had gone on a stroll to the beach, not been taken by the Kindred for three days. And yet Cora detected a flicker of annoyance in her voice—at interrupting her painting, or at being back at all, she wasn't sure.

Rolf didn't even pretend to be pleased to see her. "Come back to apologize, I hope?"

"Apologize for what?"

He let out a coarse laugh. "Right. Pretend like nothing's happened. Where do you claim to have been for three days, if not sneaking around with Leon and stealing our food? If I didn't know so much about gardening, we might have starved because of your games."

She let out a frustrated cry. "You still think I'm still stealing food? How? I haven't even been here! I've been with the Caretaker!"

Rolf's face reddened. His fingers massaged his head as his eye twitched. "Well, now it makes sense. You got him on your side against us. You're his favorite, after all. He'd do whatever you asked. Change the weather. Stop feeding us. Have you been watching us this entire time, laughing as we *starved*?"

"Of course not!" Her own head was throbbing. She squeezed her tired eyes shut, resisting the temptation to smack Rolf. *Laughing* with the Caretaker? More like the slow torture of seeing what they really did to humans. "Listen. I know you don't like me. You don't have to. I've seen more of their station and I think I know how we can get back to Earth, but we'll have to act quickly. They're speeding time up in here. If it's already the twenty-first day, they might be on to us." Cora pinched the inside of her arm hard enough to cause a steady stream of pain, glancing at the shadowy figures beyond the black windows.

Lucky had been pacing behind her, but he stopped at her mention of Earth. At the same time, the paintbrush froze in Nok's hand. Rolf and Mali exchanged a silent glance, but Cora dismissed it.

"The Caretaker took me through a marketplace," she continued. "I saw some other species. The Mosca." She glanced at Mali, whose face remained stoic. "You said they were black market traders. Well, they speak English. I heard them talking to human kids they took from Earth. They said they'd be going back to Earth soon for another supply run. If we can just find the fail-safe exit and get out of here, we could negotiate with the Mosca to get a ride back home."

None of the others spoke. Nok seemed intently focused on the tip of her paintbrush. Why weren't they happy about her news?

"Cora," Lucky said slowly, "you haven't been sleeping. You really just need to rest."

Cora shook her head in frustration. "It isn't about that. Look, I can't do it on my own. And I don't want to. Mali, you must know the hallways of this station. We'll need you to get us back to the market without anyone seeing us. Leon's a black market trader at home, so he can handle the negotiations. Cassian said they aren't loyal to any particular race. All they care about is payment. We've got all the tokens from the games, and I saw the same tokens out there too, so maybe they're worth real money. If I have to, I'll cut off my hair and use that to pay for our trip."

Nok and Rolf exchanged a troubled glance. Lucky clenched his jaw, listening and nodding as his eyes darted around to nothing in particular. He had seemed relieved to have her back—so why did she now feel ice down her spine?

"Cora." His voice was soft. Too soft. Pitying. "There's something you don't know."

The ice down her back spread to her tailbone. She looked to Mali, who only nudged a paintbrush with her toe. Rolf whispered something in Nok's ear; she let out a giggle before clamping a hand over her candy-stained lips.

Lucky didn't meet her eyes. "Cora, there's no point trying to escape. Earth is gone."

37

Cora

THE WORDS CREPT OVER her like a cold mist. *Gone?* She felt like a stranger in her own body. The wind was blowing, but she felt nothing. The air had lost the smell of flowering trees, replaced with the ozone she'd smelled the first day. *Gone?* What about Charlie? Her parents? What about her bedroom with the stars on the ceiling, and Sadie asleep at the foot of her bed, and her notebook of half-written lyrics stashed beneath her pillow? *Gone?* She didn't need to look down to know her hands were still attached to her wrists—in the same way, she still felt the pull of home.

She shook her head like he'd spoken a foreign language. "What are you talking about?"

Lucky rubbed the back of his neck. "Mali told us. She found out from the Caretaker. It happened right after they took us. That is why there's no point in trying to escape—there's nothing to escape *to*." For once, he wasn't popping the knuckles in his left hand.

The fog in her head grew, turning colder by the minute. She

threw a hesitant look at the others. None of it made any sense. If Earth was gone, why hadn't the Caretaker told her? He certainly wasn't shy about showing her the terrible things that happened in the menageries. And there were the Mosca's words in the market too. He'd talked about his next supply run to Earth like it was a foregone conclusion.

Her eyes fell on Mali, standing cryptically silent, pinching her own wrist. "How do we know you aren't lying? If you were working with the Kindred, this would be the perfect thing to say to make us give up hope. And if it was coming from you, not them, we'd be more likely to believe it."

Mali didn't answer.

"They've never lied to us," Rolf declared.

Cora threw out her arms toward the mountain range and the ocean and the farm. "This whole place is a lie!"

"No—it's a chance." Rolf had been massaging his temples like his head ached, but he abruptly dropped his hands. His voice had an edge of authority that she'd never heard before. What had happened, while she was gone, that made *him* the leader? "They've created an entire new world for us. We're like gods to them."

"A *world*? Props and tricks, that's all it is. Do you know what the Caretaker showed me, out there? Kids for sale in a market. A little girl made to do tricks. She had blond hair just like mine, but they'd cut it all off, and two of her fingers as well. They drugged her and made her curtsy and clap her hands and kiss like a deranged sideshow. That's how much they value us, Rolf. We aren't gods to them. We're playthings."

"Listen to yourself! First they give you special treatment. More tokens. Your stupid song on the jukebox, over and over.

A private tour of the Kindred's space station. And now you're ungrateful for all that they've done for you? Why in the world are they still keeping you around? You're stealing our food. You're trying to sabotage us. It doesn't make any sense! What, are you sleeping with the Caretaker or something?"

Everyone fell silent. Cora's heart started thumping. He didn't know how close he'd hit to the truth. That moment in the fountain room, his lips so close to hers . . .

No. It wasn't like that. That was sick.

The light shifted to the brightest setting, midday. The Greasy Fork door slid open, and the sound of Cora's song cranked up on the jukebox. All their heads turned.

"The diner's finally open again," Nok said in surprise.

"It's a trick," Rolf answered quickly. "I told you, she's got the Caretaker on her side somehow. She probably asked him to do this, so it would look like she wasn't behind them stealing our food. We shouldn't trust it. I have the system in the farm perfectly planned out. If we just stick to our vegetable rations—"

"I am tired of raw carrots," Mali said flatly. She started up the diner steps. Nok had a hand pressed over her stomach, practically drooling at the smells coming from the diner, but she kept biting her lip and looking at Rolf in indecision.

"Fine," Rolf said. "*We'll* eat the food. Cora, I'm in charge now, and I say that you aren't allowed in. You can try surviving off the farm for a while and see how you like it." He started moving toward the door.

"Wait—I can prove it!" she cried, standing between them and the diner. "I saw a comic book from Earth in the market. Its date was two years in the future. That proves that Earth couldn't have ended when we were taken. They *must* be lying." Cora's heart thudded to the heavy beats of music. They had to see that this was all just a trick. Just the thought of Earth being gone shrank her soul. That it was ashes now, Sadie and her family, the gap-toothed girl from Bay Pines, and the NPR reporter on the radio with his smooth voice, and her entire town, and state, and country.

No. It couldn't be gone.

Nok brushed the pink streak of hair from her face to reveal a pitying look. "You look really tired. After lunch, let's go to the beauty parlor. I'll paint your nails. We'll get some chocolates, yeah?"

Cora stared at the dot of yellow paint on Nok's nose. Was she going crazy—or were they? Rolf scooped up the paintbrush, wrapped an arm around Nok, and skirted past Cora to enter the diner. Mali went behind them, licking her lips.

Lucky was the only one left. Cora went pale, thinking of their last conversation—the one that had made her run.

It's time to grow up, he had said.

"Do you believe me, Lucky? That Earth is still there?"

He wiggled his toes in the long grass. "I don't see why Mali would lie. She doesn't care either way."

"Maybe they lied to her too." She hated the pleading tone in her voice, but she needed him to understand. "I'm not willing to take our captors' word for it. If Earth is gone, I want to see it with my own eyes. The Mosca could take us there. We have a chance."

He didn't answer, and panic clutched at her throat. "I forgive you for everything, Lucky. For lying to the police about the accident. For taking my father's money. I don't care about any of that. All I care about is what happens now. You were going to risk your life for your country back home—don't you still care about it? Don't you still want that beach, and a beer, and a girl?"

"I have a beach," he said quietly. "And I thought I had a girl too. Just drop all this talk about escape. Rolf . . . he sees you as a threat now. He thinks you and Leon are conspiring against us. He isn't going to trust you anymore, now that you're making these wild claims. Can't you just accept this for what it is? Your father's gone. All our sins are behind us. This can be the fresh start that we've always wanted."

"That *you've* always wanted. I never wanted to walk away from my problems, move across the country because I couldn't face my mother's murderer."

He clenched his jaw, then slowly shook his head. "You aren't thinking straight. You should listen to Rolf. He's a genius—he knows what's best. We still have time to obey, Cora. The twenty-first day isn't over until tonight."

She stared at him, knowing exactly what he meant. "And if I don't?"

He picked up the guitar. Flexed his knuckles. Didn't meet her eyes. "Then you're on your own."

He climbed the steps to join the others. She clutched at her necklace, feeling the weight of the charms. The golf clubs for her dad. The theater mask for her mother. How could she give up on ever seeing them again?

She spun on her heels, trying to put as much distance as she could between herself and Lucky. She followed the path through the wildflower field to the desert and climbed the nearest dune until her calves burned and her resolve gave out, and she sank to the sand.

She heaved a breath and combed back her hair. She'd seen

the date on the comic book. She'd heard the Mosca talking. If that ten-year-old Icelandic girl from the menagerie had escaped three times, why couldn't she? She should forget the others. That's how the girl at Bay Pines had escaped—alone. Thanks to Mali, Cora knew how to hide her thoughts. She just had to find the fail-safe exit, hide out in the corridors, and make her way to the black market traders. She'd take a weapon disguised as a toy—no one was cutting off her fingers to make into tea—and negotiate with them. Her hair for a ride back to Earth.

But can I really leave the others here?

She twisted her hair in her fist. Below, at the base of the dune, the shimmering ocean seemed even brighter. Cora felt on the verge of something, like pieces of a dream coming back to her, or a song she had long ago forgotten the words to. Pain fractured her skull as the ocean grew so bright she had to squint against it. Why would the Kindred turn the lights up? She clutched her hands to the sides of her head, wincing against the pain. She could almost see a shape moving among the waves. A swimmer.

The dead girl's ghost, she thought. Cora was still wearing her dress.

But—ghosts didn't exist. She rubbed her eyes. Her ears were roaring too. Her sense of balance felt off. Was it another panic attack? Or a pulsing headache, like she'd had in the bookstore?

Her hands twisted in the sand. Her head threatened to rupture. Just as suddenly, the harsh light and colors muted back into reality. The waves lapped calmly. Even her headache eased. It was as though nothing had happened. She pushed herself up from the sand onto shaky legs.

Is this how people lose their minds?

She glanced toward the tangled jungle. Lucky had told her she was on her own, but there was still a tattooed Maori smuggler out there. Leon might still want to escape as badly as she did. But she wasn't going out there without a way to protect herself. For all she knew, Leon's heart might have grown as black as the tattoos on his face.

WHILE THE OTHERS ATE lunch, she tiptoed back to the house, up the stairs to Lucky's bedroom. The guitar rested on his pillow.

Cora touched it gently, afraid the wood wouldn't be wood at all, but it was hard beneath her fingers, and when she knocked, it made a hollow sound. A memory returned of Rolf trying to play it while the others danced in the rain, so blindly happy. She picked up the guitar by its slender neck and clamped her fingers over the strings to stifle any errant notes. Then she slammed it with all her strength against the dresser.

It splintered. The long neck ripped off and strings snapped. The echo of notes faded gradually. She glanced out the window to make sure the others hadn't heard, then assessed the wreckage. She could bury the splintered wood in the mulched paths, and Lucky would never know. He'd assume that the Kindred had taken it, or Leon had stolen it, or maybe the captivity would get to him and he'd forget he'd ever owned a guitar . . . just like, in time, he would forget about her.

She wrapped the six guitar strings around her wrist like bangles and sneaked out toward the jungle.

38

Mali

NORMALLY MALI DIDN'T MIND the Greasy Fork, with its jukebox music and checkerboard tablecloths, but today everything about the diner annoyed her. She picked at her food, ignoring Nok's plea to go to the beauty parlor together.

"But you would look so pretty with curls," Nok argued.

Frustrated, Mali shoved her chair out and slunk from the room, leaving her pudding unfinished. She squinted up at the scalding sunlight and hugged Rolf's military coat more tightly around her.

She couldn't shake something that Cora had said: when Cassian had taken her to the menageries, she'd seen a little girl with blond hair shorn closely and missing two fingers. Mali had been through too many owners to keep count, but the last one had been the worst. He'd kept her and another girl locked in cages and made them fight each other or animals.

Anya.

Their owner had sold Anya's beautiful blond hair and four of her knucklebones.

Even if they'd only been together a few months, Anya had been the closest thing to a sister that Mali had ever had. Like Mali, Anya had been taken at a young age from her home—a place called Iceland—by the Mosca traders. But unlike Mali, she had never grown submissive to their captors. She had always tried to escape her owners. First at age six. Then at seven. Always talking about proving that humans were as intelligent as the Kindred. After Cassian had rescued them from the fight ring, Serassi had told Mali that Anya had died due to complications from old wounds. And yet here was Cora, saying that Cassian had taken her to see a human child he knew well, with blond hair and two missing fingers.

Could Anya still be alive?

Mali glanced over her shoulder, making sure the others weren't watching, and ran up the steps to the drugstore. She couldn't be certain if Serassi would be watching; Serassi rarely observed them herself, far more consumed with analyzing data the other researchers collected. Hormone levels, fertility rates, the science of couples and romantic liaisons—that was Serassi's particular interest, but Mali pressed her hand to the black window and focused her thoughts on wishing to speak to her.

Nothing happened for a few minutes, but then pressure came, and a caretaker appeared—not Cassian, but the female one who filled in for him when he was on emotive leave—and grabbed her. They rematerialized into a dark chamber that took shape as the medical room, where Serassi was leaning over the examination table. Mali paused. A human girl's body rested on the table. Long black hair. Very tall. A constellation mark of the Big Dipper on her neck.

It had to be Mali's predecessor.

"That will be all for now, Tessela." Serassi dismissed the substitute caretaker with a wave and then returned to her work. She addressed Mali without so much as a glance. "You requested to speak with me. Why?"

Mali circled the table slowly, her bare feet cold on the metal floor. "Is this the previous Girl Three. The one who dies."

Serassi did not bother to verify something they both knew was true.

Mali kept her distance. She'd seen plenty of dead humans before, in the worst menageries, or in cages, or cut apart by the black market traders. But she'd never seen the Kindred, with their high moral standards, deigning to handle a corpse.

"Will you dismantle her body for parts." Mali kept her voice calm. She had learned that the Kindred were more likely to respect her, and thus answer her questions, if she acted as stoically as they did.

Serassi's black eyes met Mali's. "Of course not. You know better than that. We are not like the Mosca. I am merely cataloging this girl's DNA to add it to the stock algorithm. We are creating a new program for human reproduction. Soon we will not even need the breeding facilities; we will be able to engineer your race just as we engineer our own. It will be far more efficient."

"Leon tells me that he kills her."

Serassi removed a needle as long as her forearm from the wall casings. "Boy Three is disoriented. He is mistaken if he thinks this girl died because of him. The first day they were introduced to their enclosure, I rematerialized into the cage to check on their vital signs as they woke. This girl saw me as I was rematerializing. She was afraid and ran. Boy Three did not see because I was standing behind him. The ocean has a high saline level to prevent drowning, but this girl was an expert swimmer. She was able to pass beyond the breakers. It is an oversight we have corrected; the ocean is no longer a threat, if that is what worries you." She stuck the needle into the dead girl's abdomen, and Mali flinched. "Now, you did not summon me because of her. What do you want?"

Mali felt Serassi's probing mind shuffling through her own thoughts. It had taken her years to learn how their telepathy worked and, more importantly, how to block it. She focused her energy on splitting her thoughts: on the surface of her mind, she thought about the dead girl's blue lips. But deeper, where Serassi couldn't probe, she wondered if they were examining the dead girl not for fertility or reproductive DNA, but to see if her body had evolved. Mali knew the rumors. Anya had even been the source of some of them. Anya had claimed she could sometimes hear what the Kindred were thinking, or predict what they were going to do next. Mali had tried to tell Anya to keep such information to herself, but she'd been too young to realize the danger of talking freely.

"Do you know Cassian takes Cora to the menageries," Mali said.

Serassi withdrew the needle probe from the dead girl's abdomen, checking it to get a reading. "Yes." Her voice was dismissive—she didn't have time for Cassian's foolishness. "It was risky of him. If the Council found out, he would be severely reprimanded."

"Cora says she saw a girl there with blond hair and two missing fingers." Mali stared at the dead girl's blue lips. "It sounds like Anya."

Serassi's hand paused. The probe lingered an inch above the dead girl's belly button.

"You tell me that Anya is dead," Mali pressed.

"Then why are you asking me something you already know? Are you suggesting that I lied to you?"

There was a challenge in Serassi's eyes. Something bitter cold, and Mali flinched again. On the surface, Serassi was one of the best Kindred at cloaking her emotions. But Mali had come to know her and could read some slips of emotion, just as she could with Cassian.

"You would be wise not to question us," Serassi said. The door slid back open, and Tessela entered. "Now return to your enclosure, Girl Three."

Girl Three. There had been a time when Serassi had called Mali by her name, just as Cassian did. But now the familiarity was gone. She had asked too many questions.

Tessela grabbed her, and they dematerialized back to the drugstore, facing the green grass and warm sun, though Mali hugged the jacket tighter. She stopped on the porch and looked out over their world as Tessela disappeared behind her.

The ocean lapped against the beach. The stream wound through the farm. In the distance, she could make out the highest dunes of the desert.

Cora had said that this enclosure was a lie. The artificiality of it had never bothered Mali before, because she knew there was no alternative. Earth was gone. She had never questioned that.

But now she wondered if Anya was still alive. And if the Kindred had lied to her about Anya, what else had they lied about? Could Earth still be there, and they'd only been told it wasn't to keep them complacent?

Her eyes traced the far reaches of the desert. She had only the one memory of her life before she had been taken. A carpet laid out over sand, and camels in the distance, and her mother pouring hot tea from a beautiful glass pot. She had clung to that memory of her home because it was all there was.

But maybe there could be more.

Maybe her mother was still there, and the camels, and the tea, and all of Earth. Maybe she had been wrong to have trusted the Kindred. She had thought she was different; that Serassi and Cassian were her friends, and she was more than just a human subject. But maybe they had been manipulating her the entire time, just like they had the others.

Maybe Cora was right.

Maybe Earth was still there—and maybe they could go back.

39

Cora

OVERHEAD, SPRAYS OF PALMS obscured the sky. Cora raced along the elevated walkway through the jungle. There were no mosquitoes, no thorns, no tropical snakes—nothing dangerous, just like all the habitats. A heavy rain began, soaking into her clothes.

Between the dancing leaves, she glimpsed the ruins of a towering stone palace covered in vines, and a few quaint huts, though they were likely just fabricated replicas that provided a framework for the black windows. She was drenched, so she jumped off the walkway and ran for it.

Mud gave way to sandy soil as she jogged toward the closest hut. Two of the huts were entirely artificial, but the other one had three walls and a thatched roof that at least provided a break from the rain. From the collection of belongings scattered about, she knew she'd found Leon's home.

Sickly sweet peaches from the farm filled a crate. Leaves

woven together by untrained hands made a rough mat, covered with a sheet stolen from the house. There were more sheets strung up around the sides of the huts. He had painted on them in mud, and the paintings were actually quite good. She'd never have guessed that Leon was an artist, but his strokes were certain, his shading masterful and surprisingly emotional. *The Kindred took us because we're prime specimens.* She shouldn't have assumed the only desirable trait Leon had was his strength.

Someone grunted behind her.

She twisted around. Leon was crouched in a corner of the hut, waiting out the rain too. Even so close to the ground, he was a colossus. Shadows hid one half of his face, so only the tattooed side stared back at her.

She reached for a guitar string around her wrist. "Leon," she stammered. "I came to find you."

He stayed where he was. His eyes traced over her body, lingering on the wet hair plastered to her face, then drifted to the paintings. Cora swallowed. "They're really good."

What she didn't say was that they were completely insane.

Each sheet was covered in a thousand watching eyes. Not fathomless Kindred eyes, but human eyes with irises and pupils and flecks of color he must have stolen from the painting kit.

"Yeah, wow, I didn't know you were an artist," she added, fingering the guitar string. It would only take one flick of her finger to spring the knot, and have it ready to twist around his throat if he tried anything.

His expression was hooded. He stood, slowly stretching to his full height. "What are you doing out here?"

She hesitated. It was a perfectly sane thing to say, unlike the crazed ramblings she'd expected. "I . . . wanted to find you. The others aren't thinking straight. They've basically turned against me. They're convinced that Earth is gone. I don't believe that, and I think there's a chance we can get home, but first we have to escape this enclosure. Mali claims she doesn't know where the fail-safe exit is, but she's lied to us before. She won't talk to me, but she might talk to you. The Kindred must have paired you two for a reason."

He cocked his head, taking a step toward her. "You grew your hair out. Mom always wanted you to have long hair."

He was out of the shadows now, so she could see both sides of his face, and his eyes that weren't threatening but weren't entirely sane, either. She ran her fingers through her damp hair. *"Mom?"*

"You should stop dyeing it, though," he said. "Blond doesn't suit you."

Oh—he thought she was his sister.

The level of his delusions left her jittery, a deer ready to bolt, but he loved his sister more than anything. If he thought she was Ellie, at least it meant he wouldn't hurt her. Right?

"Yeah . . . bro," she said slowly, surrounded by the blue and green and purple eyes. "So will you ask Mali for help?"

He watched the green eyes next to him, hypnotically. "It's too late for her."

"Mali? Why?" He didn't respond, and it took Cora a minute of studying the electric-green eyes in the painting to understand. Only one of their group of captives had green eyes. "You mean the dead girl."

He nodded. "Yasmine."

Uneasiness picked at Cora's palms like flea bites. "How do you know her name?"

Leon flashed her a wild look that made Cora grab the guitar string, ready to spring it open in case he lunged for her. But he didn't.

"I never told anyone," he said. "I thought you would think I killed her on purpose. She was running away from me like I scared her. I didn't mean to chase her. Or maybe I did." He cocked his head at a strange angle. "I can hear her sometimes. She walks through the forest. She likes the mountains. They remind her of home."

He went back to staring at the painted eyes.

She swallowed. Had he just confessed to *killing* the girl?

The raised platform wasn't far away. She could bolt—Leon was strong but slow. On the other hand, could she believe a thing he said? He was insane. As much as he was prone to violence, she couldn't imagine him drowning a girl he'd never met before.

"However she died, Leon, she's not still here. She can't be wandering around."

His eyes swung to her. "Of course she isn't," he barked. "It's her ghost."

He tilted his head toward the set of painted green eyes as though they spoke to him. A cold spike drilled between Cora's shoulder blades. She glanced at the nearest black window and pinched her arm.

"I need you, Leon. Brother. You're the only other one who isn't complacent here. Nok and Rolf like it here. Mali does too. She might as well *be* a Kindred. And Lucky is . . ." She swallowed, thinking of his dark eyes turning away from her. "Lucky is as blind as the rest of them. You and me, we're the only ones who under-stand that we have to get out of here. This place is dangerous."

"Yeah. I'll help them." Leon slowly slunk back to the shadows at the rear of the hut.

"Oh. Great—"

"I'm already helping them. That's why I'm out here, Cora."

At the sound of her name, not Ellie's, she grabbed the guitar strings. His mind was returning to reality, and she wanted to be ready if he did anything unpredictable.

He crouched in the corner of the hut. "For a while, everything Rolf said made sense. He and Nok were happy. Yasmine was gone, and none of you knew what happened to her. I thought maybe they were on to something about this place not being so bad." He paused. "But then I saw that girl with the scarred hands, and I knew, even without a mark, that she was the new one for me." His eyes dropped to the guitar string stretched between her hands. "I couldn't stand to be near her, knowing what they expected. Knowing what happened to the last girl they tried to pair me with. What if I snapped? What if I killed Mali too? *That's* why I'm here. To protect them from me."

Cora thought, in that moment, that Leon would continue to surprise her. He hadn't abandoned the group because he didn't care about the others, or because he was crazy. It was because he *did* care.

"You can help Mali—all of us—more by being a part of our group than by banishing yourself. Come back, Leon. Help me figure out how to escape."

He shook his head. "They were right, you know—the people back home. I'll never be the good person Ellie thought I could be. I've done things I'm not proud of."

His eyes shifted to a pile of sheets and clothes in the corner of his hut. Curiosity flickered in Cora's mind. Bedding streaked with paint was kicked into the corner. Something red glinted: Nok's radio. That was strange—Nok took it with her everywhere. Next to it was a crumpled pair of panties.

"Has Nok been here?" Cora asked uneasily.

Leon ran a hand over his face. "Ah, hell. What an idiot."

"Nok?"

"*Me.* I'm a bloody idiot. Few weeks ago, if a girl like that came to me, offering what she did, I'd have thought I'd hit the bloody lottery. But now—" He gazed off, eyes a little unsteady. "Now I know better. Or I should. But you don't understand what it's like out here. So quiet. It makes my thoughts scream in my ears. And the headaches . . ." He cursed. "She found me at a weak moment. Rolf's not a bad kid. He didn't deserve it. Not from me. Definitely not from her."

The small crumple of underwear stood out like a stain among the sheets. Had Nok come, one of those days when she claimed she was in the salon, and slept with *Leon*? Nok had always acted so in love with Rolf. It didn't make any sense; the first day, while they whispered together in bed, Nok had said that she didn't like hulking guys like Leon. So why would she do something so drastically out of character?

Cora remembered something else about that conversation. Nok had slipped up on basic London geography. She'd been lying, but Cora had thought it was harmless.

What else was Nok lying about?

Leon glanced at the pair of painted green eyes. "Get out of here, sweetheart. Don't come back."

He stomped off into the leaves. She stood alone in the

clearing, heart pounding. The sun shifted a degree to signal late afternoon, as an eeriness settled between the trees. It was too quiet. The sounds were all wrong, like the wind was moving backward.

A crash came from the woods. Maybe Leon. Maybe the dead girl's ghost—for all she knew, the Kindred could bring back the dead.

Cora bolted. She tore back toward the walkway, back to the safety of town, but her legs were so fatigued that her foot caught and she slammed to the mud.

She sat up, wincing, looking for the root she had tripped on. But it wasn't a root. It was a long, hard object the length of her thigh, bleached white, a shape she'd studied in school but had never seen in real life. Her stinging palms throbbed harder.

A bone.

A human one.

40

Cora

WITH SHAKING HANDS, CORA dug the bone free of the mud. She tried to convince herself it was from a dog or a horse, only there were no animals in the cage.

Just people.

If Cassian had taken Yasmine's body, whose bone was this?

Her stomach clenched with a swell of vomit. The bone was old and sun-bleached; it must have been there for months, maybe even years, though it was hard to tell in a place where time moved differently. She pushed herself to her feet, struggling with the mud threatening to swallow her back down.

The bone had to mean that they weren't the first kids in the cage. There had been others.

But what had killed them?

To her left, palm branches hid one of the humming black windows. She shoved the leaves aside and pounded on the glass.

"I know you're watching, Cassian! Show yourself!"

Her hair began to rise even before she'd finished the sentence. She hadn't quite believed it would work, but then she saw his reflection behind her in the panel and went still. Did she really want to know what had happened to the last group? It wasn't too late to drop the bone, stop questioning, and accept their prison.

But then she looked at the jungle mud splashed on the hem of her dress. A dead girl's dress. Any of them could be next, unless she did something about it.

She turned slowly on the Caretaker.

He cut such a striking figure against the jungle backdrop that it was hard not to be anything but awestruck. In person, he was always larger than she remembered. She couldn't help but take in all the little details that made him real: the dent in his nose. The slight scar on his chin. The way his hand flexed at his side when he was struggling to control his emotions. For a moment she forgot about the bone, and Yasmine, and she was back in the menagerie, on the soft cushions around the babbling fountain. His lips had been just an inch from hers. *I'm not interested in learning about kisses from them,* he had said, and her anger had melted away, just as it did now. Had he read her thoughts about showing him what a kiss was?

Had he *wanted* her to show him?

She gasped, shocked by her own line of thought, unable to calm her rapid heartbeat as easily as he was able to. She squeezed the bone, refocusing herself.

"What the hell is this?"

Cassian didn't blink. "That belonged to a previous inhabitant of this environment."

"A *dead* inhabitant."

The accusation seemed to slip off his smooth skin, and he cocked his head calmly. "Yes. We are able to synthetically replicate your world within these boundaries, but it requires a large supply of carbon. If humans die, it is perfectly logical to recycle their carbon. Most is absorbed quickly; sometimes there are pieces that take longer."

"This whole place is made of *dead bodies*?"

"We use a variety of carbon sources, not only human carcasses. I would place the number of bodies that have been absorbed into this environment at twelve. This enclosure is relatively new. Your cohort is only the third one to occupy it."

She squeezed the bone harder. "What happened to the other two groups?"

"The cohorts both failed. Each ward was terminated as a result of their own actions."

Cora frowned, uncertain of what he meant.

"They murdered each other," he clarified calmly, as though this information didn't trouble him in the least. But it rocked Cora; her heart seized into a fist.

"Murdered?"

"We discovered that none of the previous inhabitants of this environment were adaptable to captivity," he continued. "They grew irate. The males fought over the females. They started wandering alone instead of residing within the settlement areas. Eventually they killed each other."

"You mean they went crazy." It was a struggle to control her voice. "They couldn't handle your mind games. The headaches. The optical illusions. You pushed them too far, messing around with time and space, matching random strangers together . . . what did you expect would happen?"

She was shouting now.

He folded his hands. "Naturally, given our moral code, this was alarming. It will not happen again."

"Why not?" She threw her arm in the direction of the jungle huts. "Leon's halfway there already!"

For a second his mask slipped, and she saw indecision in his eyes. "The previous cohorts were selected solely for their desirable traits and their fertility. Unfortunately, their advanced age made them unable to adapt. That is why the six of you are all of an adolescent age. Old enough for procreation, but young enough to adapt. We spent considerable time reconfiguring the habitats to reflect the needs of your age bracket."

If it hadn't been for the heavy fatigue in her limbs, Cora would have wanted to slap him. The adults all turned violent, so they took teenagers instead. This explained the childlike nature of life in the cage: the candy store, the arcade, the prizes. As if they were six years old, not sixteen.

"Is that really what you think matters to us? Toys? Candy?" She sucked in a breath. "Is that really what you think matters to *me*?"

She clamped her mouth shut before her voice broke. She knew how desperate she sounded. The other Kindred viewed them as dolls they could toy with, but she had thought Cassian was different. She thought he saw her as a person, not a plaything.

Maybe she'd been wrong.

Cora closed her eyes, but the image of the bleached bone didn't go away. Was she truly just a chore for him—something to keep alive and healthy? What about the times he'd bent the rules for her? What about the necklace with the charm of a dog? What about the stars?

She clutched her necklace so hard that the sharp charms bit into her palm. With her eyes closed, she could almost believe she was back home. She'd wake in the morning in her own bed, with the smell of brunch downstairs, and the soft hum of the morning news on the downstairs TV.

"Cora."

Her eyes snapped open. He'd moved close enough that she tasted metal.

"I know that more matters to you. I know that you long for home. I know that you wish you had told your family more often that you loved them." He reached for her neck. The Warden's hand flashed in her head, his fingers against her windpipe. But Cassian's hand didn't tighten around her throat; it stopped on the charm necklace. His bare fingers touched it gently, almost reverently, and that nameless electricity sparked around the edges of her throat.

"How long were you watching me on Earth?" she whispered.

"Long enough."

"Long enough for what?"

"To know you, and what you are capable of. There is more to you than the other wards know. Boy Two cares for you, but he doesn't know you. Not as well as I do." His fingers curled around the charms. Their bodies were very nearly touching. Her eyes sank closed as his breath whispered against her ear.

"A smile can hide so much. A smile can be a lie." His voice rose and fell oddly. With a start, she realized he was trying to sing—but his voice was rusty and unpracticed; he must never have sung before. It was one of the songs she had written after the bomb threat at her dad's political rally.

Heat radiated from Cassian's hand, holding on to the necklace, holding on to *her*.

"A smile can make me want to scream, and leave all this behind."

He was singing her words, which she'd never shared with anyone—not even Charlie. Words she'd used to make sense of a life she didn't fit into anymore. About a little girl who was supposed to spend her whole life smiling, even when she was sad, or scared, or went to prison for a crime she didn't commit.

Her throat burned. She'd been holding her breath. It caught up with her all at once, and she sucked in air. Her chest grazed against his; electricity pulsed and the bone knocked against her leg. The *bone*. She'd forgotten the femur clutched in her hand.

She stepped back, and he released her necklace, and the spell was broken.

"Cora—"

"Get away from me." Her voice was a knife. "You're a liar. We aren't safe here at all. If you don't kill us first, then we'll end up killing each other."

He looked at her like she'd slapped him. His hand flexed at his side, once, twice, and he opened his mouth as though to plead with her. But then he straightened, and the mask returned.

"Your safety is of utmost importance to us. The stock algorithm accurately predicts—"

"Did the stock algorithm predict what happened with the last groups?"

He paused. "There is always a margin of error."

Margin of error, she thought. *Such a tidy way to explain twelve dead bodies.*

The sun was merciless. The mud tried to swallow her feet. Fear and anger and exhaustion seized her body in a tight fist, and yet the worst of all of it was the way his black eyes shifted to her, always back to her, as though she was different. His pet.

I am *different*, she realized. *I'm the only one sane enough to know we're in danger.*

"I will personally ensure the safety of everyone in this environment," Cassian repeated more insistently. "We simply require you to follow a set of basic rules." He leaned close, and all that emotion came rushing back. He could be tender; he could be cruel too. "It has been twenty-one days, Cora. You have until midnight."

With another swell in pressure, he was gone.

Cora sprinted away from the jungle. The ocean taunted her with each crashing wave that moved too slowly, reminding her that nothing was real, not this place, not Cassian's promise that they were all safe.

This is how it begins. She'd been a fool to think she could ever leave the others behind. They would die without her there to keep them sane, and the sand would swallow their bones.

She reached town just as the artificial sun dropped another level. She slowed to a walk. The only sound was the jukebox music and the beeping arcade games. No insects trilling, no barking dogs, no traffic or hum of electricity, but fears roared in her head.

Ahead, sitting on the porch swing, were Lucky and Nok. She ran for them, about to call out, but then slowed. Nok wore a look Cora had never seen before. She wasn't hiding behind her pink stripe of hair. She was facing Lucky, one hand on his thigh, purring into his ear.

She stopped abruptly.

Back in the jungle, Nok's panties had been tangled in Leon's sheets. Now she had her hands on Lucky. Cora dropped to her knees and crawled closer, through the marigolds.

As much as Cora wanted to trust her, Nok was hiding things. It was time to find out what.

41

Cora

CORA CROUCHED IN THE marigolds, bone clutched in her hand, as she made out Nok's and Lucky's voices.

"I can't stop thinking about her." Lucky's voice was broken.

"Poor Lucky," Nok cooed. "Left all alone." Cora's heart started pounding. They were talking about *her*. "It isn't you. She's delusional. She didn't even believe us when we told her that Earth was gone. You can't reason with someone like that. She and Leon—they've lost it, yeah? They weren't meant for captivity."

"So what am I supposed to do? It's been twenty-one days."

Cora clamped a hand over her mouth, silencing her breath. There was only the sound of the porch swing chains creaking. Then Nok sighed.

"You can't save someone who doesn't want to be saved. At some point you have to look out for yourself."

"You don't understand, Nok. I've hurt her before. I owe her this."

"You've done everything for her. If she cared about you in return, she'd sleep with you, to keep you from being removed."

Cora could only make out their shadows on the wall; Nok's hand grazed Lucky's cheek as she leaned in to him. "Let me help you," Nok whispered. "I don't want you to be removed, Lucky."

As if her offer wasn't clear enough, her shadow reached up to ruffle his hair seductively. There was a long pause when Cora's head filled with terrible images of Nok and Lucky making love in front of a humming black window. She wasn't sure if she was jealous or just shocked. It felt so out of character for Nok, like a script Nok had been taught to say.

"You might even enjoy it, yeah?" Nok teased.

Cora's hand tightened over the bone nearly hard enough to snap it. Lucky was silent a breath too long, and Cora's heart churned in her throat. She knew Nok wasn't attracted to Leon or Lucky, so what did she hope to gain by sleeping with them?

It's a man's world, Nok had whispered to herself, in bed the first night. *Controlling men is the only way women like you and me will survive.*

"Come on, Lucky. To save yourself."

Before he could answer, the sun faded completely and the streetlights came on, the diner sign flickered to life, and the juke-box cranked up.

A stranger in my own life, a ghost behind my smile . . .

The song floated on the air, in one ear and out the other, making Cora's head spin. Someone in the distance called Lucky's name, and Cora, still crouched in the marigolds, looked over her shoulder to see who it was.

Rolf was coming back from the farm with a crateload of peaches, and peach juice dripping down his chin to stain the front of his shirt. At the same time, Mali came down the drugstore steps, looking as cold and cryptic as always, and the porch swing creaked as Lucky stood. He and Nok descended the stairs, just a hair from where she was crouched.

They all greeted each other and chatted like this wasn't a cage in an alien space station but old friends crossing paths back home. Nok threw her arms around Rolf's neck and kissed his cheek and laughed with the others over some joke Cora wasn't privy to.

Cora pushed to her feet shakily. Crazy. They were all going crazy. She had to warn them what had happened to the last group. She came around the side of the house, bone held high.

Lucky's smile faded when he saw her. He swallowed, hard. "Cora."

The last time she'd seen him, he'd insisted on believing that Earth was gone, even despite her evidence. He'd told her that if she wanted to keep looking for a way home, she was on her own. Now he picked lint out of the pocket of his leather jacket, pulling on a loose string, avoiding her gaze.

"Lucky, we need to talk—"

"Well, decided to join us again?" Rolf set down the crate of peaches roughly. His left eye twitched. "You wouldn't happen to know what happened to the guitar, would you?" His words were gnashing teeth.

She squeezed the femur. Not a single one of them had even glanced at it. "Listen. I found this bone. The Caretaker—"

"Because it's funny," Rolf continued, in a sharp tone that was anything but entertained, "but we found some splintered wood and a guitar pick in Lucky's room. Then outside the house, the mulch was disturbed, like someone was burying something. When we dug it up, we found the broken guitar. Like someone intentionally destroyed it. And there's only one person who has a history of trying to sabotage us. *You*."

Sweat broke out on her brow. The guitar? God, why did they care about a toy when she was clutching a human bone? "Listen—"

"Is that true, Cora?" Lucky's brow was knitted with concern. He flexed his hand, but the knuckles didn't pop this time.

She knew the guitar had meant a lot to him. Music meant the world to her too, but it was nothing compared to going home.

"I just . . . I need to tell you something."

Nok took her free hand gently, like guiding the elderly. "Right after dinner, yeah? They've started feeding us again, and it's better than ever. You won't try to steal our food anymore, right?"

Cora stumbled forward, because she didn't know what else to do. She followed the others into the diner in a daze. The light seemed particularly hazy, and Lucky accidentally knocked into the pendant lamp, sending it swinging back and forth, back and forth, throwing too-bright light onto Rolf's face, still dripping with peach juice, and then Nok's grinning face stained with bright red candy, making them all look diabolical in the harsh light.

The others dug into their trays of food like animals. Mali was quiet. She didn't laugh with them or join in the conversation, but they seemed to accept her because she wanted the same thing as they did—to be obliviously happy here forever.

Lucky pushed her chair out with his foot. "I know it's been tough on you," he said as she sank, dazed, into the empty chair opposite him. His hand reached over to cover hers, his eyes soft and brown. "But all our secrets are on the table now. I know it'll take time to work through it all, but at least we're here together." He leaned in to brush his lips over her cheekbone, and she flinched at the sudden smell of wet grass. "I want to see you smile again."

Smile? *Smile?* She was holding a dead person's femur.

A cold feeling spread between her shoulder blades, but it wasn't coming from the black window. Nok was watching her from another table, with narrowed eyes that could slice her in half. Her eyes darted between Cora and Lucky as she bit into a peach.

No, Cora thought to herself. *Nok never used to be like this.* Cora could still remember the day the Caretaker came, and Nok squeezing her hand. What had changed her?

Nok sank her teeth into the peach again. Her brown eyes fixated on Lucky, and how his whole body was angled away from her as he spoke to Cora. It wasn't exactly jealousy in her eyes; more like fear. Widened pupils and a clenched jaw that spoke of desperation.

Nok needed Lucky for something, Cora realized.

Rolf wrapped an arm around Nok, scooting his chair closer, as if he'd noticed too. He whispered a few words in her ear that she didn't seem to hear. He pulled a lollipop out of his pocket and held it up in front of her face. Like a cat, easily distracted, she pounced on the candy and tore open the wrapper.

Rolf smiled.

Rolf knew exactly how to manipulate her, just like the Kindred: a rush of sugar and bright colors to momentarily distract her. Maybe Rolf had been learning from the Kindred all along, studying the ways they manipulated the captives, and studying the captives' reactions. He'd always had the mind of a scientist. Now he had Nok as his own personal lab rat to manipulate and control.

Cora's hand suddenly went slack on the bone. Lab rats. Rodents. *Moles.* Ever since the first day, Rolf had insisted that the Kindred would plant a mole among them to help bend the group to their will from the inside. Cora had assumed that Mali was the mole, and yet Rolf had sided with the Kindred right from the start.

Cora played back all the things Rolf had said: they shouldn't try to escape. That life in the cage was actually desirable. A paradise, even. He had used science and human nature to justify his arguments, and it had sounded so believable.

What if he was lying to them? What if *he* was the mole?

Cora stood so fast, her chair skidded backward. She picked up the bone like a cleaver, and the others all stopped eating in surprise.

"It's you," she said to Rolf, her voice barely a whisper, as she felt her thoughts cutting through the fog. "It's been you, this entire time. Manipulating Nok. Manipulating all of us. *You're* the Kindred's mole!"

Rolf's lips fell open in true surprise but just as quickly pressed shut. "What are you talking about now? Is this some new plot of yours?"

His innocent act enraged her, and she flew across the table and grabbed the shoulder of his shirt, dragging him toward her, the bone raised to threaten him. Nok jumped up, and Lucky pushed to his feet too.

Mali kept eating her pancakes.

"I'm talking about how you're working with them," Cora accused, "like the rat you are, trying to bend us to their will. You twisted Nok first. Convinced her to give up on escape—"

"You're crazy!"

"Cora, just calm down," Lucky whispered.

"This is just more of her games!" Rolf snapped. "You take away our food and then have the Caretaker bring it back. You insist on maintaining the seashell calendar so you can make us think time is passing strangely. You're mad that we won the guitar, so you steal it." When she started to object, his face turned red. "Are you seriously going to say you didn't steal the guitar? Just like you didn't steal the food? Or mess with our heads?"

She started to deny it, but they'd found the guitar. They knew. She hadn't taken any food, but they'd never believe her now.

Cora let go of Rolf's shirt abruptly and paced, sweat rolling down her face. "Rolf's been manipulating you all this entire time, in conjunction with the Kindred. I suspected it from the first time he tried to convince us we shouldn't fight back. He always had such a convenient explanation for everything strange that was happening, so we wouldn't question the bigger motivation of what the Kindred wanted with us. He even has a convenient story about his life back home. How he was bullied, so we'd feel sympathy for him. How he was so caught up in his studies that he never had time for the books and TV shows we all might have watched. He even has twitches and strange mannerisms like Mali does. Probably because he's never even been to Earth and doesn't know how real people act!"

Rolf looked like he had been slapped. Red splotched his pale face. His fingers, which hadn't twitched in days, slowly started their neurotic tapping against the table.

"Leave him alone!" Nok said. "It isn't true, any of it!"

Cora whirled on her. "Why do you keep defending him?"

"Because you haven't heard him talk about home like I have.

We both lived in London. We went to some of the same restaurants. He's seen *Star Trek* and he's ridden the London Eye and there's nothing wrong with the way he acts. Anyway, I wouldn't care if he *had* grown up among the Kindred, because he's a good person, and he loves me, and because we're going to have a baby together!"

She pressed a hand against her mouth. Silence echoed in the diner. Cora stared at her, stunned. Nok was still thin, but she had certainly put on a few pounds over the last few weeks. Cora had assumed it was all the candy. Was *this* why she'd been acting so strangely? Why she'd needed Lucky and the other boys wrapped around her finger?

Nok tossed Rolf a look that wavered between nervous and excited. Slowly she removed her hand from her mouth. "So, um, now would probably be a good time to tell you that I'm pregnant."

42

Cora

CORA LET ROLF SLIP out of her hands as fatigue caught up with her all at once, and she slumped into a chair. He pulled away like a frightened animal, then turned to Nok, blinking hard, fingers twisting in his wild red hair.

"Is it true?" he asked.

For a moment, no one dared to move. Lucky massaged his temple, wincing, like another headache had struck. Nok was breathing hard, cheeks flushed, as the light kept swinging back and forth.

Mali reached for another dinner roll.

"Yes," Nok said. "By almost two weeks. They can detect these things early. I wasn't supposed to say anything until I was further along. That medical officer, Serassi, has been testing me in private ever since you and I started sleeping together, with a needle so big it would give you nightmares. She materialized into the salon yesterday and told me I was pregnant." Nok pressed her hand against her stomach. A slight smile came to her lips. "She said she oversees centers where human children are raised communally, like nurseries, but I asked if we could raise it here, on our own, and she asked the Warden; she said it would be good for her research to observe human child raising in their natural habitat. He agreed."

Cora glanced at Rolf out of the corner of her eye. Did he know about Nok visiting Leon in the jungle? Trying to seduce Lucky? Did he know there was a chance the baby wasn't his?

She pushed out of the chair and took a shaky step backward, like Rolf was a powder keg and this information was a lit match.

But he blinked, and his fingers twitched, and then threw his arms around Nok. "That's wonderful!"

He didn't know.

He swung Nok in his arms, kissing her cheeks, making her giggle. Cora stumbled backward against the black window. Oblivious of her shock, Lucky pushed past her to congratulate Nok. The tension from earlier had shifted to laughter—Cora was forgotten, and the mole was forgotten, and so was the bone.

Pain throbbed between her temples.

Maybe Rolf wasn't the mole. Maybe Mali wasn't either. Maybe there never *had* been a mole. Maybe the Kindred had been setting her up to be ostracized all along: giving her unfair amounts of tokens, making it seem like she'd stolen the food, letting her out of the cage, as though they were intentionally trying to make the others jealous.

And now she'd dug her own grave by stealing the guitar and accusing Rolf.

The black window at her back hummed against her skin. She'd thought the cage was driving the others crazy, but what if it wasn't? What if it was just twisting *her*, like the others kept insisting?

They always said crazy people never knew they were crazy.

Frustrated tears tangled with pain and pushed behind her eyes. Mali was the only one not congratulating Nok. Instead, she calmly offered Cora the rest of her roll across the table. For once, her light brown eyes weren't cold.

Cora stared at her, then knocked the roll away. "It's a hell of a time to start being friendly!"

Lucky glanced over his shoulder. The smile on his face faded once he saw the tears that dripped onto her untouched plate. He pushed aside the diner chairs and pulled her into a hug, murmuring in her ear. "What's wrong? Don't you like your pancakes?"

This only made Cora cry more, because he was still so kind, despite the fact that he was totally delusional.

"I'm not crazy," Cora whispered. "This place is a prison. We're slaves here, Lucky. They're trying to turn you all against me."

"Shh," he said. "I'd never turn against you."

Over his shoulder, Nok had her hands pressed to her stomach, Rolf still kissing her cheek, but Nok's smile shifted to uneasiness when she caught Cora's words.

"At home, we were living half a life," Lucky said. "I held on to so much anger, Cora. At your dad. At *myself*. But after our talk, I finally let all that guilt and pain go, and you should too." He softly pointed his chin toward the others. "Look at how happy Nok and Rolf are. That could be us."

Nok's dress ruffled as she came toward them. She smiled at Cora, but the sweetness of the smile didn't reach her eyes. "Lucky's right," Nok said. "We were so worried, we even thought we might have to kick you out of the house if you kept making life so difficult for everyone. But you're over that, now, yeah? You want to be one of us. *Don't you?*"

Her threat was as clear as the challenge in her eyes. This was Cora's ultimatum: embrace their insane paradise, or be ostracized to the biomes like Leon, starved for human contact. And meanwhile, they'd just keep sliding further into insanity.

The bone was still in her hand.

The song ended, and there was a second of silence before it reset itself. Someone had overturned a glass of water that rolled off the table and dripped onto the floor like the ticking of a clock. *Drip. Drip. Drip.* Lucky was looking at Cora with eyes so full of hope—delusional hope—and if she said yes, they would be a couple, they would run obstacle courses and eat gumdrops and pretend they weren't rats running on a wheel for the benefit of their alien captors.

He would be happy.

She would be numb.

She had done it before—shut out the screaming voice in the back of her head. At Bay Pines, she'd given in. Back at home, too. The saddest part was how easy giving in was: a tug of the lips into a smile, voice silenced, lyrics kept to herself. Now, she'd resisted the Kindred for weeks—for what? Sunken eyes and weary limbs? Cold looks from the only people in the world who could laugh and smile and comfort her?

She rubbed her eyes with hands that felt impossibly heavy.

"Okay," she whispered.

As soon as she spoke the words, relief wound into her tired muscles. She'd had sixteen years of practicing how to give in. It came so naturally, so effortlessly, like greeting an old friend. A small voice tried to claw its way back up, but she forced a smile.

She ignored the tears in her eyes.

"And Rule Three?" Nok said tightly. "You'll even obey Rule Three?"

Lucky stopped his pacing. Cora's heart stopped its beating, as the voice tried once more to claw up her throat. Then, with a single lurch, she swallowed it back down again.

"Yes."

Her voice sounded as broken as she felt.

Genuine smiles stretched across Lucky's and Nok's faces. Mali looked as expressionless as always, until her eyes shifted to the black window, where a murky shadow flickered.

Lucky kissed Cora's temple. "I knew you'd come around. The night of the accident bound us. It was fate. Now we'll always be together."

Cora forced a wider smile. *Smile, even when you feel like crying.*

Lucky brushed away her tears. "I know you're worried. But the Kindred are so much more advanced than us. They have to know what they're doing. If they want us to be together and have kids, they must have a good reason. It's like . . . our duty, Cora. To continue the species."

He kissed her tear-stained cheek.

"Our duty," she repeated.

He gave a serious nod. "Exactly."

This was what they had done to him, skewed his ethics, made him think they were like children who didn't know what was best for themselves.

He took her hand. "We're going to be so happy."

43

Leon

LEON HAD LEARNED TO move through the habitats silently. It was difficult at first; the words *quiet* and *subtle* had never once been used to describe him, but now, as he crept through the marigolds by the side of the diner, he felt like a jungle beast.

A figure dropped over the side of the railing, landing on all fours in front of him. He let out a curse and stumbled back.

Mali stared into his eyes like she could see the very stains on his soul. Her eyes went from the mud on his hems to the sharpened stake he had made out of a rocking horse. "What are you doing."

"Hunting. Now scram."

She stood slowly. "Hunting what."

"Ghosts." He braced himself. He knew that sounded crazy, but it wasn't. Yasmine's ghost was here. He could feel her eyes. They had it all wrong, when they thought the Kindred were the ones watching.

A bird trilled and he crouched lower. The bird sounds

weren't real, either. They were Yasmine, trying to drive him mad for running her into the ocean.

Mali gave his shoulder a sharp pinch.

"Ow! What was that for?"

"Focus. I must ask you a question." She glanced over her shoulder toward the diner in the distance, where they others had been talking. "When you spy on the others, do you hear them say that Earth is gone."

He rubbed his shoulder where she pinched him. "Yeah. But they're idiots. Cora's the only one with any sense. She's right. Earth isn't gone."

"How do you know."

"Because if Earth was gone, they'd have a finite supply of humans. Us six and the rest scattered around in cages. A few thousand, at most. Barely enough to rebuild an entire species. They're supposed to be all logical, right? So they wouldn't be mucking about, letting private individuals chop off our fingers or whatever, eh? They'd have every single one of us in breeding facilities, churning out kids left and right. They wouldn't bother with this twenty-one day shit."

"That is just a theory. You do not know that for sure."

"I know human nature, kid."

"They are not human."

"They're close enough."

Mali sat abruptly, cross-legged, resting her chin on her hands. Ever since stars had appeared, the night had taken on a different color. More silver, like a riverbed. The starlight played over her dark hair, showing blacks and browns and even a hint of burnished red that Leon had never noticed before.

She stared at him hard. "Would you go home if you could."

Leon didn't answer. Home? When he'd been taken, he'd been in the middle of helping his older brother unload a truck of ripped-off gaming systems into the back of a dirty warehouse. His sister, Ellie, had called to invite him over for dinner, and Leon had said he couldn't be bothered. Now all he wanted in the world was to sit at Ellie's table, her baby gurgling beside him, their nieces and nephews tugging on his clothes, asking him to pick them up and play Godzilla.

"Would you go back," Mali pressed. "I need to know."

In the shadows, with her long dark hair, Mali almost looked like Yasmine. Only Yasmine's eyes had been so frightened as she'd run away, and Mali looked like she'd never been frightened in her life.

"Doesn't matter, kid. There's no way out."

He shoved past her, knocking her to the ground. He hadn't stormed away more than a foot before something launched itself at his back; he cursed and ducked, but the thing was moving fast. Thin arms and stringy black hair and cold, cold eyes.

"Bloody hell!" he yelled.

He spun, trying to grab Mali, but she evaded him easily. He felt a tug on his arm, pressure on his left calf, a pinch between his shoulder blades, and suddenly he was flat on his back, staring at the stars, and every one of his muscles screamed in pain.

Mali leaned over him with that flat smile of hers.

"How the hell did you do that?" he bellowed.

"You do not scare me," she said.

He tried to stand, flustered and cursing, but she seemed able to hold him down with a single finger against his forehead. Was this some sort of alien ninja shit?

"I don't scare you?" he roared. "What do you think hap-pened to the girl you replaced? You look like her, you know that? Brown skin. Long hair. Be careful or you'll end up like her too. She's dead because of me."

Mali leaned in, her finger digging into the center of his fore-head. "I see my predecessor's body. I see her wounds. She drowns on her own."

"She was running away from me."

"She runs from the Kindred. Serassi stands behind you, your first day here. The previous Girl Three sees her. It frightens her enough to flee into the ocean, where she thinks she can swim away. She does not yet understand that she is no longer on Earth."

Leon's muscles, cramped with pain, suddenly released. The pain melted away but was replaced by a rush of shock, then denial, and then rage.

"*They're* the reason she's dead?"

"They have her body. They perform tests on it."

Rage choked him. He forgot about the stringy-haired girl sitting on his chest. He forgot about how she'd immobilized him with a single finger. All he could picture was Yasmine's green eyes, so round and full of fear, and how he'd hated himself every day for driving her into that ocean.

But she hadn't been running from him.

He felt like he could breathe for the first time in days. Maybe her ghost wasn't haunting him for revenge; maybe it wanted revenge on their black-eyed kidnappers, and he was the only one who could get it for her.

Mali leaned close. "You can make a choice. You can choose to do what is right."

She removed her finger from his forehead, freeing him. He sat up, pushing her aside, leaning into his throbbing hands.

He hadn't killed Yasmine—*they* had.

He stood in a daze and stumbled to his camp, and stared at the paintings of Yasmine's haunting eyes. Mali's words lodged in his head like a splinter. He ripped down the bedsheet, and all the paintings, and then stormed deeper into the jungle.

44

Cora

AFTER THE ARGUMENT AT the diner, the rest of Cora's night was as surreal as a nightmare.

Lucky took her to see a film in the movie theater, ten minutes of a goat standing in a field while the phantom smell of popcorn choked her. He spent every hard-earned token he had on chocolates and gummies from the candy shop, which Cora forced down with a smile, never mind that they made her stomach burn. He solved the jukebox puzzle until it played a song about finding true love.

The entire time Cora smiled, and smiled, and smiled, just like her father had taught her to do. Her mind was too tired to fight anymore. It was clear that this newfound peace was shaky, at best. Lucky might believe that they were a happy little group in a perfect little prison—except for Leon, of course, insane in the jungle—but the others clearly didn't. Mali was as cryptic as ever. Rolf eyed Cora suspiciously, while Nok's smiles were so frost coated that Cora shivered like she was back in the alpine area.

Night fell, and the artificial stars appeared one by one, and Lucky followed her heavy footsteps upstairs to the bedroom they would now share. She crossed the threshold and stopped abruptly.

A quilt rested on the bed. A Persian rug was stretched on the floor. Watercolor paintings hung on the wall. A ceramic dog sat on the foot of the bed. It was like taking a dizzying step back into her old bedroom—into her old *life*. There were even constellations drawn on the ceiling.

"I wanted to surprise you." Lucky came in behind her, fiddling awkwardly with a book on the shelf. "I listened when you told me what your bedroom was like, and I've been redeeming tokens for similar prizes. I know it isn't exactly the same, but I hoped it would make you feel better. Like this was home."

She sank onto the corner of the bed. Memories spilled back, of scribbling lyrics at her desk, gazing at the stars outside, petting Sadie. She picked up the ceramic dog. If she closed her eyes, she could almost imagine she was back on Earth.

But she let the dog drop to the floor. It *wasn't* Sadie, it was a toy. The thing that Lucky didn't realize was that her bedroom in Richmond had been as artificial as the one here. She had come home from Bay Pines to find every trace of her mother gone, moved to an expensive condo in Miami that she'd only see on weekends after a long flight. As if to make up for it, her father had completely redecorated her room. He'd covered the stars she'd painted on the walls with expensive wallpaper. He'd hung elegant curtains over the windows where she used to stargaze. He'd poured thousands of dollars into giving her a room fit for a princess—or for a daughter who'd taken the fall for him—but he had only succeeded in excising everything that had made it hers.

She felt just as hollow as she had at home. She wanted those stars back. She wanted her room back. She wanted her life back—the real one.

Lucky leaned in. "I'll always look out for you." He kissed her cheek.

As he closed the door and pulled her down with him onto the bed, she couldn't find words for how catastrophically heartrending it was. His lips were on her cheek, her forehead, her neck, her mouth. He whispered in her ear how he was so glad she had been standing in the surf twenty-one days ago, how he had been so afraid she would hate him, how he would take care of her forever. Her tears were hot against her cheeks. He kissed them away without asking their reason. He said they had a chance to change the world. They would have children who would grow to have children of their own, ensuring the continuation of their species, under the Kindred's guidance. He said they were so lucky that out of all humans the Kindred chose them to entrust with this important role. He said their love was going to save humanity.

Cora had thought, when she'd so desperately agreed to obey the third rule, that she could do this. She had thought that the relief of giving in would make up for the awful feeling of bowing to the Kindred's will.

But the voice inside her was screaming now, and she wasn't sure of anything.

Lucky shrugged off his leather jacket, setting it carefully aside, not rushing anything. Cora glanced at the black window as she shed her dress. She had to believe Cassian wasn't watching. If he was knowingly letting this happen, then she really had been blind. Cassian said he'd never be cruel to her, but this was the definition of cruel—watching this happen, knowing how terrible it was. He must be able to see inside Lucky's head and read his intentions: that they would sleep together tonight, that they'd soon be as deliriously in love as Rolf and Nok, that Cora would get pregnant too, and then next year the same thing, and the year after that. It might have been paradise for the others, but it was Cora's hell.

As Lucky slid one camisole strap over her shoulder, she looked at the ceiling, at the stars he had drawn there. He'd done the best he could, but it would never be right.

A realization suddenly struck her.

That's why Cassian isn't stopping this.

Just as Cassian could see inside Lucky's head, he could see inside hers too. He knew that Lucky might have every intention of them sleeping together, but she didn't.

She couldn't.

Cassian wasn't stopping it because he knew she was going to stop it herself.

A tear rolled to her chin. She imagined what would have happened if she and Lucky had met on Earth, before the accident, just two strangers. Maybe her expensive car had broken down, and he'd come to fix it in his worn jeans with a rag in his back pocket. She might have loved him there, on the side of the road, on Earth.

But not like this.

She whispered, "Lucky, do you remember when you taught me to spar in the desert?"

He nodded against her neck. She squeezed her eyes shut. The memory was fresh: sand warm against her back, hunger to feel his lips on hers. "Of course I do," he said. "It's hard to forget having a beautiful girl under you."

"I just want to say that I paid attention," she choked. "And that I'm sorry."

She dropped her hand down, curling her fingers around the ceramic dog on the floor. If she told him how wrong all of this was, he would only smile and whisper something about fate. He would never force her to obey Rule Three, but he'd never understand, either.

She thrust her hip up, throwing him off balance, escaping the mount like they had practiced. His surprise gave her enough time to slam the ceramic dog into the side of his head, where it connected with a sickening sound.

He slumped against the bed, moaning.

Tears spilled from her eyes as she held on to him and murmured apology after apology, hating what she had done, hating the Kindred for making him into this twisted person. She pulled on her dress and gave his forehead a trembling kiss. He would wake with a killer headache, but that would be nothing compared to his heartache when he realized she'd deceived him.

The hallway was quiet. Mali's door was closed. Nok's and Rolf's voices came floating up from the living room—she couldn't go out the front door or they'd see her. She pushed up the bedroom window as silently as she could, and climbed onto the roof, dropped to the grass, and raced out into the town square, where she doubled over, feeling sick and guilty and confused, and fought the urge to throw up.

The Kindred had taken Lucky for his morality, only to twist it. They could cut off her hair, sell it to the highest bidder, cage her, but they wouldn't twist *her*.

She wiped the sweat from her face and stalked to the nearest black window. Sunrise wouldn't be for a few hours, but she wasn't going to sit around and wait.

She hurled her fists against the black glass. "Come on! Why are you waiting?"

Tears ran down her face as she smashed harder and harder, frustrated that it didn't shatter, or even bruise her palms. She wanted to feel something, even if it was pain.

The hair on her arms started to rise. She gritted her teeth and spun around.

Cassian stood before her. So calm. So collected. As formally as he had the first time he'd appeared, his cold eyes regarding her like a stranger, despite their trip to the menagerie, despite everything he'd revealed, despite the fact that he could reach into her head and see everything she had ever done and thought.

He folded his hands. "I assume by your actions that you are refusing to obey the third rule."

"That's right." She took a slow step forward, challenging him. "I'll never obey, so you might as well remove me. But I'm not going without a fight."

A flicker of emotion crossed his face. He hadn't expected this final act of defiance, but Cora had nothing to lose. They'd twisted Lucky into believing this was home. The others detested her. She was facing a lifetime of being toyed with by the Kindred. She couldn't fight them forever, but it would feel good to try.

She smashed into him, pummeling him with her fists. That electric spark came when their skin connected, and it energized her more. Unlike the illusions of the cage, Cassian was real, and so was his flexible metal armor, and it bruised her hands.

He trapped one of her wrists. "Stop this."

She didn't. It felt good to fight, even if he only stood there. She kept struggling as tears streaked down her face. She hurled accusations at him, in words and in thoughts, but he didn't respond.

She shoved him again, uselessly. "You were supposed to take care of us! You knew what the Warden was doing, but you didn't even try to stop it!"

"You do not know what actions I have taken." His voice was lower than usual. He glanced at the black window. "I am on your side, Cora. But things cannot change in the blink of an eye. The Warden is powerful. When he has a plan, nothing gets in his way. Not you. Not me."

His voice was monotone, but she detected a note of tenderness, and all the fight slipped out of her. Cassian wasn't the one she wanted to punch. It was the researchers. It was the Warden. It was whatever system classified humans as a lesser species.

"I can't do it," she said. "I can't do Rule Three."

"I know."

This was it. The moment it all ended. He might be trying to change the system behind the scenes to make conditions for humans more favorable, but it could take weeks. Months. Years. And time was up for her. He would have no choice but to lock her in a cell so she could perform cheap tricks. The others would go crazy, and without her there to stop them, they would end up bleached bones in a jungle.

"It never would have worked between Lucky and me. The algorithm got it wrong when it chose me."

She could feel his demeanor change. The pace of his breathing slowed.

"The algorithm didn't chose you."

Her eyes went wide. She forgot to fight. "What do you mean?"

His hands tightened on her wrists. "*I* did. Boy Two was selected first. Then the algorithm selected a suitable female match. Her name was Sarah. She had a high level of intelligence and morality that would complement his attributes."

"Then why isn't she here?"

She felt the telltale pressure building, knowing they were about to be dematerialized to a menagerie or a prison or somewhere she couldn't even imagine.

An instant before the pressure overtook her, he leaned in close.

"Because then I saw you."

45

Nok

NOK RECLINED ON THE living room sofa, sucking on a butterscotch, her feet resting in Rolf's lap. He kept talking about the baby, whether it would be a girl or a boy, what they would name it, but Nok only half listened as she trained her eyes on the stairs to the second floor. Cora and Lucky had gone up there, after they'd left the diner. Was Cora actually going to go through with the third rule? If so, it changed everything. Nok had been sure Cora was a lost cause. At first she'd been thankful to have another girl; back in London, she'd never have survived the flophouse without the other models, and she needed a friend here just as badly. All that had changed, though, the moment Serassi had appeared to her in the salon.

You will reproduce in thirty-six weeks, Serassi had said flatly, and given her instructions on proper prenatal health, but Nok hadn't listened. A baby. She was going to be a mom. She'd looked around the salon at all the stupid nail polish and hair machines and seen her reflection in the black window: pink stripe of hair like a silly teenager, band T-shirt pulled down over one shoulder. Mothers didn't look like that.

She couldn't do this alone.

"What do you think about Holly, if it's a girl?" Rolf asked. "Or Ivy. Maybe Violet. Anything that has to do flora. If it's a boy, it'll be more of a challenge. Alder, after the type of tree?"

"They're all lovely," she murmured.

"Do you think we'll raise our baby in this house? Or will they give us our own house in one of the other habitats?"

"I don't know." She sucked on the butterscotch, a hand pressed against her stomach.

As soon as she'd realized she couldn't raise this baby on her own, she'd set about subtly establishing influence over the others. *Controlling men is the only way women like you and me will survive,* Delphine had said. All her manager's old lessons came flooding back. Getting men to give you presents with a coy look. Bending them to your will with one smile. She already had Rolf willing to do anything for her; it wasn't hard to win over Leon, either—he'd wanted what every boy wanted. She'd win over Lucky in time too. Mali had been harder—a coy look and a smile did nothing for her, but Nok had patiently bought her friendship with painting parties and dancing in the rain, teaching Mali all the things about humanity that she hadn't ever experienced on Earth.

That had left Cora.

Cora, who had whispered reassurances in her ear when she'd huddled on the toy-store floor the first day. Cora, who had squeezed her hand when she couldn't sleep, and told her she'd keep watch. Cora, who had caught her in a lie but hadn't told the others. A girl who, in another life, could be her friend. But here, with her crazy theories about escape and desperate attacks on both Lucky and Rolf, Cora was only a threat.

Rolf was watching her expectantly. She cleared her throat.

"Maybe . . . Robin," Nok said. "If it's a girl. Or Wren. I'd like for my daughter to know what birds were, even if there aren't any anymore."

The bedroom door slammed upstairs, jolting Nok out of her thoughts. She jerked upright, swinging her feet off Rolf's lap. Lucky appeared at the top of the stairs, hunched over. Blood covered the right side of his face.

Nok gasped. She and Rolf helped him down the stairs, and she pulled off the punk shirt over her black dress and dabbed at his face.

"It was Cora," he choked. "She's gone. She ran."

"She did this to you?" Nok cried. She knew as well as anyone that Cora was growing more unstable, but *this*?

Rolf was suddenly by her side, and she saw a flash of jealousy in his eyes as she tended to Lucky's wound. She pulled back a little from Lucky, aware that if she was to keep everyone loyal to her, she was going to have to tread very lightly.

"She was scared." Lucky buried his head in his hands.

"Scared?" Rolf sputtered. "Stop making excuses for her! How many times have we given her the benefit of the doubt? We ran the puzzles because she asked us to. We collected tokens because she asked us to. We told her the truth about Earth and she refused to accept it. She even broke your guitar. And now this—trying to *kill* you? She's gone totally crazy!"

Lucky pressed a hand to his bleeding face. "I don't think she was trying to kill me."

Nok bit her lip, looking between them anxiously.

"Of course she was!" Rolf said. "She knows all about how to kill a person. You've heard her talk about making weapons out of teddy bears and things . . . I mean, who *does* that? She must have been some kind of social deviant back on Earth, some sociopath, and now her true tendencies are coming out."

Nok chewed on her lip. "If that was true, wouldn't the Kindred have stopped her?"

Rolf tossed her a look like she was a traitor for even daring to speak such a thing. "Why do you think they've kept her behind so many times? Why do you think the Caretaker keeps paying her the most attention? It's because the Kindred know that they made a mistake putting her here, and that she's dangerous. Didn't you all see in the diner—she had a bone in her hand! No explanation. Just a bone. It was probably from that first girl who died. Who's to say Cora didn't kill her and hide the body?"

"Could a body really decompose that fast?" Nok asked.

"Time doesn't work the same way here," Rolf answered curtly.

Nok flinched. Rolf had found his confidence and then some. She told herself he was just worried about the baby, and the threat Cora's instability might pose. But the truth was, Rolf had always had a jealous streak. He was jealous when she smiled at Lucky. He was jealous when Cora got more tokens.

Nok raked her nails over her scalp. Her head throbbed so hard she could barely think. "I just can't imagine Cora would do such a thing. If we could reason with her . . ."

Lucky's eyes were dazed from the head wound, and he kept clutching at himself like Cora had ripped the very heart from his chest.

"Maybe she isn't malicious," Rolf said quietly. "But we all know that she's going crazy. For her own good, she can't be allowed to just run free. None of us are safe with her on the loose. We have a baby to think of now. We need to find her and turn her over to the Kindred. They'll give her the help she needs and put her in a place that's right for her."

Nok chewed on her lip. She glanced at Lucky, who looked like he wasn't even listening. He kept pressing his fist against his heart, rubbing his chest, swallowing hard.

Maybe Rolf was right.

Pressure started to build in the air, and alarm shot to Nok's throat as she remembered it was the twenty-first day. Had they come for Lucky now? Surely they would give him another chance. She didn't want him replaced with some half-feral boy with cold eyes who might pose yet another threat to her child.

A figure materialized in the corner, dressed in black, but it wasn't the Caretaker. It was a Kindred woman with dark hair, pulled back tight in a different style knot from Serassi's. The same apparatus jutted out of her chest. The woman tugged off her thick black gloves.

"Who are you?" Rolf asked in a bewildered voice, looking just as shocked as Nok felt. "Where's the Caretaker?"

"I am the substitute Caretaker. My name is Tessela. It is my responsibility to heal any minor injuries that do not require the medical officer's attention." She pressed her ungloved hand against Lucky's bleeding temple. When she pulled back her hand, the wound was healed, the blood dried and crusted. "Due to this recent incident, the Warden has determined that the artifacts from Earth, such as the ceramic dog, are too dangerous; you cannot be trusted with them if you insist on hurting one another. The Warden has given the order to phase them out over the next week. They will be replaced with imitations."

Nok gaped. The radio with the knobs that looked like a smiling face. The painting set. The books in the bookstore. They would replace them with toys that would feel wrong and smell wrong.

As if sensing her thoughts, Tessela turned to her. "That goes for your child as well. The Warden has determined, given this violent incident, that your cohort is too unstable for a child to be raised among you. Once you deliver your child, we will transport it to the standard facility, where it will be cared for." Tessela gripped the apparatus in her chest and, with a wave of pressure, flickered away.

Nok's breath caught. Pain ripped through her head, but it was nothing compared to the panic flooding her chest. Her heart fluttered like a trapped bird. Her hands pressed against her abdomen protectively. They were going to take her baby away? All because of one fight? Her thoughts churned faster, panic rising. She had to fix this. She had to convince the Kindred—but she couldn't win *them* over with a flirtatious smile, that was for sure.

It hadn't even been Nok's fault. She had done nothing but obey the rules. *Cora* had been the one who'd broken them.

Rage started boiling inside her, heating her up faster and faster until she feared she'd melt. She had thought Cora was a friend. She had defended her against Rolf's claims. And this is what she got for her friendship—her baby ripped away?

Pain fractured behind her left eye, and she doubled over. A memory overcame her. Standing on the tarmac in Chiang Mai, in her older sister's finest dress that her mother had patched, a backpack with fifteen hundred baht and a bag of peanuts in case she got hungry. Her parents pulling her into a stiff hug, her mother trying not to cry. *Like winning the lottery,* her mother had said, and then, less than twenty-four hours later, arriving at a London apartment and realizing she'd practically been sold into slavery.

She'd grown up with strangers, forced to be photographed, observed.

Her daughter would not have that life.

Her daughter would have a mother.

Nok crouched next to Lucky, forcing herself to keep her rage tamped down. She had seen how Delphine had handled this kind of situation—not with raised voices but with soft ones. Not with fists but with whispered words.

She smoothed Lucky's hair. "You see?" She petted the healed place on his forehead. "Rolf was right. This is what Cora has done to us. They're taking away everything we have because of her violent tendencies. Even my baby. It doesn't matter if she was a good person. She's crazy now, and she has to be stopped before she ruins *everything.*"

46

Cora

WHEN THE REMATERIALIZATION WAS over, Cora found herself in a small room nearly bare of furniture. Open doorways led to two more small rooms. The space didn't have the medical chamber's austerity, nor the market's bustling chaos, nor the menagerie's faux Greek columns. But starry light came from the seams in the wall, marking it as a Kindred space.

Cassian held her tightly. As soon as he released her, she took a quick step away.

She crossed to the single window and shoved open the curtain, afraid to see a black window and know she was still being watched. But on the other side was the night sky filled with endless stars. Some so faint they were nearly invisible, some close enough to burn her eyes. In the center was a distant planet, ringed like Saturn, the blue color of water. She had to grab the curtain to keep from falling.

"This is what's outside? Outer space?"

"That is a projected image. I selected it for you." He paused. "I know you like the stars." He traced a pattern on the wall in the central room, where a cabinet slid out, revealing a square container and a single square drinking glass.

She peeked into one of the other rooms. A bed with no sheets or blankets, and a shelf holding a few blue cubes and nothing else. Had he brought her to a prison cell?

"Where are we?" she asked.

"My quarters." He spoke so casually that Cora barely had time to register before he pointed to the sitting room. "Sit in there."

"Your *quarters*? I thought you were taking me to one of the menageries."

He raised an eyebrow. "The Warden did instruct me to take you to a menagerie. And as you recall, I *did* take you to one. The Temple. I fulfilled his orders—I just didn't leave you there, drugged and caged." She thought she saw a flicker of dark amusement cross his face. "Never let it be said that my kind does not excel at finding loopholes."

He picked up the square glass and the bottle but hesitated. "The Warden recommended that I take you to a menagerie called the Harem. It is located on the seventh sector—an area frequented by disgraced Kindred and Mosca traders. They go through human girls quickly there. It is a place I do not think you would like to go. I would certainly not enjoy having to leave you there."

He was implying using girls for sex, or worse—things she couldn't even imagine. It made the childish tricks in the Temple seem positively innocent. What had she done to make the Warden hate her this much?

Cassian pointed toward the sitting room. "Sit. Please. I would not like to spend the little time we have arguing."

Cora made her way into the sitting room. It was barren, save for some metal crates pushed against the wall and a book tossed on top of the crates, dog-eared and worn. *Peter Pan and Wendy*. An artifact from Earth. It was the only thing at all in the entire room that had any glimmer of personality. Cassian picked up the book quickly and dropped it into one of the metal crates.

The bare room reeked of desolation. "Do you all live like this, so spartanly?" she asked.

"Yes, though not by choice. There is not an abundance of resources in space. Dust and rock and light can only power so much. We live a frugal life out of necessity. The technology used to create your environment works only within certain confines and requires a high amount of carbon. We could not create such luxury for ourselves." He traced another pattern on the wall. A small tray emerged, which served as a table for the glass and square container. He poured a sharp-smelling liquid into the glass and took a deep drink.

"What's that?"

"Alcohol, made from fermented lichens."

"You have alcohol?"

He glanced at her with a flicker of amusement. "Every society in the universe has invented alcohol—even some lesser species, such as your own. Intoxicants are prohibited, in general, outside of the menageries. But we are allowed to keep one container in our quarters, in case of difficulty controlling emotions."

She grabbed the glass out of his hand, downing the contents, wincing as it burned her throat in a way her mother's expensive wine never had. She held out the glass for more. "I'm definitely having difficulty controlling my emotions."

Cassian hesitated—clearly he meant the drink for himself, not her—but then refilled the glass. She took a slower sip, letting her heavy eyelids sink slightly. The room was quiet, too quiet, and she cleared her throat. "What did you mean when you said that the algorithm didn't make a mistake, but you did?"

He dragged a crate over as a makeshift chair. "It is protocol to monitor the stock algorithm's selections before the transfer from the native environment to the artificial one. I performed the required period of observation on the other Girl Two. She would have been suitable." He looked down at his hands. "I continued to monitor Boy Two simultaneously. He was performing a research operation on one of your networked computers. He found an article from the previous year about your father's employment. You were standing in the picture. Boy Two's emotions were very strong. Impossible to ignore."

Lucky had said he looked her up on the internet every few months at his library, hoping for news that would make him feel better about playing a part in her time in juvenile detention.

That whole time, Cassian had been watching?

"He felt intense guilt," Cassian continued, "which was perplexing, since he had not directly wronged you. He felt curiosity too, and very strong attraction, though that only made his guilt increase. I began to observe you as well. Call it . . . curiosity. Your experience with captivity was somewhat unusual in a female of your age and your intelligence. Such resilience is highly desirable to us, after what happened to the previous cohorts."

She swallowed. Her hand still felt dry from the femur bone.

"You had other traits—physical attractiveness, a quiet demeanor, an emotional strength—that would make for an interesting pairing with any of the three males selected. I already knew Boy Two would be more than interested in you. So I went against the stock algorithm. I selected you myself. The Warden strongly disapproved, but I argued that your resilience would make you highly adaptable to an environment such as this."

"That's what this is all about, resilience?" She clutched the glass harder. "You thought that because I was in prison before, and didn't cause disruptions, that I'd roll over and accept this prison too? You've got it all wrong. The accident and my time at Bay Pines didn't make me resilient. It left me a shell of a person. I can't face enclosed spaces. I can't face water. It didn't matter where I went or who I was around after that; I didn't belong anywhere. Not at home. Not in prison either. It changed me, Cassian."

Her fingers were trembling on the glass. He folded his own across from her, a gesture that felt startlingly human. "Perhaps we define resiliency differently. My understanding was that resilience isn't about weakness, but strength."

"Exactly. I'm *not* strong. I can't sleep and when I do, it's just nightmares. I can't even—"

Her voice failed her. She was about to say she couldn't even love Lucky like he deserved, but Cassian didn't need her to list her failures. He could see them in her head.

For a long time, he didn't answer. He must be thinking about how he'd made a mistake. He thought she was more than she was. He saw something that wasn't there. She didn't think she would ever care if the monster who brought her here regretted it, but in some ripped-bare part of her, she found that she did care. Yes, she did.

She wanted to know why he thought she was resilient.

"Because of what happened with your father," he said. "Because of the truth."

CORA'S EYES CLOSED TO the room and the starry window, as she remembered a different night long ago. It was two days after she had been released from Bay Pines.

Her welcome-home party.

The divorce had been finalized halfway through her incarceration, but her mother had flown back from Miami and drunk enough pinot grigio to be able to be under the same roof as her father, though never in the same room. They'd invited all her old school friends and her father's colleagues. Her mom had attached a silk bow to Sadie's collar. There had been a three-tiered cake and presents, as though she'd been away at a European boarding school for the last eighteen months, and not an upstate detention facility.

No one talked about Bay Pines. No one asked her how bad the cafeteria food was or if any of the girls had attacked her. Her father made a long toast to her return. Then the guests left, and her parents got into one of their marathon fights and her mother stormed out, and the maids cleaned the spilled champagne, and Cora went outside to look at the night sky.

Whether she was looking up from Bay Pines or Fox Run, whether her family was together or broken, at least the stars had always looked the same.

Her father joined her, and for the first time since the night of the accident, they were alone. They exchanged a few words about the upcoming election, and the fight he'd had with her mother over the guest list, and then he leaned over the railing, with no warning, and let his gin glass slip into the bushes below, and covered his face with his hands.

It was the first time Cora had ever seen him cry.

"I didn't know what to do," he said, between sobs that made the loose skin on his neck tremble. He was already bald by then, and his manicured fingers clutched his head as though it needed to be held together. "I'd had too much to drink. I was so angry with your mother, threatening divorce."

It had taken Cora a moment to even realize he was talking about the night of the accident, because he only ever spoke about it in vague terms, and only if he had to. As a senator, he'd always been coached in what to say, so it was rare to see him open up like this. She watched his fingers fumbling over his bald scalp, searching for something, anything. He looked older than she'd ever seen him, and it was the first time she realized that one day he would die.

"It eats at me. It should have been me. My little girl spent eighteen months in that place, and all it would have taken was a single phone call, a single confession, and you would have walked free."

He had collapsed into a sobbing collection of tired eyes and world-worn fingers and wrinkles that hadn't been there before that night.

Cora leaned against the railing next to him. She had tried hard not to think often about the night of the accident. That terrifying plunge off the bridge, the car filling with water, shivering together on the shore, her father reeking of alcohol. Sitting on the wet grass, she'd thought through what would happen next. The police would arrest him. He would lose his senatorship and his reputation. Her family would lose their livelihood. Her mother would divorce him for real. She and Charlie would lose a father.

Below, in the garden, the shattered pieces of his gin glass reflected the moonlight. She remembered each day of those eighteen months. The fights in the shower. The leering eyes of the guards. The lights that stayed on all night. At the time, it had seemed an eternity.

"It was my choice, Dad." She had glanced back through the windows at her house, where her mother slept on the sofa and Charlie played video games. She felt like she was looking into another person's life. "I wouldn't have suggested it if I hadn't known the consequences. I knew exactly what I was doing when I told the police that I had been behind the wheel. I was saving our family."

"I never should have gone along with it." Her dad sobbed. "I should have confessed. I should have served the time."

Cora had reached over and covered his large old-man hand with her small one. "It's okay, Dad. I knew what I was doing."

She had lied to him plenty back then, but not that night on the porch. It *was* okay. Her father worked too hard, and was away from home too often, but he loved her. She knew him—she loved him—and she never once blamed him for going along with a decision that she had made on her own. Lucky had it all wrong, when he thought that her father had forced her to take the fall for him. She had never been a victim. Not once in her life. It had been her idea to take the fall. There on the banks of the river, waiting for the police to come, she had practically forced her father to agree. And even after the conviction, and after the divorce happened anyway, and after juvie, and after coming home and knowing that she would never belong again, she had never once regretted it.

47

Cora

"HE'S MY FATHER," SHE whispered. "I had the ability to help him. It's what anyone would have done."

Cassian didn't answer. In his eyes she saw herself reflected: tangled hair, delicate features, dark under-eye circles. Taking the fall for her father didn't mean she was brave. It certainly didn't make her a paragon of humanity.

But she sensed that Cassian disagreed, and it was a strange feeling. He didn't see her as a victim, like Lucky did. He knew that the lie had been her idea. He didn't care about the accident or her false imprisonment or the skills she'd learned in juvie or even her high-profile family.

He cared about the sacrifice she had made.

"Humans have been cruel to you," he said. "Your father, for allowing you to accept blame for his crimes. Your fellow inmates in detention. Those in the media who unfairly judged you. And yet you bear no resentment toward them. I took you from your world because I wished to give you something better."

Her heart pounded. She never expected this. Not from him.

"I don't want better." Her voice was faint. "I want home, flaws and all. And don't try to tell me it isn't there. I saw the comic book. I know time works differently for you. Just tell me straight that it was all a lie. Earth is still there, isn't it?"

Her words reverberated around the small corners of his room. Echoed back at her, they sounded desperate, but she refused to back down. Not when everything she had ever loved was at stake.

She could tell by his flat expression that he was going to lie again. She could almost *feel* the lie forming on his lips, could almost taste its bitterness. But then he closed his mouth. "There is no short answer to that question." The flatness in his face was gone now; he was telling the truth. "Because we ourselves do not know."

She gripped the edge of the table. "How can you not know? It's a huge planet. It's either there or it isn't."

"Two hundred rotations ago, the stock algorithm ran a projection that predicted humans would destroy their own planet with a ninety-eight point six degree of certainty. We began taking the last groups of humans before the destruction was predicted to occur. So by all projections, the answer to your question is yes, Earth is gone."

"But I overheard the Mosca in the market talking about going back to Earth for another supply run. And that comic book was stamped with a date in the future."

He took the glass from her and swallowed her concerns with another pour of alcohol. "Many artifacts are counterfeit—you cannot trust the comic books are authentic. And we do not concern ourselves with the Mosca. If they believe Earth exists, perhaps they have not been back yet to verify its destruction."

"But have *you* verified it? Have any Kindred seen it with their own eyes?"

"A ninety-eight point six percent chance does not require verification."

She didn't listen to his talk about percentages and statistics. All Cora heard was that there was a chance; the stock algorithm had made mistakes before. Margins of error.

Maybe this was a mistake, too.

"You forget that I can read what you are thinking," he said. "You still hope to return to Earth, even knowing the high likelihood it is gone. Perhaps the Mosca would be able to help you, but they are an unscrupulous species. They would just as likely betray you. The wisest course of action would be to forget your dreams; if you will only agree to obey, I can request an extension from the Warden. He won't like it, but I have some sway. I could make the enclosure more comfortable for you."

On the wall, the fake stars shimmered. He had already risked so much for her—and now he was willing to sacrifice more. She picked up the glass and twirled it in her fingers.

"It isn't about the comforts of Earth. It's about what's real. My life at home was as fake as my life here. I was never allowed to be myself—I always had to be a senator's daughter. My mother couldn't be an actress, like she wanted, and it made her bitter and resentful. I could never be a songwriter, because my dad's handlers thought that if any of my songs got online, it would hurt my dad's chances at reelection. We had to be these artificial versions of ourselves, always smiling when we were sad, cloaking our real emotions, just like you do.

"If I can go home, I can change that. I can truly live, even if it's painful. I want a real relationship with my father and my mother. We can be a real family again, even with the divorce—we were making progress. I want to write songs about the things I've been through, and I want to fall in love with someone I choose, not who was chosen for me." She tore her hand away from her necklace. "You probably don't understand that."

He was quiet for some time and then very slowly rubbed the scar on his neck. "I understand more than you think. I could not have observed humanity for this long without being affected by it. The others of my kind are fascinated by the brightly colored parts of humanity: your clothing, your architecture, the tricks you can perform. I'm not as interested in those. I like the quieter part, like how humans wish on stars knowing they won't be answered. And what you told me once, about how some mistakes are worth making. I have made mistakes myself." He took the glass and downed another sip, as though he could swallow whatever memories pained him. "That is why your capacity for emotional depth intrigues me. The Kindred do not have those notions. Forgiveness. Sacrifice. They are remarkable traits."

His face had looked so otherworldly at first, like that of a god, or someone from her dreams. But now she knew he was just a person, and he was young too, and felt things like guilt and shame and the need for forgiveness.

"You should not be ashamed to be one of the unintelligent species," he said, looking into the glass. "The intelligent species are not perfect, though we may pretend to be. We can lie. We can manipulate. We can betray. Your kind are not capable of the same level of evil as mine is." He set the glass back down, and the liquid settled. It was cold in his room, but he didn't seem to feel it.

"Yes, we are." She thought of the girls at Bay Pines who bullied each other just for fun, and of her friends who had vanished after her arrest, and even of herself, who had been so careless with Lucky's heart. She took the glass and downed the rest of it. "You admit that the Kindred lie. Were you lying when you said your people had taken us for our own benefit? All your talk about swearing altruistic oaths . . ." She looked down into the glass. "It isn't true, is it?"

He didn't answer. This close, his eyes weren't just black; there was depth to them, like the cut crystal of the glass.

"Tell me why the Warden *really* had you take us," she demanded.

The angles of his room felt extra sharp. The tension was heavy in the air, nearly at the point of bursting. *No more lies. Please.*

He leaned in slowly. "Our oath is not a lie. We do see ourselves as stewards, and not just because of our fondness for humans. It is our duty to ensure your survival—and all the lesser species' survival—because the universe would lose its richness without humanity, and diversity of thought leads to the ultimate intelligence." He paused. "But you in particular. You six. There is more to it than what we have told you, and more to your enclosure."

"So you admit that those researchers *have* been manipulating us." Her vindication was immediately swallowed by anger. "But why would they mess with the puzzles? Why put us in such strange pairs? Why turn the others against me?"

"Mali has mentioned rumors to you that certain humans are beginning to demonstrate signs of perceptive ability. Some have claimed to be mildly psychic, even telekinetic. None of the claims have been verified. The six of you were chosen, in part, because of your potential to display perceptive ability, if your minds were pushed in the correct manner. Challenging your concepts of time and space, for example. Altering the weather. Putting pressure on you in terms of presenting puzzles with variable rewards."

She stared at him like he was speaking another language. All of it, everything, had been an attempt to see if they were evolving. The headaches. The irritability. The fighting among themselves. The scrape of anger clawed her once more. "It was under the Warden's orders, wasn't it? And those researchers were more than happy to screw with our heads. But we could have killed each other, like the last groups. We still could! When Rolf finds out Nok's sleeping with Leon, it could all go to hell!"

She sank forward, resting her tired head in her hands, trying to quiet the millions of thoughts warring for her attention. Her neck throbbed as though the Warden's icy grip was still there. No wonder he'd been willing to remove her—she wasn't being a good little specimen. She wished she had never awakened in that desert, and seen that ocean, with its strange shimmer and its dead body. Why had they even given them an ocean, anyway? Was it just more manipulation? There was no puzzle there. Eight puzzles in the habitats, eight in the shops—that's what Cassian had said. And each of the environments they'd found had a puzzle: the treetop ropes course in the forest, the maze in the desert, the scavenger hunt in the swamp, the musical puzzle in the grasslands, the harvest game in the farm, the temple maze in the jungle, and the sledding race in the arctic habitat.

A strange tickle spread down her back, painful but not like

a headache, and she pinched herself hard. That was only seven. That meant there had to be an eighth, and the ocean was the only habitat left. Maybe it was a puzzle they couldn't solve—because it was hidden by perceptive technology.

Because it was the fail-safe exit.

She pinched herself harder. She might not be psychic, but she was smart enough to see through their lies. She bit the inside of her cheek, tasting blood, and leaned forward. If she was right, they could all escape. "Give me another chance. Take me back to the cage, just for one more day. You might not have been the one manipulating us, but you went along with it. You owe me."

Even as she said the words, she knew they weren't quite true. How many times had he bent the rules for her?

He turned his head. "That is against protocol."

"So was taking me to the menagerie. So is having me in your bedroom, I'm guessing. Admit it—you know what they're doing is wrong. You know I'm more than a gender and a number. I'm a person. Like you."

Her heart hammered. It was excruciating, being so close to this beautiful bronzed creature who wasn't human but who was so similar. A crazy thought entered her head: *Maybe Lucky was right to be jealous.*

His hand flexed on the table, close enough that their fingers brushed, and the spark ran through her, straight to her heart.

"Why do you wish to go back," he asked, "when we both know you will never obey?"

She bit the inside of her cheek harder, masking her thoughts with pain. "Don't ask me that. Please. I can't tell you."

That's why the ocean had pulsed so strangely that

day—because her eyes knew they were being tricked. Her body knew there was something wrong with the ocean, more than just her fear of deep water.

"I would be risking much for you, Cora. If the Warden found out, we would both be severely punished."

She didn't let herself think. "That's what I want."

He paused. "Then I will help you. And I will not ask why."

Silence shrouded the room, but Cora didn't mind. It was a reprieve from the cage. From her thoughts. From her loneliness. Cassian refilled the glass, and they took turns sipping. For the rest of the night they sat in his spartan quarters and talked, and then they didn't talk, and they listened to the silence around them.

Cora's head jerked. She had fallen asleep sitting up. She tried to stand but stumbled, shaky. Cassian stood too, to keep her from falling.

"You should rest," he said. "When you wake, I will return you to your enclosure."

He was asking her if she could walk, but she couldn't find the words to answer. She just wanted to sleep. Her thoughts kept drifting back to her bed at home, the quilt that Sadie liked to curl up on. Even with all the pain, and hurt, and loneliness, she wanted that life back.

The ground fell away from her; he was carrying her to the other room as though she weighed nothing. Her head lolled, her hair dangling. Then came a temperature change and a softness as her body relaxed into the familiar comfort of a bed, though it was harder than she'd like. Her muscles unwound in a way they hadn't in weeks.

"I will wait in the other room," he said.

She shook her head. She reached out a hand to touch him, though she wasn't sure if she wanted to push him away or pull his warmth closer.

"I still have to try," she whispered.

He didn't ask her to elaborate, because if he could see in her head, he had to know what she meant: she couldn't live in a cage. And she couldn't let the others continue to slide away from humanity.

"Not now," he said. "Now, just rest."

She started to drift even deeper into sleep. The mattress dipped where he was sitting; she was tempted to roll toward that groove. He said words she barely heard, about how she was wrong when she thought she was just an animal to him. That he didn't think of her that way. But it might have just been her dreams taking over.

Her mind drifted deeper, and an hour might have passed, or maybe only an instant, but his weight was still on the bed beside her.

"Cora," he said softly, more to himself. She felt the faintest touch of his hand on her cheek, his fingers light as if they didn't know how hard to touch not to bruise her. The metallic skin of his thumb rubbed along her bottom lip.

You don't know what I'm like in private, when I'm uncloaked.

As she slipped from the waking world to sleep, she wondered if he wanted to kiss her. He had been so curious, that day in the menagerie. His desire to understand humanity had been palpable. Her heart was racing, despite the alcohol. She could still show him. She could press her lips to his—she was aching to. It was so clear now. She wasn't sure when it had begun, certainly not that first day, nor in the medical rooms. The night he gave her the stars, maybe. She wanted to show him what it meant to be human.

She moved her lips, trying to form his name.

But as soon as his thumb had brushed her lips, it was gone, and the weight beside her on the bed was gone, and then she fell asleep to the sound of his footsteps by the window, pacing back and forth, back and forth. Just like a tiger.

48

Lucky

LUCKY CROUCHED BY THE side of the candy shop, working fast in the moonlight. His palms stung from swinging through the treetop ropes course all night. Without Cora to hold the ladders, it had been difficult, but he'd managed. Now he ran his hand over the plastic water gun he'd bought from the toy shop with all the tokens he'd earned. Back on his granddad's farm, he'd learned a trick to keep the flies off horses: liquefied cayenne pepper. But if you got it in your eyes, it would blind you.

He stomped on a handful of peppers from the farm, juicing them under his heel, and squeezed them into the water gun. His head throbbed from where Cora had hit him, but he ignored it, just like he ignored the awful hollow space in his chest. He'd only felt this way twice before—once, on a bridge outside of Richmond, after his car had wrapped around a streetlight, and he'd looked over to see his mother slumped against the wheel. The second time had been when he'd met Cora's father's men in a drugstore parking lot and taken their check.

He finished filling the water gun and shoved the stopper back into it, then grabbed a jump rope he had modified into nunchakus. He glanced back at the house, where he could make out Rolf reading a book by the window. For a brief moment, he considered staying.

But the cherry blossoms wafted toward him, and he turned sharply and started for the jungle. He *knew* Cora. She wasn't that devious. Someone must have put her up to hitting him, pouring lies into her ear for weeks. He knew it wasn't Nok or Rolf, because he'd constantly been around them. He didn't think it was Mali—she had no reason to. There was only one person in the enclosure who had violent tendencies too, who could have convinced her to do such a thing.

Leon.

His chest felt even more hollow at the memory of her betrayal, and he had to lean against the railing of the jungle walkway. He pictured her face, the blue eyes with the dark rings around them from not sleeping, and her lips that had tasted so real, and he gripped the jump-rope nunchakus harder.

He ran down the walkway, dizzy from his injury and the distortions. He'd known Leon would be trouble from the start. His father had warned him about Leon's type—guys who hated authority. Guys who wanted to be soldiers not to protect the country, but because they liked blood on their hands.

He skidded to a stop as soon as he saw a collection of huts scattered around a huge stone temple. His heart pounded harder as he walked as silently as he could through the jungle. A sheet flapped in the wind, covered with odd symbols he couldn't make out in the moonlight. They almost looked like eyes. Then he heard rustling, and took out the water gun. His plan was to blind Leon first, then use the nunchakus. Four years of martial arts had to be worth something.

He pressed his back against the hut, moving slowly toward the entrance. The jungle was so quiet he could hear his own heart beating. Another shuffle came from within the hut, and he leaped inside, gun raised.

Nok screamed.

Lucky started. What was *she* doing there? She was alone, wrapped in only a sheet, her pink streak of hair hiding the left side of her face.

"Lucky?" she sputtered. "Is that a *gun*?"

He lowered the water gun, leaning on the doorway to steady his throbbing head. Her lips fell open, but she seemed at a loss for words. Lucky's thoughts caught up with him all at once: Nok wrapped in the sheet . . . how she'd come to him that day on the porch and run her finger down his cheek, and offered to help him fulfill the third rule.

Had she made the same offer to *Leon*?

"Jesus, Nok. What are you . . . Is the baby even Rolf's?"

His words jolted her out of her stupor. She dragged the sheet around her tighter, stumbling to her feet, a fire in her eyes. "I had to, Lucky. You heard what that substitute caretaker said. They're taking away my baby because of what Cora did to you. She's gone crazy. Leon's the only person who can stop her. I need him, and don't you dare judge me for getting his help this way."

She tossed the pink streak of hair out of her face. She had a wild look in her eye that had never been there before. This wasn't the same skittish, pretty girl he'd found cowering in the toy store. He'd only seen glimmers of her darkness before, like the time she'd kicked Leon in the groin.

"How's Leon going to stop her?" Lucky said. "They can't be stopped!"

A shadow filled the doorway behind him.

"What the hell is this?" Leon bellowed.

Lucky's hand tightened on the gun. *Blind him, then use the nunchakus.* But he hadn't expected Nok. He hadn't guessed that they'd been sleeping together. His stomach twisted at that feverish-wild look in her eye.

He was so tired of it all. The betrayals. The hurt.

He looked at his makeshift weapons. What had he been planning to do, *kill* Leon? He'd felt such hatred in his veins, such certainty that Leon had been the one to twist Cora, but the truth was, all of them were twisted.

He let the water gun fall and shoved past Leon, back out into the jungle.

He ran along the walkway until it bled into the forest. He followed the paths to the clearing with the treetop ropes course. He would isolate himself, like Leon had, for his own safety.

He reached for a branch, but his hand froze.

What if *he* was twisted too, just like they were, and he didn't know it? Had *he* done anything that might have made Cora run? He'd just been trying to show her that he loved her. He'd been trying to keep them both safe from removal.

The hair on his arms started to rise. He stared at it in the moonlight, and then whirled in the clearing. That pressure usually meant the Caretaker was coming. He wound the jump rope around his knuckles, ready to use it to strangle him when he appeared.

As soon as the Caretaker flickered into the clearing, Lucky jumped him. He managed to get the rope around his neck, pull it taut so it dug into the creature's metallic skin, but then the air rushed out of Lucky's lungs, and he felt himself flying across the clearing. His back collided with the mulched chips.

Before he could sit, the Caretaker was standing over him, one booted foot resting on his chest.

"I have an offer for you," the Caretaker said.

49

Cora

IN THE MORNING, CORA blinked awake on an unfamiliarly hard bed. Her vision focused on a black panel with a starry sky. The smell of ozone lingered on the air. She stretched out, reveling in having slept soundly through the entire night for the first time in weeks, and then gasped. She jerked upright. The light from the wall seams, the empty shelves . . . she'd fallen asleep in Cassian's bedroom. The events of the previous day came rushing back: how, in that murky time between awake and asleep, she'd wanted his lips on hers. It was a mortifying thought—all the worse because he must have been able to read her mind.

His door opened, and he entered. She stood in a rush, smoothing out her dress and her hair, looking everywhere but at his eyes.

"It is time to return to your enclosure."

His demeanor was perfectly even. Emotionless. Cora envied him that ability.

He led her to the control room, every move mechanical, just as it had been on the day of the medical examinations, after he'd slipped and said her name by accident. It wasn't until he had stabbed the apparatus through his chest and dematerialized them both into the peach orchard that she observed any emotion at all.

His hand flexed a little too hard by his side. "One final day. Continue to disobey, and I will have no choice but to take you to the Harem."

With that, he was gone.

Cora watched the grass blow around the place where his two heavy boots had stood. He—her jailer, her captor—was risking so much for her. She made her way toward town, winding through the maze of peach trees, trying to find the right words to convince the others to escape with her. They were furious at her, thinking she was trying to sabotage them. Not to mention she'd knocked Lucky out and run.

She reached the edge of the town and shrank behind a tree. Nok and Rolf were playing croquet on the lawn between the house and the movie theater. Those two were frighteningly unstable, especially after all the accusations they'd thrown at her in the diner. She skirted behind the row of shops until she was close enough to overhear their conversation.

Crack.

Rolf swung his croquet mallet, his force extra hard as he smacked the ball.

Crack.

The sound was strange; not like wood against wood. "Try it again," Nok ordered, a hard edge to her voice. Rolf paused to wipe the sweat from his forehead, then slammed the croquet mallet down again. Nok stooped to examine the ball. She gave him a grim nod.

"That's the right amount of force. Remember, she can make a weapon out of anything. If she comes back, she'll probably be armed, yeah? We can't take any chances after she tried to kill Lucky. Now hit it again."

Rolf hefted the croquet mallet.

Fear trickled down Cora's back. They weren't playing croquet. So what were they hitting so hard with the mallets? She dared to peek over the bushes.

Pumpkins. Big, round ones. They'd painted blue-eyed faces on them that looked an awful lot like hers.

Rolf brought down the mallet. *Crack.*

Nok nodded. "Perfect."

Cora slunk along the ground, afraid to even breathe, until fear got the best of her and she took off at a run toward the habitats. Her legs burned. Her vision went glassy. Did they really think she had tried to *kill* Lucky? What had this place done to them, to twist them into such angry versions of themselves?

She stopped running when she reached the swamp, and collapsed against a tree to catch her breath. This was going to be harder than she thought. She needed to test her theory that they could escape through the fail-safe exit beneath the waves, but that wouldn't help her much if the others had it out for her. She couldn't go to Lucky for help; she was sure the Kindred had fixed his head injury, but they couldn't fix a broken heart. That left Mali, who might as well *be* a Kindred, and Leon, who had gone completely insane—but at least he didn't hate her, so he was her best chance.

The sun shifted a degree. Noon already. She ran for the jungle, her bare feet slapping across the raised walkway through the thick underbrush. She reached Leon's makeshift camp just as a drenching rain began.

Oh, no.

The camp was destroyed. The sheets with Leon's artwork had been torn down and trampled in the mud. Rotten fruit spilled out of overturned orchard crates. No one lived there anymore, that was certain. And judging by how violently Leon had destroyed his camp, he might be even more dangerous than he had been before.

Cora flinched as rain came harder, and thunder struck high up in the sky. It made the same sound as a hideous *crack*, like a croquet mallet slamming into a pumpkin. She leaned against a tree, hands pressed to her throbbing head. The previous six inhabitants were dead now, murdered by each other. How long before history repeated itself?

She slid down the tree to the jungle floor, letting the mud streak her clothes. The rain pounded harder against the nearest black windows. Were the researchers there now, studying her fear? She balled herself tight, as though that could protect her from their watching eyes.

This wasn't some experiment.

This was her life.

Thunder cracked again. Little rivers formed in the mud. Soon the clearing would flood, but she didn't care. Even if she found the fail-safe exit, she couldn't escape on her own, knowing what grisly fate awaited the others.

She didn't hear feet approaching until a set of toes wiggled in front of her. She jerked upright. A girl stood among the palm fronds, her long, dark hair streaked with rain, so quiet and still that she nearly blended into the shadows.

The dead girl, Cora thought. *Yasmine, come to take her dress back.*

Cora grasped the charm around her neck as though it could protect her. The girl stepped out of the shadows, and light fell on her face.

Not Yasmine. Mali.

"The Warden sent you to remove me, didn't he?" Cora had to shout over the rain. She wiped the rain from her face, trying to see better, tasting salty tears. She pictured cages and drugged children. Herself in a toga, forced to do tricks.

Mali crouched in the mud. "No one sends me." Her eyes slid to the nearest black window. She pinched her shoulder. "I decide on my own to help you escape."

The rain was so loud that Cora thought she must have misunderstood. But Mali's eyes were unflinching.

"Why?"

Mali stood abruptly, rain dripping off her eyelashes. "Follow me. I will take you to a place where the Kindred cannot easily read our minds."

She moved faster than Cora had ever seen anyone go. Cora sprinted behind her. The rain lightened as they neared the edge of the jungle. The walkway gave way to stone through the swamp, and then sand as they entered the desert. The maze loomed a hundred feet away, but Mali veered away from it. She led Cora up the highest dune. From the top, they could see all eight habitats.

Cora doubled over to catch her breath. "*This* is where we can speak privately? It's the most exposed place in the entire cage."

Mali folded her legs and collapsed cross-legged in the sand. "Sometimes it is easier to hide in plain sight. It is not ourselves we try to hide, but our minds. The fewer distractions, the better." She pointed toward the dunes that stretched for miles, endless and monotonous, the perfect place for meditation.

Cora hesitantly sat across from her. "How can I trust you?"

"You have no choice." A crease formed in the center of her forehead. "You say that in the menagerie you see a girl with shorn blond hair and two missing fingers."

Drugged girls. Forced kisses. She nodded.

"Her name is Anya," Mali said. "Three years ago we are privately owned by the same Kindred official. He sells four of her knuckles to the Mosca. He tries to do the same to me, but Cassian rescues us before he can. Anya and I are separated. The Kindred later tell me she dies from an infection." Mali leaned close, a braid falling in her eyes. "But they lie."

Below, the town and the eight habitats looked like a perfect doll village. A world of lies.

Mali pushed back her fallen braid. "If we can escape this enclosure, I know the paths through the aggregate station. If you help me free Anya, then I will take you to the market and the Mosca. They help escaped humans sometimes. For the right price. Your hair will fetch a ship. Information is more expensive. A finger to know if Earth is still there. Maybe two."

She spoke so casually. Cora ran her thumb over her knuckles, feeling the hardness beneath flesh. "I'll give them all ten fingers and ten toes, if that's what it takes."

"We first must discover the location of the fail-safe exit," Mali said. "That is one thing I do not know."

"I think . . . I think I do." Cora rubbed her knuckles harder. "It has to be in the ocean. It's the only habitat that doesn't have a puzzle, and sometimes it shimmers in a strange way. It gives me a headache, like the other optical illusions." She looked off at the ocean uneasily. That deep water, nearly as dark as the river water that had swallowed her. She turned away from it with a shudder. "While I test my theory, I need you to talk to the others. They think you're on their side and that you know everything about the Kindred. Try to convince them that it's worth coming with us."

Mali frowned. "We should just go. You and me."

A breeze carried sand across Cora's dress. Artificial wind. Artificial sand. To Mali, who had spent most of her life here, the difference was negligible. But to Cora, it was everything. "One day, when we're back on Earth, you'll understand why I can't leave them here."

Mali considered this while she toyed with a braid. "I will try to convince Lucky. The others might listen to him."

"Good. Then tonight, after dinner, we'll meet by the movie theater. If everything goes right, we'll be out of here by tomorrow. I'll help you find Anya."

Mali nodded. The sun dimmed as she unfolded her long legs to head back to town. Cora didn't follow right away. She wanted one final look over their cage: the distant mountain, the red barn, the cherry tree where Lucky had told her about their shared past. The colors were brighter than they were on Earth; the temperature more even, and the weather more predictable. But she would trade a gray, rainy day in the city for a lifetime of all the brightest colors in the world.

At the base of the dune, ocean waves lapped gently on the

beach. A perfect scene straight from a postcard, and yet Cora recoiled. Ever since plunging over that bridge, she'd avoided deep water. That night had changed her. Before the accident, she had thought her father ruled the world. Afterward, she saw him for what he was: just a man, as insecure as everyone else, easily manipulated by his own daughter.

She forced herself to take a step, and then another, as sweat broke out on her temples. The thought of that cold water eating up her toes and her ankles and her waist left her shaken, but she had no choice. She took a deep breath and walked faster, then ran, and crashed into the sea with all the force she could manage. She didn't think about the murky depths or the salty chill as she waded deeper. She tensed her muscles to dive.

A force as unyielding as gravity stopped her.

Her head was roaring so much that she had hardly noticed the pressure building. It wasn't until Cassian's arms were around her, preventing her from going underwater with a grip hard enough to bruise, with raw emotion on his face—desperation— that she knew she was right. His gloves were gone, and the clips on his shirt were only half closed. The materialization apparatus jutted out of his bare skin at the base of his rib cage, where a metal port had been grafted into his body. The metallic skin around it was streaked with angry black veins, as though he hadn't had time to properly connect to the device. She flinched at the sight. He must have dropped everything to stop her.

But he couldn't stop her, not when she was this close.

He pushed her back to the shallow surf. "Don't, Cora. You can't do it. Your mind isn't strong enough."

She started. His voice was different. Less rigid. Startlingly human. Was he *uncloaked*? A rush of curiosity swelled. *You do not know what I am like, when I am uncloaked.* But she ignored her curiosity. He wouldn't be stopping her unless she was right. She had solved the last of the puzzles—the only one that really mattered.

The exit.

50

Cora

THE OCEAN WAVES WENT on crashing, even when everything else in Cora's world had ground to a halt. The salt air beckoning her toward the exit she knew was just beneath those waves—if only Cassian weren't holding her back.

More than just his voice had changed. It was his eyes. They had always been fathomlessly black, but they were cloudy now, like a broken storm, clearing into something that looked drastically more human.

Her lips parted. "Your eyes—"

"Don't," he said again, his voice so warm and rich and varied as his fingers knitted against her. "Don't go in the water. Your mind can't handle it."

Cora's head spun, still thrown off by seeing raw emotions in a man she had thought practically mechanical. "That's the way out, isn't it? I figured it out in your quarters, when you were telling me the real reason the Warden took us."

"Yes." His heart was beating wildly through his shirt. "Yes, that's the way out, but it's impossible for humans to pass through. Your physical body can do it—it's just a matter of swimming down far enough—but your mind won't let you do what it believes is impossible. You'd have to go beyond the point where you could swim back to the surface." His hand wove through her hair, and she closed her eyes, overcome by this new side of him. "You shouldn't have been able to perceive it. It's true that they've been monitoring you for signs of perceptive ability, but none of you have yet exhibited any, despite the extents to which they've pushed your minds."

"I don't have to be psychic to be smart." Her voice sounded certain, and yet her thoughts wavered. Was deduction really all there was to it? There'd been that time the ocean had shimmered so strangely. The time in the bookstore when her vision and balance had pulsed.

She stared at the waves that weren't waves at all, but just more illusions, wondering what it all meant. One of Cassian's hands still tangled in her hair and the other pulled at her waist, refusing to let her go, flooding her with that spark.

His storm-cloud eyes searched hers. "What are you thinking? Tell me."

His frantic request threw her off—she was so used to him reading her mind—until she remembered that he couldn't read minds when his own was flooded with emotions.

I'm thinking about you, she thought, knowing he couldn't read her. *Seeing you like this, uncloaked and real, as desperate as I am.*

"I can't stay here," she said. "None of us can. Through the ocean is the only way." A breeze sent a spray around them. A drop landed on the shoulder of his uniform. She touched it with the pad of her finger. "Don't you understand? None of this is real. We can't live like that."

"Not everything is an illusion." His hands pawed at her waist. "There are real oceans out there, on other planets. I'll get permission to take you there. I'll show you an ocean, or dogs, or the stars—I'll show you whatever you want, as long as you stay here."

His breath was straining against the machinery strapped to his chest. He wanted her to be like Charlie's pet rat, taken out to ride on his shoulder, but at the end of the day, always locked back in his cage.

She closed her eyes so she didn't have to look at his. Those dark eyes, the scar on the side of his neck, the nights he spent sleepless. They were more alike than she wanted to admit. She thought of that single chair in his quarters. Why hadn't she seen until then how alone they both were?

Cora had wanted so badly to feel normal for once. She hadn't belonged in Bay Pines, and she hadn't belonged back home either. Maybe she would never belong: maybe there were certain people, like her, meant to live between worlds. Cassian too. The only Kindred who felt sympathy for humans and a desire to understand them, not use them.

"I can do it," Cora whispered. "I figured out the puzzle was there without perceptive abilities, so I know I can make it through."

His hands pulled her close enough to whisper, with a voice so human she could close her eyes and almost pretend he was. "Stay here. With me. The things I have done . . ." He stopped, and swallowed. "I've made so many mistakes, Cora."

She didn't know which mistakes he was talking about, but it didn't matter. They had both made so many. In that moment, more had changed than just his eyes. In her, or in him, she wasn't sure. When she had first seen him, she had thought him such a terrifyingly beautiful creature. Their captor. Their jailer. He was still those things to her, but he was something more. She didn't want to put a word on it, and she didn't know how she even would, but she knew it had to do with the times he had asked her what it meant to be human.

This was what had changed, and it was so devastatingly simple: she had become a person to him; he had become a person to her. Human, Kindred—it didn't matter. It was just her, and him, standing in the sea.

His hand grazed the constellation markings on her neck. She couldn't help but think about Lucky, who drew her to him as if they'd been made for each other—exactly as the Kindred engineered it. She and Lucky had everything needed to fall in love: attraction, respect, a shared past she hadn't even known about. But in the same way the trees here were not quite trees, and the fruit was not quite fruit, the Kindred had misjudged something about humanity, and people, and the connections between humans. Love wasn't just a combination of matching physical and personal criteria. It was something you couldn't put into words, just a certainty, a twist of fate, a spark.

As much as Lucky drew her to him, she had never felt that spark. Not like she did with Cassian.

She pulled away, covering her face with her hands.

"Cora," he murmured, and then said her name again and again. She was shaking so hard that she leaned her head against his chest and thought about how before him, before this place, everyone thought of her as a victim—her family, her classmates, the media, even Lucky. But Cassian had never looked at her that way. He had always known that beneath the smile she'd been told to wear, she was strong.

Cora started crying because she didn't want this, and it was wrong, and she didn't know anything about him. Cassian might have been Mali's hero, but he could never be hers. How unfair, then, that suddenly she felt closer to him than anyone.

He touched a hand to her cheek. "Tell me what you're feeling."

He knew, just as she knew, that what was happening between them was wrong. That he couldn't fall in love with a human and she couldn't fall in love with her captor, but here they were.

"Please," he whispered. "Whatever you ask, it's yours. Just tell me that you feel—"

"Stop." Her hand went to his lips, silencing him. "Don't say that."

His muscles were tensing and untensing as he gave up the last remnants of his fight to cloak his emotions. He rubbed a hand over the bump in his nose, turned his head to the side and cursed. He was acting just like . . . a person. And that scared her most of all.

"Cloak your emotions again," she ordered.

"I don't want to. You asked what I was like in my private life. Let me show you." He leaned in, touching his forehead to hers, his lips a breath away. "You captivated me. I knew you were different. Strong. So full of potential. You baffled the researchers. You baffled me too. I did everything I could to understand you, and you were still a mystery."

His chin started to tilt toward hers. His lips parted. "I want to know what it feels like," he whispered.

My god. He was going to kiss her, and it was so wrong, and so was how badly she wanted him to.

She turned her head at the last second. "Don't. If you cared for me, you'd help me escape."

He balled his fists and straightened, trying to gain control over his emotions. He was a jealous person, she hadn't forgotten. And Mali had said they were unpredictable when their emotions were uncloaked. As much as Cora wanted to think of him as human right now, she had to remind herself that he wasn't.

He took a step away from her, pacing in the surf. "Is that what you want? To be away from me?"

"We weren't meant to live behind bars."

"What you are asking me goes against logic. You want to leave this place—leave me—when I've so recently discovered that you remaining close is the only thing I truly want."

She urged her foot to take a step closer. Her hand drifted to her collar, to the charm necklace that tied her to a different world. She didn't stop until she felt the heat from his body.

"I know," she said. "I'm still asking."

"Here I can at least see you, and touch you, and keep you safe from those who might do you harm. Why would I help you when I would lose even that?"

"Because I'd never be happy here. And caring about some-one means you would sacrifice your own happiness for theirs."

"That is a human way of looking at things. Not Kindred."

"Well, you said you wanted to understand humanity." He was silent, though he paced through the surf with his storm-cloud eyes still on her, and she added, "I'm not asking you to break the rules. I don't want you to be punished. Just look the other way."

He regarded her steadily, trying perhaps to see around his own mental blocks and read her thoughts. He put one hand around the back of her neck and moved closer.

His lips touched hers.

The flood of electricity broke through the dam of her lips and flowed into her chest, her arms, her head. She steadied herself against him. He hadn't kissed before. It was stiff and hungry, but he had seen her and Lucky kissing, and Nok and Rolf. He knew what it looked like. He threaded his fingers though her hair like Lucky had. Cora let everything go, then. She didn't care if other Kindred were watching.

She kissed him back, showing him how a kiss was meant to be, though she hardly knew either. He learned fast. His people might not kiss, but she could tell by his heart thumping under her hand that he enjoyed it, that he responded to it the same way humans did. Quick breath. Radiating warmth. Hands running over every inch of her back, arms, waist, like he had imagined this all in his head a thousand times. Everywhere he touched her rippled in goose bumps. He wasn't careful and gentle with her, not like Lucky had been. He knew she wouldn't break.

He was so warm, so full of energy and life that Cora never wanted to never let go. But she had to.

She pulled away from the kiss. He kept his arms around her as she closed her eyes, grounding herself in the coppery smell of his uniform. Something had happened here. They had crossed a line there was no going back from. It was a mistake—but some mistakes were worth making.

"Go at night," he said. "The ocean isn't as deep as it appears;

there's a pressure lens separating it from an equipment chamber beneath. You have to swim down far enough to reach it. The pressure will increase to the point where continuing feels impossible, but it's not. You'll break through the pressure lens. After that, you're on your own."

"Won't the Warden and his researchers be watching?"

His eyes had returned to black, but his emotions were not totally gone. He pressed his lips to her forehead very softly, and then whispered a few words in her ear before letting her go.

"Leave them to me."

He dematerialized, leaving her alone in the crashing waves.

51

Cora

CORA SPENT THE AFTERNOON hidden within the boughs of the cherry tree, until it was time to rendezvous with Mali. The jukebox music came, signaling dinner, and she heard the others' voices chatting as they ate, then the crack of mallet against wooden ball as they played croquet beneath the stars.

Cora flinched at each crack, remembering Rolf slamming it into the pumpkin. She drew her knees closer. She hoped desperately that Mali had talked to Lucky, and that he'd been able to convince the others. Otherwise, it might be her head under that mallet.

Once the cage was quiet, and the house lights turned off one by one, Cora crawled from her hiding place and ran toward the side of the movie theater. She paced nervously, jumping at every shadow. She watched the house lights carefully, praying the others were all heavy sleepers. At last the sound of footsteps came, and Cora sighed with relief.

"Mali—"

But she froze. In the starlight, a tattooed face stared back at her.

"Going to leave us, sweetheart?" Leon grabbed her before she could run. "I don't think so."

Her heart shot to her throat.

"I wasn't going to leave you!" she stuttered. "Please, Leon, keep your voice down. Don't wake the others. . . ."

"I saw you out there with that black-eyed bastard. I was under the boardwalk. I heard you say you were going to escape and he would help you." His voice bellowed. A light turned on in an upstairs bedroom, and Cora cringed.

"It's true—I do know the way out, but I'm not leaving without you. Why do you think I'm still here?"

Rolf appeared in the house's doorway, the military jacket slung over his thin bare chest, Nok behind him. Anger twisted their features. They tumbled out of the house just as Mali came down the trail, a few minutes too late. Her eyes darted to Cora's, heavy with warning.

"What are you doing here?" Nok yelled. "They're taking away my baby because of you!"

Cora straightened. What was Nok talking about?

Mali leaned close to Cora. "I cannot convince them. They strongly dislike you."

"Yeah—I figured that out," Cora whispered back. "I was right about the ocean, but we have to leave tonight. Cassian's distracting the other Kindred." She glanced at Rolf, who scooped up one of the croquet mallets. "But we'll have to get through them first."

"If it comes to this I am ready." Mali cracked her knuckles. Cassian had said that Mali was an incredible fighter, so she might be able to handle Rolf, maybe even Rolf and Nok, but not Leon too.

"Where's Lucky?" Cora asked.

Nok tossed her pink hair back, narrowed her eyes. "He left. He couldn't stand to be here anymore after you tried to kill him."

Cora chewed on the inside of her cheek. She couldn't leave without Lucky. Maybe they weren't soul mates, maybe they'd hurt each other, but she owed him this one thing.

"Things have changed, Nok. I know how to get us out of here. We can leave tonight, if you'll just come with me."

"Escape?" Rolf shook his head. "You really are stupid, aren't you? There's no way out of here."

Leon paced in front of her. "Oh, she'll be just fine. She's got the Caretaker on her side. I heard it myself. He's protecting her. She kissed him, right out in the ocean."

There was a moment of stunned silence. Cora couldn't deny it. In their eyes, she was already the enemy, and this just distanced her even further.

"It doesn't matter," Nok said, breaking the tension. "Serassi gave me a device I can use to reach her, in case there's a problem with the pregnancy. It's in my bedroom. If you leave, I'll raise the alarm. Not even the Caretaker will be able to help you."

Cora looked to Mali desperately, who cracked her knuckles a few times, stretching her neck like she was warming up for a fight. Rolf was blinking up a storm, fingers tap-tap-tapping, one eye wincing like his head throbbed.

"I'm not letting you do it, Cora." He pressed his hands against his temples. "They're taking away our baby because of *your* violent outburst with Lucky. They're taking away all the artifacts from Earth, because *you* used one as a weapon. If you try to escape now, they'll think we're too rebellious and take away the habitats, or the shops, or chain us up."

Rolf hefted the mallet and started for her. Rolf, quiet little Rolf, who Cora was certain hadn't hurt a fly before.

Mali cracked her knuckles one more time.

"Wait!" Cora scrambled against the movie theater wall. "Wait! If the Kindred aren't going to let you keep your baby, don't you want to raise it back home, where it can be free?"

"Freedom doesn't mean anything." Rolf clenched his jaw, as though a bolt of pain ripped through his skull. "We were free at home, and we were miserable, all of us. You want to send me back to those bullies? You want to send Nok back to the tiny apartment where she was a glorified prostitute? I won't let you!"

Glorified prostitute? Now it all made sense—Nok's lies and evasions about her life in London. But before Cora could think, Rolf raised the croquet mallet. Time fractured like a kaleidoscope. Mali sprang forward to stop him, but Leon lunged with a growl. They rolled to the ground, clawing at each other. Nok jumped back just before the two of them reached her.

Cora was left facing Rolf. He raised the croquet mallet.

"Karl Crenshaw!" she screamed, throwing her arms over her head. "Karl Crenshaw hit you with a cricket bat and nearly killed you. Cricket bat, croquet mallet—it's the same thing. Is that who you want to be, Rolf? A bully? A *murderer*?"

His eyes were blinking like mad, the muscles in his jaw twitching, but the croquet mallet paused above his head.

"That's not you," she continued in a rush, fighting against her own throbbing head. "That's not who you want to become."

He staggered back, just as Mali slammed her foot into Leon's face. Blood spurted everywhere. Cora grabbed the mallet from Rolf's hand and threw it to the ground. His grip on it was loosened, the mallet already forgotten. Rolf sank to his knees in the grass, looking dazed.

"Rolf, don't listen to her!" Nok screamed.

The croquet mallet gleamed in the light from the streetlamps. Still within reach. Rolf's eyes shifted to it, debating.

Cora's heart pumped harder. "Nok is trying to manipulate you, Rolf. I heard her on the porch hitting on Lucky. She's been sleeping with Leon too."

"She's lying," Nok snapped, cheeks bright red. All eyes went to Leon, who wiped the blood from his face and didn't deny anything.

Rolf's fingers started tapping again. He looked confused, like the past few weeks hadn't happened and he'd just woken here.

This is how it ends, Cora thought. *With our bleached bones buried beneath the sand.*

"Is that true, Leon?" Rolf asked in a deadly quiet voice.

Leon put a hand to his head, wincing like Mali's last punch had jarred him too hard. "She threw herself at me, brother. Sorry."

"*Sorry?* Sorry, that's it?"

Leon coughed, still wiping away blood. "What do you want, a greeting card?"

Rolf shot back something about Leon deserving to be alone, how Yasmine would have hated him, and Leon's entire body went rigid.

Cora took a step back.

Mali's hot breath came in her ear. "If we do not leave now, I do not think we will have another chance."

Rolf and Leon started throwing insults like punches. It wouldn't be long before they were trading real blows. Across from them, Nok was taking small steps backward, glancing over her shoulder at the house. Rolf suddenly lunged for the croquet mallet, and Cora dropped to the grass, afraid of the crossfire when he swung it at Leon's face. Her mind flashed to that first day, the fight between the two of them in the toy store. *I'll owe you that punch,* Rolf had said, and now he meant it. He was quick, just like his twitching fingers, and he was back on his feet before Leon could catch him.

Rolf let out a furious yell and hurled himself forward—at Nok. Not Leon. Rolf tackled her to the ground, using the mallet to pin her arms as she screamed wildly. Leon was still braced to duck the blow that was less and less likely to come.

"You said you loved me!" Rolf choked, ignoring her pleas. "I saw the way you looked at Lucky and Leon, but you told me I was just being paranoid!"

Nok screamed something in a mix of Thai and English, struggling to get away.

Cora pushed to her feet. "Rolf—"

Rolf threw Cora a look over his shoulder. "Just go! Get out of here! This is between me and Nok."

Beneath him, Nok gave one final twist, uselessly. Suddenly all the fight rushed out of her and she started sobbing, big racking tears that didn't seem like acting at all. Nok's whole life had been a struggle, it seemed. Rolf's words had been enough to put together a picture of a life in London that wasn't the jet-setting dream, but rather dirty rooms and flashing lights and bruises hidden beneath flimsy little dresses.

Rolf blinked a few times. "I won't hurt her," he said. His voice had grown softer, just like his grip on Nok, anger melting away into devastation. "I would never hurt her. But leave us alone; you never belonged here. If you can get out, then go. Whatever the consequences for us . . ." He swallowed hard, looking at Nok sobbing. "We have bigger worries right now."

Cora glanced over her shoulder toward the churning sea. "Come with us," she said.

He shook his head. "I can't. Chances are it's my baby. We might not be free, but we're safe here, and right now that's more important for the baby. But Lucky might go. Try the boardwalk. He walks there at night when he can't sleep."

The light overhead shifted. Mali pinched herself anxiously, throwing glances toward the ocean. Cora knew she would never see either Nok or Rolf again, but good-byes felt wrong. Her lips wouldn't form the words, so she turned instead, blinking hard to clear her eyes, striding toward the ocean.

"Cora, wait," Rolf called.

She turned, brushing the moisture from beneath her eyes. Nok was still sobbing, oblivious of everything. Rolf rubbed the marks on his neck slowly. "You were right, in the medical room. I was studying their technology. Those blue cubes above the doors are amplifiers. Destroy them, and the Kindred won't be able to open the doors with their minds. It might buy you some time. I'll make sure Nok doesn't sound the alarm. Now just go."

Over her shoulder, the waves were crashing. Beckoning. Mali tugged on her arm.

"Thank you," she whispered. He gave a curt nod, his attention already back on Nok. Cora turned to Leon. "It's not too late."

He cracked his knuckles anxiously, keeping a good distance from Mali, looking toward the ocean, then back toward the jungle. "I can't. This is where Yasmine is. Her ghost won't let me go."

Mali grabbed Cora, and they started running for the beach. Cora didn't look over her shoulder to see them all one last time, because she knew their faces would be burned into the space behind her eyelids.

They raced to the boardwalk, where a figure heard them coming and stood from the deck chair, in the darkness looking as vague as the night sky.

His hand drifted to the side of his skull, where Cora had hit him.

The last time she and Lucky had spoken, she had hurt him deeply. A broken head and a broken heart. She was supposed to be his partner, his match. That rainy night on the bridge would forever tie them together. He had lost his mother. Cora had spent eighteen months locked up.

But Lucky was wrong when he thought being here could be a fresh start. There were no fresh starts for caged birds. There was only as much freedom as their captors wished to give them.

His eyes found hers beneath the stars.

"Lucky." Her breath fogged in the air. "We're getting out of here. Come with us."

He didn't answer. He didn't seem surprised at all.

"I know about you and the Caretaker," he said.

52

Cora

FEAR THREADED THROUGH CORA'S veins. "Did Leon tell you?"

"The Caretaker told me himself." Lucky took a step forward, his face unreadable. "He came to visit me last night. He said you were asleep in his bed. He didn't say anything outright, just that I could have whatever I wanted if I left you alone. To tell him the type of girl I wanted and he'd give her to me." He looked toward the sea, because it must have been easier than looking at her. "I told him the girl I wanted was you."

"Lucky, I didn't know—"

"I didn't believe him. I thought he was tricking me, but he wasn't, was he?"

She swallowed. "No."

"Jesus. Why?"

"You loved me because I was a victim. But I never was, Lucky. I was the one who came up with the idea to take the fall for my dad." A month ago, if she'd met Lucky, she'd have fallen like a comet for him. She clasped her necklace as if she could hold on to that girl she'd been before, but then she released it. "Cassian knew that. He sees me as someone who can save herself."

Lucky touched the place on the side of his head where she had hit him. Cora had expected he would be furious at her. Crazed. She hadn't expected such heartbreaking hurt in his eyes.

He shook his head. "Just go. You never needed someone to protect you, I can see that now."

He turned toward the boardwalk, but Cora grabbed his arm. "You always wanted to be a hero, Lucky, but you don't need a victim for that. Be your own hero. Come with us."

Mali glanced over her shoulder, and Cora felt nervous too.

"Please, Lucky. We can go back. Earth is there, I know it."

His head tilted toward the stars that shone over a red desert, snow-covered mountains, a town where they might have been amused but never truly happy. Would the Kindred take Nok and Rolf and Leon away? Without humans, this place would be meaningless.

Lucky turned away from the shops and habitats that had made up their artificial world, facing the ocean instead.

"Let's go home."

THE THREE OF THEM stood in the sand, letting the surf whisper to their toes. "You have to swim without stopping," Cora said. "There will be a pressure lens. You have to push past."

Lucky and Mali listened intently, then waded fearlessly past the breakers. But Cora hung back. She hadn't been in water over her head since the accident. The rush of pure cold pouring in the car windows, up through the gearshifts. These crashing waves were mild and warm, but they still drenched her with fear. She waded deeper, crunching the sand with her toes, and didn't panic until the moment when a wave lifted her up and her toes didn't touch the ocean floor when she bobbed back down.

She treaded water with quick, jerky movements. *Breathe. Count backward from ten.*

Ten. Nine. Eight . . .

Lucky was a good swimmer. Mali's strokes were jerkier, less practiced, but she was strong where the others weren't: she knew the Kindred's mind games. Even if she'd never faced a puzzle like this before, she could handle the psychological pressure.

"Are you sure you can do this?" Lucky asked.

Cora took a deep breath. *Seven . . .*

"I'm sure." As soon as Cora answered, she hit a cold patch in the ocean. It chilled her certainty. She recalled Cassian's kiss and his whispered words. *Leave them to me.* He wouldn't lie to her, would he? Lying would mean death for them—and she'd looked into his storm-cloud eyes. She'd seen raw emotions there. The last thing he wanted was their deaths.

Six. Five . . .

That was what kept her going. She wasn't paddling toward death. She was paddling toward life.

Four . . .

Toward home.

"Countdown. On one, we dive," she said. The stars overhead shone brightly. A strange nostalgia crept over her. From here, she could see the diner lights still flashing, hear the jukebox music still playing.

"*Three*," Lucky said.

Cora thought about Nok, and Rolf, and Leon, and what would happen to them. Yasmine's ghost would haunt this same water. When death had come to her, Cora hoped it had been quick.

"*Two*," Lucky said.

Cora's lungs started to close up. She wondered if she would ever see Cassian again.

"*One.*"

Their heads disappeared, just as Cora filled her lungs. A second before she dived below, a figure appeared on the beach. There was no mistaking his hulking shape as he came tearing into the water.

Leon. He'd changed his mind.

But Cora was already underwater. There was no going back up. Water stung her nose. Her hair floated away. She felt like a ghost herself, like Yasmine was down there, calling to her, wanting to pull Cora down too.

Cora followed her ghost. Yasmine's death, Cora's life. With each stroke the pressure grew. The water grew colder, unnaturally so. Salt water filled her eyes, or maybe it was tears. The others were nowhere. Her chest was imploding, insisting it was time to go back for air.

She pushed past her instincts. There was no going back. The darkness was complete, a universe with no stars. And cold. The ocean really did go on forever. She imagined she was back in her father's car with river water rushing in. What if he'd never broken the door window? Time confused itself, and she was back there, trapped in the car. She thrashed against the seat belt and the dashboard and the floor. She stroked, and stroked, and bubbles burst around her as her lungs squeezed out the last breath of air. She screamed into the silent water.

She couldn't swim anymore. Her arms burned. Her lungs

demanded oxygen that wasn't there. Only water. And water. And water. No pressure lens.

Cassian wouldn't lie to me.

Her arms threatened to give out. She had nothing left in her, no heart, no soul. She saved her last thought for her mother, and father, and brother. She remembered a hike they had taken up Blood Mountain, when Sadie had been a puppy, when her father had just been a lawyer from Roanoke and her mother an aspiring actress and it was the four of them against the world. She wanted to go back to that time. And Charlie. She wanted to be in the airplane on Charlie's first flight as a pilot and be there on Sadie's last day. Most of all, she wanted to tell them that she loved them.

A calmness overtook her. The ache in her arms slowly abated. The pain through her body dissipated. If this was dying, it was quieter than she would have thought. It was black curling in at the edges of her mind, and then it was nothing.

And then, strangely, she breathed.

Air.

Cold seeped through her back, water choking her lungs; wet hair streaked her face. She blinked her eyes open and saw her own hand resting on a cold metal floor the pattern of woodgrain. Light the color of the stars bled through gaps in the walls. Her middle finger twitched.

She coughed up water, and sucked in a lungful of air.

She was alive.

53

Rolf

THE TOWN SQUARE FELT too empty without the others. Rolf had watched them disappear into the night, leaving only him and Nok, who had sobbed for ten minutes before her anger bubbled up in one last surge, and she started struggling again. Weeks ago, he'd never have had the strength to keep her from running to the house to summon Serassi. But hiking up the mountain to sled had given him stamina, and throwing apples in the farm puzzle had built muscles in his thin arms. Nok tried to claw at the ground, but he pinned her wrist.

"Not yet. I'm sorry."

"This is how you treat someone you love? Who's going to be the mother of your *child*?"

Hot fury flashed behind Rolf's eyes, pulsing in time with his aching head. She was trying to manipulate him again. It was so obvious now. As he looked around at the perfectly still trees and buildings of the cage, he felt a strangeness that unsettled him. Over the past few weeks he'd gotten used to the paths that looped them back to their starting place; he'd even stopped thinking it strange that such a beautiful girl had fallen for him. Now, anger built in him until he wanted to squeeze Nok's wrists so hard she'd cry out.

He'd done everything for her, and it still wasn't enough.

"You said you loved me too." He didn't recognize the hard edge in his voice. "You lied."

"Hell yes, I lied! I would never love you . . . you twitchy . . . stupid . . . boy!" Tears mixed with her insults. "Did you think I'd love you because you were kind to me? Because you were patient with me? Because for the first time in my life someone looked at more than my legs? I *hate* you. I do. I swear. I . . . I . . ."

She broke down into sobs. She stopped struggling and curled into herself instead, trying to hug her knees close. He let go of her hesitantly, ready to tackle her again if she tried to run, but she only sobbed harder, rocking back and forth like she had the first day. The pink streak in her hair was caught in her eyelashes, damp with her tears. She suddenly shoved it back angrily.

"I *do* love you, you idiot! Of course I do!"

His anger melted away with hers. He watched her rocking and crying, and started to touch her knee but stopped his hand. He loved her, but could he trust her?

"Then why did you cheat on me? Lucky was my friend. And Leon's a complete ass."

"It wasn't about them. It wasn't about sex at all. It was about creating a stable world for our baby. Not just getting the boys loyal to us, but Mali and Cora too. The boys were just easier to work with, because boys only want one thing. My talent manager in London, Delphine . . . I spent years watching how she made men fall in love with her. She built an empire out of manipulating men. Their money. Their connections. The stability she got from that. I learned from her, even if I didn't want to. I was afraid you and I wouldn't be enough. Not so far from home. Not in a place where anything could happen. I needed all of us together on this—and I tried to do it the only way I know how."

Rolf stared at her. Part of him still wanted to hurt her back, hurl insults just like she had. Call her a cheater. Call her manipulative. But then he surprised even himself.

He started laughing.

It was filled with pain and bitterness. He doubled over, supporting himself in the grass, his stomach cramped with angry laughter mixed with tears. It wasn't until he had wrung himself out like a sponge that she pushed the pink streak out of her face.

"What's so funny, then?" she asked sharply.

"You. And me. This place. We've both become the one thing that tormented us most back on Earth. I became Karl Crenshaw, my old bully, and you became Delphine. Cora was right about this place. It isn't paradise. And the Kindred . . ." His fingers curled in the hard earth. "Maybe they aren't what we thought they were." His fingers started twitching, *tap tap tap*, all his old fears and old bad habits coming back in full force. He pushed at the bridge of his nose where his glasses used to rest.

Some genius.

"I should have seen it. I'm an idiot—"

Nok grabbed his hand, holding his fingers still. "No. Don't ever say that. You're brilliant and that's why I love you. But you're not perfect, and neither am I. It doesn't matter." Her jaw was set with determination.

The feeling came back into Rolf's arms. He dared to look at her and saw sincerity in the lines of her face. He pulled her into his arms, breathing in the scent of her smooth hair, feeling her heartbeat against his. His skin tingled like it was on fire. It wasn't until the hair started rising on his arms that he realized pressure was building.

Nok went rigid in his arms. "Behind you," she whispered in a frightened voice.

He whirled, holding Nok tightly, expecting to see the Caretaker. Cora had said he would help the escape; maybe he'd come to make sure Nok and Rolf posed no further threat to her.

But the Kindred who materialized wasn't the Caretaker. It was a woman, and as her body took shape, he recognized the painfully tight bun, the high cheekbones.

The medical officer. Serassi.

His head spun to Nok, but she shook her head emphatically. "I didn't summon her. I promise. You've been with me the entire time."

"But if you didn't, why is she here? The Caretaker was supposed to—"

His words were cut off as Serassi approached. Behind her, another figure began to materialize. Tessela, the substitute Caretaker. Yet another figure materialized behind her. A male Kindred who Rolf had never seen, big as the Caretaker, with a long row of knots down the side of his uniform and a permanent scowl that formed heavy wrinkles between his eyes. Two more Kindred men materialized behind him.

Rolf pulled Nok closer as the team of Kindred approached.

"Rolf..." There was fear in her voice. He held her tightly. He would never let them be separated.

"This enclosure is being temporarily shut down," Serassi said in her mechanical voice. "This cohort has failed. I have instructions to take you to a holding cell in the medical chambers until the Warden determines what is to be done with you."

"The Warden?" Rolf clutched Nok tighter. Cora had told them about the Warden, the ruthless Kindred who had tried to strangle her their very first day, whose forehead was knotted with angry wrinkles.

Rolf's eyes went to the Kindred man with the hardened face. His scowl formed a deep vertical wrinkle between his eyes. Wasn't *that* the man Cora had described? Could there be more than one Kindred with the same description? Usually Rolf was good at thinking things through, but none of this made any sense. "Where's the Caretaker? Where's Cassian? We need to see him, right now."

The Kindred all stopped. Serassi cocked her head, as though for once her impassive mask might drop to reveal some true emotion; but then she straightened, and the mask instantly returned. Behind her, one of the Kindred took out an apparatus that looked like a weapon.

"Cassian is the one who gave the order for us to come. He notified us of your exact position." Serassi removed two sets of shackles from her pocket. "Cassian *is* the Warden."

Nok let out a small cry, and Rolf held her tighter. His head ached, and so did his heart. He cast a look in the direction of the ocean, where the others had disappeared, and wondered if they knew they were walking directly into a trap.

54

Cora

THE CHAMBER WHERE CORA had awakened was filled with machinery that hummed a hundred times louder than the black windows. Cassian had called it an equipment chamber, but she didn't see any vents or buttons or moving parts, only cubes upon cubes, the ones Rolf had said were amplifiers, arranged in what looked like a haphazard order—but nothing about the Kindred was haphazard.

Lying on her back, she could see the ocean stretched out overhead, a beautiful, dancing dome of water. It reminded her of an aquarium her father had taken her to, where sharks swam overhead. Only there was no glass now. If she had been tall enough, she could have touched water, come away with the smell of salt. Once or twice she though she saw a star on the other side.

We made it.

She was alive—and so were Lucky and Mali, collapsed on either side of her, stunned but breathing steadily.

Mali jerked awake and coughed up water. Her body was hunched, as though she'd bruised every muscle when she fell. Cora's own body ached in every joint. The pain made her feel wonderfully alive.

Lucky rolled onto his side, coughing. Their eyes met beneath the shimmering ocean dome. Despite everything, he smiled.

"Jesus," he said. "I thought that ocean would never end."

The thrill of victory was in their smiles, in the lightness of Cora's heart. They weren't out of the woods yet, but they were past the hardest part.

"We shouldn't stay here long," Cora said.

Mali wrung the water from her hair. "The traders are located in the lowest level. We must be cautious."

Cora nodded. They had just done the impossible, so she felt ready for anything.

"Someone came with us," Lucky said in surprise.

Cora followed his gaze to a wet patch a few yards away from them, with big wet footsteps leading to the open doorway.

"It was Leon," Cora said. "I saw him running toward us at the last minute."

Mali sniffed the puddle. "The water mostly evaporates already. He must wake long before us."

"He left us," Lucky said. "I guess I shouldn't be surprised."

Cora studied Leon's evaporating footsteps, knowing it was true, but the fact that he had left the cage was strong evidence that he had regained his sanity. "He's still rebelling against the Kindred, which means he's on our side, whether he left us or not."

They wrung the water out of their clothes so the Kindred wouldn't be able to follow the seawater trail. Every drip made Cora feel stronger. The door was propped open—Cassian had been true to his word. The only shadow in her heart was the certainty that she would never see him again. After that one glimpse of his real self, uncloaked, she wanted more. She wanted to see him smile, and laugh, and sleep at night. She rubbed her neck where the Warden had strangled her. She prayed Cassian hadn't been caught. What would the Warden do to someone on his own team who had betrayed him?

Lucky peered out the doorway. "It's clear."

Cora joined Lucky and Mali, looking up and down the impossibly long arched hallway. "Leon's tracks lead to the left."

Mali snorted. "He does not know where he goes." She pointed the opposite direction. "We must go down."

Cora frowned. "That's downhill? It looks perfectly flat."

Mali wobbled her head. Water dripped from her hair and ran in the direction she'd been pointing, though the floor appeared even. "You do not know anything about aggregate stations."

She had a good point, and Cora was happy to let her take the lead. As they jogged silently down the austere hallway, Lucky kept stopping to marvel at the light coming from the wall seams. He'd never seen those intricate archways, the metallic walls, the eerie silence like ancient monasteries.

Mali paused, listening. "I hear something."

Cora's skin started to tingle with the urge to run. What if Nok had gotten away from Rolf and sounded the alarm? The Warden would send soldiers to stop them, and Cassian would be powerless to help.

She squeezed her charm necklace. She could still feel the lingering touch of his fingers brushing her skin. Had she made a mistake in letting him take such a risk?

They waited several impossibly long seconds before continuing. The hallway abruptly branched to their left, and Mali froze. Cora heard it too.

Footsteps. Boots.

"Go the other way," Mali whispered urgently.

They followed her down the opposite direction, but the hallways only looped back. The sensation of being turned around made Cora's head throb, and Lucky kept rubbing his forehead too, but it didn't seem to affect Mali. She was faster than they were, not slowed by the strange perceptions. She disappeared around a bend, and when they stumbled after her, she was gone. The hallway stretched as far as Cora could see. Mali simply wasn't there.

Instead, five Kindred dressed in black turned the corner.

Cora skidded to a stop, choked by the sight.

"Run!" she yelled.

Lucky and Cora raced in the opposite direction, turning at each branching hallway, desperately looking for a door, but Cora had the awful feeling they were just running in circles.

She focused her thoughts and projected that she needed Cassian's help, but he must have been too far away to perceive her call, because minutes passed and he still didn't come.

Lucky slipped. Cora pulled him to his feet as they stumbled around another corner. There, at the far end, was another soldier. Black clothes, short hair, but it wasn't Cassian.

"Hurry!" Cora said, and they raced down the corridor, but the soldier was impossibly fast. He was on them in a second. His hands dug into Lucky's shoulder, and Cora knew—she *knew*—that he would never get away.

"He can't catch both of us," Lucky yelled. "Keep going!"

Cora was crying now that they had Lucky, and Mali and Leon were both gone, and she was on her own. The only way she could keep going was to tell herself that she'd come back for him. She'd head to the lowest level, and find the Mosca traders, and come back to rescue him.

She turned another corner as sweat poured down the back of her neck. A door stood at the end—a chance to hide. She threw herself against it.

Her beating heart was all she could hear as she dug her fingernails into the seam, screaming at the stupid door to open. She heard footsteps behind her and worked faster. The door didn't budge. There were no tools around, only a blue cube above the doorway.

An amplifier.

Rolf had said if she could damage it, the Kindred wouldn't be able to open the doors with their telekinesis. Maybe the opposite was also true—if she broke it, maybe she could override the door and open it by hand.

She wedged her foot in the doorway and used it as leverage to push herself up until she could grab hold of the cube. She'd been expecting something hard like plastic, but it was cold and pulsing and wet, more like ice. Shock made her let go, and she had to climb up again, her heart pounding harder.

She gripped the cube again and dropped her weight. The sudden force made the cube splinter with a jolt of electricity. She cried out as she crashed to the ground, then scrambled to the door and shoved her fingers into the seam. It opened an inch, enough to wedge her toe in. *Thank you, Rolf.* She pushed harder, and it glided open.

She stumbled through the doorway, then pushed it closed

behind her. She was in a room the size of the medical chamber, only not nearly as sparse. It was packed with a chaos of belongings, stacked on the floor, propped on a circular desk ringing nearly the entire room. Most of the clutter was unfamiliar—blue cubes of all sizes, boxes stuffed with a variety of apparatuses—but a few things seemed vaguely recognizable. Stacks of the Kindred's cerulean clothing. A communicator like Cassian wore on his wrist. Metal boxes with lids piled against the wall. It all looked haphazard, but Cora got the sense it was actually highly organized, in the same way the market had been.

She took a hesitant step into the room. Several of the black windows had been set into the walls, projecting a variety of different images. Cages. Dozens of them. Not a single one of them theirs. She took a step forward and unfolded one of the blue fabric uniforms. The material was fine, supple but strong. Cerulean, the color of authority. Fearfully, she counted the row of knots down the side.

Twenty knots. Far more than any of the other Kindred she'd seen.

She must have run straight into the Warden's personal office.

55

Cora

SHE SCRAMBLED TOWARD THE wall, but the door didn't open. She dug in her fingernails, but it wouldn't budge, no matter how hard she pulled. She must have broken it. She punched at the door. Screamed at it. Frantically, she waded back into the mess of belongings to try to find something to pry the door open. She grabbed one of the arm-length apparatuses, but it was hinged and merely slumped to the ground like liquid. She tossed it away and threw the lid off one of the metal boxes, but paused.

Comic books. Just as she had seen in the market. She pushed the first few aside, but none had a date. Her fingers caught on something hard, and she pulled out a worn hardback book. Her breath stilled as she recognized the faded cover.

Peter Pan and Wendy. Dog-eared halfway through.

The same copy from Cassian's bedroom.

Her fingers curled around the book. What did it mean, finding it here? Her mind only reached one conclusion, and a frightened sound slipped out of her throat. The Warden must have found it in Cassian's room. He must have figured out that Cassian was developing sympathies for the humans.

Had the Warden set Cassian up? Had him followed this entire time, because he knew that Cassian was no longer loyal to him?

She hugged the book tight. This explained the soldiers who'd been waiting for them to break through the fail-safe exit. The Warden must have learned of Cassian's true loyalties and gotten the information out of him. Had he tortured Cassian? Killed him? No, surely he wouldn't sacrifice one of his best soldiers. But he might have Cassian imprisoned somewhere, awaiting some awful fate.

She leaned on the desk as the strength leached out of her. They'd gotten Lucky. They'd probably gotten Mali and Leon too. Now it seemed they'd even gotten Cassian. She was trapped in the Warden's own office.

There would be no escape for her. No ride home on the Mosca traders' ship. No seeing her parents again, or Charlie, or Sadie bounding across the lawn.

She was about to slump to the floor, hugging Cassian's book as her one last tie to Earth—to him—when footsteps sounded on the other side of the door. She jerked her head around just in time to see gloved fingers wedge through the doors and manually pry them open.

She braced to fight. Braced to hurl herself at the Warden, and at least make it difficult for them to drag her away. But as soon as she saw the figure standing on the other side, she let the book clatter to the floor in surprise.

That dent in his nose. Those dark eyes filled with concern.

Cassian.

"It's you." Her voice twisted with relief as she raced for the doorway. She threw her arms around him, breathing in his scent, feeling the warmth radiating from his uniform. He wore gloves, so the electric jolt of his touch was gone, but she didn't need it to feel a spark.

"Cora." His voice was flat. He was cloaked again, but she hadn't forgotten that passion when he'd shown her his true self. It was there, below this mask. She waited for him to explain what was happening, but he was hesitating. And they couldn't afford to hesitate. She grabbed his hand and tugged him toward the door.

"We'll have to hurry. There were a lot of soldiers. They got Lucky, but there's a chance that Mali and Leon got to the Mosca's sector. We can meet them there and hide out until we can figure out how to get Lucky back. You'll have to come with us on the Mosca ship. The Warden will never forgive you, once he finds out you betrayed him. Once we're safely off the station we can talk about what comes next. Assuming Earth is still there. I can't exactly take you back with me. My parents would have a heart attack if I brought *you* home."

She was so anxious that she was rambling. She tugged on his hand harder, but it was like pulling on a metal Dumpster, impossible to budge. She tossed him a confused look.

He seemed to be in no rush.

"Cora. There are things I must tell you." He swallowed. "I told you before that I had made mistakes. Some very grave ones. I have not been honest with you—"

Confusion hardened like wax in her chest. She was about to ask what he meant when more footsteps sounded on the other side of the door. She froze. Cassian had no reaction other than to curl his fingers around hers, holding her hand, trying to comfort her.

Someone pried the door open again. She gasped as the Warden, Fian, filled the doorway. The cerulean suit that rippled like water. The row of knots down the side. The wrinkle between his eyes that made him always look angry.

She took a step backward, feeling Cassian's reassuring heat behind her. Was this why Cassian was acting so strange? Had he known the Warden was on his way? His hand still clutched hers—although at this angle, it was starting to hurt. It almost felt like he was holding on to her less for comfort, and more so that she wouldn't get away.

The Warden took a step into the room, black eyes darting between her and Cassian, and she gritted her teeth. "I swear, I'll get out again. I figured out the exit without being psychic. I opened the doors without telekinesis. We might not be evolved, but we can still outsmart you."

Fian studied her with mild uninterest and then cocked his head toward Cassian.

"We have the others secured. Boy Two is in the medical chambers after sustaining a minor injury. Girl Three is already in the holding cells. Soldiers are still in pursuit of Boy Three." His cold eyes slid to Cora. "Shall I take her to the holding cells as well?"

The room seemed to spin. Cora felt gravity pulling her like a ride at an amusement park. Why was Fian addressing Cassian with deference, when Fian was the one in charge? They were standing in Fian's office. His uniform was right there on the counter. Cassian was merely the hired help. The jailer. Disgraced and demoted to the lowest position.

"No." Cassian's voice was stiff. "I will take her myself."

"Very well, Warden."

Warden?

The word knocked the air out of her. Her head kept spinning, spinning, spinning, like the ride was going faster. He wasn't denying it. He wasn't trying to fight his way out with her. Her eyes fell on the copy of *Peter Pan and Wendy* on the floor.

Was it there because this was *Cassian's* office?

She tore away from him before he could tighten his grip. "You're... the Warden," she whispered. "You've been giving orders this entire time. Serassi, Tessela, those researchers . . . even Fian. They all work for you."

He stepped forward, towering over her. "I will explain."

"No . . . I get it now. You've been pulling the strings. You've been changing the weather, and speeding up time, and giving us headaches. You've been trying to break us—to break *me*—to see how far we can evolve."

A wave of disbelief overcame her, and she staggered against the wall. She was back in the deep of the ocean, fighting for breath, body screaming in pain. He might as well have wrapped his own two hands around her neck and strangled her, because that was what his betrayal felt like. Memories of all their times together assailed her head. The first day, where he had rescued her. The day in the bookstore where she'd admitted to herself that she was curious about him. Standing in the snow as he gave her the charm necklace back. And the kiss. The kiss was the worst memory of all, because despite everything, thinking of it still made her falter.

She had never felt so trapped, like the walls were pressing in. His black eyes took her in: the bruises on her arm where she had fallen, the salt water in her hair and damp sweat on her chest. Hope drained from her fingertips.

She didn't have words. She didn't even have thoughts, except this one: there *had* been a mole. All this time, there had been someone gathering information, learning each of their secrets, and feeding it back to their Kindred handlers. *She* had done all of that. *She* had told Cassian every last detail of their plan.

She was the mole.

His eyes found hers, and his hand started to flex at his side. Her heart twisted. It was too late for that. He couldn't pretend he felt something, when everything had been a lie.

"I will escort her to the medical sector, Fian. Leave us." Cassian reached out a hand, but Cora shied away.

"No." She took a step backward, never taking her eyes off his, until she was standing next to Fian. "I'll go with your soldier. You've already done your job." She nearly spit the last word at him. He started to speak, but she turned before he could answer and let Fian calmly slide the shackles over her wrists.

56

Cora

FIAN TOOK HER TO Serassi, who fixed the bruises on her arm methodically. Serassi didn't speak. The device in her hand didn't hum. There was only silence, which made the betrayal all the more deafening. Once Cora was healed, Serassi made her strip to her camisole and panties, and a team of Kindred came in stiff blue uniforms. One gripped her by the neck while another examined her left hand, then the right, inspecting each finger front and back like a horse at auction. A third pressed his fingers into her sides, as though counting each rib, then felt the muscles along each side of her spine. They took an excruciatingly long time prodding at her right ear.

An inspection, just as Fian had done the first day, when she'd thought he was the Warden. Cassian must have set it up that way so that he could rescue Cora, and she would start to trust him.

The team left as abruptly as they had come. She dropped to the hard floor, too shaky to stand. She imagined they were determining if she was best suited for the brothels, or the fight clubs, or the cells where children were made to do tricks. Would Cassian be the one to make the call? Maybe he'd take pity on her, after his betrayal, and spare her the Harem. Or maybe he didn't care at all.

An hour passed, maybe longer. Another Kindred came, with three knots on his uniform, and took her to a room full of plain cells. A true prison this time. When he locked the cell, she expected the hinges to groan, and the lock to *thunk*, to echo the slamming sounds of her heart. But it closed as smoothly and silently as everything in the Kindred's world.

Cora caught sight of Lucky and Mali, each locked in an individual cell a few doors down, separated from each other by an aisle. Cora tried to yell to them, but her voice only bounced around the perimeter of her cell. Lucky shouted back, but she heard nothing. Their cells must have been soundproofed.

Cora grabbed the bars.

"Are you okay?" she mouthed.

A bandage covered half his face. His other eye had a deep circle under it, but he nodded. In the cell beside his, Mali merely pressed her lips together in an expression Cora couldn't quite read, but it looked grim.

Cora let go of the bars and paced her cell, still feeling the crushing weight of Cassian's betrayal. A worry struck her, and she jerked up her head. Had Mali known all along that Cassian was the Warden? But one more glance in Mali's direction showed sunken, hollow eyes and a hardened mouth—Mali was just as disappointed as Cora was. Cassian had been Mali's friend too.

For hours, Cora paced in the cell. Serassi had given her new clothes to wear. Plain black robes with a single knot at the shoulder, which Cora could only assume was a sign of their status now, the lowest of the low. Lucky and Mali wore the same robe. The constellation markings on their necks were gone, nothing to identify them as a gender or even a number.

It was clear the Kindred weren't returning them to the cage. So what would happen to them? And what had happened to Nok and Rolf? There were no toilets, no food, which meant the Kindred couldn't be planning to keep them there for long. Words that Mali and Cassian had both hinted at scrolled through her mind: *Drugged girls. Dead girls. Private owners. Menageries.*

The door at the end of the room opened. Cassian entered.

Cora looked away. She didn't want to see those lips she had kissed. Those eyes that had cleared like storm clouds. His approaching footsteps were heavy and slow. From the corner of her eye, she saw his fingers curl around the bars of her cell. She could almost convince herself that he was feeling something. Regret, maybe. But she snatched back those traitorous thoughts. Any true emotion he had shown her had been a trick.

"Cora."

His voice was so quiet that, huddled in the farthest part of the cell, she could almost pretend he hadn't spoken.

"I brought you something." He slid an object through the bars, and her heart clenched. The little red radio with dials like a smiling face. Nok's radio. Did this mean that Nok didn't need it anymore—that they'd transferred her somewhere? And what about Rolf? She glanced at Lucky and Mali, who watched them but couldn't hear past their own cells. A part of Cora wanted to lunge for this small comfort he was offering—voices on the airwaves, a link to home—but she didn't want anything from him. She hugged her legs closer.

Cassian's hand curled on the bar. "I wish to explain."

"There's nothing to explain. You're the Warden. Everything was a lie."

"I told you that I feared I was making a mistake. You assumed I meant betraying my people. I meant betraying *you*. Lying to you gave me no joy. I almost aborted the mission when I saw the strain it was putting on your cohort, and on you. I did not want you to end up like the previous groups."

"*Dead?* How kind."

He paused. "I did not lie to you about our mission. All my actions were for your own good. Under my orders, my researchers were putting pressure on your minds to see if they could bring you to the point of mental evolution."

"So you could justify enslaving us, when we failed?"

"So we could *free* you, when you succeeded." He lowered his voice, almost as though he feared someone might overhear them. But he was the Warden—there was no one higher than him, was there? Where did he even plan to take her, if his plan had worked? She couldn't exactly picture a parade rolling down the austere aisles of the aggregate station, celebrating humanity's intelligence. The Kindred had made it perfectly clear they didn't want humans as equals.

"I pushed you to prove that humans are intelligent, as I know you can be. Anya was psychic; she read my mind on two separate occasions. When the other Kindred learned of this, they drugged her and locked her in the menagerie to hide her abilities. I was a low-ranking soldier—there was nothing I could do about it. So I set my mind to working my way up our ranks, rotation after rotation, until I was chosen by our Council as Warden."

Anya. The caged Icelandic girl who looked like a younger version of Cora. Was that the reason Cassian had thought Cora could be psychic, because she reminded him of Anya? She didn't know what to believe—if Anya had truly become as intelligent as the Kindred, why was she locked up? Wouldn't she have outsmarted them before they could drug her?

"I did see some of Anya's traits in you," he said, reading her mind, "but not because of your appearance. Because of your ability to navigate the space between cultures. Anya never fit in with any cohorts; Mali was the only friend she had. I believe it was this isolation that broke her mind."

Cora glanced at Lucky and Mali, so far away. *Isolation.* Well, she had certainly achieved that.

"Being Warden granted me certain privileges," Cassian continued, "such as a lack of oversight. I was able to circumvent the stock algorithm without being detected, and select you. I did everything I could to try to break your mind, subtle things that wouldn't arouse the Council's suspicion. It was no accident that the fail-safe exit was located in the ocean—I wanted you to have to face all your darkest fears. I gave you more tokens so the others would grow jealous and turn on you. I planted the bone in the jungle to drive a further wedge. I thought, when you discovered your past with Lucky, you would leave him. When you still showed signs of caring, I offered him a bargain to stay away from you. I needed you to be alone. Terrified. Only then would your mind truly break."

Air slipped from her lungs. All the confusion and stress she'd been through for weeks was just for his twisted experimentation.

Had he planted the comic book? The Mosca traders? Had he fabricated a chance for escape just so he could snatch it from her, and leave her even more broken? She pressed a hand to her head. What about the kiss—was that the biggest lie of all?

Give her stars. Kiss her. Make her fall in love.

Then betray her.

All she could feel was hurt. Worse than that—dead. Her heart still beat, but the blood had dried in her veins. There was no warmth. He had taken every piece of her that was alive—her heart, her soul, her trust—and smashed it beneath those metallic boots of his.

She had nothing now.

No family.

No friends.

No future.

"I did not wish to hurt you," he continued. "I tried other techniques, with the other cohorts. All of them failed—" His head jerked toward the black window. His eyes narrowed a fraction, and then he straightened instantly. He was perceiving something Cora couldn't. Someone listening, or someone coming.

She didn't care. She was the kind of broken there was no fixing.

And then her index finger started trembling. It pulsed strangely, like pins and needles were digging into it. Then her middle finger. Something strange happened to the lighting, almost like it got brighter, but only around the black window. Cora blinked, confused. Like on the beach, and in the bookshop, the sensation was in her head too, and her sense of balance, and her ability to sense temperature, and detect smells—all her senses, all at once.

The whisper of intuition, now loud as a scream. There *was* some-one behind that window, though they were blocked from her view. Two Kindred males, neither of them quite as tall as Cassian, one with a metal cast over one arm, the other with a deep wrinkle in the center of his forehead—Fian.

Pain exploded in her head. She clutched at her scalp as though she could keep her mind from fracturing. The strength leached out of her legs, and she slammed to the floor. Her muscles seized up, twitching and throbbing so fast she couldn't control her limbs.

The door flew open. Cassian was by her side. "Tell me what you are experiencing. Strange sensations. Visual disturbances."

His words found her through a fog of pain and racking tremors. He had spoken those words to her before. In the foun-tain room of the Temple menagerie, after she had collapsed. Had that been part of his plan too? Had he shown her the menagerie in hopes of breaking her?

"Serassi. Come at once." He was speaking into his wrist communicator. She had never heard him sound afraid before.

A moment later, Serassi's rough palms scraped against her head, feeling her temperature. Incomprehensible Kindred words were exchanged as her vision faded in and out. Static crack-led in her ears, deafening her, except she could hear everything perfectly—inside her own head. She felt as though she wasn't in her own body. She was almost hovering above it, in all corners at once, watching her own self as she convulsed. Cassian clutched her shoulders, holding her still, while Serassi administered some kind of drug.

"I'm sorry." Cassian was speaking to her body, though her

mind was hovering a few feet above them. "I had to betray you. It was the last part of the plan. The only thing strong enough to break you." His hand kept flexing, flexing, flexing. Serassi left to fetch something from the next room, and Cassian bent down.

His lips so close to hers. His hands gripping her shoulders.

It wasn't all a lie.

The words echoed in her head. Cassian's voice, and yet his lips hadn't moved. Unspoken words. He had only thought them. He glanced toward the door, removed his gloves, and pressed his hands against Cora's temples.

Electricity jolted through her, grabbing her floating perceptions and pulling them all back into flesh and bone. She sputtered awake, shoving him away. "Don't touch me!"

She stared at her shaking fingertips. What the hell had happened?

He ignored her. "Did your vision change? Were you able to read my thoughts—"

"Stop it!" She clamped her hands over her ears, trying to wrap her mind around what was happening.

"It's true, isn't it?" He reached an ungloved hand toward her, but she shoved him away again. "You perceived something. This will change everything, Cora. There are others, like me, who believe humans are capable of intelligence, but we are a minority. Most fear what would happen if humans gain intelligence. The right to govern themselves. The right to participate in our commerce and law. If the Council learns of this, they will try to silence you, just as they did Anya."

She drew in a sharp breath. God—was he right? Had she actually psychically perceived those two Kindred standing behind the window? There really wasn't any other explanation for something that should be impossible, and yet . . .

She slumped against the wall. She'd never even considered that the rumors might be true. It had sounded so far-fetched when Mali talked about kids becoming psychic. They lived in the real world, not a fantasy one.

But she had *seen* those Kindred behind the window.

"I don't care what you have planned," she snapped, trying to catch her breath. "I'm done being your experiment."

His enthusiasm melted off his face. "I broke you. I know that. But I will fix you again. I will make you even stronger. I am not alone. We intend to hide you in a menagerie, but I will watch out for you there. I will not let any harm come to you. I will teach you how to control and focus your ability. Cora. We can change everything, together."

That last word hung in the air. There was hope in his voice—hope her heart didn't mirror.

She gave him a cold look. "Get away from me."

He hovered by the door, as though he wished she would change her mind. After a few painful breaths he left, his boots loud, and the sound of the closing door louder.

From the corner of her eye, she saw Lucky waving his hands to get her attention. "What happened?" he mouthed. In the cell next to him, Mali hunched in the corner, watching keenly. Mali had known Anya well, almost like a sister. She must have seen Anya have a seizure like that at some time. Did she know what Cora had just experienced?

Lucky pointed at himself, then Cora, then Mali. He kept repeating one word, but Cora didn't understand until he pointed toward the door. *Escape.* He was trying to get her to cling to hope. But Cora let her head fall. Her body was spent. Escape? There was no escape for them. Even if they managed to get out, even if Leon was crawling around in vent shafts to break them free, the Kindred would only catch them again. They were in Cassian's world now, and he made the rules.

Cora picked up the little red radio with shaking hands. It felt so solid, so comforting. The last thing she had to cling to. From the speaker came the sound of a song. It didn't bounce the right way around the sharpened corners and metal bars.

Not at home in paradise, not at home in hell . . .

Cassian had taken her freedom but given her the last song she'd written, in Charlie's Jeep. Her last memory of home. She squeezed the radio, fighting back tears.

She pulled her knees in tight. Her whole body was shaking. Had Cassian's awful experiment really worked? Maybe it came from her intuition. Maybe it was a latent talent all humans had, but none developed because they didn't know it was even possible.

But she was psychic.

At least she had been, for a moment.

The Kindred thought humans were like children, naive and in need of protection, but they were wrong. She had changed, which meant humanity could change, and if the Kindred didn't think they were intelligent creatures, *dangerous* creatures, they weren't nearly as perceptive as they thought. Humans didn't deserve to be caged. They didn't deserve to be dressed up like dolls and toyed with. They didn't deserve to be used and manipulated and betrayed, even if the ends were just.

She would show the Kindred how powerful humans could be. Maybe some mistakes were worth making, but ripping her from her home was a mistake they would regret dearly.

She would make Cassian regret it most of all.

ACKNOWLEDGMENTS

IF YOU'RE READING THIS, then I owe *you* a big thank-you. Thank you for picking up this book, or ordering it from your favorite bookstore or online, and thank you for making it to the very last page. Without you, I couldn't do what I do.

Thanks also to my brilliant editor, Kristin Rens, for giving me the time I needed to make this book right, and for believing in the book from Day One. And thanks to the entire Balzer + Bray team who worked on it, through editing, marketing, or promoting: Caroline Sun, Michelle Taormina, Alison Donalty, Renée Cafiero, Nellie Kurtzman, Kelsey Murphy, Jenna Lisanti, Margot Wood, and Aubry Parks-Fried.

To Josh Adams and the Adams Lit team: This book wouldn't be in print if it weren't for you. I'll never forget sending that email that went something like "What about a human zoo . . ." and getting Josh's big "YES" back. Thank you for helping to navigate this book in all its stages, from proposal through many, many edits, and now into publication.

I had so many critique partners on this book, there are

almost too many to thank, and if I forget any, my deepest apologies: Ellen Oh, Stephanie Perkins, Alexandra Duncan, Megan Miranda (who must have read a dozen drafts), April Tucholke (who is also the reason this book made it to print), Courtney Stevens, Amie Kaufman, and Gina Montefusco. For emotional support and factual information, thanks to Carrie Ryan and Natalie Whipple, as well as the Asheville writing group. And a big thanks to the Bat Cave gang, who didn't look at me *too* strangely when I jumped up at dinner and said I wanted to write about a human zoo. To Tiffany Trent, my muse, whose real-life stories gave me the spark for this idea.

And thanks are also due to my amazing nonwriting network of friends and family: my parents, Peggy and Tim, who have long been supporters of all things books; my sister, Lena; the Shepherds; and most of all my husband, Jesse. Even if we never make it to Mars, we've made a great life together.

MEGAN SHEPHERD grew up in her family's independent bookstore in the Blue Ridge Mountains. The travel bug took her from London to Timbuktu and many places in between, though she ended up back in North Carolina with her husband, two cats, and a scruffy dog, and she wouldn't want to live anywhere else. She is also the author of the Madman's Daughter trilogy. Visit her online at www.meganshepherd.com.